A Cowboy's Fortune

The Kelly Can Saga Book 2

A COWBOY'S
Fortune

By

E. Joe Brown

Artemesia
Publishing

ISBN: 978-1-951122-76-8 (paperback)
ISBN: 978-1-951122-77-5 (ebook)
LCCN: 2023947432

Artemesia Publishing
9 Mockingbird Hill Rd
Tijeras, New Mexico 87059
www.apbooks.net
info@artemesiapublishing.com

First Edition

Acknowledgements

I need you folks as my reading family to know that I am indebted to the following folks for their unwavering support of me and my goals.

Elizabeth Layton my Digital Media and Marketing Manager.

Krista Soukup and Janelle Wilson my Publicist.

Whatever success I enjoy now and, in the future, will be because I have these talented folks guiding me as I expand my literary world. I can't thank them enough.

Dedication

To my wonderful grandchildren, Jordan, Christina, Darian, Averie, and Aiden who give me reasons daily to be proud. They inspire me to get up and do all I can do to make this a better world for them to inherit.

Chapter One
Honeymoon
February 1919

THE SATURDAY AFTER HIS wedding, Kansas City's biggest in decades, Charlie Kelly sat at the breakfast room table off the kitchen of his father-in-law's home on Westover Road. It was the largest home in the city, and its indoor swimming pool and other features made it one of the fanciest as well. Charlie enjoyed his second cup of black coffee as he watched squirrels scurry across the backyard out beyond the pool. He smiled as his mind wandered through the events of the past two years leading up to his marriage to Susan. He shook his head at how his life had changed.

How can I be here this mornin', married to the most wonderful woman I've ever met? I know she's heir to the largest fortune west of the Mississippi River. The money's great, but I'm glad I fell in love with her long before I learned of it. How she fell in love with a poor thirty-dollars-a-month-plus-room-and-board cowboy, I'll never understand. But here we are, married as of yesterday, and we'll head out on our honeymoon tomorrow.

Charlie looked up as Susan, his beautiful wife, strolled toward him. His heart pounded, and he couldn't help but admire her glistening, raven black hair as it flowed down beyond her shoulders. His eyes never left her tall, slender body with its awe-inspiring curves. Her colorful Pongee silk robe with blue, red and pink flowers was loosely tied around her narrow waist, open enough to clearly show she wore nothing under it.

"Good morning, Charlie. How long have you been up, Sweetheart?"

His eyes finally finding hers, he said, "Oh, I guess I've been here about twenty minutes. Enough time to be on my second cup of coffee and consider all that's happened these last couple of years."

1

She bent down and kissed his forehead. "Yes, a lot has happened since you left New Mexico headed for the 101 Ranch in Oklahoma. I'm glad you stopped in Elmore City along the way, otherwise we would never have met."

Charlie pulled Susan to him and rested his head on her breasts. "It sure has. When I took the job as a clerk in Jasper's store, I never expected to find the love of my life."

She gave him a hug, pressing her breasts into his face. "And I never expected to find such a strong, sexy man who could fulfill me more than any man had done before."

Charlie pushed her away gently and looked into her eyes. "I always wondered if Jasper knew about us down at the creek and sort of encouraged it."

"He knew," Susan said. "It saddens me, the tragic way he died in the fire, but it meant we could then become husband and wife."

Charlie nodded and gave her a hug. Susan had cared for Jasper, but he also knew it had been a loveless marriage because of how Susan had at first flirted with him, and then done much more. "Oh, Susan, we don't need to talk through all of this, but it did lead us to each other, and now I couldn't be happier."

She took her seat and poured a cup of coffee. "I guess you're right, we don't need to go through it, but we do need to discuss our honeymoon to Jekyll Island and how we'll get ourselves the 101 Ranch as soon as we can. You still work there for George Miller, you know."

Charlie heard Susan's father coming down the hall from his bedroom. "Susan, it's your father."

She closed her robe and cinched the sash tight as she said, "Good morning, Father. How are you feeling this morning?"

Walter Kramer entered the room slowly and sat across from Charlie. "I'm tired. Yesterday, was wonderful, but I'm still weary as I start today. Can you pour me a cup, my sweet daughter?"

"Of course." She retrieved a cup and saucer from the bureau. "And you better take it easy today and for as long as needed until you feel better."

Beverly, the cook, walked into the room. "Morning, everyone. Can I fix you all your usual breakfasts? And Charlie, I've made a pan of biscuits using your recipe."

Charlie grinned. "Beverly, you're an angel." He looked at the others, and they nodded their approval. He turned back to Beverly. "Yes, we'll have our usual. And another pot of coffee would be nice."

Walter cleared his throat and said, "Kids, I've arranged for you to use my Pullman Car to make your trip to Jekyll Island. I've always thought it's the prettiest part of Georgia." He looked at Susan. "I haven't used the car since you came home from Oklahoma. I've never taken you to the railyard and showed it to you, have I, Susan?"

"No, you haven't. I'm sure it's nice, and it'll be wonderful to have our own rail car." She gave her father a piercing glare. "How come you didn't let me use the Pullman when I went to Vassar? I had to share a sleeping car with several others."

"If I remember right," Walter said with a grin, "those others included your friends also going to Vassar and you wanted to spend time with them."

Charlie took a sip of coffee, smiled, and said, "I think he's gotcha there. Thank you, Walter. I've never been on a Pullman. What's it like?"

Walter smiled. "You'll have all the conveniences of home, and it's every bit as luxurious. When you get settled in, look at all the mahogany wood. It's not used just for trim, but entire walls."

Walter coughed and struggled to catch his breath.

"Father, are you alright?"

He wheezed a few times, then said, "I'll be okay." He took a cloth napkin and wiped his brow. "Don't look at me that way, Daughter. I'll see my doctor next week."

"Okay, Father. I'm concerned since Charlie and I are leaving town."

Walter gave a reassuring smile and patted Susan's hand. "Don't worry about me. Now where was I?"

Charlie said, "You were describin' this beautiful train car I've never seen."

"There's a full kitchen and bath with a shower. The bedroom has a bed the size of Susan's here at home. There's a dining table, and in the main room where you'll sit most of the time, it has French provincial furniture and nice side tables. The car's like this home but on railroad tracks."

Susan said, "Father, it sounds like you spared no expense when you had it built. Now Charlie and I'll enjoy it and be thankful we have it. Will we have staff on the car to help us?"

"Yes, I wanted a comfortable way to travel and do business available to me. So, you'll have a chef and housekeeper to make your trip as pleasant as possible."

Beverly brought their breakfast, and the three of them enjoyed the meal and talked about the wedding. It had gone by in a flash for Charlie, so it was nice to hear about it from Walter and Susan's perspective.

As they finished up, Charlie looked at the time and said, "I need to go meet my parents and make sure they make it to the station. Their train back to Oklahoma leaves this afternoon."

"I'll get started on the packing for us," Susan said as Charlie stood up. She leaned forward and Charlie obliged her with a kiss.

He wished he had time for more, but it was going to be a busy day. *No rest for the wicked.*

***

Early Sunday morning, the newlyweds boarded their rail car at Union Station. Their Pullman would make the trip enjoyable and comfortable. As they settled in, the housekeeper put away their luggage with the help of the porter, and the chef walked in and asked what they wanted for lunch. As the staff got to work, Charlie and Susan sat down in the expensive French provincial chairs.

"This will certainly make the trip more bearable," Charlie said.

"We've got two days here before we reach Georgia," Susan said. "Then we'll catch the ferry out to the island."

They sat in silence for a few minutes. Outside the train, the conductor was making his final check and last-minute passengers raced to reach their cars.

After a while, Charlie looked across the main room of the Pullman at Susan. "You look like somethin' may be botherin' you. Can I help?"

"Oh, I'm just concerned about Father. He seems to be getting weaker. I'm sorry, I don't want to worry you or make it seem like I'm not excited to spend this time alone with you. It's been years since I've spent time at our cottage on the island, and I've always loved visiting there. I can't wait to share it with you."

"You'd not mentioned Jekyll Island until we were planning our wedding. Why?"

"Father had considered selling what his friends call Walter's Hideaway while I lived in Elmore City. I didn't know he still had it until recently. He told me last night he keeps our staff at the cottage year-around, and they're expecting us tomorrow evening. Charlie, you're going to love the island and our cottage."

Charlie rubbed his chin. "You said year-around. I'm confused. It's your cottage, so isn't it available anytime?"

"It's available, but most folks who own property there, whether apartments at the club or cottages, are from the northeast or somewhere cold in the winter. So, they spend those winter months on Jekyll Island and return to their primary homes in the spring."

"Your father, when he mentioned Jekyll Island, said the members included the Rockefellers, Vanderbilts, Morgans, and other very rich and powerful people. I think he mentioned the Jekyll Island Club was private. Is it?"

"Yes, you must be invited or sponsored into the club, and the membership must vote you in for you to become a member. After acceptance, you must buy into the club and become a shareholder or co-owner of Jekyll Island and the private club."

Although their Pullman was near the end of the train, Charlie and Susan heard the woo-woo of the train whistle, followed by the shush sound of the boilers, then the crisp clank from the couplings between the cars, and finally they felt the jerk as the train began to move. Union Station soon faded into the distance as the train's engine created its chugga chugga sounds, working hard to gain speed as it climbed to the east enroute across Missouri to Independence, Columbia, and beyond.

A while later, Charlie turned on the sofa, looked out the nearest window, and said, "Well, we're on our way, and it looks like we've already left Kansas City. We'll be goin' through St. Louis, Cincinnati, Chattanooga, and on into Brunswick by tomorrow evenin'."

Susan joined Charlie and snuggled against his chest. "I'm going to enjoy every minute of this trip, and as I said, I can't wait to show you Jekyll Island."

***

The sun settled beyond the western horizon as the train pulled into the station in Brunswick, Georgia, on Monday evening of February 17th. Charlie looked out to see an elegant building with a slate roof and six gables. He marveled at its beauty.

As they disembarked, Charlie said, "Susan, the station's impressive; its Victorian style reminds me of the home you and Jasper had in Elmore City. The gables and the red-brown brick columns and chimneys."

"It's very nice. I've always liked Brunswick. It's lovely here, and there are shops and restaurants folks on the island enjoy while they are here. We need to catch the ferry, so let's get moving."

The Jekyll Island steamer met Charlie and Susan and ferried them the ten miles to the island's wharf on Jekyll Creek. The ride was less than thirty minutes, and land was in view the entire trip.

Charlie said, "I love what we can see, although it's gettin' dark. The air's moist. It seems like the smells are a mixture of the ocean with the pines and marshes along the shores."

Susan said, "You'll see lush foliage on the island, and yes, the smells are the salt air filled with many fragrances coming from the ocean and everything growing here."

As the boat pulled next to the wharf, Charlie pointed to the island. Over the tops of the trees, he could make out the top floor of a large Victorian building with a turret. He said, "I didn't expect to see a hotel."

Susan laughed. "Oh silly, that's the Jekyll Island Club's main building."

"Well, it looks big enough to be a hotel."

"In a way it is, Charlie. The main floor has a dining room, offices, and some meeting rooms. We'll go there and sign in and then head on to our cottage."

As they went ashore, a porter loaded their baggage onto the back of a horse-drawn buggy to take them to the clubhouse. As the horses clip-clopped along the road, Susan swept her arm across their view and said, "Isn't this beautiful? I love the huge oaks with the Spanish moss drooping down."

Charlie said, "It's somethin' special. Those are palm trees along the road, aren't they?"

"They are, and we have some on our property at the cottage. Remember, we're in the southern part of the country now, and it's warmer here."

"Oh, I can feel it. It's muggy, and I need to get out of this coat. But I'll wait until we get to the house."

They signed in, and the desk clerk provided their table location in the dining room for when they chose to come for dinner. Then Charlie and Susan walked out front where a tall older man with salt and pepper hair stood beside a carriage.

Susan smiled. "Jarvis, how wonderful to see you."

The man said, "Miss Susan, my how you've grown. Whatta beautiful young lady you are."

Susan gave him a hug, then turned and pointed toward Charlie. "Jarvis, this is my husband, Charlie Kelly."

Charlie reached out his right hand. "Jarvis, pleased to meet ya. I'd say you've been a special friend to Susan for a while."

Jarvis nodded. "Pleased to meet ya too, Mister Charlie. And yes, I remember Miss Susan as a kiddo. Now she's a full-grown lady. Let's git y'all to the cottage."

Charlie asked, "How far is it?"

"Not far, we'll be there in a few minutes."

As they passed several houses, Charlie asked Susan, "What does your cottage look like?"

"It's shingle style like many you would see in New England. Father loved what Mr. Pulitzer built and used those ideas for our cottage. Here we are, Sweetheart."

Charlie lay back in the carriage and exclaimed, "This isn't a cottage. It's as big as Westover."

Jarvis looked back at Charlie as they entered the driveway to the cottage and said, "Mister Charlie, I don't know anything about Westover, but we have nineteen rooms and five baths in these three stories."

Charlie just shook his head and smiled.

As Charlie and Susan climbed the stairs to the porch, two people stood there waiting for them. Susan introduced Hazel, a short, redheaded woman of about forty, as the cook, and a slender, young blond as Winnie, the housekeeper. They helped Jarvis to bring in and unpack the luggage.

Charlie looked at Susan. "I'm hungry. It's a little past 7:00. Is there any food in the house?"

Hazel said, "Ma'am, I can whip ya up somethin' real quick."

Susan smiled as she shook her head. "No, Hazel, how sweet of you to offer, and we'll certainly have breakfast here in the morning, but I told the folks at the reception we would come down to the club for dinner tonight."

Charlie put his arm around Susan's shoulders, winked, and said, "Let's let Hazel fix us somethin' so we can stay in together. We can see the dinin' room in a day or two." He gave her a passionate kiss.

"Oh, Charlie," Susan said with a sigh and returned the kiss.

Chapter Two
Ms. Post
February 1919

AFTER A FEW DAYS of passion, the honeymooners decided to have an evening meal at the clubhouse dining room. As they walked out the front of their cottage to Riverview Road, Susan pointed and said, "Over to our left, with those large palmettos in the front yard, is the Pulitzer cottage; the John Albrights live there now. They moved in while I was at Vassar, so I don't know them well."

Charlie said, "You keep callin' these cottages. Susan, they're large homes. Each of these easily compares to some homes in the Country Club section of Kansas City."

Susan said, "Yes, but these folks have homes in New York, Chicago, Philadelphia, or some other city that are larger and more elaborate than these. Our cottage, although large, is about half the size of our home on Westover Road."

The couple turned right and walked under a Spanish moss-draped canopy of live oaks as they headed toward the clubhouse about a quarter of a mile away.

Susan pointed to their right. "Charlie, this Mediterranean stucco two-story house is the Goodyear cottage, and I understand Frank Jr. uses it now. Frank should be about twenty-eight years old, and he's someone I remember playing with as a kid.

"Next is Mistletoe Cottage. Its owners are the Henry Porters. Henry must be in his late seventies. He's a businessman and a past member of the U.S. House of Representatives from Pennsylvania. He influenced my father to consider sharing his profits with employees. Now you know why, when we discussed the subject, I was so quick to agree. We knew Mr. Porter, and his company grew rapidly as he shared the wealth with his key leaders.

"And this three-story house is called Indian Mound. William Rockefeller owns it. You met the Rockefellers; William and his older brother, John, attended our wedding. Along with the Morgans and Goodyears. Several of our other neighbors on Riverview Road and around the island sent flowers, gifts, and best wishes."

The clubhouse came into view as they finished the walk.

Charlie put his arm around Susan and said, "Well, this island and the people here are inspirin'. Walkin' and seein' this place lit up this evenin', it's beautiful. I'm a little startled by havin' these powerful people as neighbors. It's not fear, mind ya, just me gettin' used to havin' this kinda life."

Susan snuggled into Charlie. "You'll be great, just like you have been at the 101. I do love this place. It's pretty and romantic too. The dining room's elegant, and I hope we'll have a table which gives us some privacy."

As they walked into the Grand Dining Room, Charlie noticed the maître d' looking at his boots. While the maître d' led them to their table along a wall of windows overlooking the courtyard, Charlie smiled and nodded to the other guests seated in the room. A woman seated alone at the table next to them was the only one who returned his gesture. After being seated, and sliding his hat under his chair, Charlie said, "I'm guessin' you don't see too many folks wearin' cowboy boots and hat here on Jekyll Island?"

Susan laughed. "No, probably not. You're within the dress code and you won't cause a stir." She smiled and put her hand on his. "Sweetheart, I don't think I'd recognize you without your boots and hat."

She looked around the room. "Now, what do you think about this place?"

With a disbelieving shake of his head, Charlie said, "This is somethin'. It might be fancier than the Mission Hills Country Club dinin' room where we had our weddin' reception. Those two sets of white pillars down the length of the room, the tables, chairs, and fine China all make it obvious you're wealthy and powerful to be in this atmosphere. My granddaddy would've called it 'livin' in high clover.'"

Susan squeezed his hand and said, "Well, it's true the members want to live in luxury even when they are away from their primary home and daily business environment." Looking past Charlie, she added, "My, there's a young, attractive, and refined lady at the table next to us."

Charlie nodded. "She certainly is. She's a mighty fine-lookin' tall brunette like you. Do you know her?"

"No, and she's there alone."

Charlie said, "She seems friendly enough; maybe you should at least speak to her."

"Well, okay." Susan looked directly at the lady and said, "Good evening, I'm Susan Kramer-Kelly. I don't believe we've met."

"No, we haven't. I'm Marjorie Post-Close. I'm not a member here but a guest of the J. P. Morgans. You may be acquainted with Jack and his wife, Jane. I'll be staying here a few more days."

Charlie turned and said, "I'm Charlie Kelly. The only Posts I know started the town in the Texas panhandle and made the cereal that was available from the 'coosie' at the 101."

Marjorie gave a small laugh. "Well, that's my father C. W. Post. He started Post cereals. And he built Post City in Texas on land he bought from the U Lazy S Ranch."

Charlie nodded. "I know the ranch, though I never had a chance to work there myself."

Marjorie turned to Susan. "And Susan, you must be the daughter of Walter Kramer. My father spoke highly of him."

"Yes, and I believe we share the role of being the only child of powerful men, do we not?"

Marjorie laughed. "That's one way to describe it. I heard from Jack that your father is not in good health. We talked earlier on the phone; he said he and Jane spoke to him at your wedding."

Susan leaned closer to Marjorie. "He's not doing well. He had to beg Charlie and me to come here. We hated the idea of honeymooning this far away from him." Susan hesitated, then said, "Are you here alone?"

Marjorie took a sip of wine, smiled, and said, "Yes, I needed to get away for a while. You know how life can throw you challenges, and I needed a break. The Morgans kindly offered me the use of their apartment in the San Souci across the street from the club." She noticed Susan was about to ask a question. "I'm fine," she assured her, "and I certainly don't want to bring my troubles into the celebration of your new life together."

Charlie waved his hands. "Oh no, we didn't mean to pry, and we don't need to hear any more."

Susan shot Charlie a stern look and turned back to Marjorie. "We're sorry to hear this, but if there's anything we can do to support you, we offer our help. I would love to spend some time with you to learn how you stepped into your role as the Post company leader. I know my father has done a lot to prepare me, especially as his health has failed him. But hearing your experiences would be educational and interesting."

Marjorie leaned forward. "Thanks for your kind offer and for respecting my privacy. I would love to get to know you two, and if I can be of any help to you, it would be wonderful."

The waiter arrived to get the Kellys' order, and the conversation with Marjorie ended with an agreement to meet the next day for lunch. She left as Charlie and Susan began to read their menus.

After a few moments, Susan said, "Sweetheart, a ribeye medium and a bottle of cabernet to share will suit me fine."

Charlie smiled and looked at the waiter. "Make it two ribeyes, one medium and the other medium rare. We'll have a bottle of cabernet, and you can bring it immediately."

After dinner, they walked back to their cottage and opened another bottle of wine to enjoy on their back porch. As Charlie and Susan sat within arm's length on their lounges, sipping their cabernet, Susan said, "We don't have a swimming pool, but the beach is close. Let's walk down there in the morning."

She had already unbuttoned her blouse and when she rolled over, giving her man his favorite view, he immediately responded.

"That's my Charlie; now let's make another night on Jekyll Island memorable."

***

Charlie and Susan slept late for them, arising at 7:30. After Hazel's breakfast of eggs, grits, and bacon, the couple walked to the beach across River Road along Jekyll Creek. They enjoyed the warm, for February, temperatures and the gentle ocean breeze as they strolled along the beach.

"Susan, I see us bringin' our kids here some day and it's excitin' to me. When I left New Mexico, my biggest dream was to become a cowboy at the 101."

Susan squeezed his hand. "I want kids someday, but right now, to me, our kids are banks, department stores, railroads, and a construction company."

Charlie nodded his head slowly. "Okay, Darlin'. Remember I come from a big family and that's how ya make sure yer farm or ranch is successful. I understand, as long as ya see us havin' kids someday."

"I want kids too, but with me assuming Father's position within Kramer, I need the Board to see me as no different than Father."

"Okay, Sweetheart. Since your father and I already added a kid, you didn't mention oil in your list, can we add another one?"

"What are you talking about?"

"A ranch."

***

Later the Kellys met with Marjorie, taking advantage of a windless

75-degree afternoon to enjoy lunch on the patio at the club. Susan and Marjorie ordered Waldorf salads, and Charlie enjoyed the roast beef in his French Dip.

They began sharing their personal lives and, not long into their conversation, Charlie said, "It sure looks to me like you two have a lot in common. Marjorie took over the family business in her twenties, and Walter is turning the day-to-day operation of the Kramer Group over to you, Susan, and you're in your twenties."

Marjorie smiled and nodded. "Susan, I think we both share a strong desire to take what our fathers created and make it our own, don't we?"

Susan said, "I have so much respect for what Father built, but Charlie and I have dreams requiring us to create more and move into new areas of the business world."

"It sounds like you two make such a good team, and it takes one. What areas are you two looking into for expansion of your companies?"

Charlie said, "Her father and I have been talkin' about the oil business. After watchin' friends like Harry Sinclair and John Rockefeller have big successes, he already had an interest. I'm now workin' in the oil business with the 101 Ranch Oil Company. We also know we want to own and operate ranches and be part of the beef industry. When we return from our honeymoon, I'll be immediately returnin' to the 101 Ranch in northern Oklahoma."

Marjorie said, "As I mentioned yesterday, my father built Post, Texas from ranch land. He also owned a ranch, and I got involved some in running the ranch, so I understand how you feel and I can see you being very successful."

Susan reached over and took the hands of both Charlie and Marjorie and said, "I guess we're the Three Musketeers, aren't we?"

They laughed and threw their hands up and gave out a hoot. Others nearby looked over in surprise and then shared their laughter. A solid friendship had begun.

***

The next two weeks became a mixture of daytime activities, often with Marjorie, and evenings filled with romantic and intimate walks around the island.

On Monday, March 3rd, while having lunch with Marjorie, the maître d' came to their table and said, "Mrs. Kelly, you have a telegram." He held a silver platter toward her.

Susan took the telegram as Charlie continued to tell Marjorie a story about working on the 101 Ranch. It took them a moment to realize Susan had gone very quiet. Charlie turned to his wife and noticed she had gone very pale. He reached out a hand and noticed her's were shaking.

"What is it, Darlin'?"

Susan's lips trembled and she shook her head slightly. She handed the telegram to Charlie, and Marjorie reached over to hold Susan's hands. Tears welled up in the corner of her eyes.

Charlie read the telegram:

```
Susan
Your father is in the hospital - STOP
The doctor says it's serious - STOP
Come home immediately - STOP
Curt
```

"Oh, Charlie," Susan finally managed to say, and she fell into his arms.

Charlie rubbed her back. Marjorie gave a questioning look, clearly wanting to know what the telegram said but also not wanting to pry. Charlie said, "Walter's in the hospital."

Marjorie nodded, understanding fully the importance of those simple words. She gave Susan's hand a squeeze. "I'm so sorry. Susan, my heart hurts for you, my new friend." She looked at Charlie. "You know the different ways to reach me, so please keep me informed of what you find out when you get home. Please go pack, and I'll let the staff at the front desk know what's happening. They can have the ferry ready for you."

Charlie sent a return telegram stating they would be leaving immediately.

Back at the cottage, Charlie began making the additional arrangements needed for them to leave. The next train out of Brunswick was departing later that evening.

They'd be on it.

Chapter Three
Passing
March 1919

THE TRAIN ARRIVED IN the evening on Wednesday, March 5th, and Uncle Curt met them at Union Station. Susan ran to her uncle, and they embraced. Curt whispered, "I'm sorry for how this has happened to you on your honeymoon."

"Thanks, Uncle Curt, how's Father?"

"He's very weak, but the doctor said he's stable."

Charlie said, "I've got our luggage, let's go see him."

They headed to the car and were taken directly to the hospital. Despite the late hour, Susan and Charlie were taken to Walter's room.

Walter's deep-set eyes opened weakly as they walked into his private room. Susan hurried to his bedside. "Father, I'm glad you're awake. We got here as quickly as we could."

Walter tried to rise as he said, "Oh, how I wish you kids could have stayed longer on the island. I hate this so much."

Charlie walked to the opposite side of the bed from Susan and took Walter's hand. "We wouldn't want to be anywhere else. What can we do to help?"

Walter dropped back on his pillow. "I'll admit you being here makes me better. Susan, can you find a nurse and get us all some sweet tea?"

Walter looked at Curt. "Did you bring the paperwork?"

"I did. I'll get it out."

After Susan was out of the room, Walter turned to Charlie. "How's she doing? I see stress all over her face."

"Father, she's worried about you. Nothing else matters right now to her or me."

Walter smiled. "I know I don't need to say it, but do what you can to support and comfort her, son. When she gets back in here, I want to discuss what I've been doing while you've been gone."

Susan walked in and said, "I heard the last part; what have you been up to?"

Walter raised his hand palm out, and smiled. "It's all good, and you'll be happy with me, I hope." He watched as Susan handed out the sweet tea then returned to his bedside. "Last month, we got the paperwork completed to place you, Susan, as the Chief Executive Officer and me remaining as the Chairman of the Board. I've now added that you'll be the sole owner and become the Chairman upon my death. I formed the Kelly Oil Company with Charlie as President. Curt created the necessary documents for it to operate under the Kramer Group. We have established appropriate Kelly Oil bank accounts and funded them with $500,000. Charlie, feel free to adjust the company leadership as you see fit. I know you have someone in mind to become a partner, and that's splendid.

"Kids, it's all done, and I've already signed everything. Curt has the paperwork with him, and I want to see you sign it. I don't know if I'll ever leave this place, so we'll execute the most important business transactions of my lifetime right here, right now."

Curt placed the papers on the side table. Charlie and Susan signed them, and Curt notarized them.

Walter laid back with a smile on his face and said, "Now I feel much better, and I'll stop talking and let you ask any questions."

Susan pulled an armchair close to the bed and sat. "You have been busy. I'm thrilled you have taken these steps, and thank you for showing your complete trust and approval of me and Charlie as future leaders of the Kramer Group."

Charlie wiped tears from his cheeks as he said, "Father, I don't have the right words now. But I agree with Susan, I couldn't be happier you trust us this way. We won't let you down. But tonight, more than anythin', we want to see you gettin' better and ready to come home to us."

Walter took a sip of his sweet tea, wiped tears away, and struggled to set the glass down. "I... uh... think I need to rest now. Go home, unpack, and get some rest. I'll see you in the morning."

Susan bent down and kissed her father's forehead. "Okay, Father; rest, and we'll be here right after breakfast."

Charlie gently squeezed Walter's hand and said, "Love you, and we'll see you tomorrow."

On the ride home from the hospital, Charlie said, "He sure looked weak, didn't he? Susan, I'm worried."

"Me too. But Father seemed to perk up as he told us what he had done while we enjoyed Jekyll Island."

Curt said, "Yes, he did. Well, at least he's where he can get the care he needs."

Once home, they unpacked while Beverly fixed them something for a late dinner. After eating, they had their wine by the fire and went to bed.

As Charlie climbed into their bed, he said, "This bed sure looks good. I think I'll be asleep in two minutes."

Susan scooted over and cuddled up next to him. "I'm tired too, but please hold me."

***

They hadn't been asleep long when a knock on their bedroom door awoke them.

"Miss Susan, Mr. Charlie, are you awake?"

Susan mumbled, "Wha... what is it?"

In a complete fog Charlie muttered, "Susan, what's goin' on?"

"I don't know. Kathryn, what is it?"

"Ma'am, Mr. Schlegell's here to see you. He's waiting in the parlor."

Charlie looked at the clock. "It's after midnight, Susan; this can't be good."

She sniffled and reached for a handkerchief. Her throat scratchy with fear, she whispered, "I know..."

They grabbed their robes and hurried to the parlor.

Curt stood as they entered the room. "Susan, my sweet niece, I'm so sorry to have to tell you this, but your father has passed."

Susan burst into tears and fell against Charlie's chest. Charlie assisted her to a sofa across from Curt.

Charlie asked, "Why didn't the hospital call us?"

Curt stifled his emotions as he said, "Uh... Walter... had given them my name and number in case of emergency. You were out of the state... and really, I'm glad they called me, so I could deliver this awful news."

Susan sobbed, "What... what happened?"

Curt said, "According to the Charge Nurse, he had gone to sleep and passed quietly between 9:00 and 10:00. On her 10:00 rounds, his nurse found him lying quietly and unresponsive. The doctor said his heart just wore out and quit beating."

Charlie said, "He... he didn't look good earlier when we visited... but this is certainly unexpected. Had the doctors figured out his sickness? He would spit up blood sometimes, have headaches, and he seemed to tire so easily."

Curt said, "We'll never know for sure, but the doctors told Walter they thought it might be lung cancer. They couldn't be sure what caused it because there are so many opinions on the cause of the disease; they could only offer drugs to help with the symptoms. They did have plans in place to ease his pain and discomfort."

Susan said, "What do we do next, Uncle Curt?"

Curt said, "Your father arranged everything with Eylar Brothers Funeral Home. And they have been contacted to take Walter to their facility. I'm happy to assist you in making the necessary contacts to the few family members, and the appropriate agencies he has listed on the paperwork he left with me and McGilley's. Susan, it's Thursday morning now, and the soonest we can have a service is likely next week. Let me help you."

Susan looked at her uncle. "Of course, you can help. Please take over and follow Father's wishes to the letter. I believe he wanted a private funeral service. Then we can plan a memorial service for next week. My only concern is allowing enough time for those from a distance who want to attend to get here."

Charlie said, "We'll come into the office in the mornin', and you can go over the guidance Father left us, and we'll support you however is needed."

Curt said, "Fine, and I'll leave you now to try to get some rest. I know you must have been tired from your long train ride, and now... this."

Susan said, "Uncle Curt, I know you're hurting too. Please know Charlie and I are here for you."

"Yes, please don't think you must do everything yourself," said Charlie.

Curt nodded. "Thanks, kids. I'll be fine, we knew he was in bad shape, but..."

***

The following morning, Charlie listened with coffee cup in hand as Susan called Marjorie. She held the receiver so they both could hear.

"Hello, Marjorie speaking."

"This is... Susan... my father passed during the night."

"Oh no, you sweet thing, I'm so sorry. I'll come to Kansas City."

Susan cleared her throat. "Oh you're a dear friend, but you don't need to. I would love it if maybe we could talk from time to time. Your friendship already means more than I can express. I know you can relate to what has happened."

Marjorie said, "I suspect you're right. Are you sure I can't come?"

Susan said, "Well, I would love your support. If you could attend the service..."

"Of course; and call me anytime you need me. Let's meet somewhere in Kansas City after the service. I'm so glad you have Charlie. He's a special one, Susan."

"Yes, he sure is." She gathered herself. "I better go start my day; I'll call you soon. I'm so glad you understand and are available to talk. Goodbye."

On Sunday, the family along with the household staff met in the chapel at Eylar Brothers and held their private funeral for Walter. As Walter had wished, it was a small, intimate affair, allowing them to grieve away from the public. He was then interred at Union Cemetery.

***

The Thursday after Walter was buried was the day of the memorial service. The intervening days had seemed to fly by as Charlie and Susan split their time between the service preparations and getting updates from their leaders regarding the business. Earlier that morning, Charlie had sat across the breakfast table from Susan and observed her lost in thought as if in another world. He didn't question anything; he knew Susan's focus was on the events happening in a few hours at the service.

A large crowd was already seated at Saint Joseph's, the largest and most distinguished Catholic Church in Kansas City, when Susan, Charlie, and Curt arrived. Bishop Thomas Lillis, who would lead the ceremony, stepped over and briefly greeted them. Governor Fred Gardner stood next to the bishop and offered his condolences. He would later give the eulogy. The Governor and Susan's father had been friends, and Curt, on behalf of Walter, had requested him to be a formal part of the memorial.

Lt. Governor Crossley, Secretary of State Sullivan, Attorney General McAllister, and many other political office holders attended. Some spoke briefly, and six served as honorary pallbearers. Most newspapers from across Missouri and even as far away as Oklahoma City, Tulsa, Denver, and Chicago had people attending. Flowers and correspondence had arrived from friends such as the Rockefellers, the Fords, the Vanderbilts, the Morgans, and of course Marjorie.

Susan surprised some in the crowd when she went to the podium near the end of the service and spoke lovingly of her father. After a few shared memories she knew many in the crowd would recognize, she gathered herself, wiped away a tear, and looked at Charlie. She said, "Father was very protective of me, almost to a fault. My dear husband had to save him from drowning before he was sure Charlie was the one for me."

The crowd laughed and, for the first time since arriving back in Kansas City from their honeymoon, Susan smiled.

Later, back at the Westover Road home, Susan didn't want dinner. Instead, she craved her cabernet and as much from Charlie, emotionally and physically, as he could give. Charlie understood and was supportive because he knew Susan had held everything inside. She needed to let it all go. That night, between their deep intimacy, many tears, and glasses of wine, Susan finally mourned her loss in Charlie's arms.

***

Weeks later, Charlie and Susan sat in their breakfast room and ate while enjoying the view across the patio and yard toward the conservatory. They had hosted the Kramer Group quarterly meeting with the Board of Directors the day before.

As Susan looked outside, she sighed, and said with yearning in her voice, "It's been like heaven here and over at Jekyll Island, but we do need to get you to the 101."

Charlie said, "There are some beautiful spots at the ranch along the river—big trees, clear water, seclusion. We'll find our special place there too. But we have plenty of time—"

Susan interrupted him as she reached over, patted his hand, and grinned. "I know, but we need to get on with our lives."

He put his coffee down. "Well, I guess you do have everythin' caught up after the quarterly meetin', right?"

"Yes, and how are things regarding Kelly Oil?"

"Uncle Curt and I have everythin' ready. I need to talk with Hank, and I want to do it in person." Leaning forward, eyes bright with excitement, Charlie placed his hand on hers. "I know we've been workin' the business, plannin' our weddin', and now the memorial service, so we could move to the 101, but Sweetheart, we don't need to leave for Oklahoma anytime soon. George will understand."

Susan leaned toward him and touched his cheek. "Honey, I'm fine, and getting on with our plans is the best medicine for me right now."

"Well, if you're sure, we can take the afternoon train to Ponca City tomorrow. Whattaya think?"

Susan stood. "Oh yes, let's do it. I've arranged everything needed to work the business from the ranch. I'll come back here when needed. We can pack tonight and leave tomorrow."

A big smile lit up his face as Charlie said, "I'll call George, and ask him to pick us up in Ponca City tomorrow night."

With the decision made, they finished their breakfast and went to their offices. From his desk, Charlie called person-to-person for George L. Miller. When the operator connected them, he heard George say, "Hello, Charlie."

"Good morning. Susan and I'll arrive in Ponca City at about 7:00 tomorrow evenin'. We've booked seats on the train. Can you meet us or have someone meet us?"

"I can. I'm glad you're coming. I've much to catch you up on."

"Is everything alright, George? You sound concerned."

"I'm okay; but a lot's going on. I'll fill you in. Enjoy the train trip, and I'll see you tomorrow evening."

"Okay, goodbye."

Charlie went to Susan's office and spoke from the doorway. "Susan, George'll meet us in Ponca. He sounded concerned about somethin', but he wouldn't tell me what. He's sure happy we're comin'."

Curt was walking up behind Charlie and heard Charlie's report. "What's this about someone meeting you in Ponca? Why and when?"

Susan stood and walked around her desk. "Uncle Curt, we need to get Charlie back to the 101. I'm going with him."

Curt tilted his head. "Susan, you just finished a major business meeting, not to mention your very recent loss. Charlie can go, but you need to stay here."

Susan stepped forward. "I understand how important it is for me to stay actively involved in the business now with Father gone. But I want to see this wonderful ranch my husband loves. I'll stay involved in leading the business and come back here as often as necessary. It's settled; we leave tomorrow."

Curt put up his hands. "Okay. Getting away might be the best thing for you right now."

***

Later they enjoyed their last dinner at Westover. After eating they went to the conservatory. As Charlie placed his wine glass on the side table next to his chair, he looked at Susan and watched as she unbuttoned her blouse. "Whatcha doin'?"

Eyebrows raised, she said, "Is this something new for you? You've not seen me do this before?"

He shook his head. "Well, I guess that was a stupid question. I'm happy to help ya if needed."

"Oh, I think I can do this. You better get busy yourself."

Chapter Four
Settling In
April 1919

THEY ARRIVED IN PONCA City shortly after sunset and used the lights of the depot to disembark. Charlie noticed George standing a short distance away with a dark haired, slender woman who was almost as tall as Susan. As they walked toward him, he recognized George's wife, May. He waved. "George, we're here." He stepped down to the ground, turned, and guided Susan safely to his side.

Susan said, "Thank you, Sweetheart." She turned to the porter and offered a substantial gratuity. "Thanks for your help." She looked back at Charlie. "Sweetheart, can you take our bags?"

"Yes, I've got 'em. Here comes George and May."

George immediately looked at Susan and tipped his hat as he said, "We're saddened to hear of your loss."

May said, "And Susan, we're sorry we could not attend the memorial."

Charlie said, "I'm sorry folks. Where's my manners? Susan, this is George Miller and his wife, May. And this of course is Susan."

Susan nodded. "So happy to meet you. And thank you, and I understand. Now we're here to start our new life at the ranch."

They all climbed in the Miller's Buick and rode out to the 101.

A quarter of a mile away from the ranch headquarters, Charlie leaned over to Susan. "Can you see the roof peeking through the trees?"

Susan's jaw dropped. "My goodness yes, it's a big building."

Charlie grinned. "Wait and see."

A few minutes later Susan said, "When you described the ranch to me, Charlie, I didn't imagine it was as big as this. Why this is busier than Elmore City!"

Charlie laughed. "Yup."

Driving through the main gate, Susan reached up to the front seat and tapped May's shoulder. "This beautiful house is amazing. I'm so thrilled for you.

May said, "Thank you, Susan. We're proud of our home. We must have you over for supper after you have a chance to settle into your new house. You'll live close by, and I look forward to your company."

George added, "Susan, you're welcome in our home anytime. Charlie's office is next door to mine on the ground floor. I hear your home in Kansas City is wonderful."

Charlie said, "It's impressive and then some. We enjoyed a private patio and the conservatory with its swimmin' pool daily."

Susan said, "Charlie's right, it's a beautiful place, but we don't have a hundred and ten thousand acres like you have here."

George pulled up and parked in front of the house the Kellys would call home. Charlie unloaded their bags, and before they said their good-byes, he asked George, "Are you sure there isn't somethin' we need to talk about tonight?"

George looked Charlie in the eye as he placed his hand on Charlie's shoulder, squeezed it, and said, "It can wait until the morning. You two get settled."

"Okay, I'll see ya at breakfast."

***

Charlie rose with the roosters as always. He tried to be quiet so he wouldn't wake his new wife. Because of the small bed and tiny house, he failed miserably.

Susan yawned. "Wha… wha… what time is it, Honey?"

"Daybreak, probably about 6:00. I'm sorry, Sweetheart, I tried to be quiet."

"Okay. I'll get up with you. What about breakfast? I didn't check the cupboards last night. Do we have any food in the house?"

"No, part of my deal here at the ranch is I eat my meals at the café for free and you can eat there too."

"Did George know your appetite when he made the deal?" Susan giggled. "I doubt it. Go ahead and I'll go later. I know you're supposed to meet George early this morning."

"We usually start our business day at the café. I'm leaving, and I'll see ya later. Maybe we can go for a ride this evenin' and explore along the Salt Fork, okay?"

He bent over and gave Susan a long kiss.

Through a wide grin Susan said, "Sounds good to me; go meet George.

I'm sure I'll find plenty to keep me busy today."

As Charlie approached the front of the café, he saw George coming down the steps of the White House. Charlie went inside, sat at George's table, and waited for him to arrive.

The waiter, a stoop-shouldered, grizzled former ranch hand, came over. "Mornin' Mr. Kelly, glad yer back. Ya went to Kansas City, right?"

"I did, Jed. My wife and I arrived last night. She's at the house and should come by later this mornin' for her breakfast."

"Do ya want yer usual coffee, eggs, bacon, biscuits and gravy?"

"I do, and it looks like Mr. Miller's comin' through the front door now."

"I'll get ya both a cup o' coffee and come back with yer food soon."

Charlie stood as his boss approached him. George grinned and offered his right hand, greeting Charlie with a tease in his voice. "Good day, Mr. Kelly. I trust you slept well?"

Charlie smiled. "Mr. Kelly? Hey, I'm still the cowboy you hired months ago. Last night was okay, but we're gonna get us a bigger bed. The one there worked great for just me. But..."

"Say no more. I think we may need to move you folks into the big house. One of the visitor's suites is larger than the little house you're in now, and it has a nice-sized bed. I considered giving you one of those rooms anyway when I moved you into your job. Ask Susan to come down to the office later, and we'll discuss it."

Charlie grinned. "I will. I know she'll appreciate the offer."

Jed put their coffee mugs on the table. George took a sip and said, "It sounded last night like she grew up in a beautiful home in Kansas City, and your three-room house is probably smaller than her old bedroom."

"You'd be right. Susan told me the Kansas City house has somethin' like seven thousand square feet and sits on a little over an acre. It's a good size piece of land for bein' in the city."

They talked about the weather and a few jokes George had heard while they devoured their breakfast. When they'd finished, they went straight to their offices.

As they entered the White House, George said, "Get a pad of paper and pencil from your desk and come to my office."

In a few minutes, Charlie was seated in a stuffed chair across the desk from George, waiting for his instructions.

"Charlie, it's good to have you back, and a lot's changing here. But first, tell me about Kansas City, Susan, and what you two have planned as you see it right now."

Charlie cleared his throat, took a deep breath, and said, "What a mouthful of words and questions, but I'll do my best to answer ya.

"First, let me thank you again for meetin' Susan and me at the railroad station last night. I'll have to say, Kansas City is a big and beautiful city. Susan owns a good-sized piece of it. Well, I guess maybe I should admit *we* own it. Susan had her Uncle Curt, the company attorney you met at the weddin', draw up paperwork makin' everythin' owned by us both. Her father, right before he died, formed a new oil company under the Kramer Group based on some discussions he and I had before the weddin'. I'm the President of Kelly Oil Company. Susan's the Chairman and Chief Executive Officer of the Kramer Group."

"Charlie, I read about it in the newspaper. Maybe life at the 101 is going to be boring and too small a world for you now."

"George, I don't want you to think that for a moment."

George said, "Well, okay, but I've got to ask this. You and Susan are wealthy. My guess is you could buy this ranch and not have to get a loan. You don't need us or this job, so why are you here?"

Charlie smiled and said, "If I were you, I'd have questioned me that at the weddin' or before Susan and I left Kansas City. We've talked, and we have some deep, sincere reasons for bein' here. Her father created the fortune we own. She may have had some influence over it this past year as her father's health failed. I may have done a tiny bit over these last few weeks. But the Kramer Group is somethin' she inherited. We didn't create it. We do want to sustain it, grow it, and create our own legacy."

"That's admirable, but again, why are you here?"

"George, I couldn't stop talkin' to Susan, her father, and Curt about you, your brothers, and this ranch and all its industries. I have such admiration for you and what you do. I want to understand more about your approach to business management and how you make the 101 all it can be."

George smiled at Charlie's comments and said, "But I see you leaving someday to achieve your goals."

"True, but it doesn't have to be soon. It might take years. I suspect you and I have a lot to do. Can we get back to the 101 now?"

George nodded. "Sure." George leaned back in his chair and laughed. "Now, I know I don't need to worry about the size of the numbers scaring you in our daily conversations."

George and Charlie talked for a while about general issues around the ranch, then George said, "What plans do you have for Kelly Oil?"

"I'm still thinkin' on it. I didn't get to discuss any specific ideas with Susan's father. I have discussed some things with E. W. Marland's man, Hank Thomas, but I need to have another talk with him before I say anythin' further."

George said, "Marland has indicated he may make some changes soon, so that's why I asked. To help prepare you for some decisions you'll help me with. I need to discuss with you the drilling locations for some new wells Marland has identified to me. The Bar L part of the ranch will likely be our next big oil field. If it does as well as what you and Hank found in Payne County, we'll pump somewhere in the millions of barrels a year out of it alone."

Charlie gave George a concerned look. "The Bar L's tall grass has been one of our prime pastures for runnin' cattle over the years. Does your brother Zack have plans for it again this year?"

George nodded. "He does, but we're going to drill some exploratory holes anyway to see what we find. Over these past few years, the oil business has been more profitable than our cattle or any of our agriculture businesses. I need you here with me when I meet with E. W. sometime in the next day or two. You'll help address several issues he's identified."

Charlie said, "I guess he's back from Pennsylvania and ready to run the 101 Oil Company again?"

"Yes, he was able to get all his personal matters settled and returned last week. But he seems different somehow."

Charlie didn't respond, but wondered, *What does that mean?*

George said, "Charlie, call Susan and have her come up here. We need to talk about housing."

"Will do."

Charlie waited at the head of the front porch stairs and then descended to meet Susan. He gave her a kiss and led her inside the house.

As they entered George's office, he stood and walked around his desk to meet them. "Welcome to the White House, Susan."

She said, "This place is grand. You have something special here. I'm sure you're proud."

"We are, but the real joy for us comes when we share it. In a way, that's why we need to talk."

George took the couple upstairs, where he unlocked a massive door and led Charlie and Susan into a sizeable furnished suite which rivaled any hotel in the country.

After taking the couple on a quick tour, George asked, "Susan, how would this do for you and Charlie to have as your home here at the 101?"

Susan's eyes sparkled as she said, "This is wonderful. Are you sure about this?"

George nodded. "Yes, and you need to know that before Charlie left, I thought about offering him one of our guest rooms here on this floor. I decided a bachelor wouldn't need something like this and gave him one of our small new houses instead. Now you're a couple, this suite seems more appropriate."

Charlie said, "So, I had to marry Susan to get somethin' this nice, is that what I'm hearin'?"

With a grin, George said, "Yeah, I guess so. I can always let you go back to the little house."

Susan laughed as she broke in. "Be quiet, Honey. No, this is fine, George." She swept the area with her right arm. "I notice there's no place to cook?"

"You're right. We're in a guest suite for a distinguished visitor, who would be fed by our chef downstairs in the dining room. Another option is to have food delivered to the room."

Charlie said, "Susan, I remember from Elmore City that you're a great cook, and you seemed to enjoy it, but we would have about the same situation in the little house."

Susan smiled. "Well, we have a cook in Kansas City, so this is fine, Charlie."

George said, "I hope Charlie has told you part of his compensation is housing and food. He would have received the house and his meals at the café. I'm offering to expand the offer to include this suite. You both can order your meals from the chef downstairs or go to the café."

Charlie looked at Susan and said, "What do you think, Sweetheart?"

"Charlie, this is wonderful." She looked at George and smiled. "It really is wonderful."

Charlie looked at George. "Well then, we'll take this suite and thank you for the offer."

Susan added, "Yes, this is very generous." She turned to Charlie, poked him in the chest, and said, "Now, you better work your butt off for this man."

They laughed, and George said, "This is a nice way to end your first day back, Charlie. You two take whatever time you need to get your things out of the house and move in here. Take these keys to this suite, and you can give me the keys to the house after you move out. I'll see you at breakfast tomorrow."

Susan took George's right hand in both of hers, tilted her head, smiled warmly, and said, "Thanks, George."

***

The next day, Charlie met Susan for lunch at the café. She was at the table waiting when he arrived. After ordering their food, Susan said, "Sweetheart, we need to discuss how we plan to get around to places at a distance while we're here at the 101. A horse will not always work for us.

At least not for me."

"Well, I guess we need a car. I'm sure we can get what we need in Ponca City. George bought his Buick there."

"Then we need to go to Ponca City. Do you think we can get George to take us?"

"I'm sure he will."

After finishing lunch, they went to George's office. Charlie knocked on George's door. "Sorry to interrupt you, but we need to buy an automobile. Do you know what's available in Ponca City?"

"Why do you want an automobile? I don't use mine much. I still prefer my horse."

"We both think we'll need one for business purposes and to enjoy it. We plan to visit my family later this year. They live south and east of Shawnee. We would rather drive than ride horses travelin' on a long trip."

"Okay, when I bought my car, I looked at several different manufacturers. There's a lot more than Fords available in Ponca City."

Susan looked at Charlie and said, "Father loved his Cadillac, we have one in Kansas City, so let's see if we can get one for us here."

Charlie nodded and George said, "The place I bought my Buick also sells Cadillacs. I'm sure you'll find something there, and Truman will give you a good deal."

Twenty minutes later, they pulled up at the dealership and began looking at several Cadillacs. Susan found one she admired. It was a blue 1919 Cadillac Coupe.

Charlie walked up beside her and said, "This is smaller than the sedan we have in Kansas City. And different from the Marmon Limousine-Town Car we've used on special occasions, like the funeral."

Susan said, "Yes, it is, and I love the blue color, and the size is just right for us because we don't have Bernard here at the ranch. You can drive us anywhere we need to go, right Charlie?"

Charlie said, "Sure, Sweetheart. This blue one's my favorite too." He looked at George. "Whattaya think, George?"

"It's mighty nice. The paper in the window says it'll cost ya the better part of $4,000. But I assume price is no problem."

Susan said, "It's a lot of money for anyone, but we can have Uncle Curt wire the owner whatever it takes."

George said, "Here comes Truman. I asked the person at the desk to have him join us."

Charlie said, "Thanks, George. My goodness, he's a big man."

George said, "He is that. But you're bigger." George turned to greet the man. "Truman, it's good to see you. I've got you some customers here ready to buy a new Cadillac if you can make them a good deal. Charlie... Susan... this is Truman Drummond. He's the owner here. Truman, meet Charles and Susan Kelly. These are fine young folks, and you're going to want to know them."

Truman said, "Pleased to meet you. Are you sure a Chevrolet wouldn't be more your speed?"

Susan cocked her eyebrow, grinned, and shook her head. "No, we like Cadillacs. We have one at our home in Kansas City along with our Marmon Limousine."

Truman stepped back, smiled, looked at Charlie, and said, "My goodness, who are you?"

Charlie crossed his arms and said with a business tone, "We own the Kramer Group. I'm sure you've heard of it." He pointed at Susan. "Deal with her. She knows what she wants."

Truman wrung his hands and said, "My goodness, yes. I meant no offense, ma'am, but most folks in their twenties are hoping to find something on my used lot we can help them afford. I'm sorry..."

Susan said, "Mr. Drummond, no offense taken. What's your cash price on this blue coupe today?"

"Mrs. Kelly, I'm happy to sell it to you for $3,500, and I'll prepare it for you to drive away today."

Charlie and Susan looked at each other and shrugged. Susan turned to Drummond and said, "Sold. We need to borrow your phone to make a call to Kansas City."

Truman said, "Please follow me to my office."

Chapter Five
New Opportunities
May 1919

ON A **MONDAY AFTERNOON,** as Charlie and Susan walked back from shopping at the mercantile, they saw a heavy-set man in a business suit standing on the White House steps with George Miller.

Susan took Charlie's hand. "Sweetheart, do you know who's with George?"

"It's Mr. E. W. Marland. Of course, you haven't met him."

George waved and hollered, "Come join us." As they got to the bottom of the steps, he smiled and said, "Susan Kelly, I would like you to meet E. W. Marland. I'm sure Charlie has told you about him. He runs our 101 Oil Company. Charlie has spent a lot of his time with him for the past six months or so."

The big man leaned forward and tipped his hat. "Good to meet you, Mrs. Kelly."

Susan nodded. "And I you, Mr. Marland."

Marland turned. "And how are you doing today, Charlie?"

"Doin' fine, E. W."

Marland eyed Charlie and grinned. "I was about to leave because I've business waiting on me. George has some news for you both, and we'll need to talk in the morning. How does 9:00 here in his office sound?"

Charlie looked at Susan, George, and back to Marland. "We'll be here."

Marland smiled, nodded, and turned to leave. He paused. "Again, pleased to meet you, Mrs. Kelly."

George waved to Charlie and Susan. "Let's go inside, we need to talk."

In George's office they sat in overstuffed leather chairs near the fireplace.

George scooted to the front edge of the chair cushion. His eyes sparkled. "Let's sit here for a minute and discuss our future." He smiled at Charlie then turned and focused on Susan. "As I told Charlie back when I made him my assistant, the oil business is snowballing, and it's the most profitable part of our 101. That's why I needed and wanted him to help me. I had functioned as E. W.'s main contact with the Miller family. The growth in oil demanded more focus, and I couldn't give it the time it needed and stay on top of everything else here at the ranch. Charlie has been a great help."

Charlie added, "And things are goin' well as I see it."

George said, "I couldn't agree more."

Susan placed her hand on Charlie's forearm. "Sweetheart, your role supporting George sounds like a great opportunity, and it's what George needs."

Charlie squeezed her hand. "Susan, you're right. George, ya know I'll continue to live and breathe the oil business or whatever it takes."

George said, "Good, but I have a new opportunity I need to discuss with you. E. W. has just informed me he has decided to devote more of his time expanding into a new business taking him out of state more and more. He needs to sell his part of the 101 Oil Company and focus on Marland Oil. I told him about you and the Kelly Oil company. He's ready to discuss the possibility of you buying him out. Charlie, I favor it, and you and I can continue to work together. This time as partners."

Charlie hesitated, then said, "I... uh... I'm interested, but you've always said you needed my help to keep track of everythin' here at the ranch. How'll ya manage?"

George leaned back. "True." He scratched his chin. "I think Joe's boys, George William and Joe Jr., have worked with us long enough now they can step into the ranch management function and do more. That'll allow me enough time to work with you in the oil business. You know and love this place and will partner better with me than Marland."

Charlie smiled at Susan, looked back to George, and nodded. "I couldn't agree more. I'm excited about this opportunity. The oil business is where a lot of money's made, and I want to make a bunch of it."

George grinned. "You might get your chance. I'm calling it a day and heading upstairs."

Charlie smiled. "We'll be up to our suite soon, but I think a steak for supper sounds good. Ya with me, Honey?"

Susan stood. "Oh, I'm already out the door, you better catch up."

**

The couple hustled to the café and found the dining room empty except for the waiter. Charlie and Susan sat at the table near the front window and gave Jed their order for T-Bones, baked potatoes, and sweet tea.

Between bites, Charlie said, "Can you believe this is happenin'?"

Susan laughed and lightheartedly reached over and boxed his right ear. "For the umpteenth time, Sweetheart, yes, I can. This timing's unbelievable, but I thought you would get this chance to build a profitable oil business here in Oklahoma."

After his last bite, Charlie leaned back. "Let's take a walk and discuss things."

Susan put her fork down. "I'd like to."

As they walked under the canopy of a blackjack oak grove along the river, Charlie continued his thoughts. "I agree I expected success in the oil business here, but this is happenin' much faster than I expected. George has been tellin' me for some time they're makin' more money from oil than from any other area. The meatpackin' company's doing well too, but oil is king. I can't wait to hear what Marland has to say."

Susan leaned against the trunk of a large tree. "My only concern is the timing of this could keep us from going down to Maud to visit your folks sometime soon. I want and need to spend more time with your family. But I agree buying out Marland will move up the date of Kelly Oil being a profitable oil company."

Charlie grinned big as he said, "Don't worry, we'll get down to see the folks."

Susan sighed. "I know we will."

Charlie kissed her and said, "And someday we're goin' to add cattle ranchin' to the business too. Heck, there's probably opportunities we don't even know about or expect we'll add as well."

Susan teased, "With the kiss I thought maybe you might get romantic. But no, now we'll talk cattle ranching?"

He kissed her again, smiled, and said, "Oh, I guess that conversation can wait."

They walked back to their suite, and with bellies full of steak and potatoes and their heads filled with dreams, they crawled into bed and snuggled, content with their better-than-good life.

***

Charlie stared out one of the windows in George's office and smiled as several cowboys rode out the ranch's main gate the following morning. He turned and walked over to Susan. "Marland's parkin' his truck. He'll get here in a minute."

George said, "Good, let's sit at the conference table. Charlie, you and Susan sit on this side and E. W. can sit across from you two."

Marland entered the office carrying a brown leather satchel. With a large smile on his face he said, "Good morning, everyone. I trust we all got plenty of rest last night."

Charlie offered his hand. "We sure did. Susan and I are lookin' forward to our discussion."

George pointed as he said, "We have coffee over on the counter, and E. W., here's your seat."

Marland nodded. "Mrs. Kelly, you look beautiful today." He turned to Charlie. "No offense, Charlie."

Charlie smiled. "None took."

Susan put her hand over her heart. "Why, Mr. Marland, you flatter me."

They all shared a laugh then spent a couple minutes getting their coffee before they returned to the table.

George glanced at Marland and began the meeting. "I brought the Kellys up on the basics of what you and I discussed yesterday. They seemed interested, so I think you best share your wishes directly with them."

Charlie and Susan nodded their agreement.

Marland pulled paperwork from his satchel, spread it on the tabletop, and said, "George and I've had a good run the last few years here with the 101. I think there's still money to make and probably a lot. Now, I need to focus my efforts on opportunities away from here with the potential to grow my company substantially in other states as well as here in Oklahoma. I'm willing to divest my business interests on the 101 Ranch property and oil fields around Yale, Cushing, Morrison, and Skeddee. Yale and Morrison have drilling rigs in place. I won't give up my assets in pipelines and refineries, but I could arrange access to them at a cost. I can share other companies and investors who may want to buy me out."

Charlie put up his hand palm out. "I don't need to hear any names from you because only one name matters: Kelly Oil Company."

"Who's this Kelly Oil Company?"

"Me," Charlie said with a smile. "You're talkin' to the President of Kelly Oil. I thought George told ya..."

Marland leaned forward. "He said something about the Kramer Group. When did this happen?"

Charlie nodded at Susan, took a sip of coffee, turned, and eyed Marland up and down. "I had several conversations with Susan's father in Kansas City. While we honeymooned at Jekyll Island, her father had the Kramer Group attorney create the legal documents to make Kelly Oil Company happen. I'm the company President."

Marland grinned. "My, what a wedding present. I don't mean to get too nosy, but did he also provide startup funds?"

Susan stifled a laugh. "Money we have. Now it's a matter of whether we want to spend it."

Marland's jaw dropped. "Whattaya—"

Charlie interrupted, "More to the point, we would require equipment as part of this deal. Which would have been my next step. I will need to put together equipment and drillers as I explore for leases. What are your thoughts about includin' equipment in a deal with me?"

Marland stood and walked across the room as he lit a cigar. "I know all about the Kramer Group, and Susan, I'm sorry for your loss. I know money isn't the issue here, but I can't afford to give you more than three drilling rigs with the necessary support equipment. It's the best I can do."

Charlie rose and walked to where Marland stood. "What will all of this cost me?"

Marland hesitated, then turned to Charlie and said, "$300,000, and you must come up with $100,000 now, and I'll carry $200,000 on a note for a year."

Charlie didn't flinch. "I'll give you $150,000 cash today. I'll make a call, and we can wire it to your bank this afternoon."

Marland's jaw dropped as he reached back to find his chair. He sat still for a minute, focused on Charlie, and said, "Uh, ahem, let me give you my bank account. I have it here in this paperwork."

They shook hands, and Kelly Oil took a significant step toward becoming an operating oil company.

Charlie said, "Let's create a memorandum of agreement with George as our witness, and I'll call our attorney and have him create the appropriate contracts and work the transfer of the deeds after he's wired us the funds."

Susan stood and said, "Charlie, this went much more quickly than I expected, but E. W. wanted to sell, and you wanted to buy. It doesn't hurt you two have worked together these past months either."

Marland said, "She's right. This deal was an easy one to close. And George, it's easy for you to work with your man here, don't you think?"

George leaned back. "I'm a happy man. It's been good working with you, Marland. But I know Charlie and I will work great together."

Charlie and E. W. made calls to attorneys, and they agreed on dates, times, and locations for closing the deal.

Marland hadn't made it to his truck when Charlie said, "George, we can make this easy for us. I know what your contract with Marland had in it about the distribution of costs and profits. I'm fine with those numbers, but I want to add somethin' to the arrangement."

"What, Charlie?"

"I want to continue to use my office next door, and Susan and I will continue to live here in the White House for the foreseeable future. Not forever, but we need time to determine where we'll move permanently."

George leaned back, his arms crossed his chest, and he grinned as he said, "Fine, but now I'll have to charge you rent."

Susan bent over, laughing. "Now, there's a real businessman for you. Did you see that coming, Sweetheart?"

Charlie stepped back, stifled a laugh, and stroked his chin as he said, "Of course I did."

***

The next morning, Charlie and Susan were sitting together having a late breakfast when Charlie said, "I need to talk to Hank today if I can get ahold of him."

A voice from the doorway of the café said, "Well, I'm here. What do ya need to tell me?"

Charlie and Susan turned to the doorway. Hank Thomas stood at the entrance with a smile. "I heard from Marland yesterday afternoon about some deal he did with an outfit called Kelly Oil. Ya wouldn't know anythin' about that?" He joined them at their table.

"I might know a thing or two about them," Charlie said.

Hank ignored Charlie and beamed as he said, "My goodness, this beautiful lady must be Susan." He put on a show as he bent at the waist and offered his hand.

Susan smiled, took his hand, and said, "It's my pleasure, Mr. Thomas; please join us."

Hank grinned at Charlie, sat, and Jed brought him a cup of coffee.

Charlie said, "You're here? I thought ya still had some work at the Morrison lease."

"I did. I called Marland about what was happenin' there and he filled me in."

Susan said, "Marland didn't waste any time. What did you hear, Hank?"

"Marland said you agreed to purchase all rights to land, leases, and equipment supportin' his oil field work with the 101 Ranch. I hope the deal includes what we've done and are doin' in Payne County."

Charlie patted Hank's shoulder. "It sure does. We'll own the Yale, Cushing, Morrison, and Skeddee oil fields."

Hank took a sip of his coffee. "I couldn't wait to see ya; it's why I'm here. This is better than what we've been talkin' about this past month. I didn't see this opportunity comin'."

Susan put her hand on Hank's forearm. "As I think you know my father created the company after he and Charlie had talked. Father believed in you two and your dreams. I know he would have wanted you to take advantage of something like this."

Charlie said, "Now all we need to know is, are ya part of it?"

"Yes, buddy, it's why I'm here."

Susan said, "Charlie and I have talked about this a lot. I agree you'll get half the net profit for your efforts. I only request we recover our start-up costs before either of us takes anything out. Hank, your expenses and whatever Marland paid you are part of the startup costs, so don't worry when you don't see income at first."

Charlie said, "I think it was a good idea Susan's father created Kelly Oil as a company under the Kramer Group. It gives us tremendous resources if some great unexpected opportunities come along. But our focus is to stay independent and grow from within."

Hank said, "So, who will create our contract?"

Charlie grinned. "I called our attorney yesterday afternoon. Based on our discussions over the past few weeks I assumed ya would come with us. Susan is goin' to Kansas City in a week to run the Kramer Quarterly meetin', and she'll bring back copies of all the contracts. But we need to think like Kelly Oil startin' today. Did ya settle things with Marland?"

"Yes, he knows I'm here and why. I also talked to my three main crews. I'm bringin' them with me. I don't think that'll surprise Marland because most of them I brought with me when he hired me."

Susan leaned back in her chair. "You two are set up. This deal was way too easy. The oil business can't be like this all the time, can it?"

Hank and Charlie grinned at each other and shook their heads. Charlie said, "No, Sweetheart. But Hank and I have wanted and planned for this."

They spent the rest of the morning and early afternoon together. Charlie and Susan enjoyed listening as Hank updated them on every drilling site and oil field which was now part of Kelly Oil.

Chapter Six
Cushing
May 1919

A **WEEK LATER, AS** they walked to the café to eat supper, Charlie said, "I'm going down to Cushing and Yale tomorrow to work with Hank. They're setting up to drill another well on the Yale site. There have been issues with the weather. It's been raining down there for more than a week. It's probably muddy, but he's sure we can get things started soon."

"Are you coming back tomorrow night?"

"No, I'll stay down there at least through next week. I need to spend as much time with Hank as I can."

"I understand, but I'll miss you. I had a call from Chester Abrams this afternoon while you talked with George, and I want to discuss his ideas with you."

As they entered the café, Charlie said, "Well good, let's get our table and talk about it." They sat down and after ordering, Charlie said, "What did Abrams have to say?"

Susan said, "Chester has made great progress developing the business model and locating suppliers for our new department store. He's ready to find the initial location."

"Sweetheart, that's great news. We're still thinkin' Oklahoma, right?"

"Yes, and I would like a town we could get to easily. Somewhere in this part of the state. What do you think?"

"Susan, I have an idea of a place, and I think it'll meet every item on Abrams' checklist. You'll like it too, because I'm there a lot, and you could go with me."

"Where is it, Charlie?"

"It's Cushing. The town's growin' but is still small enough to fit Abrams' ideas."

"Oh really; do you have any more information?"

"Why, yes, ma'am, I sure do. Accordin' to what Marland told me a while back, Cushing is approachin' about six thousand people, and that's five times more than the census in '10. With all the refinin' companies and the businesses they spawn, he thinks the town could grow half again larger over the next ten years. With the oil business there and it already bein' the hub of the farm and ranch industry in the area, any new business like we're talkin' about should do well."

Susan nodded. "Makes sense, Charlie. We could have our Strawberry Hill construction company send a crew down and build on a site we purchase."

"We could, but I noticed some new construction on the same street as the hotel when I went there recently with Marland. Before we invest in construction, let's check if we could lease in the new buildin'. It appeared to be a block long. The sign in front of the construction site said they're buildin' to lease."

Susan smiled. "You are a natural businessman, Honey. We should lease if it's an option. Can I go with you tomorrow? We can stay at the hotel you mentioned, and I'll check everything out and call Chester."

"Sounds like a good plan. We can see where we are with the Yale oil field and the Abrams retail project and determine if we both need to stay in Cushing for a while."

"Good idea. I'll start packing tonight," Susan said as their food arrived. They both showed their hunger as talk stopped and they dove into their chicken-fried steaks.

***

Charlie and Susan loaded their Cadillac and filled the car's tank at the ranch's gas pumps. Then they headed for Cushing, planning to eat lunch at the Hotel Cushing.

As they pulled onto the main road headed south toward Perkins, Susan said, "This is wonderful. We get to have a little alone time today. And I get to see some new countryside. This is fun."

Charlie reached over and gently caressed Susan's breasts. "I always have fun when I'm with my sweetie. You look beautiful today, and I'm glad you chose to wear pants and a button-up shirt. Sweetheart, no one fills out pants and shirts like you."

She smiled and cuddled against him. "You're a little horny, huh, Honey?"

Charlie laughed as he said, "In case you haven't figured it out already, let me make it clear. When I'm with you, I'm horny."

Susan looked at the road ahead, and with no vehicle in sight, she unbuttoned her shirt. "If you promise to keep us safely on the road, I'll expand your scenery a little."

Charlie glanced over. "Consider it a guarantee, my dear."

Susan opened the shirt and exposed a beautiful chemise; then, she pulled each breast out to the daylight and into Charlie's view.

Charlie grinned big. "This is what I call travelin' first class."

"So, I assume you'll expect something like this anytime we're going somewhere in our Cadillac?"

"Consider it a given, Sweetheart. You're the most beautiful woman I have ever laid eyes on, and what you did tells me you love me and you want to give me pleasure. So, yes, I would love it if you did somethin' like this whenever we're alone in the car."

"This is a way to show you how much I love you. And you always show me how much you love me in ways that make me feel special. And many have nothing to do with how wonderfully handsome you are."

The drive to Cushing was pleasant, allowing them time to plan the next two weeks.

As Charlie slowed to a stop, he said, "Here's the Perkins turn-off. We'll go east for about fifteen to twenty miles." With a smile and warmth in his voice, Charlie looked at Susan and said, "I love this car. It's so easy to drive, but I'm sure it's the company makin' it seem like this went by much quicker than the same trip with Marland."

Susan playfully giggled. "And much more entertaining, I hope."

Charlie reached over again and gently caressed her bare breasts. "Yes. Words can't describe how I'm feelin'."

A few minutes later, Susan noticed the oil refineries as they arrived on the west edge of Cushing. She held her nose and asked, "What's the smell?"

"Sweetheart, it's the smell of money, lots of money."

"Is it sulfur I smell?"

"Yes, but sometimes it's somethin' else. Sulfur's probably the most common. To a rancher, the smell of a cattle feedlot means money. To an oilman, it's the smell of a refinery. Both would smell bad, in most people's opinion."

She looked at Charlie and started to button up her shirt. Charlie frowned, and Susan said, "Don't pout. You'll get more later. But there's more traffic, and we're coming into town now."

With a sigh, Charlie said, "Yeah, I guess ya better."

She patted his leg as they entered the town limits. Charlie stopped in front of the hotel and went inside while Susan waited in the car.

At the hotel desk, Charlie said, "I'm Charles Kelly. Do you have a suite available? I plan to keep it for up to two weeks."

"We do, sir." The clerk looked Charlie up and down. "It costs twenty-five dollars a night."

"That's higher than the last time I stayed here," Charlie said.

The clerk hesitated. "The oil boom's driving up the cost of everything."

With a grimace, Charlie said, "I'll take it. Let me go to my car and get my wife and our bags."

Charlie leaned through the open car window and told Susan, "They have a suite we can keep for two weeks. Let's get our bags and move in before we eat lunch."

"Okay, how much does it cost us?"

"More than I like. The clerk said they raised the rates because of the oil boom."

"You didn't answer my question, Charlie."

"It's twenty-five dollars a night."

"My goodness, twice what I would have thought."

"Well, it's three times what I thought, so we both are surprised. But I agreed to take it. Let's go sign for it."

After they checked in at the front desk, rode the elevator to the top floor, and unpacked, they returned to the lobby and found the restaurant. They sat at a window table and watched the activity along Broadway. Susan sat with her back to the dining room, which allowed her to unbutton her blouse just enough for Charlie to enjoy her cleavage.

Susan smiled and said, "I want to see your handsome smile, but a respectable businesswoman must keep to her standards of decorum."

Charlie nodded and said, "I agree and certainly appreciate your beautiful curves."

When the waiter arrived, Charlie saw him smile the whole time as he took their order.

Susan sipped her sweet tea and said, "He seemed to enjoy your view too."

Charlie grinned.

Susan said, "After we eat, you can walk me to the potential store location you described."

Charlie nodded. "Afterward, I'll call Hank's office and arrange to meet him."

They enjoyed their lunch and talked about Susan's first impression of Cushing. Susan was practically the only woman in the restaurant—all the other guests looked like either oilmen or bankers—and she was enough to have their waiter make extra stops at their table to "be sure" they had everything they needed. Charlie grinned as the waiter stopped by to top off a coffee cup he had barely touched.

"Why are you smiling?" Susan asked.

"Because I'm eatin' with the most beautiful woman in the room, and I think every other man in here's jealous of me."

Susan smiled and took a surreptitious look around the room. "I do believe you're right, Darling. Good thing I didn't unbutton more, or there might have been a riot." She dabbed at her mouth with her napkin and set it across her plate.

Seeing Susan had stopped eating, Charlie said, "Are we ready to take a walk?"

"How far is this construction site?"

"It's less than two blocks. We passed it as we drove down Broadway."

"I'm ready. I'm glad it's nice and close."

As they left the dining room, Charlie noticed their waiter wore a sad expression now that he had to go back to serving the staid oil company executives and bankers. Charlie took Susan's arm, and they left the hotel, turned right, and began their walk.

As they approached the site, Charlie said, "This next block is all new construction, and we'll want to check the sign on the corner for some contact information."

"They must have razed a building or two which stood here before. They are using similar materials and techniques used by our Strawberry Hill folks in the Country Club area in Kansas City. Their work does look like good quality. I do want to meet with whoever is doing this."

"There's a construction crew still workin', so we can ask them for information."

Charlie and Susan walked the block from end to end and returned to where the crew appeared closest to them.

Charlie hollered, "Hey, fellas, can I talk to your boss?"

A man walked over. He seemed almost as tall as Charlie, and bigger around his middle than his chest. His ruddy face and smile said I'm-a-friendly-sort. He turned to Charlie and said, "Hello, I'm Stanley Farley, the superintendent. How can I help you?"

Susan responded, "I'm Susan Kramer-Kelly, and I'm interested in the status of this building." Stanley turned to her with a surprised expression. Susan said, "I'm looking to locate a new business here in Cushing, and I need a site. When would be the earliest a business could move in here and start operating?"

Stanley's eyes had drifted to Susan's cleavage. He looked up and said, "Uh... We're targeting Thanksgiving. That would be the basic building, and if a tenant has specific needs, we could need additional time."

Susan noticed his struggle to look her in the eyes. She smiled and said, "Who would I need to talk to for detailed leasing information?"

"Uh, ma'am, Mr. Sam Holder's the owner. He's here tomorrow morning for a meeting with the City of Cushing's inspector to discuss some questions I've brought up regarding codes. I'm airing dirty laundry here. I'm from Chicago, and we had certain ways we addressed plumbing. They want something else here. I don't want to do it my way and find I must tear everything out and do it again."

Charlie said, "Really smart on your part, and it's good your owner wants to get it right the first time too."

Susan said, "It's Stanley, isn't it?

"Yes."

"I'll arrive here at 9:00. I want to discuss leasing options with Mr. Holder. Can you make it happen?"

"Yes, he'll easily finish with the inspector by then. I'll tell him to expect you."

Susan smiled again. "Good, I'll see you then."

As they walked away, Charlie said, "I think he'll remember our conversation for a while. He couldn't take his eyes off your chest."

With a wily grin on her face, Susan took Charlie's hand and said, "If a man's mind is there, I have him where I want him. You don't mind it do you?"

"Hell no! I'm happy to share your beauty, just not your affection and our bed."

Susan squeezed his hand. "Father said I caught myself a smart one in you. My goodness, I love you so much."

Chapter Seven
Sam Holder
May 1919

EARLY MORNING IN THEIR suite at the Hotel Cushing, Charlie stood at the wash basin shaving as Susan sat at a table brushing her long, beautiful raven hair.

Charlie said, "I called Hank in his office in Drumright while you bathed. I'll meet him at the Yale site at noon today."

She paused and looked toward the bathroom. "Good. Then you can join me this morning when I meet with Sam Holder."

He rinsed off his razor. "Yep, Hank had some things he could do in the office, and I wanted to go with you, so it worked out."

"Have they started drilling yet?"

Charlie walked out of the bathroom. "It's been too muddy to get the equipment out to the site. We'll discuss things and create a plan to get started."

"I hope you don't get the car stuck out there."

He bent down and kissed her cheek. "Gettin' the car stuck's the last thing we need. I'll park out at the road and walk in."

***

They had a leisurely breakfast and headed out of the hotel so they'd arrive at the construction site at 9:00.

As they walked west on Broadway, Susan said, "I want to get a commitment from Sam Holder out of this meeting today. I want to know an occupancy date and what influence we can have on the size and layout of the space. And he should give us a price on the cost per month to lease the space."

"Are you planning to commit to something before you talk to Abrams?"

"No, but I may put a retainer in place with Holder to buy some time for a discussion with him."

"Good thinking, Sweetheart. I guess you'll call Abrams later today."

"I will."

They saw the construction site was busy with workers as they approached the building. The sound of hammers and the shouts of men filled the air. Susan looked around and pointed to a group of men looking over a set of construction plans. "There's Stanley."

Charlie waved. "Stanley, can we talk to you for a minute?"

Stanley gave a final word to the men who went into the building. He rolled up the plans and approached them. "Sure, Charlie, wasn't it?"

"Yes, and you remember Susan."

"Good morning, ma'am. You folks wanted to talk to Mr. Holder."

Susan said, "Yes, is he here?"

"He is. Let me get him for you."

Stanley walked across the construction site and returned with a man who appeared to be in his late forties. He was of medium height and build and had dark hair and a bushy mustache.

Stanley said, "Sir, these are the Kellys."

Holder said, "Thanks, Stan; I'll take it from here." Stanley nodded and went back to the job.

Holder turned to Charlie and Susan. "Good morning; I'm Sam Holder. I understand you have some questions about the building we're constructing. How can I help you?"

"I'm Susan Kramer-Kelly; he's my husband, Charlie. We own a company expanding soon into Oklahoma. Charlie's involved in the oil business, and I'm working on a project that may be interested in using this site. Do you have some time now to discuss this?"

Sam's eyebrows rose, and his head tilted. They'd apparently piqued his curiosity. He smiled and said, "I must drive to Oilton after lunch, and I have about an hour of work to do here. But yes, I have some time. I recommend we find a better place to have this conversation."

Charlie said, "I have a meeting around midday too. We're stayin' down the street at the hotel. How about their café, and we can have a second or third cup of coffee?"

Sam smiled and said, "Good idea." He turned and called over to Stanley, "I'm down at the hotel with the Kellys for a while."

After the short walk to the hotel, the trio found a table away from the front door and ordered coffee.

Susan began. "I'm looking for a location to put a small department store. It's our initial venture into Oklahoma. When do you plan to have the property ready for occupancy?"

"I'm targeting December. Depending on the weather, anytime within the month. How much space are you looking for, and do you have any specialized needs?"

Susan replied, "Those are fair questions, and I don't have the details to give you good answers. I can get answers for you within a day or two. My man heading up this project is in Kansas City. I'll call him this afternoon, and we can address all your questions."

"Very well. I planned to have fifteen to twenty storefronts in this block. The final number depends on the requirements of the clients. You just mentioned Kansas City and you said your name is Susan Kramer-Kelly, right?"

"Yes, is there a problem? I hear the concern in your voice."

"Maybe not concern, but are you affiliated with the Kramer Group out of Kansas City?"

Charlie grinned. "Sir, we are the Kramer Group."

Holder nodded and said, "I've heard of the Kramer Group, and we'll work with you to meet your requirements, but of course, we'll need them as soon as possible."

Susan said, "I understand. We own a construction company in Kansas City. It would help if you had lead time to acquire your resources once you know your requirements. I can get you what you need as soon as I talk with Chester Abrams, our project manager."

Holder leaned back in his chair and said, "Now, this feels a little strange. I know the name. Do you mean Chester Abrams from Cleveland, Oklahoma?"

Susan said, "Yes, why do you ask? Do you know of him?"

"I do. I renovated a building for Chester a few years ago in Cleveland. He's excellent to work with and a true professional. If you have him with you, Mrs. Kelly, he's a real asset for your expansion."

Susan said, "Sam, can we all use first names now?

"Of course, Susan."

"Good. We plan to open, at the minimum, dozens of stores across Oklahoma, Kansas, and Texas. If we choose to make this our first location and we make a good team, this could become a long-term relationship. We'll want to lay out our stores similarly to create continuity and likely more profit."

Sam smiled as he said, "I'm getting more interested the longer we talk."

They continued the conversation for another hour, getting to know each other better. Then the three went their separate ways. Charlie headed to Yale. Susan went to their suite to call Abrams. Sam went back to the construction site. They would meet for breakfast Sunday morning at the hotel.

***

Charlie drove to the Yale site and found Hank talking with his crew.

Hank walked to him and said, "We'll start setting up this afternoon. Everything has dried out enough, and I want to get to drillin'."

Charlie tilted his head as a smile grew. "I guess you don't need me to help make any decisions then, do ya?"

"No, but I'm glad you came out. There's an auction of Osage County leases comin' up soon at Pawhuska. We need to be there."

Charlie asked, "Where's Pawhuska?"

"It's about forty miles east of Ponca City. It'll take an hour or more to get there."

"It might. In the Cadillac, maybe less. It depends on the roads."

"Good. Colonel Walters, the auctioneer, usually starts the auction at 10:30 in the morning."

"Who's this Colonel Walters? Was he in the Army?"

"No, Colonel is his given name. I hear he was named after some famous relative who died in the Civil War. Most of the big oilmen in Oklahoma will attend this auction. As I said, we need to be there."

"Then we will. What's the date?"

"I better check my notes back at the room. You're free to go and support whatever Susan has goin' and then go back up to the ranch. I'll let ya know what's happenin' here and give ya the auction date."

***

Later in their room, Charlie stood looking out the window as he said, "Well, the drillin' started at the Yale site, and Hank and I'll go to an auction soon. I've got plenty to keep me busy."

Susan said, "We both do. I spent several hours talking with Chester. He liked what he heard about Cushing. He's familiar with this town. Cleveland is only about forty miles from here. We discussed what he needed to complete in seven months, getting all the agreements with suppliers in place, staff hired, business accounts set up, and working with the construction company here."

"That's a lot to get done, isn't it?"

"Normally, yes, but we have his experience, contacts, and all our resources within the Kramer Group. We agreed we could do it. Since the building right now is not much more than the outer shell, he's willing for me to negotiate a lease, and he'll come here and work with Sam to help them design and build it to suit us."

"Great, Sweetheart. We're lucky to have seen this town and all the growth to support a new business. This timeline seems fast for me. What does Chester think?"

"He sounded excited, relieved, and wanted to get down here as soon as possible. Charlie, how about we drive around town for a while? We can get to know a little more about the area."

"Okay, sounds like fun and a good use of our evening. Are you ready to go now?"

"Soon; let me have a few minutes to freshen up."

Charlie walked over to the coffee table and picked up the newspaper. He settled on the sofa and read the front page of the Cushing Daily Citizen.

In a few minutes, Susan stood in front of Charlie. "I'm ready; let's go explore, Honey."

He looked up and found her in pants and a button-up white silk blouse. They clung to her curves. The same combination had been entertaining on the drive from the 101 and had become one of his favorites.

"Yes, you are, Sweetie. I'll happily drive you anywhere."

They went east on Broadway and into a neighborhood of homes within a few blocks.

Susan said, "My, there are some nice houses on this street." She pointed. "Look at the beautiful Victorian over there, and across the street is a Craftsman."

"Some of these are large." Charlie pointed. "Look at this one coming up on the left. With those huge white pillars, it looks like Mount Vernon. I've only seen a picture of President Washington's place, but I assume it's big."

"I went to it when I was back east in college. It is, but you're right, this home is beautiful and stately."

They discovered homes of varying sizes for about two miles. Charlie turned left on a road that had more houses. They were fewer and smaller than on Broadway.

Charlie looked at Susan and said, "I can't believe I didn't see ya unbuttonin' your shirt. My how the scenery has improved."

"Well, thank you, sir. Do you know where we're going?"

"Yes, I do. Main Street is directly ahead of us. I remember it as a main road going east to Drumright. It lies north of Broadway and Moses, the street we entered the town on. I plan to go back west using it."

"I'm glad you're driving; I'm just along to enjoy the view."

"No, Susan, I'm the one enjoyin' the view."

They stopped at a gas station and store, and Charlie watched as the gas jockey filled the gas tank.

Susan buttoned her shirt partway and went inside. She came back with a big smile on her face. "I swear the man inside almost forgot to charge me for these RC Colas."

Charlie laughed. "I'm not surprised; the view you gave him must have been worth a lot more than the two colas."

She looked down and gave an impish smile as she saw that she was unbuttoned more than she'd expected. "Oh well, I guess I made a memory for him. He seemed like a nice man."

"I'm sure he appreciated you and your free spirit. I love how you're serious about business and the important things in our life together. But I also love your fun-lovin' sexy spirit. You're my Theda Bara or Lillian Gish, although they certainly don't have your curves. To me, you're more sensual and beautiful than either of them."

Charlie paid for the gas, and they got back into the car. Susan looked at him, her face showing every ounce of love and passion within her. "Sweetheart, I love how you see and believe those things. We're so lucky to have found each other. Our lives are wonderful, and I'll always want to be your everything as you are mine."

She handed him one of the cola bottles, and they clinked them together, and each took a sip.

As they turned east on Broadway, heading back to the hotel, Susan turned in her seat to face Charlie and said, "I'm impressed with what Cushing already has to offer. Jasper created a successful business with a much smaller population in Elmore City. You said Drumright is growing fast or faster with much less commercial support. Which means we're getting here at the right time."

Charlie looked at her. "I agree, and I wonder if we should consider contactin' Rice Coburn about gettin' into the construction business here. There's a demand for what Strawberry Hill can provide."

"Not a bad idea, Honey. I'll call Rice on Monday. He needs to meet Sam too."

They completed their loop and parked back in front of the hotel. They went inside, found their table available, and ordered supper.

Charlie reached over and took Susan's hand. "I'll guess I'm free to go with you in the morning to meet with Sam. Hank and I agreed the site was dry enough to move our equipment into place. They've started drilling, and Hank won't need me here until the week of July 6th. I assume we'll negotiate a lease arrangement and have Abrams come to Cushing as soon as possible?"

"Yes, I asked Chester to come and provide all the operational require-ments to Sam that'll drive the store's design. He wants a fifty-foot front and a partial two-story space."

Charlie said, "It'll surprise me if Sam doesn't agree to whatever we need, but we won't know until breakfast tomorrow."

Chapter Eight
Back at the 101
May 1919

AS PLANNED, **C**HARLIE **AND** Susan met Sam Holder at the hotel restaurant for breakfast. After some discussion, Susan created and signed a memorandum of understanding for leasing the storefront. Susan and Sam forwarded the agreement to Holder Construction's and the Kramer Group's attorneys to develop the formal leasing agreement.

Sam said, "Mrs. Kelly, Susan, this has been a wonderful and fortunate meeting. I guess we have Charlie to thank for this."

She reached over and squeezed his arm. "Yes, we're grateful Charlie's down here in Cushing and involved in this oil boom. Sam, you and I both can take advantage of the growth caused by the discovery of oil in the area."

Charlie said, "Susan and I are wrapping up our business here in Cushing today and are goin' back to the 101 Ranch. We plan to git back here on Sunday, June 6th. Chester arrives here that evenin' on the Rock Island train."

Susan said, "Sam, let's meet for breakfast on Monday the 7th."

He nodded. "I look forward to seeing Chester."

Charlie said, "Good, we have a plan. We'll get you guys goin' on Monday, and I'll head up to Yale to check on the drillin' operation."

Susan said, "We've finished here, and Charlie and I need to get on our way. Sam, again, it's been great meeting you, and we'll see you in two weeks or so."

Sam said, "You two travel safely." He grinned and said, "Keep the Cadillac between the fences."

Charlie and Susan went up to the suite and packed their bags. Charlie reserved the suite for June 6th and beyond as he paid their bill. He also added a room for Abrams and his wife to use upon arrival. Driving away, the Kellys headed north toward Yale this time.

Patting Susan's thigh, Charlie said, "I wanted you to see the Yale site, and also, this road north, I hear, is better than the one we came in on."

Susan said, "Okay, and I want you to see something too." She unbuttoned her shirt.

"You're an angel, ya know it?"

"I know how to please my man. Didn't you say this is something you would enjoy as we traveled in our Cadillac?"

"Yes, I did." Charlie cupped a breast. "Amazin', Sweetheart."

Susan smiled and squeezed his hand around her breast.

Charlie said, "I called George while you bathed and dressed. He knows we're comin' back today."

She turned to face him. "What did he say?"

"All he said was he's got some things he needs to talk to me about, so I guess it's good we're going back."

Charlie turned right at the road's junction to Yale and drove the short distance to the property. He pulled off on some level ground and pointed to the oil derrick where they would drill the well.

"Hank thinks this gonna come another gusher."

Susan looked at Charlie. "A gusher of lots of oil, right?"

He returned her gaze. "Yep, lots of oil and money."

She pulled him to her. "Sweetheart, now it's a Kelly Oil Company oil well that'll come a gusher." She kissed him.

Charlie returned the kiss. "You're right, and we'll make big money from it."

They got back on the road and returned to the intersection. Charlie turned right, heading north to Pawnee.

Charlie put his arm around Susan, and she nuzzled into his chest. Their coupe had them close anyway, but he wanted to hug and caress her as they went down the road.

Susan looked up and said, "I love you, and I'm so happy as your wife and lover. I'm excited to see where life leads us."

Charlie gently squeezed her to him. Susan stretched and kissed him on his cheek. They enjoyed a pleasant afternoon and arrived back at the ranch before supper.

After taking their bags to the suite, they found George still at work.

George looked up as they entered his office. "Welcome home, you two. Sit down. Tell me about Cushing."

Susan sat on the edge of her chair as she said, "There's a great deal more to it than I thought. The downtown buzzes with activity, cars, trucks, wagons, and horses."

Charlie nodded and said, "And I'm glad I got to see Hank. It's good to get the old team back together."

George said, "I've met him but don't know him. Smart men have called him a genius at finding oil."

Susan's eyes sparkled as she said, "There are some lovely estates in Cushing east of downtown. And speaking of the downtown area, I signed a letter of agreement to lease a brand-new storefront still under construction in downtown Cushing. This store is the first in our new Abrams' chain of small department stores."

George replied, "What exciting news. So, Charlie gave you the idea for Cushing as a good place for the store, right?"

"Yes, he's just too smart, but don't tell him I said it, okay?"

They laughed, and Charlie said, "I can't help it."

George said, "It's late; what I was going to have you do, Charlie, can wait till morning. Could you get with Boss? Marland wanted to drill several wells this year on the Bar L land. Boss has told Zack it would reduce their grazing land to the point it'll force us to sell off so much of the cattle we might as well get out of the business."

Charlie said, "So you want me to talk to him? George, I may want to drill there too after talkin' with Hank. How about I ask to ride out there and let him show me his concerns."

"Good. You get it, and I knew you would. I'm sure glad you could come back now."

"I'm happy to help with this. Hank and I set up a drillin' rig, and it'll start operatin' by tomorrow. They've had so much rain in Payne County over the last month that the location where we'll drill almost became swampland."

George stood and said, "I'm glad you have it going. Go have supper and take it easy this evening."

Susan said, "We will, and you and May do the same."

Charlie and Susan walked to the café and found their favorite table waiting for them.

Susan said, "I'm ordering their ham steak tonight; how about you?"

"Sounds good to me. With some sweet tea, and I'm fine."

Over their meal, Charlie brought up something he had been thinking about for a while.

"Susan, my brother Jess has been workin' for the past year at a store similar to the one you and Jasper owned in Elmore City. Could we offer him a chance to work with Abrams as he opens the Cushing store?"

Susan asked, "Do you think he would want to?"

"I don't know, but are you open to explorin' the idea?"

"Of course, but he would need to want it, and he would need to have the skills, knowledge, and abilities we would want. Or should I say Abrams would want? It's his project and business to run, not mine."

"You own it."

"Remember, Charlie, we own it. Please think about this: How would you like it if someone gave you a business to run and made all the decisions for you? After learning more about it, Chester chose Cushing. I gave him the information he needed, and he made the decision. I only sealed his deal with Sam."

Charlie said, "When we're next in Maud, you make sure you ask Jess enough about his role at the store and whatever else you need to form an opinion about his qualifications."

"I will and certainly can offer my opinion to Chester if Jess wants a shot at working in the Cushing store."

"Wouldn't it be great? We can offer Jess a better future than he'll find anywhere else in Oklahoma. But you're right; he must want it. Thanks, Sweetheart."

After their meal, they walked to the barn. Charlie needed to see his buddy—his horse, Tony.

Charlie rubbed Tony's muzzle. "Tony, how are ya, my old friend? You look so good. I've missed ya so much."

Susan said, "You can tell he missed you too. How about we go for a ride tomorrow afternoon?"

"Let's do it. I haven't shown you my favorite places around the ranch. I know we once watched the sunset and enjoyed a nice spot and a beautiful evening, but there are others too. We can have supper at the Salt Fork Bar. You need to meet Mabel Little Feather."

"I do, huh? Is she an old sweetheart of yours?"

"Oh, definitely. Mabel's probably over 40 years old, five feet nothing, two hundred pounds, but I do love her to death."

"What?"

Charlie laughed. "She's a good friend and a great lady. But the description I gave you is not too far off."

"How do you know her?"

"Her bar's where all the hands go to get a cold beer and just be guys. It's on the edge of a settlement called White Eagle. The 101 is so large there are several small towns within the ranch's fence line. White Eagle is one of them."

"Well, it's settled," Susan said.

Chapter Nine
Boss
May 1919

CHARLIE LAY UNDER THE covers on Monday morning and planned his day with Boss. *We'll ride together over the Bar L portion of the 101... But, right now, all I want to do is look at my beautiful lady lying asleep.*

Charlie did all he could to get out of bed without waking Susan. He failed when he bumped the bedpost and jarred her awake.

With a sigh, Charlie said, "I'm sorry to wake you, Sweetheart."

Susan yawned and replied, "It's okay. I wanted to go have breakfast with you anyhow."

Charlie asked, "You haven't met Boss, have ya?"

"No, and as much as you've mentioned him, it's about time."

They dressed and walked to the café.

Charlie said, "What are you plannin' to do this mornin'?"

"I thought I would see if I could meet George's sister, Alma. I heard she was to arrive this past weekend from Kansas. We have Vassar College in common."

Charlie smiled. "I've never met her, but I'm sure you two will hit it off great."

They went into the café and found the dining room empty. They took their table, and Jed ambled over with two mugs and the coffee carafe.

"Mornin', folks, how's the day startin' fer ya?"

Susan said, "It's a bright, sunny day already." She looked at Charlie. "You'll have a perfect day for horseback riding."

"Yer usual this mornin', folks?" Jed asked.

Charlie turned to Susan with a questioning look and said, "Yep, thank ya, buddy."

Boss walked in. Charlie waved to Jed. "He's joinin' us."

Boss took a seat at the table with Charlie and Susan.

Jed looked at Boss. "What'll ya have?"

Boss raised his hand. "Just coffee. I ate earlier with the hands at the chow hall."

Charlie said, "Boss, this is my wife, Susan." He placed his hand on Boss' shoulder as he said, "Boss is the foreman for the ranchin' operation here at the 101, Susan. I owe a lot to this man."

Boss said, "Miss Susan, I've heard wonderful things from everyone I know who has met you. I expected a pretty lady. But you're all that and much more. You can call me Boss, but somehow it doesn't seem right for you. My momma gave me the name William. I'm Bill Bellamy, so feel free to call me Bill if you like."

Susan smiled and said, "With the respect Charlie has shown when he has described you, I consider it an honor to call you Bill. But... I'm happy to call you Boss. From me, it would be a term of respect and endearment."

"Miss Susan, you're a wonderful lady." Boss laughed and turned to Charlie. "Young man, do you have any idea how lucky you are?"

"I pinch myself every day, Boss. I still can't believe it."

***

After breakfast, Charlie and Boss went to the barn, saddled their horses, and rode out the gate and across the Salt Fork before either one broke the silence.

Finally, Charlie said, "What do you want from this ride over to the Bar L today, Boss?"

He looked at Charlie and grinned. "You mean besides a nice day ridin' with one of my favorite hands?"

"Yep."

With a serious tone, Boss said, "Marland has been workin' mighty hard to get access to the Bar L property for drillin' oil. I've been pushin' back to keep the area strictly for grazin' purposes. Now, since Marland is out of the picture, George wants to get your opinion on all this; so today, we'll ride over there, and we can figure out what we agree on."

It took about an hour and a half for them to get out to the area of the Bar L that Marland had coveted. Along the way, Charlie reflected. *The 101 is still a beautiful place. The tall grasses, rolling hills, and bottom land to the South Fork still draw me to it.*

He looked at Boss, "It's been a long while since we rode across these acres. A piece of me misses it every day."

Boss reined his horse to a stop. "I miss seein' ya on horseback. Charlie, as you can see, this is not the best land for plowin' and growin' crops. On the other hand, the cattle love grazin' out here, and they put on weight fast. This is some of the best grazin' land on the 101."

Charlie gazed from horizon to horizon, taking in a view including wheat fields and oil derricks in the distance to an alfalfa field and the native grasses close by. He nodded at Boss. "I expected it was this area, and I see your point. This pasture is much better than down in the southern sections. I know you use the southern area too, but this grass will take care of two or three times the cattle per acre compared to the area south of White Eagle."

"Then you do see it. Marland said if he thought he could find more oil south of here, he would drill there first. But his experts are sayin' they want to move into here next year."

"Boss, are you aware of the financial bottom line here at the 101 over the past couple of years?"

"No. I know we haven't made as much from cattle lately, but I have no idea about any of the rest of it."

"The oil business is where the 101 has made its money for several years. Even the produce farmin' has done better than the cattle business. George is feelin' a lot of pressure to make money however he can to keep the ranch goin'. For him, right now, that means he has to focus on oil."

Boss replied, "So, what you're sayin' is E. W. Marland and the oil company have been callin' the shots? Now it's you and Kelly Oil, which means you'll get what you want. Do I have a clear picture of my world?"

"Let me say it this way: If the oil revenues keep climbin', and the cattle business doesn't, George and I will need to drill on the Bar L. Probably not this year, but it may happen sometime in the next two years. Right now, I've got my men busy down in Payne County. I'm involved in some sites there better than anythin' up here. The only difference between me and Marland is I'm a cowboy who loves the cattle business. But now, Boss, I'm an oilman who wants to make a profit."

"I liked ya better when ya were just a top hand that I could order about." There was bitterness in his voice, but Boss smiled too.

Charlie could see the predicament that Boss was in. George was asking him to do the impossible, to make the cattle business profitable again, but that time was long gone. If the cattle business was able to break even, they'd be doing well. It told Charlie that his own thoughts about Boss were right. This man didn't deserve to end his many years of working this fine ranch in this way. But Charlie didn't have a lead line that he could offer to Boss. Not right now anyway.

They rode over to the Salt Fork and followed it back to headquarters.

Along the way, Boss and Charlie discussed their futures.

When they could see headquarters in the distance, Charlie tilted his head, looked at Boss, and said, "How much longer do you plan to stay here and run this cattle operation?"

Boss looked off in the distance. "You ask a good question, and your description of what is happenin' here could decide it for me. I'll be fifty years old next spring. I can't cowboy full-time anymore. Hell, I've been runnin' this outfit since my late twenties. I can do this for another ten or maybe fifteen years, but it may not be an option. Why do you ask?"

"I'm goin' to have a ranch of my own, hopefully someday soon, and I could use you and maybe Tom and a few hands of your choice to help run it."

"Now, where are you goin' to get that kind of money? I know somehow you started this oil business, but..."

Charlie said, "I already have it, but I've not come across the right opportunity. The beautiful lady you met this mornin' is worth several times more than the Millers. As she always reminds me, it's *we* are worth a lot."

"You married into a lot of money, did ya?"

"I did, but the beauty of it is, I didn't know it when we fell in love. I learned it only a few weeks before our weddin'."

"I guess it's none of my business, but where did she get her money, Charlie?"

"From her late father, Walter Kramer of Kansas City. Have you heard of the Kramer Group? You know, banking, railroads, retail stores, construction, and so on?"

"Oh my God, even an old cowboy like me has heard of him. You mean you're rich?"

"Yep. Boss, we're worth more than you can imagine. I'm still gettin' used to it."

Boss's eyes widened, and his jaw went slack. "Why are you here, Charlie?"

"I've learned a lot from George, and now I have a chance to grow an oil company since Marland was ready to sell. Susan and I both want to build our empire. As I told someone recently, we're grateful for what her father left us, but we want to build upon it and create our future legacy too."

Boss shook his head and said, "Charlie, if there's a cowboy who could do it, Kelly can." He smiled big at the old phrase Charlie had earned while being a ranch hand. "Don't forget me when you make it."

"Boss, my friend, why do ya think I asked you about your plans? I may make you an offer someday. I'll own a ranch, and I don't necessarily say it'll have a hundred and ten thousand acres, but it'll be a nice outfit. I'll want good help to keep it nice."

They rode in the front gate and said their goodbyes as they headed to separate barns.

Charlie gave Tony to the stable boy to unsaddle and rub down. Then he went directly to George's office to provide him with an update on the morning spent with Boss. At the office door, he knocked and waited.

George looked up. "Charlie, come in, and how did it go with Boss?"

"One of the best mornin's I've had for a while. Now don't take it wrong. I haven't had many bad ones recently. But it's great to spend time with an old friend."

"What's your opinion on the Bar L?"

"It's by far the best grazin' land you have, and if the 101 is plannin' to stay in the cattle business, it should be the last area we drill on."

"Charlie, you know where we're making our money right now."

"Yes, and I know you won't use all of the Bar L at once, but I think we should wait for a year or two and have a solid plan on how to minimize impact to the cattle operation before openin' the Bar L to drillin'."

"Well, okay then. We have enough costly things pressing us in other areas, like wild west shows, without taking away our profit from the cattle business. Thanks, and what did you tell Boss?"

"The same thing. I made it clear the cattle operation wasn't king here anymore, although it still makes money. He understands the oil business is puttin' more money in the bank for the 101 than anythin' else."

"Good, you did the right thing. Money's getting tight for the cattle business, and I have a lot of experienced hands that are earning top dollars for their work. Boss needs to see the big picture, and it's good you see it too and are the one to give it to him."

Charlie stood and headed to the door. "If there's nothin' else, Susan and I are takin' the afternoon for me to acquaint her with the 101. I better git on outta here."

"Good, Charlie. Go have fun."

Chapter Ten
Beautiful Country

May 1919

AROUND MIDDAY, CHARLIE AND Susan were walking toward the ranch café when Tom Grimes, coming from the direction of the bunkhouse, joined them.

Charlie offered his hand. "Hey, Tom, how are ya? I've someone I want ya to meet."

"Charlie, it's been a long time, buddy. Is this lovely lady your new wife?"

"Yep, this is Susan." He turned to her. "He's Tom Grimes, an old friend and my first lead man, or supervisor, here at the 101."

Susan smiled, offered her hand, and said, "Tom, it's great to meet you. Charlie has talked about how his first lead man had become someone he valued as a friend. Now, I have a face to go with stories."

Tom said, "Thanks." Not wanting to stare, he turned to Charlie. "You're one hell of a salesman to have convinced this beautiful lady to marry you."

Charlie grinned. "Yeah, yeah, yeah, I know, but don't tell her what a bum I am. I have her sold."

Susan laughed as she said, "Would you like to join us, Tom? We're having lunch at the café."

Tom frowned. "I normally would say yes, but the cook should have a sack of sandwiches waitin' for me. I'm takin' them to a baseball game in Ponca City. The hands formed a team, and we're in the tournament finals today."

Charlie said, "Let me know how the team does. Goin' to the game sounds like a lot of fun. But I've promised Susan we'd go out and explore some of the ranch today. It's great seein' you. We'll catch up another time."

"Yep, come find me sometime. We need to catch up, and I'll also fill you in on the team."

"I will, sometime soon."

After lunch, Charlie and Susan went to the barn, where they saddled their horses and rode out.

Not long after passing through the main gate, Susan said, "Honey, do you have a plan for the afternoon?"

"I do. I want to show you how grand the ranch is. Over the next few hours, you'll see several places that will surprise you. You're goin' to see hills, grasslands, thick growths of trees along the river, washouts or gullies, and oil derricks surrounded by cattle."

Susan clasped her hand to her chest. "All those things are on this ranch?"

Charlie leaned toward her and whispered, "Yes, and hopefully, the colors of the wildflowers will take your breath away."

"Charlie, your voice trembled with excitement. I can't wait for you to show me."

"Let's go then." He spurred Tony to a trot.

Charlie led Susan down to the trees along the Salt Fork, and they followed the river south and east for several miles.

Susan said, "This is amazing. I didn't expect so many trees."

"Some call it a woodland, a thicket, maybe a grove of trees. When I lived in New Mexico, people called it a bosque. You find it along rivers and creeks. The more water you find, the more trees. It makes sense. It's nice."

Looking up into the blackjack oaks, Susan said, "I hear songbirds. Many more than you hear in the city."

Charlie smiled and nodded. "We've so many crops growin' on the ranch, providing plenty of food. Some birds are here year-round."

Susan gushed, "The trees have their leaves, which are beautiful." She pointed up. "The variety of leafy trees mixed in with the evergreens makes these woods amazing."

"A little further, and we'll take a break and sit on the bank of the river and enjoy a waterfall."

Where they stopped, the horses could easily walk to the water's edge, drink, and have grass to graze. Charlie and Susan used a fallen tree as a comfortable place to sit and enjoy the waterfall.

Susan gazed out at the scene. "What a wonderful sight, Charlie. It reminds me of the creek in Elmore City. I'm so relaxed here; I want to close my eyes and dream. You must have come here before. Is this a favorite place of yours?"

"It is now. I found this small clearing on one of my first days with the crew as we rode out to repair the fence further south. I checked it out but didn't stop. I thought of it on our train ride from Kansas City."

Susan moved close and put her arms around Charlie. She pulled him to the ground, got on top of him, and passionately kissed him.

"Charlie, Sweetheart, thanks for this. We've only been out a short time, and I can already see the beauty of this place." She popped a few snaps on Charlie's shirt and reached inside to caress, squeeze, and kiss his chest.

"It's still early, and I hope you'll enjoy it all." He returned her intimacy by kissing and gently caressing her breasts through her camisole.

A few minutes later, they climbed back on their horses without closing their shirts. They looked at each other and grinned.

Charlie said, "Sweetie, about a quarter mile from here, we'll cross the river on a bridge and head mostly south a few miles. We'll come upon the small settlement known as Bliss."

Susan laughed and said, "Well, I was wondering when we might see civilization again. Just teasing you, Sweetheart. Lead the way; I'm enjoying it all."

"I'm glad. The 101 is nothing but beautiful country."

After a while, buildings appeared in the distance.

Susan stood in her stirrups. "Is it Bliss?"

"It is. It's small, but it's the area where Colonel Miller started the ranch about thirty years ago."

"Charlie, look at me." She smiled. "I hear passion and excitement in your voice. You love this place. It's your sanctuary. You'll have your own ranch, your own sanctuary; this I promise you, my Darling."

He looked intently at her. "Susan, I love you, and thanks, Sweetheart. Yes, I'd love a ranch, and this one has always been my dream. The right situation will come along, and we'll buy our ranch. I want you to know I consider a ranch only a part of the empire we'll build. The most important thing to understand is, without you, none of it matters."

They buttoned their shirts, rode into Bliss, dismounted, and tethered their horses.

Charlie said, "Let's walk around for a while. It won't take long to explore the entire town."

Susan asked, "Not because I'm hungry, but are we going to have an afternoon snack?"

"I thought we'd stop at the location where I found the rustlers and the missin' cattle. Corralin' those guys, as you know, led to George wantin' me workin' directly for him. I can share the entire story with you while we eat."

With a slight grimace, Susan said, "Honey, um, I, um, I'm sure it's a pretty location, but maybe I don't need to hear the details of what happened there."

Scratching the back of his neck, Charlie grinned. "Oh, sure, uh, I guess a cowboy would find it interestin', hell, maybe even entertainin', but a lady? Maybe not."

Back on their horses, Charlie led them toward the area with ravines, gullies, and the location where he'd found the rustlers.

Charlie looked over at Susan and enjoyed how she had opened her shirt again.

"Hey, Sweetheart, we're less than ten minutes from our snack site. Does that make ya happy?"

"Perfect, Charlie, I'm ready; what's for dessert?"

Without hesitating, Charlie grinned and said, "You."

Susan laughed. "That works both ways, you know."

They rode down through the ravine where Spencer had fallen. Then they followed the trail, which led to a clearing.

"This is where I found the cattle." Charlie pointed. "There's a nice stand of trees near a natural spring over there. We can stop here in the shade, and the horses can have all the fresh water they can drink."

Susan said, "Great, let's get out of the sun. I know it's May, and today has been nice but warmer than expected for this time of year."

Charlie took the blankets from behind his saddle, the sack of food, and two Thermos canteens out of his saddlebags. They found a shady flat area near the pool to sit and eat.

Susan said, "I'm hungry. What did you bring for us?"

"Let's see what we have here. How do fried chicken and baked potatoes sound to ya?"

"We have fried chicken?"

"Here ya go, see for yourself."

"So, we do. I was expecting a snack, not a second lunch." She grabbed one of the canteens. "It's sweet tea, I hope."

Before she started eating, Susan stripped to her panties. She laid her shirt and pants across some shrubs nearby. Charlie did likewise, and they got comfortable in the near eighty-degree weather. It made for an intimate meal.

After finishing her second piece of chicken and licking her fingers, Susan said, "While you spent time with Boss, I got a telephone call from Marjorie asking how we're doing. She had called the Kansas City offices and got our phone number here from Uncle Curt. Although she and her husband Edward appear headed for divorce, she's fine."

Charlie nodded. "I hate hearin' it, but it doesn't surprise me. Did ya see George's sister, Alma?"

"I did; she's an interesting person. We had a good visit. She loves her life in Winfield, Kansas, and has little interest in the ranch. Now, what's the temperature of the water in this pool?"

"I have no idea; why?"

"I'm going to cool off." She gracefully stepped out of her undies, waded in, and found the water to be about the same temperature as their pool in Kansas City. "Perfect. Do you want to join me? It's about five feet deep in the deepest point."

"I'm comin'. You can't have all the fun."

The pool spanned about forty feet across, so they had a good time swimming and playing their usual intimate pool games. After about twenty minutes, they climbed out, dressed, and rode off.

Charlie said, "I know you've mentioned more than once you enjoyed the beauty of the rolling hills, the wildflowers, and the colorful leaves, but what has impressed you most today?"

Susan thought for a moment, then said, "The size of this place and how familiar you are with it. I think some men are intimidated by its magnitude. Not you, and your passion and love for the land is obvious."

"I'm glad we've had this opportunity today. This afternoon, you've seen some of the areas dedicated to the cattle business. We could do it again soon and see other parts of the ranch. As we work our way toward White Eagle, I expect to see some oil equipment. We'll take it easy and keep enjoying this day together."

The ride to White Eagle involved a few stops for special views of the wildflower fields, so they arrived on the edge of town late in the afternoon.

Charlie said, "Here we are, Mabel Little Feather's Salt Fork Bar. Are you ready for supper and maybe a beer?"

"After the chicken, I'm not starving, but I'll have something to eat. I hope Mabel has something other than beer."

Charlie said, "She'll have somethin' for you. Let's tie up our horses close to the water trough so our buddies can drink." He looked at Susan's cleavage, smiled, and said, "You didn't put your camisole back on, did you?"

Susan tilted her head to one side, pursed her lips, and said, "No, is it a problem? I guess I can go around back and dress again."

Raising his hands and smiling, he said, "Oh no, it's not a problem. I wouldn't change a thing other than maybe one more button undone."

Susan laughed. "Well, I thought so. You like showing me off, don't you?"

"Yup, you got me there. Guys can look all they want. It's only fair to share your beauty with the world. But you're my wife and lover; I won't share that."

She unbuttoned one more, and they went inside and found a good-sized crowd. After their eyes adjusted, they chose a table in the corner, went over, and sat.

Mabel walked out from behind the bar. "Charlie Kelly, you haven't been in for a long time. It's good to see you. Who do ya have with you? I'm Mabel Little Feather. Welcome to the Salt Fork."

Susan didn't wait for Charlie to answer. "Hello, I'm Charlie's wife, Susan. I'm happy to meet you. Charlie speaks very highly of you and your business."

Mabel said, "I'm glad to hear it, coming from Charlie. He's been a true friend. He gave me his grandmother's recipe for biscuits, and now everyone's upset if I don't make 'em every day. He's a keeper, and you must know what I mean."

Susan smiled and nodded. "I certainly do, and it's why he's mine."

Charlie said, "Okay, you two, stop it, and let's order."

Susan said, "Mabel, what do you have to drink besides beer?"

Mabel replied, "I have wine, water, and colas. Tonight, the food's limited to beefsteak and beans."

Charlie said, "We'll each have beefsteak and beans. Susan'll have a glass of red wine, and I'll have a beer. Okay, Susan?"

"Perfect, and Mabel, again, it's so nice to meet you."

Someone walked across the room toward them as Mabel left their table.

Charlie stood as he recognized Pete.

Pete clapped his hands as he approached the table. "Charlie, you ole son-of-a-gun, how are ya? And who's this you have sharin' your table?"

"Pete, this is my wife Susan, and Honey, meet Pete Logan, one of my best friends and fellow ranch hand here at the 101."

Pete tipped his hat. "Mrs. Kelly, it's my pleasure. And Charlie's a friend for life, but he's no longer a ranch hand like me, as you already know."

Charlie said, "Sit with us so we can catch up."

Pete pulled out a chair and sat. "For a few minutes. I'm here with a few fellas. We're gonna head back early tonight for a poker game at the bunkhouse. As great a friend as Charlie is to me, I mostly miss him from these poker games. He's terrible."

They laughed.

Pete struggled to keep his eyes off Susan's cleavage. Charlie watched as Susan grinned at Pete's problem.

Pete looked at Charlie. "How and where did ya meet this fine lady?"

Susan placed her hand on Charlie's forearm and cleared her throat. Pete returned his focus to Susan and her cleavage as she said, "Charlie worked at a general merchandise store in Elmore City owned by my late husband and myself. We became good friends back then. My husband died in a fire at the store. Charlie stayed and helped me settle everything, and then he came here to the 101, and I returned to Kansas City. It was my home before marrying my first husband. You probably heard the rest from Charlie."

Pete said, "I'm sorry for your loss." He looked at Charlie. "I had no idea. I did know ya had some gal you wrote to."

Charlie nodded. "Pete, I didn't share the Elmore City story with anybody. Even George Miller learned about it only when I needed to go to Kansas City last December."

Pete tapped the tabletop and said, "Well, I'm happy for ya both. Susan, you caught him as ya said, and ya caught a good one."

Her face glowed as Susan said, "I know I'm lucky, and he says he's lucky too, so we're two mighty happy people."

Pete stood and said his goodbyes, and went back to his table.

Charlie said, "He's a good guy and the first hand I met when I arrived. My goodness, he enjoyed the view, didn't he?"

Susan giggled. "He sure seemed to like what he saw. But you know, he never showed anything but respect. Yes, he's a good guy."

They finished their meal, rode back to the ranch, and arrived at the barn about an hour after sundown. The young man at the barn took their horses to rub them down and feed them.

As they walked to the White House, Susan said, "I'll never forget today and how I got to hear from others what I already knew about my Charlie. They see you as I do. I also now understand why this wonderful place influences you and your happiness. I now know how important it is for us to own a ranch. I adore you, Charlie Kelly."

She gave him a passionate kiss.

Chapter Eleven
The Auction
June 1919

CHARLIE WAS STANDING AT the sideboard in his office and pouring himself a fresh cup of coffee when the phone rang on his desk. He picked up the phone's candlestick and receiver. "Hello, this is Charles Kelly."

"Charlie, it's Hank. Things are goin' well here at Kelly-Payne #1. We're goin' to start on #2 soon. Are ya available tomorrow to go with me to the oil lease auction I mentioned to you here last month?"

"Yep, I can go with ya. Tell me again, where is it?"

"About forty miles east of Ponca City in Pawhuska, up on Agency Hill near the courthouse and Osage Council buildin'."

"I remember now. Sure, Hank, let's do it. Susan won't miss me as she's leavin' later today for Kansas City to attend the Kramer Group quarterly meetin' on Wednesday. She'll come back Thursday or Friday. Do ya have your eye on somethin' in Osage County?"

"I do. Marland and I looked up around Burbank a while back, and some of those areas are comin' up at this auction. Marland and some others will likely show up there as well."

"Speakin' of Marland, you remember the young Indian, James LeClaire, he hired to help in the office?"

"I do; why?"

"I kept him on, and he's sharp. I'm startin' to let him do more and more around here. I can see someday we let him handle what we have here on the 101."

"We need to be in Pawhuska. Susan can take care of the rest of Kramer, and James can cover things here while we build our oil company. Can ya come up here today so we can go together in the mornin'?"

"I'll get there for supper."

"See ya then."

***

Susan walked into Charlie's office. "Sweetheart, I'm packed and ready to go to the train station, but I'm hungry. Let's eat, and then you can drive me to Ponca."

"Good idea. My word, your train leaves in two hours, doesn't it?"

"It does, but we'll make it just fine. My luggage is ready and at the front door."

They had a nice lunch at the café, and then Charlie sent her off at the train station. It was a long goodbye as they kissed and embraced each other until the whistle blew. Charlie knew she would call him when she arrived, but it felt strange to part since he and Susan had been doing practically everything together since before the wedding.

He returned to his office to stay busy, then had supper at the café with Hank. After supper, he went to the office to wait for Susan's call. He was missing her something fierce, and it was hard to keep her out of his mind. He was relieved when the phone finally rang.

They spoke briefly about the train ride and how Charlie had stayed busy all afternoon. It was no substitute for them being together, able to hold each other in their arms, to caress and explore each other's bodies. But Charlie felt the emptiness in his heart lift just a little as they said their loving goodbyes.

***

The following morning, Charlie and Hank met at the café. As they drove to Pawhuska, Charlie said, "You said last night at supper we would bid on properties around Burbank, Shidler, and Webb City. We're passin' near those towns on our way to Pawhuska. Do ya have a favorite? Should we stop and look it over?"

"Yep, I do. We can drive through, but we don't need to stop."

They had the time and drove through Burbank on their way. Hank pointed to the area he was interested in as they drove through the small town. "The three parcels located outside of Burbank will be a package deal. I'm sure of it. And I'm sure there's a lot of oil under them. If you want to make your mark with Kelly Oil we've gotta get 'em. Then, any others in the area are certainly worth somethin', but we want the Burbank parcel first. I know we'll hit it big there."

"Then we'll get it." Charlie nodded as they headed on toward the auction site.

"Marland talked about a big tree outside the courthouse in Pawhuska called the Million Dollar Elm. I'm guessin' it's where the auction is."

"Right, Charlie. Millions of dollars have been spent under that elm over the past few years."

In a short time Charlie pulled into the parking area at the courthouse. There were already a lot of people waiting for the auction to begin. Charlie parked his car, and he and Hank got out and walked toward the largest elm tree Charlie had ever laid eyes on.

Charlie said, "You didn't exaggerate about Agency Hill and this huge elm tree. Why, it's bigger than the three-story courthouse. No wonder it's become famous."

"Charlie, as I've said, there's been millions of dollars spent here since these auctions began back three years ago."

The pair wandered through the crowd to find a good spot near the elm. Charlie noticed several well-dressed men standing in a group at the edge of the crowd. He said, "Hey, there's Marland over there talkin' with a man in a fancy business suit."

Hank grinned. "He's Frank Phillips. The man's made a fortune already, drillin' over around Bartlesville. He could be one of our main competitors today."

Hank pointed out the other men in the group. "That over there is Bill Skelly. He's made money over around Tulsa. Standing next to him is Harry Sinclair."

Charlie said, "I've heard of Sinclair through Susan's father. I'd love to talk with him sometime."

Hank nodded. "Ya could learn the whole oil business from him. See that car over yonder? I believe that young guy is likely George Getty's son, Paul."

"You weren't lyin' when ya said there'd be a lot of competition here. What are our chances to git the Burbank lease?"

"I think we'll do fine, but it may cost us. It depends on who bids against us and how much they know about the site and potential."

Charlie said, "I've got $15,000 set aside to acquire leases or land outright. It's enough, isn't it?"

"It should be, but you never know for sure. With these big names here, things could get pricey."

Colonel Walters, a distinguished man of fifty-plus years, stood upon a stage erected to support the auctions and looked at his pocket watch. The crowd became as quiet as if they had just walked into church. He said, "Alright, everyone, it's 10:30. Let's get this day started."

During the first part of the day, the auction focused on properties in the eastern county around Barnsdall, Skiatook, and Hominy. Phillips and Skelly picked up most of them.

Hank leaned over to Charlie and said, "No surprise, those two love the eastern properties, and they bought those parcels at a reasonable price."

Getty bid on and won a lease near Haskell. Soon enough, a property outside of Webb City came up for bid. Sinclair opened with a bid of $1,000.

Hank turned to Charlie and said, "We're gettin' into an area we want."

Charlie said, "Then bid."

Hank raised his hand. "$1,500."

Sinclair, Skelly, and Getty looked over and glared at Hank and Charlie. Sinclair held up his hand and shouted, "$2,000."

Charlie grinned. "He's not happy."

Hank nodded. "We can let this one go."

Sinclair took that bid.

Colonel Walters quickly announced the next properties up for bid were from the Shidler area. Hank and Getty both bid on them again, and eventually, both acquired several properties around Shidler.

Walters finally described the three-parcel package of 1,250 acres near Burbank. "What's my opening bid for the oil rights on this fine piece of Osage Reservation land?"

Charlie decided to do the bidding this time and said, "I'll bid $1,000."

Marland finally made a bid as he called out, "$1,250."

Hank leaned over and said, "Charlie, does he know how bad you want this?"

"Not from me. This is your fault since ya said ya went to Burbank with Marland before we started Kelly Oil."

Then a new voice from the back called out, "I bid $1,500."

Charlie and Hank turned and looked over their shoulders. "Who's that guy?" Charlie asked.

Hank shrugged. "Don't know him."

Sinclair, Skelly, and Getty, along with everyone else stared at Charlie as if to say, well, what are you going to do now?

Charlie returned the looks with a smile and raised his hand. "$1,750."

Colonel Walters said, "$1,750, do I hear $2,000?"

Marland said, "$2,000."

Charlie looked back again, and saw the stranger look across the crowd. He followed the stranger's gaze to see where he was looking.

Charlie shook his head, and his jaw dropped. "Hank, that looks like the guy we had Pinkerton run off from our Yale well last year."

Hank strained to see the man. "You mean Willard?"

"Yeah, it's him."

Willard's eyes met Charlie's across the crowd. He scowled at Charlie, then nodded to the stranger, who turned, raised his hand, and said, "I bid $2,500."

Charlie grimaced as Willard gave Charlie the same smile that a rattlesnake gives it prey.

Walters said, "$2,500, now do I hear $2,750?"

Hank leaned over and said, "It looks like Marland and Phillips are walkin' away. They did spend a lot of money earlier. Good, this is the property we want. Don't lose it."

Charlie looked over at Willard and returned the smile. "$3,000."

Willard walked up next to his man and said something privately. His man looked up and said, "$4,000."

Several people in the crowd gave an exclamation.

Charlie immediately walked toward Walters, raised his hand again, and kept it high. "$5,000!" He turned to look at Willard and his man.

Willard looked like he had just swallowed a lemon.

The whole crowd was murmuring now and eyes were turned towards Willard and his bidder.

Hank said, "They've not seen excitement like this in a long time."

Colonel Walters leaned forward from his platform and pointed at Willard's man. "Bids $5,000 to you son."

Willard's man waved his hands as he shook his head no.

Walters shouted, "Sold to this young man here in front for $5,000."

Whistles and shouts erupted from the crowd.

Charlie looked around and saw Willard and his partner walking toward him. Willard's partner walked past without a word. Willard glared at Charlie and hissed, "You'll regret this!" As he moved past, he dropped his shoulder into Charlie; the jolt was enough to knock Charlie's hat to the ground.

Charlie wasn't going to take that from anybody, but before he could react, Hank patted Charlie's back and said, "Good job, partner." He bent down and picked up Charlie's hat and gave it to him. "I believe we'll make a lot of money in the Big Hill township around Burbank."

People begin to immediately crowd around with congratulations. Charlie watched Willard walk away as his anger slowly subsided. He also saw the group of Marland, Skelly, Sinclair, and Getty standing together. Skelly and Sinclair had stony faces, Getty nodded enthusiastically, and Marland smiled and nodded in approval.

Charlie looked at Hank and as he put his hat back on. He smiled and said, "Glad to hear it. That's why I'm in the oil business. But I'm thinkin' we've resurrected an enemy."

***

Charlie and Hank returned to the 101. They talked about their plans for the Burbank site all the way back. At the ranch Hank said his goodbye. Charlie went to his office and saw that there was a telegram from Susan saying she'd return tomorrow afternoon. Charlie smiled, knowing he'd have her back in his arms soon.

The next day Charlie busied himself with 101 Ranch and Kelly Oil paperwork. He also sent a telegram to the bank to pay for the leases he'd acquired yesterday. After lunch Charlie was happy to pick Susan up at the Ponca City train station. They embraced each other on the platform, and she kissed him passionately like they'd been apart for two weeks and not two days.

During the ride back to the ranch, Charlie put his arm around Susan and said, "Did ya do somethin' to your hair? It looks especially beautiful."

Susan snuggled tighter against Charlie and patted his thigh. "That's one of the things I love about you. It's only been a couple of days apart, but I've missed talking to you, not to mention other things."

"I can't wait to get you home so we can do those other things. But, for now, how was the meeting?"

Susan said, "The meeting was fine, nothing special, except Jim Townsley of Missouri Concrete asked us to meet with his lead man, Zane Krebs, outside Tulsa sometime soon. He indicated they have an interest in adding another quarry. He would like Zane to bring us up to date on it. I think we have a winner in Jim. He's got lots of business smarts and will fit in beautifully as we expand Kramer."

She turned to Charlie and said, "And what have you been doing while I made business deals? Being lazy with Tony?"

Charlie laughed and filled her in on the auction excitement. He mentioned Willard, but stressed that he wasn't a concern. He enthusiastically talked about the other oilmen and the great leases Kelly Oil had acquired.

Susan said, "Maybe we should be apart more often; we seem to conquer the business world better when we divide our forces."

"Maybe so, but being apart was awful. I don't enjoy buying leases as much as spendin' time with my sweetheart."

Chapter Twelve
Letter from Maud
July 1919

SUSAN STOOD AT THE door of Charlie's office, going through the mail. "Honey, we have a letter here from your family." She held up an envelope.

"Come on in, Sweetheart. I haven't got a letter from the folks for a long time."

"I was told it arrived Monday. We both were gone." She handed it to him. "Well, open it; let's see."

"Okay." He tore it open and read:

Dearest Charlie and Susan,
I hope you two are well; we haven't heard anything since the wedding. We are doing good and would love it if you could visit us for Dad's birthday this coming Saturday. We have not been able to go to the big ranch to see you, but we hope you can take the time off to come here. This is too long between times together. Everyone else is still living at home, but I don't know for how long.
Dad sends his best. He is still running the gasoline station and is becoming real good at repairing automobiles. He likes working with his hands, so he's happy. Jess is still helping the owner run the mercantile in town. Dan is still doing some cowboying at a ranch up near Earlsboro.
As you know, Annabelle finished her last year at

Maud High School. My baby is practically grown. Please let us know if you are planning to come down since you missed her graduation.

Love,
Momma

Susan said, "We must go. It has been too long, and shame on us for missing your sister's graduation."

"You're right." Charlie hung his head. "I've been so focused on gettin' our life together and started in the right direction I've lost track of things like this. I remember Momma's letter, but I was busy on a project with Hank. We better go see them soon, because I've gotta mend some fences with Momma and Anna."

Susan gave him a stern look then said, "I can't wait to see everyone again, and your momma's so sweet, and she may find a way to forgive you."

"Mom's an angel, but as ya can tell, she can get ya told if you're out of line. It sounds like my brothers are doin' okay, and I need to take a gift to Anna to make up for missing her ceremony."

Susan said, "A girl always likes a box of chocolates, but you need something else to make up for this."

"Chocolates are fine, but that's not enough. But, I don't know what else to get her."

"Leave that to me. We'll get chocolates on the way and I'll take her shopping while we're there."

"That's fine, we'll do that."

Susan asked, "When can we leave?"

"I'll talk to George and make sure we're caught up on everything. I think we might be able to get away on Friday."

"I can do the same with Abrams. Friday sounds good. Can you call and arrange a room somewhere along the way for us?"

"I'll get us a room at the Norwood in Shawnee. We'll stay there Friday night and drive into Maud the next morning. I stayed there on my way to the 101 after leavin' Elmore City. It's a nice place."

***

They loaded the Cadillac on Friday morning and went to the café for a late breakfast. After ordering their food, Charlie said, "I heard ya on the phone while I shaved. Was it Chester?"

"Yes, he reminded me to ask about your brother Jess. He's beginning to think about staff, and I had mentioned Jess is working for a mercantile in Maud. We must also stop in Cushing on Monday on our way back here."

"Great. We'll mention it to him. Here comes our food."

Twenty minutes later, they drove out of the main gate. As Charlie turned south, he looked over at Susan and said, "Let's talk about our future and how we plan to get there."

Susan turned in the seat and faced Charlie. She said, "Talk to me; tell me what you mean when you say our future?"

"Where we are in five years, and at the end of the 20s. What do we need to create to get there? Although we've talked about it before, what philosophy or criteria do we base our decisions on?"

"Honey, it's a conversation we need to have. It should happen when we both can focus entirely on the subject and each other. I'm glad you're bringing the subject up; it means we're both serious about becoming successful and powerful in business. We can—"

"Susan, sorry for buttin' in. I'm not just sayin' in the oil business and maybe ranchin' too. Your father was smart in how he got involved in several different businesses. As you have said, he also had friends and associates he would spend time with and give and take advice from."

Susan said, "All that's true. How about we get to Shawnee, settle into our room, have supper, and then discuss this."

Charlie looked over at her again. She faced him with her beautiful smile and shirt open down to her lap. She had her mind on another subject.

Charlie smiled back at her and said, "Okay, we'll have the conversation tonight."

They drove on, enjoying the nice weather and the nice views. Charlie enjoyed the views inside the car as well as out.

They passed through many small towns like Cushing, and Susan discussed how many possibilities there were for Abrams to expand in the state. Charlie pointed out the many ranches they passed and what he knew about their operations, and also how many new oil wells there were. They seemed to be growing like wildflowers after a summer rain.

They stopped at a roadside diner for a quick lunch and then arrived on the edge of Shawnee in the late afternoon. The highway became Harrison Street, and Charlie stayed with Harrison, heading south toward Main Street.

Susan said, "There's a gas station, we should fill up now. Hey, it's a Marland Station. Is that E. W. Marland's company?"

"Yes, and we should give him our business, right?"

Susan laughed and said, "Oh yes, we must."

After filling the tank, they drove south on Harrison Street and turned west on Main. In about a mile, they got to Broadway Avenue.

Charlie said, "Our hotel's in the first block north of here. We can go directly there, or there's a spot I passed last year where we can stretch our legs first."

Susan stretched and said, "Let's stretch our legs. We don't need to get to the hotel right away."

"Great, I'll show you Benson Park. I rode Tony over to the entrance, but I didn't go into the area."

As they pulled into the parking area, Susan said, "This is amazing, Sweetheart."

They could see an expanse of green lawn surrounding a lake from their car. They got out of the Cadillac and walked toward the lake.

"Shawnee seems like another good candidate for an Abrams store," Susan commented as they watched ducks swimming in the lake.

"It does. It's the county seat and looks to be growin' like Cushing is."

They continued their stroll around the park. Families walked along and children played. They saw a stage where some workmen were making repairs. They eventually circled back to their car.

"Thank you, Charlie," Susan said. "That was a nice way to end the afternoon. But now I'm hungry again."

Charlie laughed. "Well, let's go check in. The Norwood has a fine restaurant."

They left the park and drove to the hotel. Charlie parked the Cadillac in front, and they took their bags inside. As they entered the lobby, Charlie pointed to a fireplace and stuffed chairs and said, "This is where I sat with Clay Stephens after we met in Cattlemen's Restaurant. I ate the best steak ever in there. Clay said they buy his beef for the restaurant."

Susan tilted her head to the side, smiled, and said, "That's a pretty big compliment considering some of the steaks I've had at the café on the 101. You better not let George hear you say that." Charlie laughed and Susan continued. "Why don't you call Clay right now? Maybe he could come into town tonight and meet us for supper."

"I guess I could. I'll give him a call."

Charlie found a phone along the wall. He picked up the earpiece from its cradle and said, "Operator, I need Clay Stephens at the Double Bar S Ranch east of Shawnee."

After three rings he heard, "Hello, you've got the Double Bar S, Clay speakin'."

"Clay, it's Charlie Kelly. We met at the Norwood Hotel last year."

"Charlie Kelly, I remember you. Did you make it to the 101?"

"I did. I now work directly with George Miller, and I'm married too."

"My word, you don't waste much time, do ya?"

"My wife's with me, and we're stayin' the night at the Norwood. We wanted to invite you to join us for supper tonight. And bring your wife too."

"We can do that. What time, and I assume we'll meet at Cattleman's?"

"Yep, how about 7:00?"

"Fine, we'll see you then."

Chapter Thirteen
Dinner and an Invitation
July 1919

THEY SETTLED INTO THE Presidential Suite. Susan took a quick shower to clean up after the drive, while Charlie unpacked their bags then read one of his books.

Susan stepped out of the bathroom, drying her hair with a towel and wearing her silk robe. "I believe I owe you a conversation about our future plans," she said as she sat down on the sofa.

Charlie set his book down. "I don't know if I want to talk now," he said as he leaned over and placed a hand on her robe, opening it slightly.

"We'll have time for that later," Susan said. "I want to talk now before the Stephenses arrive for dinner. You must have had something on your mind earlier today. What is it?"

Charlie leaned back and placed his hand on Susan's thigh. "You're right, Darlin'. I know you've been able to tell how much ranchin' means to me."

Susan patted his hand. "That was clear from the tour of the 101 that you gave me. And like I said then, I know how much you love the ranch. You had mentioned then about wanting to own a ranch someday."

"That's true, and I hope we can do that in the next few years. I want it to be the right place and the right time to make it happen. I've been keepin' my eye open for the right opportunity."

"I'm glad to hear that, and I couldn't agree more. But Charlie, we don't settle for something when it comes along. We get what we want when it's right for us."

Charlie smiled and gave her a kiss. "I knew there was a reason I loved you. That's what I wanted to talk about on the drive. That I want to find the right opportunity for ownin' a ranch. The right time could be soon because I know who I want to help run my ranch, and if I don't act soon they may not be available."

"What do you mean?"

"George has told me that the cattle business at the 101 isn't as profitable as it used to be. I get the impression that he may be thinking about letting some of his top hands go because he can't afford to pay them."

Susan nodded. "Salaries are always one of the biggest expenses any business has. I get your point though. If the right opportunity comes along, for a top-quality ranch and the right people to run it, then we need to be ready to act."

"Exactly what I was thinkin'." Charlie leaned over and let his hand slip inside her robe and gave her a kiss.

"I told you we don't have time right now," Susan said as she broke the kiss.

Charlie looked over at the clock hanging on the wall. "Sure we do."

Susan playfully pushed him away. "Uh-uh, you still smell like the road. You need to take a shower before our guests arrive."

"Well, why don't you join me?"

"I've already had my shower. You should have thought of that sooner." She gave him a push toward the bathroom and Charlie reluctantly went to get cleaned up.

***

A few minutes before 7:00, Charlie and Susan walked down the stairs to the restaurant. A tall, broad-shouldered man and an elegant blond lady entered the front door, and Charlie turned to Susan. "There's Clay and his wife." They walked across the lobby to greet them.

"Clay, it's good to see you again," Charlie said.

They shook hands, then Clay stepped aside and said, "Let me introduce my wife, Julie. And, my dear, meet Charlie Kelly."

Offering his hand, Charlie said, "It's wonderful to make yer acquaintance, ma'am." He turned. "And this is my wife, Susan."

Susan said to Clay, "I'm so happy to have a face to put with your name." She turned. "Julie, I look forward to getting to know you." She laughed. "Oh, and you too, Clay."

"I reserved a table for us, so let's go into the restaurant," Charlie said.

The maître d' led them to a separate dining room dedicated to the Presidential Suite. After the party was seated, he said, "Your waiter will join you soon." He closed the French double doors behind him as he departed.

Clay said, "Julie and I eat here often, but I've only been in this private room once. Are you guys staying in a suite?"

Susan replied, "Charlie made the reservations. I thought he meant to impress me, but I'm wrong. It's you he wanted to impress."

Charlie leaned back. "Now, wait a minute. I wasn't tryin' to impress anybody." He looked around the table and grinned big. "But, how amma doin'?"

The waiter, dressed in a white dinner jacket with a towel draped over his left forearm, entered the room, interrupting their laughter. "Welcome, and what can I get you folks to drink?"

Charlie said, "Bring us a bottle of red wine to start."

Clay leaned forward and said, "Julie and I enjoy the cabernet here."

"Oh, that's our favorite too," Susan said.

After the waiter departed, Clay scratched his head and looked at Charlie. "I may be wrong, but has George Miller started paying his cow-pokes better wages than I remember?"

Charlie smiled but before he could say anything, the waiter returned with the wine. He opened the bottle and poured out four glasses.

The waiter turned to Clay. "Good evening, Mr. Stephens. I assume you and your wife will want your usual medium rare ribeye steak?"

Clay nodded. "Yes, Gilbert, thank you."

Susan said, "You must be regulars here." She handed her menu to Gilbert. "I'll take a ribeye medium. Charlie, that leaves only you to complete our order."

"I'll take a ribeye, medium rare, thank you."

After the waiter left the room, Clay tried again. "Let's split this bill. I'm sure you're doing well at the 101, but the Millers don't pay cowboys Presidential Suite money."

Susan jumped in before Charlie could respond. "George Miller's not the only person Charlie has impressed since you two met. Let me complete the introduction here. My name before Kelly was Blackaby, as in Jasper Blackaby. As you already know, I'm his widow. Charlie and I had become close friends, and he amazed me as he helped with everything after Jasper's death. This all happened shortly before you met him. We continued to correspond, and Charlie came to Kansas City last year before Christmas, and we married on Valentine's Day. My father passed away in March, less than a month after our wedding."

Clay said, "Well, I'm sorry for your loss but happy you have each other. He's still a dollar-a-day cowboy, isn't he? Now, wait, I'm sorry. It's none of my business. I apologize. My only excuse is I took a likin' to this guy about a year ago. I had hoped to hear from him again. Gettin' together tonight sure is nice."

Susan responded again before Charlie could get in a word. "He's mighty likable, for sure. There's more to the story. I also had a name before Blackaby. People knew me as Susan Kramer of Kansas City. And—"

Clay sat back in his chair. "Did you say Kramer? As in Walter Kramer and the Kramer Group?"

Susan smiled and nodded. "That's me."

Charlie finally got a word in. "Clay, I didn't know anything about the Kramer Group until I arrived in Kansas City. Wait a minute. I meant to say I didn't know her as a Kramer. Like most people, I had heard of her father and the huge empire of companies he had created."

Julie said, "What a wonderful, romantic story. Charlie, you fell in love with Susan because she's a beautiful, sweet young woman. And it's obvious she loves you."

Charlie said, "That's the truth of it. Now I know you want to ask me why I'm still workin' at the 101 Ranch."

Clay said, "It's my next question, for sure."

Charlie placed his elbows on the table. "I'm no longer cowboyin' for a dollar a day." He slowly shook his head. "But it doesn't mean I'm not Charlie. I'll always be a cowboy at heart. Before goin' to Kansas City, I had become George Miller's assistant, primarily workin' in the oil business. Occasionally, he'd send me out to check something on the cattle side, but my main efforts have been in oil over in the Cushing oil fields."

Susan added, "Charlie has made it clear he still loves cattle and ranch life, and I'll admit to my growing fondness for it as well. But now he has some personal plans, including working with George from a different perspective."

Julie leaned forward, bright-eyed, and said, "Tell us, Charlie; I'm so curious."

Charlie said, "When Susan and I returned to the 101 from Kansas City a few months ago, George had a big surprise waitin' for us. E. W. Marland had informed him he wanted to sell off his investment in the 101 Oil Company. Susan and I already owned the Kelly Oil Company under the Kramer Group. Her father had created it as a wedding gift shortly before his death. We met with Marland, and Kelly Oil purchased Marland's drilling and exploration interests in the 101 Oil Company. I've already added some additional resources to the company, and we're up and running. I plan to build the company as we add to our business empire."

Clay said, "Charlie, you have been very busy. What brings you to Shawnee?"

"We're on our way to Maud to visit my family and celebrate my father's birthday. We must be back in Cushing on Monday."

Susan said, "I've only met his family once, at our wedding. This visit's our first get-together as a couple with them. I'm excited and a little scared."

Julie said, "I don't know why you're scared. Don't worry; his folks will love you."

Charlie said, "Julie's right. They already love her. I'm sure Susan knew it at our weddin'. There'll be no question after another day or two with them in Maud."

The food arrived, and somebody ordered another bottle of wine. The conversation continued as they ate. They all shared stories, and everyone got to know each other better. Clay related how everything was going at the Double Bar S and how he and Julie had met each other. Charlie talked about the oil business in Cushing and related the events at the lease auction. Susan talked about their honeymoon on Jekyll Island and also said that they were starting to think about owning a ranch so that Charlie would have his own little island of calm in Oklahoma away from all the oil business.

Later, as they stood in the lobby and said their goodbyes, Clay asked, "Could you guys arrange to come to the Double Bar S on your way to Cushing? I want to continue our conversation about your dream of owning a ranch."

Charlie looked at Susan then turned back to Clay and said, "We would love to."

Julie said, "Come up Sunday on your way to Cushing. I'll have a nice brunch prepared for us."

Susan said, "Charlie, I would love it; what do you think?"

Charlie said, "Consider it done."

Clay and Julie left, and Charlie and Susan went to the mahogany-walled bar for one more glass of wine. Although the place was empty except for one guy at the bar, they took a quiet and very private table for two in a dimly lit corner.

Susan said, "I like the Stephenses a lot."

"Yes, I liked Clay the first time I met him last year. The Stephenses own the largest ranch in this part of Oklahoma. I look forward to seein' it."

"He seemed interested in what you're doing. Why do you think he wants to talk to us about owning a ranch someday?"

"I don't know. I'm curious to know what Clay is thinkin'."

"Whatever it is, I think that Clay may be another of those people who will be important to get to know better as we work to build our empire."

"Yep. He's well connected to people in the beef industry all the way to the Chicago Mercantile Exchange."

Susan grinned and leaned back into the tall booth. She unbuttoned her blouse enough to show Charlie her cleavage as she said, "I'm glad we came in here. Before going to the suite, I wanted this romantic moment."

Charlie smiled as he reached over and gently squeezed her forearm. "Susan, this evenin' with the Stephenses may begin a significant part of our future. And finishin' the day in this beautiful atmosphere with you is all I could ask for."

Chapter Fourteen
Birthday Celebration
July 1919

CHARLIE AND SUSAN HAD breakfast early at the hotel and were on the road south when Susan said, "I'm excited to spend more time with your family. I know I've said it a hundred times since we left the 101."

"I know you're a little nervous. It's *our* family now, and they love you. By the time we leave tomorrow, Momma will say somethin' like 'Susan, you're welcome back anytime, even if Charlie messes up and leaves ya.'"

"Oh, you're being silly, but I hope they welcome me that way. I'm a city girl who's learning the country ways. I'm happy doing it, but although you thought so in Elmore City, I'm not a good cook. I don't sew; I don't know how to do much of anything most country women do."

"Susan, remember me sayin' back in Kansas City, I not marryin' you for your cookin', sewin', or cleanin'? I married you because you are my best friend, and I love ya for bein' you."

"I remember, but you aren't your mother or sister."

They had headed east toward Seminole when Charlie said, "I've been to Maud before, but Clay told me last night about a shortcut. He said to watch for a sign about five miles east of town. It'll point south and say 'Maud nine miles.' I don't want to miss it."

"Okay, I'll watch for it. I guess we're maybe thirty minutes from their house."

Charlie pointed and said, "See the sign, and there's the road." He turned south.

In a few minutes, Susan pointed. "Look, I see a water tank, or do you say tower?"

The water tank said MAUD on its side, and they pulled up to a lovely white house with a big tree in the front yard.

With big eyes and a bigger grin, Susan said, "Charlie, the house is darling. It looks fairly new, don't you think?"

"Yes, it's not old. I'm really proud for my folks."

They got out of the car, walked to the front door, and knocked.

A voice from inside said, "Comin'."

The door opened, and a beautiful, young blond woman stood tall in the doorway.

She screamed, "It's Charlie! It's Charlie and Susan, Momma!"

She opened the door and jumped into his arms.

Charlie said, "Annabelle, you just keep gettin' prettier."

"It's Anna, Charlie, or Ann. I'm an eighteen-year-old woman now."

"My mistake, Anna." He held out a box wrapped with a colorful paper ribbon. "For your graduation. I'm sorry I missed it."

Anna took the box and opened it to see several paper-wrapped chocolates nestled inside. "You did miss it, but I suppose I'll forgive you since you brought me a present."

"That's not all," Susan said. "Later this afternoon, you and I can go shopping for something special. At least more than just a box of chocolates."

"Hey!" Charlie exclaimed. "Those were your idea."

Susan playfully swatted Charlie's arm, and Anna laughed as she popped a chocolate into her mouth.

Anna said, "Thank you, Susan, it's wonderful to have a sister who understands a woman's needs better than all the men around here."

Charlie said, "Well, let's get inside and—"

Ellie appeared in the doorway at that moment and said, "Oh my, there's my boy. Charles Ashley, you finally brought your beautiful wife home to visit."

Ellie turned to Susan, and they embraced, and each melted into the arms of the other. The rest joined in as Charlie grinned from ear to ear. They walked inside and into the front parlor.

"Where's Dad and my brothers?" Charlie asked.

"They're at work, silly," Anna said. "If you'd a called or sent a note you was a comin' today, they'd have gotten the day off." She popped another chocolate into her mouth with a smug smile.

Ellie took the box away from Anna. "Go take the auto over to the shop and tell your father that Charlie and Susan are here. You can tell Jess too while you're there. And give a call out to the ranch so that Dan knows. He can be here in time for supper."

Anna nodded and hurried past Charlie and went out the door.

"Do you want anything to drink?" Ellie asked.

"No, we're fine for now, Mom."

They took seats in the parlor and Ellie began to tell them everything that had happened since the wedding. In about thirty minutes, the front door opened, and Joe and Jess walked inside.

Joe walked over to Charlie, put his hand on Charlie's shoulder, and said, "Charlie, so good of you to come down for a visit. I hope everythin's goin' well for you two." He turned and opened his arms to Susan. She did the same and they hugged. "And Susan, you are as beautiful as ever."

"Pop, it's hard to believe, but she's more beautiful on the inside."

"I'm proud for ya, son. It was great to see ya put the ring on her finger."

"I still can't believe someone as beautiful as Susan ended up with someone as ugly as you, brother," Jess said as he limped over and gave Charlie a slap on the back.

Charlie and Susan both laughed. Susan gave Charlie a wicked grin and said, "Well, it took some time to get used to his tall, lanky figure and those awful bowlegs. But now he's sort of grown on me."

They all laughed.

Anna said, "Oh it's so good to finally hear someone love Charlie the way we do, despite all his faults."

Charlie took off his hat and rubbed his hand through his hair. "Well, if this is goin' to go on, maybe I should go back to the 101. At least I know that Tony loves me."

Susan smiled and grabbed Charlie's arm and pulled him close. "That's because you give him sugar cubes and apples." She gave him a quick peck on the cheek.

"We'll, if you aren't goin' to leave right away, Charlie, let's go get some drinks and catch up," Ellie said.

The women led the men to the big, cheerful, and brightly colored kitchen. They filled their cups with coffee, returned to the front room, and found a place to sit.

Joe eased into a rocking chair with a quilt draped across the back. "Son, what have ya been up to?"

"Quite a few things have happened since the wedding," Charlie said. "Ya knew I was working with George Miller supporting him in the 101 Oil Company."

Susan said, "Let me tell it. After learning that Charlie was working in the oil business for the 101 Oil Company, my father decided to create an oil company under the Kramer Group. He surprised us and did it while we honeymooned. Now we own the Kelly Oil Company, and Charlie has bought out E. W. Marland's part in the 101 Oil Company. So, we're in business with the 101 Ranch, and George Miller is our partner. I'm working with one of our new companies to open a department store in Cushing."

Jess asked, "Charlie, you went to the 101 to become a top hand and one of their best cowboys. I've wondered since the wedding, why are you workin' in the oil business?"

"Yer right, Jess. My dream was always to become a top hand and I never thought I could be anythin' more than that. I did reach my dream. I eventually worked directly for the Cattle Foreman. I had become a top hand, and last summer, I had my crew and was responsible for most of the repair and upkeep around the ranch.

"Then two amazin' things happened. I saved a ranch hand's life and caught and brought in some cattle rustlers. Because of those two things, I got introduced to the Miller Brothers. Boss, the Foreman, knew I had finished high school and was good at math." He turned and smiled at his mother. "He also had become somewhat impressed with my decision-makin' skills. During a conversation with George Miller, Boss learned he needed help. Boss recommended me to him. George hired me as his assistant at a considerable pay raise."

Jess said, "Well, great, but now you and Susan could buy the 101, right?"

Susan said, "Jess, we could buy it several times and have a lot left over, but Charlie is happy working with George as a partner, and so far, as we know, the 101 isn't for sale."

Anna said, "Wow, all of this seems like a fairytale to me. My brother leaves Fort Sumner, New Mexico, not a great deal older than me now, and in about two years, he's wealthy beyond my understanding."

Charlie smiled at her and said, "I'm still yer brother and will always be."

Susan smiled and said, "Anna, Charlie's very much the man I met in '17. He still makes decisions following what he learned in this family. Over the past year, hc has grown and learned a lot about the world around us and himself. But he's still the big brother you knew and loved when he left home."

Anna replied, "Thanks, Susan." She smiled. "I've finally got a sister; ain't that grand?"

Susan said, "I'm excited to have a sister too. I want to get to know you better." She turned to Charlie. "Why don't you, Jess, and Mr. Kelly get supper ready before Dan gets here, and I'll take Anna and you mom to the mercantile to get Anna's graduation present?"

"Susan," Joe said, rocking forward in the chair, "you can call me Dad or Father."

With a gentle smile and a quaver in her voice, she said, "I've always loved the term Dad. My father preferred Father. Dad seems friendlier and a lot more tender to me."

Joe said, "Dad, it is then; from now on." He turned to Jess and Charlie. "It's a nice warm day, why don't you boys get everythin' set up out back under the trees for us to eat outside?"

Anna said, "Come on, I'll drive us over to the mercantile."

As the women got up to leave, Charlie asked his father. "What are you gonna do?"

"Someone has to supervise."

***

Dan arrived as Charlie and Jess were getting the meal prepared. "I see you managed to arrive after most of the work has been done," Charlie said in greeting.

Dan smiled and gave Charlie a hug. "I learned it from you to work smarter, not harder. Where's Ma and the others?"

"Susan took Anna to the mercantile to buy her a graduation present and Momma went with them."

"So we got stuck with the cooking and setting up," Jess said as he rubbed flour over the chicken they were about to fry.

"I hope Charlie's makin' his biscuits," Dan said.

"Already got them in the oven."

Joe walked in and greeted Dan as he set a jug of sun tea on the table. "How's the horse business goin'?" he asked as he got the sugar from the pantry.

Dan filled them all in on what he was doing at the ranch, and Jess told them what was new at the mercantile. Charlie listened to each of them, happy to hear how they were both finding their own trails to follow. But also thinking about how each might be able to work into the plans Susan and he had as well.

As the chicken fried in the skillet and Charlie took the biscuits out of the oven, they could hear the family car pull up outside. Susan, Anna, and Ellie all walked into the kitchen. Anna carried a large parcel, and Charlie could see that his mother was wearing a new hat.

"My, Charlie, why don't you ever cook at home?" Susan asked from the doorway.

"Because we live in a room without a kitchen and take all our meals at the ranch café," Charlie replied as he slid the biscuits into a bowl.

Susan smiled and walked over to give him a kiss. "Anything I can do?"

"We're almost ready. Why don't you take the plates and silverware outside."

Susan nodded and helped Dan to set the table. In a few minutes everything was ready to eat. Everyone gathered around the table under the tree, the deep blue Oklahoma sky overhead.

Ellie said, "My, this looks wonderful. I'm so glad my boys are so helpful. Thank you."

Joe sat down at the head of the table. "I am too. I'm so happy that all of you have been here for me. I know I haven't always been the best father to you all as you grew up."

Charlie said, "We never doubted that ya loved us, even if it may have been a struggle at times. We're proud to call you Father."

Everyone agreed, and they all sat down and began to serve the food.

As they ate lunch, Charlie said, "Jess was tellin' me about his work as we were fixin' supper. Why don't you tell Susan what you've been doin' at the store?"

Jess set down the biscuit he'd just bitten into and wiped his mouth as he swallowed. He turned to Susan and said, "Well, I sort of run the place. Mr. Halsey is getting within a few years of retiring and has turned everything from ordering product, keeping his books, and hiring new help over to me."

Susan said, "Jess, that's wonderful. It sounds like Mr. Halsey sees the skills and trustworthiness every business owner looks for in their employees. Congratulations." She turned to Charlie. "Have you filled Jess in on our plans in Cushing?"

Charlie spoke around the piece of chicken he'd just taken a bite out of. "Not yet, I was waitin' for ya to get back from spendin' all our money on my little sister."

Anna lifted her parcel and pulled out a fancy sun hat with a silk lace trim. "Why Charlie, are you sayin' ya don't like my new hat? It's gonna go real nice with the dress I'm gonna make from the fancy cloth that Susan also bought me. I tried to spend as much of yer money as I could, but Susan assured me it was alright."

Susan laughed with the others and turned to Jess. "We have recently signed a lease for a new small department store up in Cushing. We hope to have it up and running by the end of this year. Charlie and I mentioned that you were working in a store to the President of this new chain of stores for the Kramer Group. We wanted to gauge your interest in coming to work for him."

"A department store, like Macy's or J. C. Penney?" Jess asked.

"Similar to that," Susan said. "But a bit smaller in scale to what they have. Chester Abrams has the idea to open small stores in the cities that are fast growing down here in Oklahoma. The Cushing store will be our first one, but we plan to open more in the coming years. This is a chance to get in on the ground floor, so to speak."

Jess leaned back in his chair. "Wow, I never thought about something like that. I had thought that maybe running the mercantile here was as far as I could ever get, but that would depend on if someone bought it from Mr. Halsey when he retired, and it stayed open."

"Well then it sounds like you may be interested in talking with Mr. Abrams."

"Very much so. If it means a new opportunity, then I'm all for it."

"Oh, but you'd have to move to Cushing," Ellie said.

Jess looked a little guilty. "But, Ma, this is the chance I would never have had here."

"I know, dear, it's just sad any time one of my children leaves the nest."

Jess turned back to Susan. "What would you have me doing, and when do you think Mr. Abrams might want me to start?"

Susan replied, "Maybe as soon as next month. Chester said he needs at least one sidekick soon to get the first store started. He needs to handle the inventory, hire the staff, and get everything ready for the grand opening. He wants an assistant to help with everything, and when Charlie mentioned your experience and hard work, Chester was interested in meeting you. I will meet with him this week and I can let him know you're interested."

Jess said, "I'm interested, but shouldn't I interview with this Mr. Abrams before we make commitments?"

Susan smiled and nodded. "Of course, it's his and your decision, but he does like my counsel at this point in this new venture. When could you come to Cushing?"

"I don't know. I need to check with Mr. Halsey and go to the bank and..."

Charlie said, "Jess, this is our idea, and we don't want you to risk anything with your job. We're lookin' for you to provide us with your opinions as the most experienced retailer in the Joe Kelly family. We'll pay your way to Cushing and back and your expenses while you're there. We'll provide you with a stipend for your services as well. All you need to do is get your employer's approval for you to come for a week."

Susan said, "That's what we want and are offering. If you like what you see, and you and Mr. Abrams seem to make a good team, then an official offer will come."

Jess picked up his glass of sweet tea and held it up as if to make a toast. "Well, count me in. I can send you a telegram on Monday letting you know when I can come."

Charlie nodded.

Susan turned to Dan. "Charlie has told me that you are working on a ranch near here. What do you do there?"

Dan set down his fork and said, "I'm the lead horse trainer. I have a crew, and I also take out some hands and we ride the fences and do repairs. We're a fairly small outfit, but I'm enjoyin' myself."

Charlie replied, "It sounds like you've done 'em a good job, and now you've got a responsible role at the ranch."

Dan said, "Skip Burkey, the owner, is known around the state for his cuttin' horses. He runs about five hundred head of cattle too."

Charlie said, "Mighty fine, my man. You're a top hand, no doubtin' it."

Dan said, "Thanks, brother, it means a lot comin' from you."

Susan took a sip of her sweet tea and asked, "Has Charlie told you what he's thinking about doing?"

Dan looked at Charlie with a quizzical expression. "No, he ain't. Are ya keepin' secrets from us?"

Charlie laughed. "No secrets. Just nothin' has happened yet. Susan and I have been talkin' about buyin' a ranch someday, when the right opportunity presents itself. When that happens we want to bring you on as one of the top hands."

Dan asked, "Do you have any location in mind where you want to own a ranch?"

"Nothin' firm. I have a friend with a ranch up near Shawnee. We're goin' to visit him tomorrow on our way up to Cushing."

Dan smiled, then asked, "Who's your friend up near Shawnee?"

"He's Clay Stephens at the Double Bar S; I'm sure you've heard of him."

Dan's eyes got big, and he nearly knocked over his glass of tea. "Holy shit, Charlie."

Ellie said, "Dan, I'm ashamed at your language."

"Sorry, Ma, but Clay Stephens is huge. He's the biggest thing in cattle going other than the 101 and the Drummond spread up around Pawhuska. He's your friend?"

Susan said, "We had dinner with Clay and his wife at the Norwood Hotel last night, and they invited us to visit them as we headed back to Cushing. He wanted to talk to Charlie about his dream of owning a ranch someday."

Joe said, "I'd say you kids are doin' a lot right. He's a highly respected man in these parts. If you can do business with him, you can be sure things are above board."

Joe said, "Sounds like you have plans for the boys. What about Anna?"

Susan said, "While we were shopping, Anna and I had a wonderful talk. She was curious about what I did for the Kramer Group, and I told her everything I do. Anna, do you want to tell them?"

Anna put her hands on the table and pushed her empty plate away. She straightened her back and said, "I want to go to college."

Joe said, "Not many colleges around here have spaces for girls, unless you was plannin' on bein' a teacher."

"And we haven't saved nearly enough to send you to college," Ellie added. "What with buying the house and the auto, even if it is a few years old."

Susan nodded at Anna and turned to face Joe and Ellie. "Dad, and Mom, if it is alright with you, I told Anna earlier that I could get her into Vassar, the college that I attended. I would be happy to pay her tuition, room, and board while she attends college there."

"As long as I keep good grades," Anna added.

"After she graduates then I can get Anna a job within the Kramer Group at a high level. I have something in mind we can talk about later."

Ellie looked like she was about to cry, and Joe turned to Anna. "Is this what you want, daughter?"

"It is, Pa. I love the idea of getting my degree and being useful in the family business."

"All my children are leaving me," Ellie said, dabbing at her eyes with a napkin.

"I'm still around," Dan said.

"Not for long if I know Charlie," Joe said. "Soon as he finds his ranch you'll be on the next horse out of here."

They all smiled and Dan had to agree that was the case.

Ellie said, "It's time to have some birthday cake and celebrate everything. Daddy's a year older now and—"

Joe laughed as he said, "Enough, we don't need to share details. Everyone knows I ain't no spring chicken."

"Cake?" Jess asked. "We weren't told to bake a cake."

Ellie smiled and said, "Another present from Susan. We ordered it from the bakery in town earlier. And Mr. Smith said it would be delivered just about now."

As she spoke, a delivery van drove up to the front of the house. Anna jumped up and grabbed Dan to help her bring the cake to the table. In a few minutes they returned, carrying a large sheet cake covered in white frosting. They set it on the table, and everyone stood up to sing Happy Birthday to Joe.

Chapter Fifteen
Buying a Ranch
July 1919

CHARLIE AND SUSAN ROSE early and said their goodbyes to the Kelly family with promises to visit more often. They told Jess where he could send a telegram about his availability to meet with Chester, and Susan told Anna she'd be in touch about getting into Vassar for the coming semester. Everyone hugged and cried and it took longer than anticipated for them to get on the road.

As they arrived at Highway 9, Charlie said, "We go right here for a couple of miles, and we'll see the Earlsboro turn-off. Then we go north about three miles. We'll see a sign and an entrance gate into the ranch. We'll turn left onto a road leading back to the house. Dan's familiar with the ranch and told me what to look for."

Susan said, "You sure look good in your hat, boots, denims, and flannel shirt."

Charlie smiled and replied, "You're in my favorite outfit too. You look beautiful."

Susan unbuttoned her shirt and opened it, showing she wasn't wearing a chemise. She asked, "Is this okay with you?"

"Perfect." He reached over and caressed her left breast and smiled broadly.

In a short time, the sign and gate appeared on their left. Charlie pulled onto the road leading to the Stephens' house. Susan buttoned her shirt, leaving a little cleavage showing. A broad, single-story home was spread out before them at the top of a hill. Charlie parked the car and they both got out. Susan looked out at the horizon and admired the view.

"I didn't expect so many trees," she said.

"That's how you know you're in Pottawatomie County."

They took hold of each other's hands and walked to the house. A deep, covered porch ran the length of the house. Charlie could tell Julie had been cooking by the smell of bacon as he and Susan knocked at the front door.

Clay opened the door and said, "Welcome to the Double Bar S; you guys made it for brunch."

Susan said, "Thanks, Clay." She hugged him and stepped aside to allow the men to shake hands.

Charlie added, "You have a beautiful place. I enjoyed the drive in from the highway."

"We benefit from being bottomland of the North Canadian and Little Rivers through this part of Oklahoma. Let's join Julie in the kitchen."

As they entered the kitchen, Julie stopped cooking, turned, and gave Susan and Charlie each a hug.

Julie pointed as she said, "I've got the table ready, so go sit down, and I'll bring the food over."

Susan asked, "Is there anything I can do?"

Julie replied, "No, everything's ready, and you got here at the perfect time."

The kitchen was beautiful. The large windows on the east side of the house allowed the morning sun to brighten the entire area. The breakfast nook on the house's west side accommodated a table and chairs for twelve people. The table allowed a view of the backyard and the closest pasture.

Susan looked outside. "You have a pool. I love swimming pools. We have one at our Kansas City home, and I miss it."

Charlie said, "We'll need to go up there in September to attend the Kramer Group quarterly meetin'. We'll git a few evenings of swimmin' in while we're there."

Clay said, "Charlie, I want to show you around the barns and shop area after we eat. I hope you have time, because this afternoon I thought all four of us could ride out to let us show you the property and some of the herd."

Charlie looked at Susan. "We had planned on arriving in Cushing tonight since we both have business to attend to tomorrow."

Susan jumped in and said, "But we can push those back if needed. I would love to see your beautiful ranch."

Charlie turned back to Clay. "I'm glad you want to show us the ranch. I'm excited to see your spread."

Julie said, "Susan, I would like to show you the house, my studio, my garden, and around the yard while they do the tour of the barn and other buildings."

They sat down and enjoyed the meal. Even though Charlie's mother had insisted they eat something before leaving the house, Charlie and Susan both piled food onto their plates. The talk was pleasant, picking up from their conversation at dinner the other night.

After eating and a couple of cups of coffee, Clay finally stood up and said, "Come on, Charlie. Let me show you the operation."

The men grabbed their hats and headed out the back door and down the hill. Although smaller than the barn system at the 101, Charlie was impressed with the quality of construction and the designs used to create effective and efficient work and storage areas.

Charlie stepped back, his eyes wide, pointing as he said, "Clay, did you design the barns and shops, or did you hire someone to do it for you? This area is first class."

Clay said, "Thanks, Charlie. All of this was my idea, but as the construction company built it, the crew supervisor offered some thoughts, and I listened. The way we oriented the main barn to address the typical winds in this valley has been a big help."

They continued walking around and talking for the next hour or so, and Charlie began to see Clay as someone he would like to visit a lot more than his current life would allow.

Charlie said, "Clay, what you have shown me and your description of how you use it is a work of art to people like me. If this ranch was a paintin', it should hang in a famous museum or someone's collection."

Clay responded, "Your kind words are appreciated, and the questions you asked let me know even though you're young, you have experiences and imagination many men my age don't have. I continue to believe you and Susan have a bright future ahead of you. Let's go back to the house and get something to drink."

"Well, thank you for those kind words. And somethin' cool sounds good to me. The weather this week sure has been nice and warm."

They found the ladies in the den enjoying glasses of sweet tea.

Julie said, "There's a fresh pitcher of tea in the icebox. Help yourself, and then come join us."

Clay said, "Will do. Come on, Charlie, I know where we can get a cookie or two to go with our tea."

As they walked into the den with their tea and cookies, Julie said, "Did you bring some cookies for us?"

Charlie said, "Um, well, um, Clay..."

Julie laughed and said, "We already had some. I just had to kid Clay. Honey, you're a terrible host."

Clay said, "Dadgummit, I stay in the doghouse, don't I?"

Susan said, "Is it big enough for two? Charlie didn't think to bring us cookies either."

They relaxed as they drank the tea and nibbled on the cookies. Charlie told Susan how impressed he was about the barns and other buildings that Clay had built.

After a while, Clay stood up and asked if they were ready to go on a ride. They all agreed and were soon outside. Four horses were already saddled and waiting for them, their reins tied around the railing of the back porch.

They rode out to the north end of the property, and Clay pointed to the west. "Charlie, a man stopped by the ranch several months ago and wanted to lease this area for drillin'. You mentioned you're in the oil business now; I could have been too. But I passed on his offer."

"This does look a lot like the anticlines we're drillin' on up near Cushing. Maybe I should have Hank come down here to give his professional opinion."

"Maybe we can talk about that later tonight," Clay said.

They rode on, with Clay and Julie pointing out their favorite spots on the property.

After a while, Susan looked at Clay and asked, "How long have you had this property?"

"Over twenty years. I was about your age when I bought it from my father's friend. I bought the land, a small cabin, and a starter herd of cattle. Julie and I had just married, and we built all this together."

Charlie turned in his saddle. "You're quite a team. Susan and I are doing our best to become a good one too."

Susan patted the neck of her horse. "Oh, we already are. We need to find a place like this for you, Charlie. I want you to have your sanctuary to come home to."

Clay asked, "What do you mean, Susan? Sanctuary?"

Susan thought for a minute about her answer, then said, "Everyone needs a place to go when they need quiet, calm, and a place to get away and recreate themselves. In my case, it has been my swimming pool and patio area at home in Kansas City. I could go home from the office, lose myself and all the day's troubles with a swim, and have a glass of wine there on the patio. I've seen Charlie on the back of a horse at the 101 after a hard day, wearing a smile and laughing like a kid. I saw the same smile on him today here, riding and enjoying your beautiful ranch. He loves the challenges he's experiencing with the Kramer Group and the oil business at the 101, but he needs his sanctuary. I think it's a ranch and being on horseback."

Clay said, "I see. How about we ride back to the house now? I can have one of my hands take care of the horses. I want to continue this conversation in our den with a glass of wine and food. Julie instructed our cook to prepare an evening meal for us. It should be ready by the time we get back."

They rode back with Clay showing Charlie and Susan more of the area's beauty. A couple of hands met them and took charge of the horses. Clay held the door open, and they all went inside the house.

After settling in the den, Clay said, "Talk to me about your goals. It sounds like they at least include owning a ranch."

Charlie looked at Clay. "I've dreamed of owning a ranch from well before I met Susan. But we have responsibilities to other businesses we don't want to end. I want to do something special in the oil business as well. I also have a younger brother who has done well at a ranch in these parts. I want him to have a role at any ranch I own."

Clay said, "Who's your brother? I thought I knew most everyone around here."

"My brother's Dan Kelly; he is—"

Clay interrupted, "Over at the Bar B, next to us. I've been trying to steal Dan away from Skip for six months. He's great with horses and mighty good as a lead hand."

"Dan will be thrilled to hear you say that. He was telling us yesterday how impressed he was with your operation."

Clay nodded to accept the compliment. He then stroked his chin. "When are you planning to buy a ranch? Would you consider a partnership?"

Charlie responded, "I might entertain a partner, it would depend on several things, but it could work for me."

Susan gestured to Charlie, turned to Clay, and said, "Well now, Clay, to answer your first question. Charlie and I have discussed this. We would buy anytime we find the right situation. We only want to consider a profitable quality ranch."

Clay said, "I have an idea for you. Skip's close to seventy years old. I don't know if Dan has mentioned it to you, but Skip knows he needs to sell the place. But he loves his horses, and he loves your brother. They have grown close over the past year. I have considered buying it, but I need to spend more time at my Wanette property. Would you be interested in Skip Burkey's place if the deal's right?"

Susan and Charlie responded in unison, "Yes."

Charlie added, "Dan has told me a lot about the Bar B and even though I've never seen it with my own eyes, I trust my brother when he tells me how good the place is."

Clay said, "Good, and I might have another idea. It could make you a part-owner of the Double Bar S. If that would be of interest to you?"

Charlie said, "Tell me what you have in mind, Clay."

Susan added, "Do you know what Skip wants for his place and how big it is and—"

Clay said, "Sorry, Susan, back to the Bar B. It's three thousand acres of quality land. His house and outbuildings are good but older than ours here. He's asking $75,000 for it. It's a fair price and includes all equipment and livestock."

Charlie asked, "What did you mean when you mentioned a partner-ship in a ranch?"

"I want to move down to the ten thousand acres we have at Wanette, and I want to buy another five thousand acres next to it. I have asked around to find someone interested in buying this place or buying into it so I could purchase the land down at Wanette."

Charlie asked, "The extra land, will you need to build or improve it to make it work for you?"

Julie said, "No, it's what we need as it is. There's a house, barn, and several ponds on it now."

Susan said, "What do you want for this place, lock, stock, and barrel?"

Clay asked, "You want all of it, now?"

Charlie said, "We would purchase both ranches now and give you whatever time you need to transition to Wanette. I'll let Skip stay there and work as long as he wants. I'll hire Dan to watch over the places, but I have a couple of top hands up at the 101 that I hope will come down here and run these for us. So, what do you need for this place?"

Clay looked over at Julie and, with a wide grin, said, "Are you ready, Honey? We've been saying we're ready for the past year, but no one had the money to buy us out. These folks might."

Julie said, "I'm ready, but it may take us a few months to get the place down there bought and ready."

Susan said, "Julie, we won't need you out soon. Hey, we still have a lot to do up at the 101, and we have our place in Kansas City too."

Charlie smiled and said, "What would you want to buy you out, Clay?"

Clay said, "I have been asking $200,000 for everything. All we'd take is our horses, saddles, and tack."

Susan looked at Clay and back to Charlie and said, "If we can get the Bar B for $75,000 and Clay says it's worth it, it'll give us eight thousand acres." She nodded at Charlie. "I'm happy to do it. What do you think?"

Charlie said, "Clay, we can have earnest funds wired to you on Monday and arrange a closing date where we'll give you the balance. Is it a deal?"

Clay said, "It's a deal. I'll assist you in purchasing the Bar B if you like."

Charlie said. "I'd appreciate it if ya would. Do you think we can see Skip today?"

Clay replied, "I'll call him now. It's still early evening." Clay went into his office to use his phone. He returned quickly and said, "Skip says he can see us tonight."

Charlie said, "Tell him we'll come right over. And, you and Julie, join us, please."

On the way over to Bar B, Charlie said, "Clay, yesterday I got a fairly detailed description of Skip's outfit from Dan. I wanted to buy it when he talked about it. I know it's gettin' dark, and I won't get to see much, but with Dan's description and your judgment, I have all I need."

In another hour, Charlie and Skip shook hands on the deal. Skip agreed to stay on for at least six months for a smooth transition. Everyone felt good about the deal. Skip seemed especially pleased the buyer was the big brother Dan had always spoken about with pride.

The couples returned to the Double Bar S, and as they entered the den, Julie said, "I know we've already had wine, but we have a nice bottle of champagne that I think we need to open, don't you?"

Susan said, "Perfect."

Chapter Sixteen
Expect the Unexpected
July 1919

MONDAY MORNING, THEY ENJOYED breakfast with the Stephenses. Julie introduced Susan to Attie and Cleta, her housekeeper and cook. Julie explained that the two women had been working on the ranch for several years. Julie told Attie and Cleta that Susan and Charlie were going to buy the ranch, and Susan offered to keep them on in their same roles. Charlie and Clay did the same thing with the ranch hands as they were getting ready for their day at the barn. Everyone seemed to be pleased with the arrangements, and Clay's foreman promised to make the transition as smooth as possible for everyone involved until the Stephenses moved down to Wanette.

Charlie and Susan finally said their goodbyes, with promises to wire the initial money for the ranch on Tuesday. As they left the ranch, they decided to head back to Maud to share the news with the Kellys.

As he pulled out on the highway, Charlie said, "Sweetheart, I'm excited to share the news with our family. We now have two quality ranches to start our Kelly Farming and Ranching Company. I didn't plan to buy anythin' this soon, but I am glad we could jump at the opportunity when it came along."

Susan said, "We had a chance to purchase high quality, and we would have been foolish not to jump on it. We'll use money from the settlement of the Blackaby Estate. In the long run, this starts the Kelly Ranching and Farming Company. We have time to share this with the leaders in Kansas City and transition into running everything down here under the Kramer Group. I'm not worried."

"I'm not worried either. It's just me gettin' used to havin' the resources to buy somethin' at a fair price when I see it and not question if I can afford it."

"Charlie, I think about it too when we're spending a quarter of a million dollars. But we have it, and it's all about determining the best way to spend the money. In this case, the decision is easy because these ranches have been successful, and the pleasure of ownership also has value."

Charlie reached his right arm around Susan and pulled her to him. He said, "I'm so happy. How can someone so beautiful on the outside have so much beauty on the inside?"

"You bring out whatever goodness is in me by the way you have respected and treated me. You're so loveable, and all I did last night was support your decision as you acquired two key pieces of our empire."

Susan popped the snaps on Charlie's shirt and reached inside to caress his chest. She said, "I'm the lucky one and I know with every passing day, our lives get better."

As they pulled to a stop in front of the Kelly house, Charlie honked the horn on the Cadillac. Anna came out of the front door smiling with her hands against her chest. She squealed, "What are you guys doin' back here?"

Joe and Ellie also came outside to see why Charlie and Susan had come back, and everyone began asking questions. Charlie raised his hands and said, "Hey, everyone, quiet for a minute, and we'll happily tell you why we came back here this mornin'."

Joe couldn't help one more query. "Everything's okay, isn't it?"

Susan said, "Yes, Dad, everything's fine. Tell them the news, Charlie."

Charlie cleared his throat, smiled, and said, "We had a wonderful visit with the Stephenses and Skip Burkey last night. As it turned out, both wanted to sell their ranches. You're lookin' at the new owners of the Double Bar S and the Bar B ranches. They have very different reasons to sell, and we found the opportunity too good to pass up."

Joe said, "You're serious? You bought both ranches at one time?"

Susan said, "They both were available and fit perfectly into our plan."

Anna asked, "So, it means Dan's workin' for you, big brother?"

Charlie said, "Yep, didn't I tell you I hoped to own a ranch, and I hoped he would help with it?"

Joe said, "Of course, but this soon? I didn't think..."

Charlie raised his hand palm out, grinned, and leaned against the Cadillac. Then he folded his arms across his chest and said, "I don't have time to head up to the ranch to tell Dan in person today. Skip said he'd fill Dan in on the details this mornin'. I want him in a leadership role at the Bar B, and Dan will be able to help out while Skip gets ready to retire."

Joe looked directly into Charlie's eyes and said, "You don't waste any time, do you, son?"

Charlie returned his gaze and said, "When I have a plan and know what I need to work it, I don't hesitate when I see what I want."

Joe said, "Good. You've figured a lot out at a young age, and it's sure goin' to benefit you and Susan."

Ellie said, "Y'all come on in for a spell."

Charlie said, "We can't. We had planned to git to Cushing by lunch, and now it won't happen. We've already had to move the meetings we had planned for today to tomorrow."

Susan said, "We just had to come back and tell you our good news."

Anna, Ellie, and Joe each gave their congratulations and promised to tell Dan if he hadn't heard it from Skip by the next time they saw him.

Charlie and Susan returned to the road, heading to Cushing.

Charlie said, "I thought everythin' went well. We have some business to discuss with Curt tomorrow. We need him to draw up the contracts and wire Clay and Skip the earnest money."

Susan said, "I know we have talked some about this already, but what are your plans for staffing the ranches with leadership?"

Charlie said, "The 101 is makin' more money from oil than anywhere else. They even make more from produce some months than meatpackin' and any sale of beef. So, I know people like Boss and Tom are beginnin' to wonder how long they may have their jobs. Nothin' may happen soon, but it likely could in a year or less. I want them to come to work for us."

"I like your plan. You always go for the best, don't you?"

"I got you, didn't I?" He reached over and caressed her breasts through her shirt. "Like I said, nothing but the best."

Susan opened her shirt, took his hand, and returned it to her breasts. She said, "I'm all yours, Sweetheart, and I feel like I got the best when I got you."

***

They arrived in Cushing in the afternoon, checked into the hotel, and unpacked in the suite. The phone rang; it was Chester Abrams checking on them. He had arrived the day before, as they had previously arranged, and had been surprised to get a note from the hotel clerk that Susan and Charlie were delayed.

Susan told Chester, "We had an unexpected meeting yesterday about a business opportunity we couldn't pass up. I'm sorry if our delay gave you any concern."

"No concern, just unexpected. But I suppose the unexpected should always be expected in business."

Susan agreed and they arranged to meet for dinner that night.

Charlie and Susan got cleaned up and then went down to the restaurant. Chester was already there, seated at their favorite table by the window. He greeted them and they all sat down and placed their orders. As they waited for their food, they started discussing their plans for the department store.

Charlie asked, "How's your work on creatin' sources for merchandise been goin'?"

Chester said, "Excellent. I've started with the home goods, because I expect that to be the core of the business, but I eventually want to expand into other departments for the store as well—like furniture, hardware, toys, and everything else the big department stores offer, just at a smaller scale. I've negotiated with all the major textile companies back on the east coast to provide the fabrics. We'll have sewing patterns from McCall's, Simplicity, Pictorial Review, and Woman's Life. Ready-to-wear can come from the houses used by J. C. Penney, Montgomery Ward, and Sears and Roebuck. I'm talking with The Singer Company to become a distributor and not limiting it to Oklahoma. And finally, we'll have all the required thread, needles, and other accessories."

Susan asked, "Do you recommend having any seamstresses on staff?"

Chester said, "Yes, I want to have as many as four. They'll do typical seamstress work, and I want to have Sewing Classes as part of our services."

Susan said, "This sounds great. Let's discuss it more tomorrow morning. Chester, I think you know Sam Holder from some work he did for you in Cleveland, right?"

"Yes, he's a good guy and does great work. Why do you ask?"

Charlie said, "He owns the construction company buildin' the site we've leased. He's meetin' us at the site in the mornin'."

Chester said, "Wonderful, I'll enjoy working with him again."

Their food arrived and they busied themselves with eating for a bit. Finally, Susan said, "Speaking of a good guy, remember Charlie's brother? He's helping run a mercantile in Pottawatomie County."

"Yes, I recall you mentioning him. Jess, isn't it?"

"Correct. He's Charlie's older brother. You may have met him at the wedding. We talked to him about your need for a right-hand man to help you get the store up and running here in Cushing. He was excited by the chance to work with you."

"That's good to hear. But I'd like the opportunity to get to know him better before I make any decisions."

Charlie said, "Jess said the same thing. He wants to meet you and let you interview him about the position before agreein' to anythin' outright."

"Well, I already like the way he is thinking."

Susan smiled. "He did seem sharp as a tack and likes challenges."

Chester responded, "I'm interested, and if we both like what we see, the timing is perfect."

Susan said, "We'll let him know. He sent us a telegram today letting us know he can be up here at the end of the week to meet with you."

"We'll make all the arrangements for him," Charlie said.

They finished their meals and all of them ordered drinks. They talked about Cushing and how Charlie was working on a project in the oil business nearby.

Charlie looked up to see Hank walk into the restaurant. He stood and waved to him.

Hank said, "Hey, good to see you, and I hope you had a nice visit with the family."

Charlie said, "We sure did, and we bought a couple of ranches too."

"You what? Well, that explains why you were late getting up here. Wasting your time buying silly ranches."

Chester said, "I can't believe what I just heard. You bought two ranches?"

Susan laughed and said, "I'm a sucker for a cowboy. Whaddaya do?"

Hank sat down and shared what he had been doing. "I've started drillin', and it looks good. I have the three crews and a backup or two hired. We'll go around the clock till we hit the oil pocket I know is there. But tell us about the ranches."

Charlie and Susan shared their weekend with them. The waiter came over and they all ordered dessert and coffee. They continued to catch up as the food and drinks were served.

As they finished dessert, Charlie asked Hank, "When will you start your day tomorrow, and when do I need to be there?"

"I'm always there at dawn, but we won't start till later. Charlie, you don't need to come out there. But if you want to, noon's fine."

Charlie said, "Susan and I'll need a few hours to handle some business up the street here and by phone with staff in Kansas City. I'll see ya at noon."

Hank said, "Take whatever time you need, and I'll see you tomorrow. I need to do a couple of things and get a good night's sleep, so I'm outta here."

Chester said, "Me too. Let me know when to expect Jess."

Charlie and Susan stayed and ordered a bottle of cabernet to enjoy while discussing the last few days' events.

Chapter Seventeen
Plans and Sanctuary
July 1919

CHARLIE OPENED HIS EYES. The sun was already up, and it probably had been for a while. He looked over, and saw Susan wasn't in bed.

He said, "Hey, where's my Honey?"

"In the front room, enjoying my first cup of coffee. I let you sleep. I could tell you didn't get settled last night until after midnight."

"What time is it?"

"It's 7:30; we're doing fine. Chester and Sam won't expect us until later."

Charlie rolled out of bed, went to the kitchenette, and poured himself a cup of coffee.

He looked at Susan. "When did you dress? You look beautiful in your new blouse with those pearl buttons. I'll feel underdressed next to you with my denims and flannel shirt. Though I don't want to change before I go to the well site."

"Well, now, listen to you talking about fashion. I need to dress for business today. But I agree you should dress for the oil fields."

An hour later, they were sitting downstairs in the restaurant, drinking their third cup of coffee, when Sam Holder walked in and joined them.

Sam said, "Good to see you, and I hope your time with your folks included food and a lotta fun."

Susan said, "Good to see you too. We had a wonderful weekend. I hope you did too. Chester should get here anytime. Oh, there he is."

Charlie stood and said, "Chester, I believe you know Sam."

Chester beamed as he said, "I sure do. Good to see you, Sam. I'm looking forward to working with you."

Sam replied, "Chester, we worked great together before, and you're coming in at just the right time."

Waving at the waiter, Charlie said, "Let's order our food and get goin'."

Chester and Sam carried the conversation as they caught up on what they had been doing since they'd last worked together. After finishing breakfast, the group walked toward the construction site. The discussion transitioned to Sam's crew and the building as the work site came into view.

Sam pointed at his men as he said, "We're building an entire city block of storefronts. We've focused on the far end of the block over the past thirty days." He pointed. "Your store takes up about twenty percent of the block and is on this end. Susan asked for the corner location to give you the option of having doors and signage on Broadway and Harrison."

Chester smiled at Susan and said, "Thanks, we think alike."

Charlie said, "Look at how busy the streets are. This town is hoppin'."

Sam said, "It's been busy since we started building, what with all the drilling for oil that's been going on. I hear some driller named Hank Thomas is expecting to hit another big one out north of here near Yale."

Charlie laughed and said, "I sure hope so. That's my well you're talkin' about."

Sam's eyes got big as he looked at Charlie and said, "No, foolin', it's your well? People say this guy Thomas is seldom wrong. Where he drills, he hits oil or gas or both. He even admits he feels this one's big."

Charlie smiled and said, "Let's hope so, but we're here to discuss buildin' a store. This block is our location, Chester. What do ya think?"

Before he could respond, Susan said, "Sam, walk up to where our storefront ends on Broadway, so Chester can tell the size and get a feel for how much space we're talking about."

"Happy to, Miss Susan." Sam walked up past what would become the sidewalk and stopped about fifty feet away. "I'm standing where your store would end," he yelled. "The outside dimensions of your space are fifty by one hundred, giving you five thousand square feet of sales space."

Chester said, "I think that amount of space for the sales floor will meet our needs." He started to walk into the building, with Sam, Susan, and Charlie following him. Sam made sure the construction workers knew they were there and guided Susan around the piles of lumber and kegs of nails.

"Sam, I see you have some work done inside," Chester said. "How much can I change with no cost increase?"

Sam smiled. "Depends. I know that doesn't answer your question, but you know if your requirements make me move a weight-bearing wall, it'll cost you quite a bit. But some things may cost you nothing."

Susan said, "Chester, as Charlie would say, you don't have free rein, but I do want to give you a chance to try your new ideas out at this store. So, you and Sam work together to design and estimate the cost to build what you need. Then give the cost to me before you place an order for the materials."

Chester nodded and began to describe his vision of the interior of the store to Sam. He made sweeping gestures with his hands to express his thoughts, with Sam nodding or shaking his head as they walked through the space.

Charlie said, "Susan, I think we can let these men work, and you and I need to call Kansas City."

Susan nodded. "I think you're right." She raised her voice to be heard over the construction noise and called to Chester and Sam who were already halfway across the store. "Gentlemen, let's have breakfast together tomorrow. Okay?"

Chester nodded at Susan and went back to looking at the space, pulling out a small notebook and a pencil from his jacket pocket. Sam hurried over so he didn't have to yell.

Sam said, "Fine, but can we meet at 7:00 instead of 9:00? I can get my crew goin' at 6:30 and join you; it works better for me."

Charlie said, "That makes sense. Let's get an earlier start."

Susan sighed, "I guess this girl doesn't get her beauty sleep." She laughed and said, "Men."

Charlie and Sam laughed with her, then Sam went to catch up with Chester. Charlie and Susan went directly back to their suite to call Uncle Curt.

Sitting on the divan next to the phone, Susan said, "Charlie, let me talk to Uncle Curt first. I have some ideas about where to pull the money from to buy the ranches."

Charlie asked, "Can we talk about it first, then call him?"

"Oh, sure, Honey. I thought of what I would recommend to Uncle Curt while I had my morning coffee. Remember when we drove back to tell your folks about buying the ranches, I had mentioned using the Blackaby Estate money for the ranches?"

"I do," Charlie said. "I figured that was already settled. Is it more complicated than that?"

"No, I had put the money from Jasper's estate into several common stocks of blue-chip companies. I wanted to make a little money but have it easily available if we needed it. I'll have Uncle Curt create a separate account for ranch support and sell enough stock to be able to put $600,000 in it. We'll then draw $200,000 out to pay Clay and $75,000 out for Skip, and that'll leave $325,000 in there for developing the ranches to our liking."

"I hate to ask, but will that leave anythin' from the estate?"

Susan smiled and patted Charlie's leg. "We'll have about $1.8 million left in those investments. Don't forget, we have over $8 million in various accounts and investments that I built up from my father's seed money when I graduated from Vassar. Remember, my degree is in Economics. I know something about how to make money. But you have more natural ability and a much more creative mind than I do. That's why we make such a good business team."

Charlie gave a low whistle and rubbed a hand through his hair. "I knew you was wealthy beyond what the Kramer Group did, but I didn't know it was that much."

"When we talked about how wealthy I was before we got married, I didn't tell you the exact amount because I was afraid I would scare you away. You were a cowboy at heart—and you still are—and I was afraid that if you knew exactly how wealthy I was that you might see me as out of reach. I also didn't want you to marry me just because I was rich on my own. That's how Goodenough thought of me. But now I know that wouldn't have scared you at all. I'm sorry for keeping you in the dark about this."

Charlie put his arm around her shoulders and gave her a kiss on the top of her head. "Darlin', I didn't know you was worryin' 'bout that back then. Thank you for tellin' me."

He let go of the hug and picked up the phone and handed it to Susan. "Go ahead and give Uncle Curt a call. I like your idea of paying cash for these properties. But as we develop them, we might want to use those accounts as collateral and borrow at a low-interest rate."

"Charlie, you're being creative. Some businessmen don't think like you. We can discuss the details about everything later."

She took the phone and had the operator place a call to the Kramer office. After a few moments, the Kramer switchboard operator came on the line and Susan told the woman that she wanted to talk to Curt. In a few seconds she said, "Uncle Curt, it's Susan. How are you?"

Susan held the phone so that Charlie could hear Curt's reply. "Susan, it's so good to hear your voice. What can I do for you?"

"I need to move and spend some of the money in the Blackaby investments to support the ranching projects we are starting."

"What ranching projects? I recall you and Charlie mentioning you wanted to own a ranch someday. I thought that was years away."

"We thought so too, but two of the finest ranches in Oklahoma just became available to us. One of the beauties about this is they are neighboring ranches, and we are friends with one of the owners, and Charlie's younger brother works at the other ranch. We have a plan for transitioning management, but we need to get ownership first."

"What do you want me to do?"

Susan gave him the details about the amounts and how she wanted him to set up the account.

"I got it and can start on this immediately. But again, Susan, are you sure about this? It seems so sudden."

"Yes, I'm sure. Charlie and I have already discussed this. This is what I want to do."

Charlie made a motion that he wanted to speak to Curt, but Susan shook her head.

"Well, it's just I had no idea Charlie wanted to buy any ranches. At least not this year," Curt said.

"We both want to buy these ranches, Uncle Curt," Susan said.

She looked at Charlie and mouthed, "Let me handle this." Charlie shrugged and put up his hands.

Into the phone Susan said, "Uncle Curt, I have known for a while now that Charlie needs a sanctuary in the same way that I use the pool at home to get away from the Kramer business. These ranches are Charlie's sanctuary. And these *profitable* ranches will earn us money, unlike the pool at home. We won't find a better deal anytime this year, and maybe not next year either. This is what I want to do."

After a period of silence, Curt said, "Uh... I can certainly sell the stock to get the money. It will take a day or two to make the sale and the money to be deposited in an account that I'll need to set up at the Kansas City Bank of Commerce. I'll also need the contact information for Clay and Skip and I'll draw up papers to create this new company. I'll call later today if I need more information."

Susan thanked him and they chatted for a few more minutes to catch up on other business that Susan had been working on. Then she made her goodbye and hung up the phone.

She turned to Charlie. "We're ranchers now!"

Charlie gave her a hug and kissed her. "I love you, Darlin'."

He broke the embrace. "But now I gotta go see to the oil business."

Chapter Eighteen
Nothing But Good News
July 1919

AFTER SPENDING THE AFTERNOON with Hank and the drilling crew at the new Yale site, Charlie walked into their hotel suite. He found Susan on the phone talking and laughing with someone. She said, "Charlie has walked in, so I'll let you go. Goodbye."

Charlie laid his hat down. "Sweetheart, who was on the phone?"

"Your brother, Dan. He called from the Bar B to let us know they scheduled a phone installation at your parent's house for this Friday."

Charlie smiled. "Now we can stay in touch better."

"Dan said Skip is so happy we're buying the place and how Dan's staying to work the horses. I told Dan to remind Skip we wanted him to stick around for a while."

"Yes, we need a few months to create a solid transition if I can convince Boss and Tom to come down and help us."

She stood and put her arms around Charlie's waist. "I'm sure you will. We can afford to pay Boss and Tom more than they are making now, can't we?"

He kissed her forehead. "I was able to look at Clay's books Saturday night, and the answer is yes. I thought we would offer Boss the salary he makes now at the 101 to manage both ranches. It's still a smaller outfit than the 101, and I want to give him a percentage of the ranches' profit as an annual bonus and an incentive for growth. Tom and Dan will become the foremen at each ranch. They'll make a good salary, and I think we should also give them a percentage of the ranch profits with the same thing in mind."

"How much of the profits had you considered sharing with them?"

"I thought Boss would get fifteen percent from each ranch, and Tom and Dan would get ten percent from their ranches. And again, this is from net profit. No profit, no bonus."

"It's ideal. Another time you're showing me your good business instincts."

He nuzzled her neck. "Thanks. Are ya hungry? I'm ready to go down and eat."

"Yes, let me freshen up. It won't take me long."

Fifteen minutes later, Susan walked out of the bedroom, looking beautiful, and Charlie immediately noticed she'd only buttoned the bottom two buttons on her four-button blouse. It brought a smile to his face.

Susan said, "I'm ready; let's go."

They found their usual table ready for them. The staff had grown accustomed to what Charlie and Susan wanted.

Charlie picked up the glass of wine that had already been poured for them and asked the maître d', "What are the specials for tonight?"

The maître d' said, "The ribeye you love is our special tonight. I anticipated you might want it and had glasses of your favorite cabernet already poured. I see your waiter is coming. Have a nice evening."

Susan smiled. "Thanks, Alexander. You're getting to know us all too well."

Charlie said, "Yes, thanks, my friend."

The waiter arrived and took their order for the ribeye steaks.

Susan sat back, provided Charlie with his favorite view, and said, "I missed you today. I guess spending every hour together for the past ten days spoiled me. See what you missed today, Sweetheart?"

Charlie grinned and said, "I can see I paid a mighty big price spendin' the day with a bunch of ugly roughnecks." He placed his hand on hers. "You're amazin'."

Susan leaned forward, teasing Charlie with a bit of cleavage, and said, "We have tonight, so let's enjoy it."

***

On Tuesday morning, Charlie and Susan walked into the restaurant to see Sam and Chester already at the "Kelly" table.

Sam said, "We beat you. This is a first for us. We arrived a few minutes ago. We've already helped ourselves to the coffee that was waiting here on the table."

Charlie and Susan took their seats and poured their own cups of coffee. "I'm thinkin' we may be gettin' too predictable," Charlie said as he took his first sip.

Susan smiled. "I'm happy with their attentive service. Reminds me of being home."

Charlie turned to Chester and asked, "Did you and Sam get anythin' figured out yesterday?"

"Yes. The location and structure are perfect. Sam's done a wonderful job there. He and I dickered over possible layouts and adding in a mezzanine in the back to put offices and workspace for seamstresses. That way we have more area on the ground floor for sales space and the receiving area. We don't have any costs yet, but Sam's promised me I can have the layout I want."

Sam set his coffee down and said, "We're early enough in the construction, so Chester's proposed changes are less of a headache than I was expecting." He smiled at Chester. "My crew doesn't need to change much."

"Chester, you're more excited than I have ever seen you," Susan said. "Things are good?"

Chester laughed, saying, "Yes, I guess there's no hiding it. I'm happy with the town too. Talking with Sam and some others at the hotel, it's obvious Cushing is growing fast. Sam and I took a drive around the town yesterday afternoon and could see new construction happening all over the place. People are moving in permanently with all the new refineries and pipelines. Our timing is great."

"I told him he might as well call his wife and tell her to pack her bags," Sam said.

"Chester, I'll talk with Mr. Schlegell today," Susan said over her coffee cup. "I'll authorize a move for you and Emily whenever you're ready. Charlie and I drove around here a few weeks back. There are some lovely homes here."

They ordered their food and had a pleasant breakfast with Chester and Sam describing Chester's vision for the new store.

After Sam and Chester left, Charlie and Susan went to the suite and called Curt. "Uncle Curt, this is Susan. I have some news for you. Charlie and I hope you have some for us too."

Curt said, "I do have some for you. But first, what do you have for me."

"I'm authorizing you to move Chester and Emily to Cushing. Chester loves the layout he'll have for the store and likes Cushing for the first store location. Charlie and I thought he would, and you should see how he's beaming with excitement."

"Excellent news," Curt said. "The news I have for you is good too. I have called and talked to both Skip and Clay. I have all the information I need from them to create the contracts and any other paperwork to transfer the deeds to the Kelly Farming and Ranching Company. I also have the account set up at the bank and the stock sale will happen today. In fact, it may have already happened as I told the broker to make the sale first thing in New York. He'll wire the money to the new account. You'll soon become proud owners of two ranches in Earlsboro, Oklahoma."

"Wonderful, Uncle Curt. My list for you today is short. But one more question: Can you have all the paperwork ready and checks in the right hands so Charlie and I can close the purchase on the ranches with our signatures by the end of July?"

"I'll make it happen."

"Thanks, Uncle Curt. I love you."

"I love you too, Susan. Goodbye."

Susan turned to Charlie and said, "Everything's going perfectly on the ranch purchases."

"That's what I thought. Everythin's movin' fast. It means we'll have a lot to do when we get to the 101. I need to talk to Boss and Tom as soon as we get there."

Susan said, "I'll start creating a list of what we need to do between the ranches, the oil company, and the new store."

"Thank you, Honey. I need to drive out to the drill site and spend time with Hank. I'll see ya at supper."

***

Charlie and Hank sat on crates as they watched the crew work through the final few steps of getting the oil rig ready to drill.

Hank said, "I'm goin' to go up to Burbank in a week or two and do some more investigatin' on our new leases so I can have a plan ready for at least three well sites. I want to start drillin' up there soon."

Charlie stood, stretched, and looked across the oil field. "You should know somethin' here in a week or two, right?"

"Yep, as long as we stay on schedule. We've had a few mysterious things happen the past week or so that have slowed us down."

"Mysterious?" Charlie asked.

"Oh, nothing much. Misplaced tools or a motor that we thought was full of gas, but it turned out to be empty. Stuff like that." Hank pulled off his hat and stared over at the drilling rig. "Maybe I'm just workin' my crew too hard. I keep pushin' them because I want to get finished here. I also need my crew over in Drumright, who're finishin' my last commitment to Marland, up and drillin' on our property in Burbank."

"Well, it looks like yer still on track here. Maybe I can come over to Burbank and join ya from the 101."

"That would be good," Hank said. "I'll have a better idea of where I want to place our first well there when you do."

Charlie and Hank continued to talk about their plans. By the time

Charlie left the well site, the crew was drilling, and Hank was focused on the action.

***

That evening, Charlie walked into the suite and said, "I'm back. Are ya hungry?"

Susan answered from the bedroom, "Starving, and I'm ready like I promised."

"Let's go down and eat dinner."

The maître d' escorted Susan and Charlie to their table, which was already set with a bottle of cabernet and two glasses poured. As he held out the chair for Susan, he said, "I have taken the liberty of ordering you your usual dinner."

"Thank you, Alexander," Susan purred.

Alexander smiled and returned to his station.

Susan raised her glass. "We need to toast our buddies working on our new storefront."

Charlie raised his glass and said, "What exactly are we toasting?"

"Two men who have worked hard the last couple of days. They gave me an estimate to complete the construction and meet Chester's requirements."

"Great, to Sam and Chester, salute," Charlie said, mimicking the toasts they'd heard while at Jekyll Island.

"Salute."

"Now, what's the number? We wanted to keep it under $100,000, right?"

"Right, and Sam assured me that all of Chester's 'wild ideas' can be done for around $75,000."

"You didn't give them a dollar figure to work to, did you? All you said was we need to keep expenses down, right?"

"Yes, and I still need to give my go-ahead. I told them I would sleep on it and see them at breakfast."

"Sweetheart, you're a devil. But I love ya."

Charlie leaned back and took in Susan's beauty. The same view as last night, and it was a view he loved.

Chapter Nineteen
A Gusher
July 1919

O VER THE NEXT TEN days, a pattern developed where Charlie joined Susan, Chester, and Sam for breakfast and a walk to the storefront, followed by a trip to the Yale drill site to spend the rest of the day with Hank and the crew.

On July 28th, Charlie arrived in the late morning at the well site. He got out of the car at the road, and Hank ran to meet him.

Hank said, "Hey, buddy; we're hearin' rumblin' comin' up through the hole. Me and the crew have a feelin' we may hit soon."

Charlie looked up at the site. He could see that the equipment and work hut had been moved away from the derrick. "I see you've already got most of your tools and equipment stored back away from the derrick. You must expect to hit oil today."

Hank led Charlie away from the car. "Yep, and—"

Before they could get ten feet from the car, the ground rumbled, and a deep, low roar came from the direction of the derrick. Charlie could feel his feet begin to vibrate with the noise. It sounded like a locomotive was barreling down the tracks straight toward him. It was a familiar sound he remembered from last year when he had witnessed his first gusher.

Hank cupped his hands around his mouth and shouted toward the derrick, "It's about to blow!"

The crew was already running from the derrick floor. In just a few seconds, black gold spewed out of the hole.

It burbled up at first, like an artesian spring, and Charlie thought it may not be as big a gusher as they had hoped. Then, in a swish of a horse's tail, the oil exploded out of the hole. Debris flew in every direction, and oil fell down like a sticky, smelly, black rain that covered everyone and everything in a wide area, including Charlie, Hank, the crew, and all their equipment. Even the Cadillac was not spared.

The pressure from the hole kept the heavy flow going for some time and everyone danced around to celebrate another true gusher.

As the gusher subsided, the crew went back to the derrick and attached a cap to close off the flow.

This was another celebration and a testament to Hank's genius of finding oil on what would become known as the Kelly-Payne #2.

***

Charlie arrived back at the hotel in the afternoon, with Hank in the passenger seat, just as Susan was walking up the sidewalk toward the hotel from the direction of the construction site. She was wearing a beautiful red and white dress and white heels. Susan stopped and stared, her mouth hanging open as Charlie and Hank stepped out of the car.

Susan stomped her foot and said, "Charles Ashley Kelly!" She put a hand on her hip and pointed at the Cadillac with the other. "What in the world have you done to my pretty blue automobile?!"

Hank had the good grace to hang his head in shame, but Charlie just grinned, streaks of oil still marring his face. "We struck oil!"

"Oh, I couldn't tell," Susan said, sarcasm lacing each word. Then she threw her hands up into the air, gave an unlady-like squeal of joy, ran toward Charlie, and jumped at him.

Charlie caught her in his strong arms and swung her in a circle. A few strangers on the sidewalk were shocked by the display and hurried on, while Hank stood there and shook his head while laughing uncontrollably.

Charlie put Susan down. Her dress was covered in oil almost as much as Charlie was. "I guess I owe you a new dress now in addition to a new car."

Susan poked him in the chest. "You betcha, buster. But I'm so excited I may forgive you about the car." She turned and glanced at the Cadillac. "Maybe."

Hank walked around to the front of the car and idly used an oily handkerchief, as if he was a chauffeur, to polish the headlamp. "I'm sure this will buff right out," he said.

Susan turned to Hank and pointed a finger at him. "You!"

Hank jerked back as if shot, then Susan ran over and gave him a fierce hug. "You are an amazing man. I'm so glad that Charlie has you on his team."

Charlie could see Hank blush under the smear of oil that covered his face.

She stepped back and held out her hands to both Charlie and Hank. They each took hold of one of Susan's hands and she led them toward the hotel entrance. "Now, let's go celebrate!"

***

The following day, Charlie made arrangements with the hotel staff to celebrate the completion of Kelly-Payne #2. Despite them still working to clean the oil from the carpets in the reception area the hotel staff was happy to set up the ballroom for the celebration. Hank told the drilling crew to meet them at the hotel that afternoon to celebrate the gusher.

The celebration had been going on for a few hours when Charlie and Susan pulled Hank aside.

Charlie said, "Susan wants to know what's next?"

"I think you should shoot the car and put it out of its misery."

Charlie and Susan laughed. Charlie had met that morning with a mechanic who said he could have the car looking as good as new by tomorrow. "No, I mean about Kelly Oil."

Hank took a sip of his beer and smiled. "The other day, the day before the gusher, I drove up to the Burbank leases. I didn't get a chance to mention this when I got back, because we struck oil that day, but when I got there, I found a bunch of surveyor's flags all over our properties."

"Well, don't you need to survey the site to know where to drill?" Susan asked.

"Not exactly," Hank said. "You survey the site to make sure that when you do drill you are on the land that you have the rights to be able to drill. But I haven't had time to hire a survey team to do that yet."

Charlie stood a bit straighter and set his glass of wine down. "You mean somebody is trying to rustle our lease out from under us?"

Hank shrugged. "It could be, or it could be an honest mistake. But I'm concerned enough that I hired a local rancher to let me know if anybody else is snooping around the sites. I pulled up all the survey flags I could find while I was there."

"Don't you oilmen have rules that you are supposed to follow?" Susan asked.

"We do," Hank said. "Or we're supposed to. There are a lot of crooked people in the oil business, all of them looking to make a quick buck. If they can't get what they want by legal means they're happy to do it illegally."

"But not us," Charlie assured Susan.

"Should we be worried?" Susan asked.

"I'm always worried when I work a lease," Hank said. "I'm just good at hidin' it. I'll take a few more precautions for Burbank now, but I'm not concerned. I can send some of these guys," he pointed to the oilmen celebrating in the room, "up to the site to keep an eye on it. I'll be headin' up there with them."

"What about the well we just brought in?" Charlie asked.

"I'll leave some men here to finish things up and get the pump squared away. I had thought about doing some more exploration here—I think there's a spot just east of number two where we can increase our output from this field—but I want to focus on Burbank for now to get it started and let others know that it is our claim."

"Can we afford to split our crews that way?" Charlie asked.

"We'll be thin for a week or so," Hank admitted, "while the crews at Drumright finish up. But since we are in the final stages here and only doin' the preliminary work up at Burbank, we'll be fine."

Charlie picked up his glass of wine and held it up for a toast. "Well, we've got the funds. My guess is our new gusher is goin' to make us a tidy sum. Let's start addin' to it."

Chapter Twenty
Making an Offer
July 1919

THE FOLLOWING MORNING, WHEN they stepped out of the hotel, the Cadillac sat in the parking area, the blue paint gleaming in the morning light. Susan gave an approving nod and said, "I guess I'll forgive you now since you got all that ugly oil off my pretty automobile."

"You seemed okay with that ugly oil the other day," Charlie said as he tipped the bellhop.

"Oh, I still am, but I was going to hold you to replacing my car if your mechanic couldn't get it cleaned up."

"I think we could afford it now," Charlie said as he got into the car.

"Maybe," Susan allowed, "but we just bought two ranches. How would Uncle Curt react if we told him we needed to sell more stock to buy me another car because you'd ruined this one?"

As Susan closed her door, Charlie laughed and said, "Boy, good thing I dodged that bullet then."

As they pulled away from the front of the hotel and headed out of town, Charlie said, "This past month was good for us."

"I can't imagine how it could have been better." Susan giggled. "Well, maybe if you hadn't kissed me all covered in oil." She made a face and stuck out her tongue. "But all in all, not a bad month."

Before they got to the Yale turnoff, Charlie asked, "Do you want to stop at Yale for breakfast or wait and eat in Pawnee?"

"Let's wait until Pawnee. I want Yale behind us. I still think of the man shooting at you last year when I think of Yale. I would much rather only remember the gushers."

Charlie said, "I still think of it as the place I began learnin' the oil business."

They stopped for breakfast at a place called Sadie's Café in Pawnee. Back on the road after eating, the summer sun soon warmed the car. Susan pulled open her blouse and they drove with only her chemise covering her. Charlie didn't mind, and they drove along in comfortable silence and intimate touches as they headed north.

Just after lunchtime, Susan sighed and put her blouse back on as the Cadillac rolled in the main gate at the 101.

Susan said, "It seems like forever since we left here."

"It sure does. And the place looks mighty good. The trees are full of songbirds, the grass is greened up, and the White House is still big and beautiful."

Charlie collected their bags, and Susan led him up to their suite.

She said, "Put the bags over there, and I'll unpack later. Did you see the light on in George's office? Why don't you go see him and get your visit over?"

"I'll do it, and then we can take a walk."

He went down to George's office and found him going through paperwork. Charlie knocked on the door jamb and said, "Good afternoon, George."

"Charlie! My, it's good to see you. When did you get in?"

"Less than fifteen minutes ago."

"Come sit down, tell me about your trip."

Charlie sat in the chair across from the desk and described their experiences and what it felt like to have oil drench you like a heavy rainstorm.

George smiled. "That all sounds very good." He leaned back in his chair. "I need to bring you up to speed on what's happening here. As you already know, following the spring cattle gather, the sale wasn't very profitable, with the price of beef down, and we didn't have as many cattle to sell. We barely covered expenses."

"Isn't it because you've givin' up grazin' land to use to drill for oil and gas?"

"It's partly that. The cattle we sold had been fattened up really well on the Bar L grazing areas, but with the war now over for almost two years, beef prices are staying down, and it won't likely change over the next few years. I'm going to have to tell Boss to let more of the hands go. We already let some go in May."

"How did the meatpackin' operation do?"

"Much better than the cattle. But nothing's topping our oil business. Now, Joe wants to get back into show business with the Wild West Show and the movies. He seems to think that people will flock to the shows, hankering for nostalgia about the west after the war and the Spanish Flu. But I'm not so sure. The last time we had the show going we hardly made any money on it, and I think we'll lose money doing it, but he insists we get it started again next year."

"George, I've some ideas. Wanna hear 'em? Maybe some ya might not like to hear."

"Sure, Charlie; what's on your mind?" He leaned back in the chair to hear what Charlie was going to say.

"Last week, Susan and I purchased two ranches in Pottawatomie County. I want to make offers to Boss and Tom to come work for me down there."

George jumped out of his chair and came around his desk as he yelled, "What! Are you out of your mind? Do you think I'll let you steal my top hands?"

Charlie stood up, the chair falling over, and took a step backward, hands up, palms out, and said, "George, take it easy. I think this will benefit both of us if you give me a chance to explain my plan."

"No, Charlie!"

Charlie raised his voice. "George, hear me out."

At that moment George's secretary opened the door and poked her head into the room. "Is everything okay?"

That caused both men to realize that they'd been behaving like greenhorns. George told her that everything was alright and, with a look of not really believing her boss, she closed the door.

George sat back down. "No, I've had enough bad news for one day. Let's talk later, but you need to know I won't let you have Boss and Tom."

"Okay, maybe we both need to cool off. Susan wants to take a walk before supper, and I need to get down early after the drive. Can I come to see you tomorrow and discuss everythin'?"

"My temper may not have cooled off by tomorrow," George said. "I'll let you know."

Charlie picked up the chair and set it in front of George's desk. He'd turned to walk out when George said, "Charlie. It is good to have you back."

***

Charlie walked into the suite and asked Susan, "Are you ready?"

Susan had changed into a riding skirt with a pink silk top with pearl snaps on it. She picked up her hat and said, "Waiting on you, Sweetheart. Are you alright?"

"No, but I'll be fine; let's go."

Susan gave Charlie a questioning look but didn't say anything.

Charlie hurried out of the White House and down the steps, his long legs carrying him ahead of Susan. She had to practically run to catch up to him. Charlie stopped and took a deep breath, smelling the summer grass and wildflowers that grew along the path. They gave off a soothing aroma and he let them calm him after his talk with George. He held out his arm for Susan to take. They walked along arm-in-arm the quarter mile to the trees along the Salt Fork.

Charlie said, "Let's sit over here on the bank and pretend we're back on Rock Creek."

"Charlie, you're a natural-born romantic. I love it." She opened the pink silk blouse she had put on and let her breasts enjoy the sunlight. "I would do this on Rock Creek and hope you would make love to me."

Charlie took her in his arms and kissed her passionately, caressing her breasts as they plunged into their world of limitless bliss.

***

The following day, Charlie knew where he could find Boss. He always got to the chow hall early. After breakfast, Boss would saddle his horse, Ole Paint, and ride to the high point on the 101. There, he would spend time looking over what he considered the finest ranch in the country.

Charlie went to the café and ate breakfast. He walked to the Miller barn, saddled Tony, rode out, and found Boss sitting on Ole Paint as he expected. He rode up beside him and looked over and nodded.

They sat their horses in silence. They both seemed to enjoy the view of the grasslands, the cattle, the river, and Charlie even enjoyed seeing the oil derricks.

Boss finally said, "You're back from the Payne County oil fields, I see."

"Yep, it felt good to saddle Tony and ride out this mornin'."

"I don't think you're here by accident. What's on your mind, son?"

"You. I want to have a sincere talk with you about my future and how you could impact it in a big way."

"Whatever do ya mean, Charlie?"

"Remember in May when I told you I was lookin' for the right property to buy to own my own ranch someday?"

Boss nodded his head.

"Well, Susan and I just bought two ranches in Pottawatomie County near Earlsboro. They neighbor each other. One is a high-quality, five-thousand-acre cattle outfit. The other is a three-thousand-acre horse training ranch."

"I'm happy for you kids. Is there a reason you came out here to tell me about it?"

"Because, like I mentioned back in May, I want to hire you to run them for us."

"Whoa, why would I leave this?" He raised his right arm and pointed to the horizon.

Grassland spread as far as they could see, dotted here and there with a few oil derricks. Thick stands of cottonwoods and other trees covered the bottomlands where the Salt Fork flowed. It was a beautiful sight and Charlie remembered the first time he had seen it.

Charlie turned in his saddle and said, "The cattle part of this place is barely makin' it now. You had to let a bunch of hands go a while back, and George told me last night you may give more their walkin' papers soon. I know you're safe for a good long while. But the work here is changin'. Oil's king here now. Susan and I bought two great places. The cattle ranch is runnin' pure black Angus beeves. We'll own several bulls who are famous as sires. The barns and outbuildings are as nice or nicer as the ones here. The horse outfit has high-quality barns and pens. They raise quarter horses and train them for cuttin' and reinin'. Both outfits are well-known and specialized. And most important of all, they are profitable."

"It sounds like you're describin' the Stephenses cattle ranch and maybe Burkey's place next door. I've known Skip for years. I don't know about this, Charlie. Don't they have enough hands?"

"Yes, but let me tell ya my plans. I want to bring Tom with us and have him become your lead on the cattle outfit. My brother, Dan, has worked at the horse ranch for over a year and has become an expert workin' the horses. He'll stay there and handle the horse outfit for ya."

"I can see you've givin' this some thought." Boss looked out at the scene before them. He remained quiet for several moments then said, "What has George said 'bout this?"

Charlie leaned forward and patted Tony on the neck. "I tried to talk to him 'bout this yesterday. He and I don't quite see eye-to-eye on this yet."

Boss gave a snort. "I betcha don't. I've known George L. since he was eight years old and, despite the differences he's had with his brothers on how to run things, and him gettin' into the oil business, cattle has always been his first love. He would ride with me in my early days here, and I taught him everything I know about being a cowboy. I bet he was rather upset when you suggested hirin' me away from him."

"Ya might say that," Charlie said with a smile. "And Tom."

Boss nodded and moved his reins to keep his horse steady. "I have a lot of respect for Tom. I'd pick Tom to join me at your ranch ahead of everyone else." He hung his head and then turned to Charlie. "Listen to me. I sound like I've made a decision."

"It doesn't surprise me ya know the places and their owners. Let me give you the rest of the story. I know the workload is lighter at these ranches. The herds are smaller, and Dan and Tom will be there to assist you. But I'll still pay you as much as you make now. You'll have a house on the property. We've cooks already there to feed ya and the hands. Now, Susan and I want you, Tom, and Dan bad enough we are goin' to share some of the ranch profits with you. You'll get fifteen percent from each ranch. Tom and Dan will get ten percent from the ranch they help ya run. Those bonuses will be paid every year at Christmastime. I know it's a lot more than ya make now. And I promise I intend for these outfits to last for generations."

"Dadgummit, Charlie, this is mighty temptin'. You know I turned eighteen as a hand on this ranch. I'm almost fifty now. George W. hired me in '89 back when Gid Guthrie was still the Trail Boss here; this has been my home since."

"But it may not be for much longer." Charlie spoke quietly, knowing that the words would sting. "The Bar L is going to be leased for drillin', either to me or to someone. As soon as that land is no longer available for grazin' the cattle, business here will not be able to recover and George will be forced to make more drastic cuts to the hands."

Charlie tilted his hat back just a bit and looked at Boss. "I'm givin' you an opportunity to continue to do what you love to do and are good at. Hell, you are the best foreman in Oklahoma. Maybe even the entire West. It would be a shame for you to be put out to pasture before your time. I want you to come work for me. Think on it and let me know your answer soon."

"I'll give you an answer now. I'll take the job, Charlie. Everythin' you said about this place is right. Unless a lot changes, the 101 won't look much like this in a few years." He pointed to the expanse of land before them. "It'll be covered with oil derricks bearing your name on them. It's excitin' for me to think I could have a chance to continue doin' the only thing I have ever loved."

"Boss, you've made me a happy man."

"But I won't do anything until George gives his okay. I won't double-cross a man that I love and respect like George."

"I'll get his permission," Charlie said. "For now, we can just say we were talkin' about our respective futures."

"I may have an idea on how you can convince George."

Chapter Twenty-One
Downsizing
July 1919

CHARLIE WALKED INTO THEIR suite at 101, smiling from ear to ear. On the phone, Susan said, "Yes, I would love to meet you for lunch. We need to get together more often, May. Our men see each other all the time; we should too. Wait, Charlie just walked in. I'll see if I can drag him over to the café with me." Susan hung up the phone.

Charlie said, "Well, I am hungry, but I don't want to interrupt anythin' if you have plans with May."

"Nothing specific. I'm sure she'll be fine if you join us."

"Did you get all the business with Chester and Curt taken care of this mornin'?"

"I did, but we can talk about that later. Let's go eat." Susan grabbed her hat and practically pulled Charlie to the door.

When they arrived at the café, Charlie saw that George and May were already seated. Charlie hesitated for just a moment; he had not expected George to be there. He wasn't quite ready to talk to him yet and figured that George felt the same way after how their conversation had ended yesterday.

Susan gave another tug on his arm and guided Charlie over to the Miller's table. Charlie and George gave polite smiles to each other as Charlie and Susan sat down but said nothing.

May looked at Susan and said, "It seems like forever since we talked."

Susan grinned and put her hand over her heart. "May, I think it's been well over a month."

They both laughed.

Charlie said, "We have a couple of comedians for wives."

George nodded. "But I don't think they're good enough for Joe to hire them for the show."

May stood, put her hands on her hips, and looked sternly at George. "Maybe you can sleep in the barn, Mr. Miller."

They all laughed, and it was as if last night's showdown had never happened. May and Susan looked at each other and nodded.

May sat back down and said, "It's 'bout time you came to your senses, George."

"You too," Susan added, poking Charlie in his shoulder.

George and Charlie looked at each other as if hoping the other would save him from their respective wives.

Susan said, "May and I don't know what happened with you two yesterday, but you're both acting like—"

"Stubborn asses," May finished.

"It's just a business thing," George said.

"It's not a big deal," Charlie said at the same time.

Both women glared at their men, and Charlie and George fell silent.

Charlie looked at May and Susan and gave a little laugh. "I guess our wives are right. This business thing is not as important as our friendship."

George nodded and said, "Of course they're right. You and I are smart enough to respect what our wives tell us." He held out his hand across the table and Charlie shook it. "I do have something we need to discuss in regard to yesterday's matter. Please come to the office after we eat."

Charlie said, "Sure."

"Now, if the two of you are done actin' like children," May said, "let's eat."

***

Charlie stepped into the office doorway and said, "George, I'm here. What did you want to discuss?"

"Have a seat over by the fireplace. After yesterday, I think it's better if we talk as equals."

"Is anythin' wrong?"

"I got more information from our business office this morning. We going to have to sell off more cattle and reduce our cattle business personnel by more than I thought, and sooner than I had planned. To get costs down to where we can keep a cattle operation, I must also cut some of my higher priced people."

With a voice filled with concern and compassion, Charlie looked George in the eye and said, "I'll admit, George, I've seen this comin' for some time. I had only been here a little more than five or six months, but with what I learned about business from Jasper Blackaby, I could see the oil business becomin' more important to the ranch than anything else."

"Sometimes I wonder if we made the right decision back in '08 to sign that agreement with Marland. Things were a lot simpler when we didn't have to worry about all the oil stuff."

Charlie nodded. "But without the oil business you might not have been able to keep the whole ranch going all these years."

"That's true. It's been a blessing and a curse at times. And yesterday afternoon you said you'd bought two ranches in Pottawatomie County. I'll admit, when you said that I felt envious of you, and then when you told me you wanted to hire away my two best men I let that envy turn to anger."

"I can understand that, and it was wrong of me ask that of you out of the blue like that."

The two men sat in silence for a moment. Finally, George said, "You said that this could benefit us both. Tell me what you have in mind."

"As I mentioned yesterday, Susan and I purchased two ranches. I didn't know the information you just told me about the change in the ranch's finances, but I have been payin' attention to what Susan talks about with everythin' she does with the Kramer Group. I know that good employees are often your highest expense. When a business is falterin', like the cattle business is here, you have to make tough decisions. I think I came to the conclusion that you just did this mornin' some time back."

George gave a weak smile. "Susan has been good to you in many different ways it seems."

"Boss and Tom are two of your most expensive hands. They are also my two best friends who are cattlemen. Not havin' to pay their salary saves you more than lettin' go a dozen regular hands. Their skill will not be needed as much as you reduce the size of the herd here. You can move a talented hand into the foreman position who can handle the smaller size of the operation and not have to pay them as much as you do Boss."

"I think I see where you're going with this but you're jumping the gun here, Charlie. I can fix this; I just need some time. And Boss and Tom can't go anywhere; I need their experience to help me."

Charlie got up and walked over to the fireplace before responding. He finally turned to George and said, "My friend, listen to me. I just said Boss and Tom are your biggest expenses when it comes to your hands. You've gotta reduce your costs in the cattle operation to stay in the business."

"I can do that without getting rid of my best men."

"If you don't get rid of your best men, you won't have a cattle business to run."

George leaned forward in his chair and sighed. "That's what I'm worried about. I need their experience to guide us through this problem of downsizing the cattle operation. But if I keep them on then we won't have a business to downsize at all."

Charlie said, "Then listen to what I want to do. I think it will solve your problem and get me what I want too."

"If you want to get rid of a competitor, you only need to wait a few months." There was some bitterness, and fatalism, in George's words.

"I don't want that," Charlie said. "You know how important it is for all the cattle operations in the state to work together, even if we may be competitors. But even more important is how much I love the 101. I don't want to see you go out of business. Just give me a listen."

George sat back and looked at Charlie.

"I want to hire Boss and Tom right now." George started to say something, but Charlie held up his hand to keep him quiet. "And I want them to continue to work on the 101."

George shook his head. "Charlie, you're not making sense. Why would you pay my men's salary?"

"My men. I'd be payin' them to help you transition the cattle operation here to a smaller size. That gives you the capital you need to make changes without worryin' that you'll go broke payin' their wages. They'll also be trainin' their replacements at the same time."

"And I'll have to pay *them* just as much."

"No, ya won't. Because your cattle business will be smaller, you won't have to pay a new foreman and top hand the same wages. And you'll have fewer hands as well. Because you are givin' these hands more responsibility, they will accept the new salary you give them."

George sat up a bit in his chair. "And I suppose you are going to tell me who to promote?"

"I am, but it wasn't my idea. This is comin' from Boss."

George looked annoyed. "You went and talked to Boss before I agreed to anything?"

"I did because I needed to know that my idea would work. He has a lot of respect for you and won't do anythin' that you don't agree to."

"So, who do you think I should promote?"

"Thad and Pete. Boss said Thad had become a top hand and a new man with his attitude change after almost dying. The more Boss gave him, the more responsible he became. Pete can handle any crew out there now, so he could replace Tom. Both those guys won't have the same job or cost you as much as Boss and Tom because the outfit's becomin' much smaller with fewer beeves and hands."

George remained quiet for a long time. He then scooted to the edge of his chair and said, "I think your idea is a good one. I can't imagine this place without Boss, but I could pay for several regular hands with the money I pay him. Tom makes a good salary too. I felt awful when I read the numbers from our accounting folks earlier. Being able to keep them on to make the transition and teach Thad and Pete the ropes is a good idea. I guess you can afford their wages if you just bought two ranches. Are you ever going to tell me about them?"

Charlie told him about the Double Bar S and the Bar B, and then they shook hands, agreeing to Charlie's solution for the problems facing the 101. Charlie excused himself and went to find Boss.

He went straight to the main barn and found Boss and Tom together. "Well, I'm here with some good news." When Boss and Tom turned around, he grinned at them.

Boss said, "Did you and George work out your differences?"

"We did, and he likes the solution you and I came up with."

Tom looked between Charlie and Boss. "What in tarnation are you two talkin' about?"

Charlie's grin got even wider and said, "Tom, how would you like to come work for me on my new cattle ranch?"

Tom's mouth fell open. "Your what?"

Charlie spent several minutes explaining to Tom about the ranches he had bought and about the deal he had just made with George.

Boss said, "I'm glad ya did the deal, Charlie. I'm fine with helpin' George, and we should still be able to get down to your place by the end of the year."

"Hell, with Thad and Pete, we may be able to get this transition done by October," Tom said. "I know it will be tough, and a lot of hands will be let go, but it's the only way the 101 Ranch can stay in the cattle business."

"Yep," Charlie agreed. "This will help George create a new cattle operation to improve things financially and allow us all to make a solid transition to our future."

Chapter Twenty-Two
Welcome to Kelly Oil
August 1919

CHARLIE SAT IN THE 101 café sipping his coffee as he pondered his next move. He was looking at a proposal he had written up to start drilling operations on the Bar L in the new year. He was also thinking about the expansion plan that Chester had just given Susan a few days before about opening the second store in Oklahoma. Chester had hired Jess, and his brother had already picked out the top five locations where he felt new stores would be successful. Charlie was happy that his older brother was already making a big contribution to the business. The only thing that concerned Charlie was that he and Susan had only been able to spend a few days of quality time at their new ranches. He wanted to spend more.

When the front door opened, he put his coffee cup down. "George, it's good to see ya. I've already started on my breakfast, but let's talk for a while."

"Sure, how have you been? Have you spent any time at your ranches?"

"I was just thinkin' about that. Susan and I've split our time between Cushing, the Kelly Oil drillin' sites, and here. So, I've spent less time at my ranches than I would like."

George had sat across from Charlie, and Jed brought him coffee.

George nodded. "Thanks, and I'll have my usual, Jed." He took his first sip. "Things around here are moving along. Boss and Tom have guided the sale of the necessary cattle, and Thad and Pete, as you and Boss expected, are fitting into their new roles better than I could have hoped. They've done a fine job of learning the business side of things and they're doing so well I suspect Boss and Tom can join you in Earlsboro within a month or so."

"That sounds mighty good, George." Charlie took a bite of bacon. "I've got another personnel decision I'd like to share with you." George gave him a look over the top of his coffee mug. "I hope to add someone to my payroll from your staff. He's worked with Marland, Hank, and Horse Chief Eagle over the past few years. He's also a fine cowboy."

George set his coffee down and leaned on the table. "Who are you trying to steal from me now?" He sounded gruff but he smiled as he said it.

Charlie chuckled. "It's James LeClaire."

"The Ponca Indian?"

"Yep, and a member of the Edward LeClaire family. He's been a solid arbiter whenever an issue has come up regardin' any of the lands the 101 has leased from the tribe, regardless of whether it's because of oil, cattle, or something else. Susan and I are goin' to move to our new ranches later this month. I want someone here at the 101 full-time I can trust who knows the history of the ranch and all the business relationships includin' with the Ponca, Otoe, and Osage tribes. The Ponca tribe and your family sponsored James to attend Northern Oklahoma College over at Tonkawa."

"I remember," George said, taking another drink of his coffee. "He graduated with a degree in Business Management."

Charlie nodded. "He'll work for me, and you can turn to him for answers to questions involvin' Kelly Oil and the oversight of leased 101 Ranch land where other oil companies are drillin'."

"Sort of what you did for Marland?" George asked.

"Yep. Now I want James to do it for us. What are your thoughts, George?"

"You've given me a lot to consider, Charlie." George leaned back in his chair and rubbed his chin. "I have other responsibilities pulling at me daily, as you know. I know that James will be good at doing the same thing you were doing for Marland. Are you willing to cover his salary?"

"Yes. As I said, he'll work for me. James is a smart, savvy, educated man, and I trust him to do the right thing and keep us both aware of what's happenin'. I'll continue to come here as often as possible, but havin' a dedicated member of my company here and focused on the day-to-day operation is best."

Jed placed George's plate in front of him. George took a bite of buttered toast, leaned back, and said, "You're right. I know James has shared office space with Joe Jr. and George Jr. for the past several months. I'll have him come to my office this morning, and we can discuss this with him together."

Charlie stood and picked his hat up off a neighboring chair. "I need to go check on Tony. I'll see you at your office to meet with James, okay?"

"Good; I'll have him there."

***

As Charlie entered George's office, the young man sitting in a chair across from George immediately stood and said, "Mr. Kelly, it's been several months since we last talked."

Charlie smiled. "Yes, it has, James. My, you seem much bigger than I remember."

James returned his smile. "I've put on a few pounds. Glad to see you again." He held out his hand and Charlie gave it a firm shake.

George walked to the head of the conference table. "Let's sit here."

Charlie sat with his back to the wall and George sat to his right. James sat across from Charlie. George had a notepad in front of him and looked at what he had written.

Charlie cleared his throat. "I see George has made some notes, but let me begin. James, you're here because I have a new job within the Kramer Group; and I feel you're the right person for it. I've discussed this with Mr. Miller, and he agrees."

James seemed a bit surprised. "Would this have to do with Kelly Oil?"

"I knew you were sharp," George said. He chuckled and nodded at Charlie to continue.

Charlie leaned in. "Yes, my wife and I have bought ranches in Pottawatomie County, and we're movin' there later this month. I need someone here at the 101 as my eyes and ears to be responsible for the day-to-day operation of Kelly Oil. We can discuss the details of what it means, but I'm offerin' you the job of bein' my on-site lead man workin' with George to address whatever needs doin' supportin' the oil business on this ranch."

George added, "James, you've been involved in the past with this type of work, representing the tribes and through other activities you supported for Marland. I'm comfortable that you can handle this. What do you think?"

James rubbed his neck. "So, I'd be working for you, Mr. Kelly, at Kelly Oil and working with you, Mr. Miller, as I operate the Kelly Oil business here on the 101?"

Charlie grinned. "Yep. I'll pay you well, and we'll arrange for you to have whatever you need for office space, phone, and whatever."

George said, "Charlie, if you agree, we can provide James with your old office next door. I'll make the space rent-free to Kelly Oil. And you can rent the little house for this young bachelor that you used before you married Susan."

Charlie looked at George and grinned. "That sounds fine, but we haven't heard James say he'll take the job."

James jumped to his feet and offered his hand to Charlie. "Oh, I'll take the job."

Charlie shook his hand and said, "Okay, I haven't mentioned your pay yet. What do ya need?"

"Between what Horse Chief Eagle gives me from the tribe and what I make here from the ranch, I get seventy-five dollars a month."

Charlie scratched his chin for a moment. "I assume the part from the tribe will continue, but I'll pay you $200 a month to start, and if everything works out as I think it will, there's a bonus at Christmas time and a raise in January."

James' eyes sparkled as he said, "Yes, sir, Mr. Kelly, it's more than fine with me."

George stood. "Well, I guess we've settled this. If it's alright with Charlie, I'll say welcome to Kelly Oil, James. And I look forward to working with you."

Charlie said, "Of course that's alright, George. Let's go over to the café, James. We can enjoy a few cups of coffee and work out the details."

***

After an hour or so of discussing what Charlie had done in a similar role supporting George and allowing James to ask questions, Charlie stood and said, "I think you need to go and start workin' on your new office and git the key from George for your new house."

James beamed. "I'm so excited about all this. I can't wait to share this news with everyone, especially Horse Chief Eagle."

"I need to go find Boss and git an update from him. I'll see ya before too long and certainly before Susan and I move out."

Charlie found Boss outside the main barn talking with Tom, Thad, and Pete. As he approached the group, he said, "I assume you're plottin' your next bank job, right?"

After the laughter died down, Boss bowed, saying, "What can we do for ya, Mr. Kelly?"

Charlie grinned. "Watch it, Bellamy. Ya could be lookin' for a job by sundown."

Again, everyone laughed, then Charlie said, "I need an update on how things are goin'."

Before anyone could say anything, Thad stepped over to Charlie, hugged him, and said, "Thanks, buddy, for the recommendation and kind words ya gave Boss and Mr. Miller."

Pete said, "That goes for me too. I don't know how I'll ever repay ya."

Charlie felt emotions coming out and hesitated a second or two.

"Fellas, the truth doesn't have to hurt, ya know. Ya both are top hands; I'd trust ya with my life. So, I was happy everyone could see in ya what I saw."

Tom said, "Now that's settled; let me answer your question. Boss and I are leavin for the Double Bar K on Monday."

"Monday?" Charlie asked, shocked at the date. "I was talkin' with George this mornin' and he said it would be a month."

Tom said, "George just wants to try and keep us around longer. These guys are up to speed on everything, and Boss and I are no more than distractions here at this point."

Boss added, "We're excited to git there and start our new life, and these two are ready to take charge here."

Thad scratched his neck. "I know it's old news, but I haven't had a chance to congratulate ya on startin' Kelly Oil and buyin' out Marland."

"Yep, Marland was wantin' to sell out and spend more time elsewhere. Now, I've promoted James LeClaire to my day-to-day operation lead here at the ranch. I'll come back as often as I can, but James is in charge."

Pete grumbled, "Ya stole another fine cowboy from us, huh?"

Charlie grinned. "I sure did. But ya know he'd been doin' office work for a while. Ya got plenty of help as I see it."

Pete laughed. "He's a good one, and I'm happy he's gettin' a chance to use his schoolin'."

Boss said, "You sure know how to pick 'em, Charlie."

"Thanks. This is all good news, fellas. I need to see my wife and call Hank, so I'll see ya soon."

***

As Charlie walked into their suite, Susan said, "Hey, this phone call's for you. It's Hank."

"Great, I was hopin' to talk to him today." Charlie walked over and Susan handed him the receiver. "Hank, what's up?"

"Charlie, I'm at the Burbank site. Can ya come over and let me show ya around?"

"Yep, I'll come over there. Want me to drive all the way out or meet you somewhere?"

"I'll pick you up at Flossie's Café in town."

"I'll meet ya there soon."

In about an hour, Hank was driving Charlie out to their leases with his company truck. As they approached the first well site, Charlie could see the top of a derrick poking up from behind a hill. "You already got one up?"

Hank said, "Yep, the crew is movin' fast. They're almost finished gettin' the derrick up. We should start drillin' tomorrow." He pulled to the side of the road so they could see the derrick.

"That's excitin', buddy. After the recent incidents I was worried we would be delayed."

"Yeah, I still don't know how these things are happenin'. We're spendin' more than I'd like to replace missin' tools and damaged lumber for the derrick. I'm close to havin' a man stay out here full time to keep an eye on everythin'."

"Do ya think it's necessary?"

"I don't know. It's an added cost 'cause we'd need to pay them for their time."

"If it keeps us from havin' delays, I'll approve it," Charlie said.

Hank nodded as he pulled back onto the dirt road. "Before we stop, I'll show you the next two locations we'll drill."

"Good. You've seemed so sure we'll hit some big ones here."

About a half mile away, Hank stopped the truck. They got out and walked over the area of the lease, and Hank showed Charlie what he had in the way of possibilities for the future. They spent a few hours discussing not only the Burbank site but also talked about Yale and Morrison.

As they walked back to the truck, Charlie said, "Buddy, ya better git me back to town. Susan and I need to have dinner together tonight. Things are comin' together faster than I could ever have hoped. I'm thinkin' we can move to the Double Bar K tomorrow or, for sure, on Friday. But I need to hear what's been happenin' with all she's been doin' first."

Hank gave Charlie a friendly slap across his back. "Ya sure gotta lot on your plate, my friend. Okay, let's git ya back to your car."

Chapter Twenty-Three
Life Begins at the Double Bar K
September 1919

O**N A HOT SEPTEMBER** evening, Charlie enjoyed his second glass of cabernet on the patio of their Double Bar K Ranch house. With great pleasure, he watched Susan exit their pool after her regular nightly dip.

Her wet naked body glistened in the light of a full moon, water dripping off her nipples. She toweled off, then poured herself a glass of wine and sat on a lounge chair beside Charlie.

Susan wrinkled her nose and grinned as she said, "I thought you would join me."

"I planned to, but Attie came to the back door and said I had a phone call from Hank. He's all excited about somethin'. He'll be here for breakfast in the mornin'. He said he's gotta talk to us in person."

"Well, we haven't seen Hank for a few weeks."

"I'm sure he wants to update us on the activities in the oil fields. I wonder what's on his mind. I hope he has some good news about Burbank."

"If he's excited, Burbank is a good guess. It's blazing hot tonight, even with this light breeze. I'm taking my wine and going back to the pool. Coming?"

"I'm with ya." Charlie dropped his clothes and dove in.

***

The following morning, Charlie and Susan enjoyed their coffee at the breakfast table, which overlooked their patio, pool, and offered a view of the barn and corrals in the distance.

Charlie said, "I love this view out these picture windows, but I prefer the view you're givin' me. Your amazin' cleavage is more beautiful than anythin' I could enjoy out these windows."

Attie stepped in, frowning as she said, "There's a man at the door. He said he's Hank Thomas, and you're expecting him."

Charlie smiled. "Please bring him here. He's joinin' us for breakfast."

Susan laughed. "Attie's a little watchdog, isn't she?"

Attie led Hank to the breakfast nook at the back of the house.

As Hank entered the room, Charlie stood. "Ya found us; welcome to the Double Bar K, Hank. By the way, you've now met Attie, our housekeeper."

Hank nodded. "My pleasure, Miss Attie." She nodded and left the room without a word.

Hank turned, his eyes immediately captured by Susan and the view Charlie had been enjoying. "You're as beautiful as ever." He shook Charlie's hand and said, "I still don't git what she sees in you."

They laughed as Cleta, the cook, walked in.

"May I take your breakfast orders?"

Susan said, "Yes, thank you, Cleta. Hank, meet Cleta, and what would you like? We have most anything you could want."

He leaned back in his chair and smiled. "Great, nice to meet ya, Miss Cleta. I'll have three eggs scrambled, bacon, and toast."

Cleta asked, "Any potatoes with it, and how do you want your coffee?"

"Potatoes, any way you have them, is fine, and coffee, black."

Cleta turned to Susan and Charlie, smiled, and asked, "Your usual breakfast this mornin'?"

Charlie looked at Susan and replied, "Yes, and could you bring a full carafe of coffee and leave it here for us? Thanks."

Susan couldn't wait; she placed her hand on Hank's forearm. "Hank, what's got you so excited that you had to drive all the way out here to tell us?"

Charlie leaned in. "Yeah, buddy, what's on your mind?"

Hank took a deep breath and said, "I'm so happy with our progress in Burbank. Marland's also got a drill site nearby, but our site's better than where he's located. I hear a lot of talk about Seminole and down in Garvin County. But Burbank's where I'm seein' all the big companies movin' into. I also hear some folks are startin' to add security guards to their crews. I know of several competitors who are losin' roughnecks because of vandalism and threats of gunfire. We need to address this."

Charlie said, "Hank, you said you were goin' to have a man live at the well site to keep an eye on things."

"I did. And our mysterious incidents have stopped happenin', but I've been talkin' with several of the other outfits and they're worried. One man was injured by a stray bullet over at a place called Whizbang and had to be taken to a hospital. It's gettin' to be like those boom towns you heard about when people struck gold. There's too many men, too many saloons, and not enough common sense."

"In my experience," Susan said, "that much money tends to cause men to lose their minds. Oil money is flowing into Oklahoma faster than the oil is coming out of the ground."

Cleta arrived with their breakfast and set a carafe of coffee on the table. Charlie poured cups for all of them and took a drink of his coffee. "There's enough in the bank account to cover ya addin' more crews and guards if needed."

"I'll do that," Hank said, biting into a strip of bacon. "These sites will more than pay for it." He finished the bacon and spent several minutes talking about how the sites were better than he had even hoped. He was animated, shifting in his seat and using his hands to explain his plans to put as many wells as he could on the land to maximize their profit.

When Hank finally slowed down and he could get in a word of his own, Charlie said, "I've never seen ya so excited and so sure of anythin'. Go for it. And let's keep an eye on Seminole and Garvin County too."

"I'll go through Payne County on my way back to Burbank and pick up another crew, and I'll look at addin' guards. Now, let me add this to your list of things to consider. As I got close to your ranch, the land to the north of your house looked as good or better for oil potential as anythin' in Payne County. Ya know how much money was made up there."

"Yep, and I also know Clay Stephens, the man we bought this place from, said several wildcatters approached him wantin' to drill on the land to the north."

Hank took another sip of coffee. "Charlie, I'm sure we'll find oil here below your ranch."

They continued to talk about where they might drill.

Susan put her foot down on drilling on their land, at least for the time being. "Go spoil someone else's view first before you spoil ours."

Hank tried to explain they could do it without spoiling her view, but Charlie had to finally promise to not drill on their land unless it was absolutely necessary.

Hank finally pushed his chair away from the table and said, "Cleta, can ya hear me?"

"Yes, sir, what can I get you?"

"A wheelbarrow, if ya don't mind. I'm goin' to need help gettin' to my truck after such a fine breakfast."

Cleta dried her hands on a dishtowel as she stepped into the doorway, looked at Hank, and winked. "Sorry, Sweetie, wheelbarrows are not in my pantry. You better talk to Mr. Kelly."

The three at the table laughed and enjoyed another cup of coffee.

After Hank left, Susan said, "Charlie, tell me again what you have planned for this afternoon."

"I'm meetin' with Boss to go over the improvement projects we want to finish here before cold weather. Between now and then, I need to study the paperwork we received from Uncle Curt to prepare us for the meetin' in Kansas City next week."

"I thought I might take the Cadillac, drive to Maud, and visit your mother. I'll go by your dad's gas station and fill the car up. We need to leave tomorrow if you still want to go through Tulsa and see the Missouri Concrete Plant."

"I do. Get the gas, and I'll see you for dinner. Tell my folks hello, for me. I'm goin' to my office till lunch."

"I'll leave soon and be back here in time for an early supper."

***

Boss stopped by the house after lunch, and he and Charlie rode out on the property. Thad had put Tony onto a train car for Charlie a couple of weeks back and his old horse was taking a liking to his new home, especially since Charlie tried to ride him every day if he could. Boss showed him the finished water wells and the two expanded ponds they'd need to provide more water for the cattle.

Boss said, "You told me the previous owner ran about seven hundred head, and you wanted to add 200 more. We've enough acres of native grass, but I knew our ponds wouldn't handle the additional cattle. We drilled the additional wells and are now in good shape."

"This is great, Boss. Let's ride over so I can see how the house we're buildin' for you is comin' along. I know you're ready to move out of that room down at the north barn."

"Ya betcha. The construction crew you brought in from Kansas City has about finished it. They work faster than any I've ever seen."

"They'll get a nice bonus if they finish by the end of next week. It's your birthday next Friday, isn't it?"

"How didja know, and why did it matter?"

"Susan and I want you to have a nice place to call home. We know you're a bachelor, but it doesn't mean you shouldn't have a comfortable place to make you proud. And Susan found out from May Miller when your birthday is. It became a convenient date to give as a target for the boys with the hammers and nails."

"Charlie, it's mighty nice of ya. I shore 'preciate it."

They rode about a half-mile north, and a wood-frame house stood in a beautiful stand of blackjack oak trees.

Charlie looked over at Boss and said, "It's a nice-lookin' house. It looks finished from here."

Boss said, "You'll hear hammers and such when we get closer. The workers are still busy inside."

"By the time Susan and I get back from Kansas City, you should have moved in. Let's have a look inside.

As they dismounted, Boss said, "Charlie, I thank you and Susan for this. I had my house at the 101, but I didn't have anything this nice."

Even though it wasn't finished Charlie could identify the two bedrooms, a good-sized livin' room, a kitchen, and an indoor bathroom. They finished the quick tour on the front porch. "This porch will be nice to sit out on and watch the sunset at the end of day."

Boss turned to Charlie, "What do you think I'll be doin'? I work for a livin', unlike you oil barons."

Charlie laughed and slapped Boss on his shoulder. "Well, I know yur getting' up there in years. I figured you'd need ta slow down some."

"I'm not ready ta be put out ta pasture yet, young man."

They both laughed and returned to their horses and rode back to the main house.

Chapter Twenty-Four
Concrete and Oil Men
September 1919

CHARLIE AND SUSAN WERE on the road early. As Charlie climbed into his seat, he said, "Sweetheart, I'm goin' to take the best roads we can, and that means it'll not be the shortest drive. It may add an hour or two. And it's a little out of the way, but we'll go through Seminole. We won't stop, but Hank mentioned it yesterday, and I want to see what the place looks like."

"Okay, better roads make for a more pleasant drive. We'll still get to Tulsa before dark anyway, right?"

"We should, and I want to. I don't like to drive in the dark, especially when I don't know the roads well."

As they drove past some businesses in Seminole, Susan said, "This town is about the same size as Maud. Maybe a little bigger but small compared to Shawnee."

Charlie nodded. "I see what ya mean, but Hank says there's oil to be found around here. If that happens, this place could become another Cushing."

They stopped for breakfast at Flo's Café.

As she buttoned the top two buttons on her shirt, Susan asked, "Did I tell you I talked with Uncle Curt yesterday?"

Charlie shut his car door as he said, "No, how's he doin'?"

"He's great, and everything is prepared for next week's meeting. He talked to Jim Townsley yesterday, and Jim has his site manager at his concrete plant near Tulsa ready to meet us tomorrow morning."

Charlie opened the café door for Susan. "Good, I look forward to meetin' him."

They enjoyed their chicken fried steak and eggs breakfasts and then headed north toward Chandler.

East of Chandler, Charlie said, "These rollin' hills around here remind me of the land up at Yale we drilled on."

"Does it make it more likely for oil to be here?"

"I'm not an expert like Hank, but it seems that he likes it better when it's not flat."

She giggled, put a hand under each of her naked breasts, lifted gently, and said, "I guess Hank would like these mountains, then, wouldn't he?"

Laughing, he said, "Honey, I promise you a guy don't need to be an oilman to love those babies."

She smiled and then looked out the windshield. "There's a town ahead."

Charlie said, "This good-sized town we're coming into is Bristow. It looks like a good place to stop and fill the car's gas tank and check the radiator water level."

As they pulled into a Marland Gas Station, Susan said, "While you buy the gas, I'll walk next door and get us a couple of Coca-Colas."

"Sounds good, Sweetheart." He teased her with, "Did ya remember the buttons on ya shirt?"

She turned and showed him. "I've buttoned the bottom two again." She gave him a wicked grin. "Is it okay, Mr. Kelly?"

He grinned too, and nodded his approval.

Susan appreciated the smooth road east of Bristow, and at Kellyville it became a paved road for the rest of the trip into Tulsa.

Susan shifted in her seat to allow more breeze to hit her body and said, "This is wonderful; no more bouncing around. It hasn't been bad today, but this paved road will save us time, and maybe we can see Jim's man today."

Charlie nodded. "We could, so let's go directly to the hotel and call out to the plant. No, wait a minute. I remember a sign back where the pavement started that said 'Sapulpa four miles.' Curt said the plant's in Sapulpa. We need to stop and call from there."

"Good thinking, Charlie. I have the number in my bag. I'll dig it out."

In a few minutes, they drove into downtown, found a hotel, and went inside.

Susan walked to the registration counter. She smiled at the clerk and said, "Good afternoon, I'm visiting Sapulpa for the first time. I need to call someone for directions to his location. May I use your phone, please?"

The clerk nodded and said, "Of course, here you go," and handed the candlestick phone to her.

Susan smiled, thanked him, and called the site. "This is Susan Kramer-Kelly; who am I talking to?"

"Hello, Mrs. Kelly, I'm Zane Krebs. I recognize who you are and thought you might call. I'm your site manager."

"My husband and I would like to visit you now. We're in Sapulpa."

"Of course. I expected you tomorrow, but this works better for me too."

He gave them directions to his office, and they arrived in ten minutes.

Zane, a man about thirty-five, five-foot-ten, and of medium build, gave Charlie and Susan a thorough tour of the plant, describing their processes for creating cement and providing production numbers they expected to achieve annually.

They returned to the office area, and Zane offered Charlie and Susan coffee. Zane said, "Let's sit around the table in the next room."

Charlie took a sip of coffee and said, "Zane, I know it's late, and you probably have more than enough work to finish before you call it a day, but I have a question for you."

"What is it, Mr. Kelly?"

"How much do you know about the use of cement in the oil drilling process?"

"Enough to know it's an area we should explore. Jim and I recently talked about it at some length, and he wants to expand into the business if we can find the interest and the funding."

"Well, Zane, guess what? You have both of those looking at you right now."

"No, shit! Sorry, Mrs. Kelly, sometimes my manners fall short."

Susan grinned and said, "Zane, you should hear me if I stub my toe."

"Do you have any oil companies contacting you to see if you can support them?" Charlie asked.

"I did have one about a month ago. Ever since I heard Erle Halliburton down in Duncan set himself up with a mixing box late last year, I have wondered why we couldn't do it too."

"We should. I'll take the lead on this, but you could become a key player here in Oklahoma with Jim's approval. Zane, the oil business is about to explode, and I want us to explode with it. Kelly Oil will become your first customer. The company we form to support the oil business with cement might eventually become a separate company. Missouri Concrete and Kelly Oil both benefit from it."

"I'm excited to hear this, and I'm ready to do whatever you need," Zane said.

Susan said, "I recommend you call around and ask questions. Learn all you can as fast as you can. We need to know what the drillers want, and we need to know what Halliburton is doing to provide the products and services he has developed."

"I can do that. Should I tell Jim this is a priority for us now? Our focus here has been supporting road building and construction. We may not have the capacity to do that and take on the oil business too."

"What do you need to make that happen?" Susan asked.

"Another quarry for starters. More men to work the quarry. More trucks to haul the concrete." Zane said, ticking the items off on his fingers.

"I'm telling you now this should be a priority. We'll make sure that Jim knows this. You start looking at what you'll need and get it to Jim," Susan said.

They all shook hands and agreed to stay in touch, then Charlie and Susan got back on the road to Tulsa.

Susan turned to Charlie and said, "My goodness, that was a much more important meeting than what I had expected when we stopped here."

"I agree, and I'm glad you think that too. The Kramer Group needs to be a leader in all parts of the oil business."

***

Charlie and Susan drove into Tulsa and found the Hotel Tulsa. After getting settled into their suite, freshening up, and changing clothes, they looked at the brochure provided in their room and decided to eat at the Hotel Tulsa's Topaz dining room.

The maître d' met Susan and Charlie at the dining room entrance. "Welcome. Do you have a reservation?"

"Yes, we are the Charles Kellys."

The maître d' checked his book and nodded. "Of course, you have the Presidential Suite on the 12th Floor; please follow me." He escorted Susan and Charlie to a private table.

Charlie noticed a well-dressed young man following their every move as they approached their table. He watched the man stare at Susan. She was wearing a luxurious red dress, and it showed off her curves and beautiful breasts. Charlie smiled at the man as he and Susan seated themselves.

Their waiter arrived. "Welcome. Here are your menus, and what can I get you to drink?"

Susan replied, "Water, and I'll give you an update after I determine my entree."

Charlie nodded. "My plan as well."

The waiter left, and Susan said, "I think I'm going with a steak. I know I'm so predictable, but we're cattle ranchers, after all."

"Sweetheart, we both seem to order the same thing all the time, but if it's what we like, so what?"

Charlie took Susan's hand. Out of the corner of his eye he could see the well-dressed man still looking at them. "Seems you have an admirer."

Susan turned her head and smiled. "Maybe he is looking at you?"

"At this ol' cowpoke? I don't think so."

The waiter returned with their waters and to take their orders. "Have you determined what I can get for you?"

Charlie said, "Yes, we each want a porterhouse with a baked potato, and bring us a bottle of your best cabernet, please."

"How would you like your steaks prepared?"

"She'll want her steak medium and make mine medium rare."

"Thank you, and I'll have your wine for you momentarily."

After the waiter departed, the young man couldn't wait any longer. He stood and walked to Charlie and Susan's table. He was handsome, maybe a few years older than Charlie, with sharp blue eyes and short brown hair. "I don't believe I've met you," he said with a slight Minnesota accent, "but I'm guessing we're neighbors. They place the occupants of the 12th Floor suites back in this corner. I apologize for invading your privacy, but I don't see many folks my age dining near me."

Susan smiled and provided him a perfect view as she purred, "I'm sorry, who are you?"

He took a deep breath and stumbled over his words, "I... I'm Paul Getty, uh, J. Paul Getty, and you are?"

Charlie answered, "We're the Kellys. I'm Charles," he nodded in Susan's direction, "and this is my wife, Susan Kramer-Kelly. We're on our way to Kansas City."

"Kramer. Are you the daughter of the late Walter Kramer?"

"Yes," Susan said, "and you must be the son of George Getty. My father worked with your father on a project back in the aughts. Are you also an oil man?"

"He sure is," Charlie said. "He picked up a couple of leases when I was at the auction up in Pawhuska."

"I thought I recognized you," Getty said. "You out bid that fellow for the big Burbank leases. People are still talking about that."

Charlie smiled. "We did. By year-end, you'll hear more about the Kelly Oil Company. We're new in the oil business but have highly experienced people with us."

Getty said, "I should leave you folks alone. I wanted to introduce myself since we may see each other from time to time. May I ask, will you be here tomorrow evening?"

Susan said, "I believe so. Do you have something in mind?"

"I've some older friends who also live here at the hotel off and on. They're here now, and I'd like us to share a meal tomorrow night. I'll make the arrangements."

Charlie said, "Who are these friends?"

"You saw them at Pawhuska, though we didn't have the chance to meet while there." He was talking to Charlie but still looking at Susan. "Harry Sinclair of Sinclair Oil and Bill Skelly of Skelly Oil. I know they've been eager to meet the young man that amazed the crowd at Colonel Walters little auction."

Charlie smiled inside because he could see Getty was captivated by Susan. The man couldn't take his eyes off her.

Charlie said, "Mr. Getty, we'll be here. How about at 7:00 for dinner?"

"Excellent. I'll leave you two alone and see you tomorrow night."

After he walked away, Charlie looked at Susan and said, "Interesting. He said they've been eager to meet me since the auction. But he's an oil millionaire, as are his friends. The funny thing to me is I'm not sure whether his friends want to meet us for social reasons or to meet their competition. And will Mr. Getty want to talk oil or be around you?"

Susan giggled and asked, "Charlie, are you jealous?"

"No. I kinda enjoyed watchin' how your brains, poise, and beauty intimidated a powerful man."

Susan said, "As I have heard you say, they can look all they want but never touch. If my looks take them off their game, great, we'll use it. I'm interested in meeting some men already making it big in oil, aren't you?"

"Yes, I'm looking forward to tomorrow night."

Chapter Twenty-Five
Touring Oil Country
September 1919

CHARLIE AWOKE FIRST. **H**E lay still in the massive French Provincial bed and watched, with complete adoration, his amazing wife sleeping. He eventually reached over and gently caressed Susan's breasts.

"Good morning, beautiful."

"Wha... uh... Good morning." Her eyes fluttered open.

Charlie kissed her cheek. "Let's go exploring today; whattaya say?"

Susan yawned. "Sure, uh, okay."

"I guess ya still need to wake up, huh?"

She reached over and took ahold of his manhood. "I'm ready, are you?"

He rolled over to her, and they postponed breakfast.

***

After their morning exercise, they finally got ready for the day and ordered in a light breakfast of coffee, fruit, and pastries.

Charlie looked up from his newspaper at Susan, smiled, and said, "I'm the luckiest man alive. We have a beautiful life together, don't we?"

"It's wonderful. You aren't lucky. You just happened to be the man I looked for all my life and didn't know it until you came into my life in Elmore City." She gave his hand a squeeze.

"Susan, I looked at a map last night. We can drive up to Bartlesville and come back through Pawhuska, Pershing, Barnsdall, and Owasso on our way back into Tulsa. Osage County is where Skelly, Sinclair, and Getty have all made some of their money. I want to drive it."

"Then I'm for it. Another day in the Cadillac with you'll be fun. And we get to see some new country too."

They headed north to Bartlesville after breakfast and enjoyed bright sunshine and moderate temperatures.

As they arrived in Bartlesville, Charlie said, "I've studied the Getty family; they made a fortune here, and I may ask him about it tonight. Frank Phillips, who leads the new Phillips Petroleum Company, his company's run from here in Bartlesville."

"Sounds like you've been reading more than your philosophy books lately. My father knew Frank because Phillips seriously considered starting a bank in Kansas City. The war broke out, and those ideas quickly changed."

"I'm surprised your father never got involved in the oil business. He knew George Getty, Sinclair, and now you say, Phillips."

"He thought about it when he talked with Phillips. Then father took ill and never acted on anything."

"Maybe that's why he was so willin' to help me start Kelly Oil. He may have realized that he was missin' out on a business opportunity for the Kramer Group."

"You may be right. Father often talked a lot over dinner about the oil business, and he was impressed with what Sinclair was building with his company."

Charlie and Susan agreed Bartlesville had become a lovely city, and they continued to Pawhuska. The road all day had been a mixture of improved gravel and paved. As they left town, it returned to gravel.

Charlie reached over and pulled Susan to him. She snuggled under his arm and said, "I enjoy driving with you. These trips are pure pleasure for me."

"Me too, Susan. We need to do this more."

Some buildings came into view, and Charlie said, "This is Pawhuska."

Susan said, "Isn't this the location of the famous elm tree? I want to see the place where you made your first big impression on all these other oilmen."

"Sure." He smiled. "Ever since that day, I've wanted to meet those oilmen as well. Hank and I saw the three men we're havin' dinner with tonight at the auction, and I knew that if I wanted to make Kelly Oil the best oil company it could be I would need to learn what they did to become successful. The Burbank leases we got at the auction is a start, but I know I still have more to learn. I'm hopin' that Sinclair and Skelly are willin' to share their knowledge and aren't just tryin' to figure out how to buy us out. I want to become the next Osage County oil millionaire."

Susan looked up at Charlie, hugged him, and said, "A gusher is all it'll take to give Kelly Oil a seat at the big boys' table. You'll get there soon, Sweetie."

"I appreciate the confidence, and I agree. The tree's at the top of this hill."

A few minutes later, Susan stood next to it at the Osage Nation's Tribal Council House. Susan spread her arms under the large boughs and spun in a circle. "This is a lovely spot. Though I think having all the men here at the auction would take away some of its beauty."

Charlie put his arms around her and gave her a hug. "It is certainly a lot prettier here with you under it."

"I say we find a place to eat before we go back on the road. Are you ready to eat, Charlie?"

"I'm startin' to git hungry. I think there's a café down the hill here."

They returned to the car and drove away from the Million Dollar Elm. Charlie wished they had a longer drive as he was used to the way that Susan unbuttoned her shirt as they drove. It had become a pattern on any day they could spend together, full of intimacy and focus on each other. It all would lead up to an evening of lovemaking.

"Charlie, there's a café in the next block. Do you see it on the right? Bennie's Eats, what a cute name."

"Yep, we'll stop, eat, and rest a spell. As my daddy used to say."

They found a corner booth next to the front window and seated themselves. As they looked at the menu, a waitress walked up and said, "Welcome to Bennie's, and what can I get you to drink?"

Susan said, "We'll both have Coca-Colas. Thank you."

Charlie asked, "What's this 'Grilled Cheese Sandwich'?"

The waitress said, "We get asked a lot. Our owner Bennie was overseas in the war, and they always had grilled cheese sandwiches. He loved them and said he would always have them on his menu. It's melted cheese between two slices of toasted bread."

Susan said, "Yum, I want one."

"Make that two; I gotta try one."

They loved their sandwiches, gave the waitress a nice tip, and thanked the owner for adding grilled cheese sandwiches to his menu.

As the edge of town, Charlie told Susan, "We're about fifty-five miles from Tulsa, but halfway there, we hit the paved road, so we should git back to the hotel before 6:00."

"Good, we'll have time to rest and shower before our dinner tonight with the oil barons."

Charlie asked, "Do we need to have a plan for tonight, or do we just enjoy our evening and hope to make some new friends?"

"We take this opportunity and make something happen. We have plans for this year and are on a business trip to Kansas City, so we have things we can discuss."

Charlie nodded. "I agree we have things we can share, but we must be careful to keep most things to ourselves. These guys won't be above stealing a good idea, and they have the money to do something with it."

"You're right, Sweetheart. We need to end this drive with a plan, so when we go to dinner, we agree on what we share and don't."

***

They arrived back at the hotel and went directly to their suite. Susan went to shower, and Charlie found a notepad and pencil and began putting ideas down before dinner. He knew he wanted to learn more about these men and their oil business.

When Susan finished her shower and began drying off, Charlie said, "Can you hear me? I want to discuss some ideas with you."

"I can, but I'll step into the room with you. What's on your mind?"

"Tonight, I want to know more about the Haskell site and anythin' happenin' up around Bartlesville from Getty. Sinclair has become known as the big fish in the oil business. He's into every aspect of the oil business. He's gettin' into banking as well. Skelly's known as a prominent oil businessman with other interests outside of oil. He's already explorin' aviation and radio. Both are new industries with a lot of promise. I hope we can get them to share some of their views on the oil business and what other companies excite them."

"Honey, you obviously learned a lot from Father when you talked business."

"Yes, he made sure I knew the successful men in Oklahoma he knew."

"Charlie, that's a lot to expect to cover in one dinner. They'll likely want to know what we're doing with the Kramer Group, Kelly Oil, and the ranches. I agree those are all good ideas, but you may need to pick and choose which ones you pursue."

"I'll keep it in mind. These men interest me, and I've read anythin' I could find about them. You know I read everythin' I can includin' the Wall Street Journal when I can get it. It's usually several days late, but it does help me keep up with the big guys."

"Father had it placed on his desk every day. He considered Charles Dow a brilliant man, and Clarence Barron, who owns the Journal, Father considered a close friend."

Susan was still naked. Charlie grinned. "As much as I enjoy your current outfit, I guess you need to get dressed, and I need to clean up and dress."

"You're right; it's after 6:00. Do you have an outfit you prefer?"

"I'm going to wear my gray seersucker three-piece suit. I'll wear a white shirt and a navy tie. Ya can wear anything you want. With your beauty, ya won't disappoint me or any of our dinner partners."

"Okay, I'll wear my white Isadora beaded blouse. It's low cut and shows cleavage. I don't have a camisole the right color to wear with it, so there'll be nothing under it. I have my gray slacks, which should match your suit well. We'll be stunning."

"That sounds impressive, Sweetheart."

Chapter Twenty-Six
Vandalism
September 1919

AS THEY ARRIVED FOR dinner, the maître d' walked briskly to meet Charlie and Susan. He said, "Mr. Kelly, you have a phone call at the front desk from a Mr. Thomas. He said it's important."

Susan said, "Oh my dear, what do you suppose Hank wants?"

As he turned toward the lobby, Charlie looked back at her and said, "I don't know, but I doubt it's good."

He got to the desk and asked, "Which phone's Mr. Thomas on?" The clerk pointed to a phone on the wall. Charlie picked up the receiver and said, "Hank, what's happened?"

"Charlie, the Burbank site has been damaged."

"What? How did this happen? Was there a storm?"

"No storm, Charlie, it was sabotaged."

"How did that happen?" Charlie asked, trying to keep the frustration out of his voice. "I thought we had hired security for the site?"

"I can tell yer mad, but I did have security there. But the man phoned me that he was sick and couldn't work his shift. I was drivin' out to the site to cover for him. As I arrived at Burbank #1, I saw a man get into a Ford truck. He wasn't part of my crew but I immediately knew him. It was the guy who shot at us back at Yale. I'll never forget his face."

"He worked for that scumbag Roland Willard," Charlie said. "I know he was mad when we got the leases at the auction, but we hadn't heard anythin' from him since then."

"I know. I've not bothered thinkin' 'bout Willard either since the auction. That's my fault. I should have anticipated he'd try somethin'. But it was his guy, I'm sure of it. He sped off before I could bring my truck to a complete stop."

Charlie said, "Damn it all to hell! I wonder what he's up to?"

"Well, a few seconds later, an explosion sent me to the ground with debris flying everywhere. I was unhurt and got up and walked over to the derrick."

Charlie sighed. "Buddy, that's too close. What did ya see?"

"The pipin' between the pump and the tank used to transfer the oil after the well comes in was a mess. Since we haven't struck oil yet, the tank's empty. My guys had the valves closed and the pump wasn't yet hooked up. We're ready for when the well comes in. The damage is limited to the pipes. The idiot didn't know what he was lookin' at. We were lucky this time. The derrick, pump, and tank are undamaged."

Charlie said, "Hank, I'm sure you expect me to bust a gasket, but I'm just glad you're alright. You've gotta go to the sheriff's office in Burbank or call Pawhuska."

"I just left the well site, and I'm callin' from a gas station in Burbank. I'll see the sheriff. As I said, this guy got to his truck as I arrived. A minute later, there's the explosion. Charlie, it's Willard's goon."

"I believe you. We need to get the sheriff involved."

"I'll go to the sheriff's office in Burbank and then to the hotel in Ponca City."

Charlie said, "Good, and I'm callin' Pinkerton right now and have them send an agent with a copy of the Yale file to Burbank tomorrow mornin'. I want Willard and his goon behind bars this time."

"I'll talk to my lead man tonight and get a crew out there to repair everything," Hank said. "But I want to increase our security. Pot shots and fights between roughnecks is one thing, but when they start lobbin' dynamite we need to have more protection. We're close on our first well and I was hopin' to have them start another well close to Burbank #1. I guess I'll have to put them on the repairs and delay the other well for a week. They'll get the repairs started tomorrow."

"Okay, and I'll bring the Pinkertons out for protection."

"Charlie, I'll meet them at the sheriff's office in the mornin'." Hank hung up.

Charlie placed his call to the Pinkerton's office in Oklahoma City and made all the arrangements needed for tomorrow morning. As he returned to the restaurant, he found Susan waiting outside of the restaurant for him.

Susan asked, "What did Hank want?"

Charlie told her what had happened.

Susan gasped and put her hand to her mouth. "Is Hank alright?"

Charlie assured her that he was. "I called Pinkerton. I told Hank we ain't wastin' time. Dead or behind bars is where Willard and his goon are headin'. I want it known you don't mess with Kelly Oil. We'll come after ya and not stop till we get ya."

As they walked into the restaurant, Charlie said, "Susan, I need to go to Burbank tomorrow. I can't get done what I need to by phone. I want Willard found and arrested."

"Honey, let the police or whoever handle this. I don't want you getting hurt, or worse. You're a businessman now, not a cowboy going after cattle rustlers."

"Honey, I will always be a cowboy."

Chapter Twenty-Seven
The Big Three
September 1919

THE MAÎTRE D' LED **CHARLIE** and Susan through the restaurant to where J. Paul Getty, Harry Sinclair, and William Skelly waited at the table. Susan knew how to make an entrance, so she stepped in front of Charlie and began immediately putting her smile, grace, and other assets to work.

Getty stood and said, "Gentlemen, let me introduce Susan Kramer-Kelly and her husband, Charles."

Susan slightly bowed as she accepted each man's handshake, providing the visual she intended.

Trying to keep his eyes on her smile, Sinclair stood and said, "Harry Sinclair. It's my pleasure, Mrs. Kelly. My condolences about your father, I considered him my friend."

"And he spoke of you often," Susan said.

Also aware of her assets, Skelly stood and said, "Bill Skelly. So glad to make your acquaintance, Mrs. Kelly."

Seeing her plan was working, Susan said, "Please, gentlemen, it's Susan." She looked at Charlie. "We're all friends, right, Charlie?"

With a wily grin, he said, "Absolutely. It's Susan and Charlie for the rest of the evenin', agreed?"

Getty ushered them to their seats, placing Susan next to him. Charlie sat at the end of the table beyond her. Sinclair and Skelly sat across the table from Getty and Susan.

"I apologize for being late, gentlemen," Susan said. "Charlie had an urgent matter that had to be attended to."

The waiter arrived immediately, took their drink orders, and left menus so they could select their meals.

"Nothing serious, I hope," said Getty.

Charlie weighed how much he wanted to tell these men. They might see an attack on his well as an opportunity that they could take advantage of. But he also knew they had experience with similar issues, and maybe being straight-forward with them could create a trust with these men.

He leaned in, elbows on the table. "One of our wells was just vandalized. We are reasonably sure we know who instigated it and will have the authorities and Pinkerton involved immediately."

Getty said, "I recently had some vandalism at a couple of rigs."

Susan placed a hand on Getty's arm. "What a shame." She sighed, offering an understanding nod.

"Thank you, Susan."

Charlie glanced around at everyone. "Hank, our partner, arrived as the thug was leavin' the site, and he recognized the guy from some trouble we had last year."

Skelly asked, "Who is it?"

Charlie shook his head. "I forget the thug's name, if I ever knew it. I'm sure he's a small-time operator who thinks he can bully people."

Getty offered, "Charlie, I'll let you know what I can find out."

"It's okay, Paul; I called the Pinkerton folks. I have Hank there to meet with Pinkerton and the locals, and I'm going there tomorrow."

Susan smiled. "Well, we didn't expect to start this evening with such a depressing report. We're sorry. Can we change the subject?"

Sinclair smiled. "We sure can, but first, here comes our waiter."

After the waiter delivered the drinks and left with their meal orders, Getty said, "I've mentioned to Bill and Harry you're on your way to Kansas City. Can you tell us a little about what brought you to Oklahoma? Marland said you had been working with him on the 101 Ranch, and that you used to be a cowboy?"

Charlie smiled. "I was just tellin' Susan that I'm still a cowboy. But yes, I used to work on the 101 as a top hand. George Miller saw somethin' in me and asked me to come work for him. That's how I started workin' with E. W. on the oil business."

"And did you two meet at the 101?" Skelly asked.

Susan answered, "No, I met Charlie down in Elmore City when he worked for my late husband, Jasper Blackaby. We got together after I returned to Kansas City upon Jasper's death."

"And how did you come to own an oil company?" asked Getty. "Charlie, you were a new face to all of us at Colonel Walter's auction this spring. Marland gave us some details, but he said the rest of it was not his to tell."

"I think I know the answer to that," said Sinclair with a smile. Getty and Skelly turned to look at him. "Walter had been thinking about getting into the oil business for years. I don't know why he never did before, but I'm assuming that once he met young Charlie here and knew he was working for Marland, he saw his opportunity."

Charlie and Susan shared a laugh. "That about it," Charlie said.

"Do you live here in Oklahoma now, or is Kansas City still home?" Sinclair asked.

Charlie looked at Susan, and she nodded for him to go ahead. "Both, actually. We own ranches over in Pottawatomie County. We also have the estate in Kansas City."

Skelly said, "It sounds like you are into ranching too."

Susan said, "Yes, we are. We own a horse ranch for breeding, raising, and training cutting horses for ranch work, and a cattle ranch for breeding Aberdeen Angus for market and managing the breed."

Sinclair put down his wine glass and remarked, "Susan, I expected Charlie to answer me. I know you aren't a cowgirl."

"Oh no, I'm not. But maybe someday. Charlie's the expert and he's been teaching me a lot about the ranch business."

Sinclair looked at Charlie, smiled, and said, "Wow, I'm impressed. We all know how hard it can be to start an oil company, but to also get into ranching at the same time has to be difficult."

Charlie smiled, nodded, and said, "I appreciate it. I gained a lot of experience workin' in the top of both industries while at the 101. George Miller and E. W. Marland are some of the best and I learned from both."

Getty said, "I don't know Mr. Miller, but I know E. W. and now I'm starting to evaluate how much of a competitor you will be to the rest of us." He laughed and the others all laughed with him good naturedly.

"Yes, I learned a lot from him and he may be regrettin' it since I stole his top guy from him when we formed Kelly Oil earlier this year."

All three oil men fell back in their chairs and had a good laugh at Marland's expense.

Sinclair said, "After Pawhuska, Marland said we should be on the lookout for you, that you were going to be a big name in the Oklahoma oil business. Since you already hoodwinked E. W.'s best man, I can see he was speaking the truth."

Skelly said, "Harry, you're right. Charlie, I'll admit I thought you were making a mistake when you got into that bidding war over the Burbank leases."

Charlie smiled. "Yep, and since you two didn't bid, I figure you think I overpaid, right?"

Sinclair took a sip of his wine and then said, "Well, maybe. E. W. said the fellow with you was Hank Thomas, his lead exploration man. The way E. W. spoke about Hank, I take it he's the one you hired away from E. W.?"

Before Charlie could answer, the waiter returned with their food. After the waiter left, Charlie said, "Let's eat while our food's hot. Harry, you're right though. I made Hank my partner even before I formed Kelly Oil."

Everyone had ordered the prime rib special and didn't hesitate to start eating.

Susan eventually said, "Harry, I wish I was around more when you and Father were getting to know each other. Now I hope we can get to know each other just as well."

"Were you with your late husband at that time?" Getty asked.

"No, I was attending Vassar while Harry and my father were becoming best of friends."

Getty put his fork down and said, "What did you study? Did you plan to become a teacher, a nurse—"

Susan looked him in the eyes. "Economics, Paul."

Getty's jaw dropped. "Oh, then you were preparing to—"

She didn't hesitate. "Run the Kramer Group."

Sinclair raised his hand and said, "I knew your father and his businesses, but my friends here may not be as well-versed in his business dealings since they only care about getting the oil out of the ground, not what's done with it after they sell it to the refineries. Why don't you tell them what you are in charge of as the CEO of the Kramer Group?"

Susan turned in her chair so all four men could see her better and said, "My father started the Kramer Group in banking. But over the years, he expanded into construction, railroads, and retailing. We will have assets in Illinois, Missouri, Kansas, Oklahoma, Texas, New Mexico, and Colorado by the end of the year."

Getty cleared his throat and asked, "Now, you've added ranching and the oil business?"

Susan responded, "Yes."

Getty turned to Skelly and said, "Better hope they decide to stay out of aviation and radio, or they may put you out of business."

Skelly laughed at the jab. "I think there's enough opportunities in both industries that I wouldn't be worried if they did." He then leaned over to Susan and said in a loud whisper that everyone could hear, "But I'd be obliged if you waited a few years."

Everyone again laughed and Charlie added, "Susan and I hope to come across as young, confident entrepreneurs here for business, not just pleasure, although this evening has been a lot of fun."

Skelly said, "I agree; it has been pleasurable. I'll also say this. Susan, it isn't fair to any man to have your beauty added to the obvious fact that you are a brilliant business leader."

Susan laughed with the men as they continued their conversation over another glass of wine, getting to know each of the other oil men better.

After dessert, Charlie said, "Harry and Bill, each of you have refineries. Susan and I have talked about creating an end-to-end oil business. Would you be willing to share what has been your biggest challenge as you expanded your businesses?"

Sinclair scratched the back of his neck and said, "I've been successful in finding oil, but there has always been such a fluctuation in the oil price, so I couldn't depend on just drilling for my regular income. And finding the right talent at the right time has been the hardest thing after I realized I needed more control over my place in the industry."

Skelly added, "I agree with Harry. Finding the right people with the talents you need and the trustworthiness required to become your employee or partner is tough. Sometimes they can prove it by stepping up and putting their money up to share the risk, but sometimes you don't need or want a partner. You need an employee."

Charlie said, "We find that problem isn't just in the oil business. Harry, you're in the banking business too. We own banks in Missouri and Texas and are now interested in adding Oklahoma. What can you tell us?"

Sinclair said, "I'm sure I could learn more from you than I could teach you. We might do some good things for each other through shared experiences. The one thing I know is this oil boom offers opportunities to expand any banking system. I'm considering that, but I fear that I may be out of my depth when it comes to banking." He turned to Susan and added, "I wish your father was still around as I could use his advice."

Susan nodded. "Maybe we could still offer you that advice. Gordon Brayton learned everything he knows from Father. I'd be happy to get you and him together, if you'd be willing to teach us what you know about the oil business."

Harry nodded and said, "I think that is a reasonable offer."

Charlie turned to Skelly. "Maybe someday we can discuss a similar arrangement with aviation."

Skelly nodded. "I wasn't wrong earlier when I said there are a lot of opportunities there. It's going to be the next big thing in transportation. I believe, in the near future, aviation may allow the movement of people and merchandise faster and farther than anything we have now."

"Well, I'm not quite ready to venture into a new industry now," Charlie said. "I think two per year is my limit." The others laughed. "But someday I may want to talk to you more about these opportunities."

The evening wound down. Eventually they were the only ones left in the restaurant, and the maître d' and waiter were politely, but impatiently, waiting for the group to finish. They all finally finished and stood up. Susan wobbled just a bit and Charlie put his arm out to steady her.

"Charlie, are you trying to take advantage of me?"

Charlie replied, "Of course not, Honey."

She smiled big and said, "Well, why the hell not?"

The others roared with laughter.

They all made their goodbyes. Getty and Skelly headed out of the restaurant. Sinclair stepped up and said, "Please call me. I want to discuss our proposal to help each other further."

Susan said, "We'll stay in touch, right, Charlie?'

"You're so right, Sweetheart."

Chapter Twenty-Eight
Burbank and Kansas City
September 1919

IN THE MORNING, **CHARLIE** and Susan went down to breakfast at the Topaz. Charlie still wanted to head over to Burbank, but Susan had convinced him to at least have breakfast first.

As they finished their meal, Charlie reached over, took the carafe of coffee, and filled each of their cups. He picked up his cup, took a sip, and said, "I think last night may have been the most important event for us since our weddin'. All three of our dinner companions are financially successful, and Paul's young like us and already extremely successful in oil."

Susan nodded. "I agree with you. Sinclair opened the door for us to develop personal and business relationships with him. We should do something special for Paul. Because of him setting up last night, we'll likely have some very productive years in oil and banking ahead of us."

"What could we do for Paul?" Charlie looked around the restaurant. "I would ask him now, but he hasn't come down to breakfast. I agree we should do something. He talked about how he likes our Cadillac. Said he loved the two-door coupe look. It's spiffy and fast. It seemed to excite him."

Susan placed her hand on Charlie's as she said, "I tell you what, I will reach out to Gordon while I'm in Kansas City about Sinclair's proposal. If that can lead to productive conversations about working with, or maybe even partnering with, Sinclair, then we should consider purchasing a Cadillac for Paul."

"Susan, are you sure? That's an expensive gift. I was just thinkin' of invitin' him out to the ranch."

"I'm sure, so let's consider it our plan for Paul. Last night created an opportunity for us with Harry, and by rewarding Getty for the introduction, it will help us cement a relationship with him."

"Susan, that makes sense. I see you takin' the lead sharin' what Sinclair needs to understand in the world of bankin'. I'll learn refinin', distribution through pipelines, and the retail side of the oil business from him. There's no way to know the impact it'll have, but I'm excited at the possibilities."

Susan leaned forward, tilted her head, and said, "Do you see us spending more time in Tulsa? If so, do we get a suite here at the Hotel Tulsa? Or do we buy a house?"

Charlie hesitated a moment. "I think we start with a suite at the hotel, and dependin' on what happens, we might need to have somethin' permanent. We might need to open an office in Tulsa for the Kelly Oil Company."

Susan squeezed Charlie's forearm as she looked directly into his eyes, smiled, and said, "You're right, if Skelly, Sinclair, and Getty are here, and they mentioned many more oil men have offices open or about to open. Tulsa is where we need to focus our efforts."

Charlie patted her hand and replied, "I think we're goin' to spend quite a bit of our time in Tulsa this year."

As they finished their coffee, Charlie said, "You're my everythin'. Everythin' good in my life starts with you."

She gazed over at him, raised her cup, and said, "I adore you, Charlie; my happiness starts with you."

***

They left the restaurant and headed up to their suite. As they entered the room the telephone rang. Charlie picked up the receiver. "Hello, this is Charles Kelly."

It was Hank, and he sounded furious. "You won't believe what's happened. Willard's goon came back during the night while I was making my report with the sheriff and damaged the pump. My guys say it's a total loss and we will have to replace it. I went back out there this mornin' and couldn't believe it. There was sand pourin' out of the fittin's. I'm filin' more paperwork with the authorities."

Charlie swore. "I was plannin' on comin' over this mornin'. Now I wish I had left last night."

"There's nothin' ya could have done, Charlie. The bastard must have been hidin' and waited for me to leave the site to file the report with the sheriff. That's when he went back to damage the pump. And we're not the only ones that got hit. Some of Getty's guys are here and doin' the same thing. I guess he's been vandalized too."

Charlie turned and sat on the sofa. "We had dinner with Getty, Sinclair, and Skelly last night. Getty mentioned somethin' about vandalism. Ya have any idea about where Willard and his buddy are?"

Hank said, "Not really, but I met with the Pinkerton agent already. They'll set up a security squad to protect our site. They're workin' with the sheriff because both locations are crime scenes now."

"Will they allow you to get the site back operatin'?"

"Hopefully, I'm allowed back out there tomorrow. The sheriff's men are still doin' somethin' out there today."

"Have your crew start doin' whatever repairs are required as soon as possible. I'll come to Burbank. Do you know if Getty is comin' out there?"

"Yes, I heard his foreman say he left early this mornin'."

"Okay, I'll arrive there by lunchtime. Maybe he and I can help get this sorted out. By the way, is the Pinkerton man the same one we had in Yale?"

"Yes, it's Bailey Muldoon, and he brought the complete file on what happened there. They took pictures of Willard and his sidekick back then, so the authorities here have them to show the locals."

"Well, good. One of the reasons I was goin' to come to Burbank was to go over to Ponca City and check around at the hotels and restaurants for Willard. I'll never forget the asshole. I'll let you go, so I can get on the road."

As Charlie got off the telephone, Susan walked into the suite's living room. "Is everything alright? It didn't sound like it."

Charlie looked up and grimaced. "We had more damage at the Burbank site last night. Hank said someone destroyed the pump. He and Getty both are filing paperwork this mornin' for the sheriff."

"Getty?"

"Yes, he must have had more vandalism last night too, or this is for what he mentioned to us last night."

Her face turned serious as she said, "We must get that asshole behind bars as soon as possible."

Charlie stood up and went to put some clothes into a valise. "I'm going to get on the road. I told Hank I'd be there by noon."

Susan asked, "So, you think it's still necessary for you to go? Can't Hank handle things there? That's why you pay him, isn't it?"

"He'll do fine, but I need to go. You don't need me in Kansas City."

"That's not true," Susan said, a small waver in her voice. "I always need you by my side. I don't know why you have to deal with this in person."

Charlie paused and turned to face Susan. "Oh, Darlin', I'm not doin' this to make you upset or to prove anythin'. This Willard fellow is dangerous, and I want the authorities to know that. They will listen to me more than they will Hank because I'm the owner."

"I guess I can understand that," Susan said. She kissed Charlie's cheek. "Then it's what we'll do. I'll call Uncle Curt and tell him about the change in plans."

Chapter Twenty-Nine
Charlie Almost Gets His Man
September 1919

CHARLIE PULLED INTO BURBANK just after noon and found Hank's Kelly Oil Company truck parked at the sheriff's office. He went inside, and saw Hank sitting with a gray-haired man in a sheriff's uniform and Bailey Muldoon from Pinkerton's Detective Agency.

Bailey stood as Charlie entered and said, "Good afternoon, sir. I'm glad to see you, but I wish it were for a more pleasant reason."

"Bailey, you're lookin' good. Yes, it appears we may have our old adversary back." He looked over at Hank and the uniformed gentleman and nodded.

Hank stood and said, "Charlie, meet Sheriff Luther Goddard."

Sheriff Goddard was already standing as he offered his hand. "Mr. Kelly, sorry to meetcha because of trouble, but it's a pleasure to make yer acquaintance."

Charlie gave a friendly and firm handshake. "Sheriff, I'm happy to see you're all together, except I don't see Getty."

Hank said, "He left a while ago with his lead man heading out to Shidler. He hopes to come back this afternoon."

Charlie pulled a chair over and joined them. "Fill me in on what ya know."

Bailey indicated to the sheriff he wanted to respond. "Sir, we haven't found Willard or his man, but we do have their pictures at every hotel and restaurant in the area. One hotel clerk in Ponca City said he thought they had someone stay overnight several days ago who could have been Willard."

Sheriff Goddard said, "It, of course, means nothin' to a judge, but it gives us hope our buddy Hank's right it was Willard's man who was gettin' away."

Charlie said, "Well, we need to find them. Sheriff, can Hank have the drillin' site back in the mornin' so we can git the repairs done and git back to findin' oil?"

"Yes, Mr. Kelly. We'll finish today; I expect my guys and the Oklahoma Bureau folks back here from your site anytime."

They spoke for a few more minutes, then left with an assurance from the sheriff to call them if he found anything useful.

As they walked out of the sheriff's office Charlie said, "I want to drive over to Ponca City and talk to that hotel clerk. It's our best lead."

Muldoon agreed. He got into his own vehicle and Hank got into Charlie's Cadillac. They drove the twenty minutes to get to Ponca City and arrived at the Arcade Hotel.

Charlie went into the reception desk but the clerk that may have seen Willard was on a lunch break.

Charlie wanted to go back to the cars and start driving the town to see if they could find Willard but Muldoon said, "Let's grab a bite ourselves, then we can talk to the clerk when he gets back.

As they were walking across the street to the diner, Charlie spotted Getty getting out of a car. He called over to him and Getty joined them for lunch.

As they finished eating, Hank said, "I want to catch Willard just as badly as you do, Charlie, but I'm wantin' to get back out to my crew at the well site. Soon as the sheriff gives his okay I want us to be back at work. I can't spend all my time here huntin' for what may be a dry hole."

Charlie nodded. "I can understand that. How will you get back to Burbank?"

Getty said, "He can ride with me. I'm going to check on my guys, and hopefully, we're back drilling too."

Charlie looked at Bailey and said, "Let's go find Willard."

Bailey pointed to the hotel and said, "Let's see if the clerk is back from his lunch."

Charlie said, "Let's go."

They walked back to the hotel, but the clerk who saw Willard still wasn't there. Charlie did his best to control his temper.

"We'll try it your way now," Muldoon said. "Let's drive and stop at different businesses and show them Willard's picture. Maybe somebody else saw him."

Charlie agreed, and they got into his car and went drivin' north out of town. They stopped at several bars, restaurants, and gas stations but nobody recognized Willard. They continued north out of Ponca City.

As they entered Newkirk, they pulled into a Marland gas station to fill up the Cadillac and Charlie spotted a Model T sitting next to the building. Charlie was surprised to see Willard sitting in the car.

Charlie pulled up to one of the gasoline pumps and said to Muldoon, "Willard's here."

Muldoon looked and said, "I'll be damned, it is Willard. You watch him and I'll go into the store and look for his goon."

"Okay, be careful."

Muldoon went inside the station, and after a few minutes, Willard got out of his car, walked around it, and headed toward the station's front door. Charlie decided to go after him. He walked briskly toward Willard and was about to grab him when everything went black.

Chapter Thirty
Sharing Information
September 1919

CHARLIE SAW LIGHT AND heard talking as he began to awake. "What... wha... what happened?"

"Willard's man attacked you, and they both got away." Bailey pointed to a young boy and said, "The boy said you got hit by a big man, and then two men drove away, heading toward Kansas as fast as their car could go."

Charlie got to his feet. "Well, do we go after them? Or maybe have the sheriff call all the authorities north of here to lookout for those two."

Bailey patted Charlie's shoulder. "I've already called Sheriff Goddard. He's sending an officer to create a report, and he's contacting all the authorities north of here."

Charlie said, "Is it a siren I'm hearin'?"

"Yes, it's the officer. We'll give him what he needs, and then we need to get you to a doctor and have him examine you."

***

After a thorough examination, the doctor told Charlie, "Young man, you're fine, but you'll have a headache for the next day or two. Don't exert yourself, as it'll worsen your headaches."

The sheriff had contacted every law enforcement office from Ponca City to Wichita, but Willard seemed to have vanished.

Muldoon drove Charlie back to Tulsa. He followed the doctor's advice and took it easy through the weekend. The only thing he did was talk to Susan on Monday morning before the Board meeting.

When Charlie mentioned getting hit on the head, she screamed, "Oh my, Charlie! Are you okay? I need to come there—"

He interrupted her, "Sweetheart, I'm fine. I promise you I'm okay."

"Damn it Charlie, I was afraid you'd get hurt. I told you to let the authorities find Willard. I need you there when I get back. I can't imagine living without you."

"I hear ya and understand. I guess I don't always git it right, but I try."

"We've got some big plans, Charles Ashley Kelly, and those plans don't mean anything to me without you sharing them. Are you listening?"

"Yes, Sweetheart. I promise I won't go huntin' after the bad guys myself no more. Now you go meet with our leaders and tell me how things are in our businesses."

Charlie had hardly placed the phone down when it rang. "Charlie, it's Hank. I thought you should know we started drillin' again on Sunday. The boys didn't wait for me to start preppin'. This mornin' we're hearin' rumbles, buddy. We're gonna hit somethin' soon. I thought we might not need to go too deep. Somethin' about the lay of this land up here. It could blow anytime, and I think it's a big one."

"Good to hear, Hank. I'm stickin' around the hotel today but plan to git out there tomorrow."

***

Later in the afternoon, Susan called. "I've got a lot to share with you from today's meeting. Are you up to hearing the highlights?"

"Sure, and we can go into the details when ya git back here in a day or two. But first, Hank called, and he thinks we may hit oil real soon out at Burbank."

"Wonderful, Charlie."

"Yep, now go ahead and fill me in on your day."

"Okay, here you go. KMS is flourishing, and adding the Rock Island routes opens four new states. Owen is looking into more ways the railroads can support the oil boom like you requested."

"Great, that will help us a lot to keep the oil movin', but I think our future is goin' to be in buildin' pipelines to carry the oil. But havin' KMS addin' to not only our capacity, but haulin' other people's oil too is a good thing."

Susan said, "Yes, and Anson Peabody's excited with what he sees happening in Cushing, but he does seem jealous of Chester. Anson wants to go to Cushing and see it. Hartsfield is thriving everywhere. People are employed and shopping in the stores more than before the war."

"Our timin' gittin' Chester on Board was just right."

"I agree, Charlie. Rice gave a wonderful update on Strawberry Hill. But I had to push him to get him to see Tulsa and all the construction going on there after I described what we experienced. He'll join Anson and me in

Oklahoma. I recommend the 19th for a meeting in Cushing. More to come."

"So, we have a couple of fellas who gave ya some trouble at the meeting?"

"A little. They're still adjusting to me as a woman leading the Group, and let's face it, we are a lot younger than those guys."

"True. What about Jim Townsley and the concrete business? He needs to see Tulsa too, and we need more discussion about how concrete impacts the oil business."

"Yes, I shared your ideas with him, and we'll see Jim in Oklahoma soon. Gordon's also interested in Oklahoma, Texas, and the oil business as it applies to banking. We may see him in Tulsa and maybe down in Dallas soon. But his interest in the oil business stirred up the room some. Although you and I didn't take any funds away from anyone when we acquired and set up Kelly Oil and the ranches, they aren't comfortable with the Board being out of the decision-making process when expansion is involved. Father typically talked with some or all of them when he funded a new business. Gordon knew about it when Father created Kelly Oil, but no one else did. We haven't needed Kramer funds to acquire the ranches, but we are putting them under the Group for future growth and development, so they had their questions."

"Susan, it's excitin' to hear some of our leaders see the opportunities we do. The others can and maybe should have questions, but they'll come along."

"Yes, I think they will. After lunch, Uncle Curt led off the afternoon session by sharing the information he took at the morning session. He added everything up, and the Kramer Group's worth just under $6 billion, and we are now among the top three companies in the United States. Gordon added, since Kramer's privately owned, you and I are in the realm of Rockefeller and Vanderbilt wealth. I don't know, but we're doing fine."

Charlie said, "Did ya share anything about our new friends?"

Susan laughed. "As I said, the comment from Gordon caused a stir, but I got the floor and shared how we recently had been in conversations with some of the most powerful men in the oil business. I emphasized how important it is we act on these connections quickly. I also described how Harry Sinclair's oil company is doing amazing things by positioning itself throughout the entire process of finding oil, transporting it, refining it, and distributing the final product through a retail outlet he owns. We want to do the same thing with Kelly Oil and more. I told Gordon we want to provide banking and finance services for companies like Sinclair. I told Rice we could build gasoline stations, refineries, and the houses where the workers live. I told Owen that oil and gasoline must be transported to the retailer and, ultimately, the end user. I told them you opened a discussion about this with these men, and they seemed to see the merit in my suggestions. They agreed we could continue to explore the subject."

Charlie said, "Sweetheart, it sounds like ya had a tough day. Anson and Rice will come around. When are ya headin' home?"

"There are a few more things to cover with the Board and documents to sign in the office with Uncle Curt in the morning. I'm scheduled on the afternoon train tomorrow and should arrive in Tulsa around 7:00. Can you meet me?"

"Of course, and I can't wait to see ya."

Chapter Thirty-One
A Cowboy's Gusher
September 1919

CHARLIE DECIDED TO GET up with the roosters the following day and head to the Burbank #1 well site. As he arrived, security guards met him. They didn't believe Charlie when he said he had a right to be there. Charlie admired their dedication to keeping strangers off of the site but was thinking maybe he should have worn something other than his cowboy hat, denims, and ranch shirt so they'd take him seriously. Charlie tried to walk past the guards so he could get Hank's attention, but they put their hands on Charlie to stop him.

"Look, fellas, I know yer just doin' what I asked ya to do, but I'm the boss and that's my well yer preventin' me from getting' to."

"Sure, buddy," one of the guards said and started to push Charlie back to his car.

"Okay, sorry I have ta do this to ya." Charlie turned and punched the man in the gut. He doubled over, and the other guard started to yell and tried to pull out his gun.

Just then Hank hurried over. "Whoa! Whoa! Hold on. What in the hell are you doin'? He's Charles Kelly, the President of Kelly Oil."

The guard pulled his hand off his gun and helped his friend. They both immediately apologized.

Charlie said, "I guess we all overreacted here, but I'm glad to know it's hard for anyone to git on this well site."

A rumble rose from the derrick. Hank said, "That's the third time in the past hour. We're going have oil spoutin' sometime this mornin'."

Charlie smiled. "I think ya just needed me to arrive."

Another rumble came immediately, along with the wonderful train sound, and the black gold flowed.

After they had the well capped, Charlie said, "You must have had an extra pump out here. I didn't ask ya yesterday when ya said ya planned on comin' back out here."

"Yes, we used the one planned for the next well up the road. I wanted to get this one goin' again. It was lookin' good before the damage."

"Good; I'm sure, based on my welcome here this morning, there haven't been any other threats to deal with."

"Nothing at all, but I don't think we want to let our guards go."

"Absolutely not. Well, I'll go back to Tulsa and call Susan with the great news."

***

After cleaning up back at the hotel, Charlie telephoned the Kramer offices in Kansas City. His call arrived during the wrap-up of the quarterly meeting. The switchboard operator said Susan was unavailable, so Charlie asked to speak to Curt.

"Hello, Charlie," Curt greeted him as he got on the line. "Susan's already over at the boardroom for the meeting. Is it important?"

"I just got back in from our Burbank #1 well. It has come in a huge gusher of Oklahoma top-rate crude oil. We're going to be a Million Dollar Company in a matter of weeks. I say it because Hank told me every indication is this well has tapped a much bigger oil field than he and I opened up last year at Yale, for Marland Oil. He said it should double the Yale well's production, and Yale alone has already provided Marland with more than a million dollars in profit."

Curt said, "Let me call you back from the conference room." Curt hung up, and Charlie waited a few minutes before the phone rang. Charlie picked it up.

"Another gusher!" Susan said in greeting.

Charlie could hear the room explode into a celebration, even over the telephone. He also heard Susan say, "Uncle Curt, could you call down to Federico's and have them bring up some champagne and appetizers?"

Charlie managed to get Susan's attention over the noise. "Let me talk with Gordon. I want to have Gordon come to Tulsa this week. I'll call Harry Sinclair and arrange a meeting at his office on Friday. I want Gordon and Hank there with us. We'll discuss Sinclair's proposal to teach me the oil business, and we'll teach him the banking business."

"Yes, Honey. Let's strike while the irons are hot."

Gordon came to the phone. "Congratulations on the gusher!"

"Thanks, Gordon. I'd like ya to come to Tulsa. Susan and I met Harry Sinclair recently, and he's part owner of the Exchange Bank in Tulsa. They do a lot of business with oil companies and want to broaden their customer base. He has been successful in the oil business in ways many have not. We want to learn more about his oil business, and he would like to know more about bankin'. I want to set up a meetin' and include you."

Gordon said, "Why would we share our banking business model with a competitor? And why would he do what you describe? I'm all for getting into banking in Oklahoma, but is this how we do it?"

Charlie said, "I hear your concern, but come to Tulsa and let's see where a meetin' will lead us."

"You're the boss, but I'm concerned."

"I'll let ya know when I set up a meetin' time."

After his discussion with Gordon, Charlie placed a call to Harry Sinclair.

"This is Sinclair."

"Harry, it's Charlie Kelly. Do ya have a minute to talk?"

"Sure. How's my new friend?"

"Great, Harry. I just talked with the President of our banking system, Gordon Brayton. He can be in Tulsa this Friday. Susan and I would love to meet with you and Gordon to discuss your ideas. You offered to discuss our working together, and we want to follow up on it. Are ya available to spend some time with us?"

"I have some free time Friday. I know this seems unusual, since we are each competing in banking and the oil business, but I liked what I saw at dinner the other night and Walter and I were close friends. It only seems right to me that I trust Walter's daughter as much as I trusted him."

"I'll admit to ya, Gordon has already expressed his concerns. He feels we shouldn't share our business secrets with anyone. I told him he should at least listen to the proposal."

"Charlie, I'll clear my calendar for you. We can start as early as you like."

"How about startin' right after breakfast, and we'll go as long as we need? All day if it takes it."

"I'm okay with it."

"Let's use the private dining room at the Hotel Tulsa; see ya then."

Charlie ended the call and called Susan in Kansas City. "We'll meet Sinclair at the Hotel Tulsa Friday morning. Tell Gordon he needs to come to Tulsa. I want to have Hank there too, if possible."

Chapter Thirty-Two
Possibilities
September 1919

THE NEXT DAY, HANK called. He had a difficult time controlling his excitement as he said, "Charlie, I just negotiated with a guy I met at the Pawhuska auction a few weeks ago. We now own mineral rights to some land near Seminole and Earlsboro."

"Hank, how excitin'. And I know we agreed from the beginnin' of Kelly Oil you would find our locations to drill, but have those areas been places you've spent time checkin' out?"

"Yes, back before we drilled for Marland at Yale. I mentioned them to Marland, but he didn't want to go south of Cushing. Charlie, I already love the area around your ranches, and we'll make some great money with these leases, I promise."

"Okay, I'm happy if you're happy, buddy. What's the latest in Burbank?"

"As you know, the pump's in place, and we're negotiatin' with a truckin' company to take our oil to a refinery here in Ponca City."

"Okay. I need ya in Tulsa tomorrow."

"Tomorrow?"

"Yes, I've set up a meetin' on Friday with Harry Sinclair of Sinclair Oil."

"I know who he is. Why are we meetin' with him? How do you know him?"

"I'll fill you in on everythin' later. Come to Hotel Tulsa and ask for me at the registration desk."

"Okay, I'm gonna stop by Burbank, but I'll be there tomorrow."

"Great, I'll see ya then."

***

On Thursday, Charlie picked up Susan at the train station. Gordon wasn't with her, and Charlie said, "Where the hell's Brayton?"

Susan's jaw dropped. "Charlie, Sweetheart, are you okay?"

"He's supposed to be with you. He sounded awfully negative about our meetin' with Sinclair on the phone, and now he's not here."

"Charlie, settle down. There was a problem at a branch in St. Louis. I agreed he would stay and handle it, then come on the evening train. He'll be getting in here very late."

Charlie apologized, and they went directly to their room.

Shortly after 5:00, the phone rang and Susan answered it.

She said, "Hank, where are ya?"

"I'm downstairs in the lobby. Should I get a room?"

"Hold on, I'll hand the phone to Charlie." She turned as Charlie came out of the bathroom. "It's Hank, asking if he needs to get a room."

"Hey, buddy, yes, you're here on business. Kelly Oil pays for it. Susan and I'll meet ya in the restaurant at 6:00."

"Gotcha, see ya then."

***

Susan and Charlie got into the elevator wearing outfits they had clearly coordinated. Both wore tan pants, Charlie wore a navy-blue blazer over a white shirt, and Susan wore a silk navy blue blouse with a low neckline.

On the elevator ride down to the lobby, the operator was an older man who seemed mesmerized by Susan. His height put his eyes at the perfect spot to enjoy the view of Susan's cleavage. Susan's silk blouse sparkled, and the neckline did not leave anything to the imagination. Charlie smiled and said, "Darlin', you won't go unnoticed tonight."

They spotted Hank as they approached the restaurant and waved. He was dressed nicer than Charlie and Susan had ever seen him in dark slacks, leather shoes, and a white button-down shirt.

Susan stepped in front of Charlie and offered her hand to Hank. "Good to see you, Hank. You look successful."

"Thank you, Susan. I feel like it. And I noticed the restaurant has a rule against denim. I figured my work attire wouldn't get me in the door." They all laughed.

"Anything particular on your mind, buddy?" Charlie asked.

"Yes, but let's get a table first; the restaurant's packed already."

Susan said, "There's a table for us, don't worry."

The restaurant was full, with nearly every table taken, and the low murmur of conversation filled the room. Charlie stepped over to the maître d' and said, "We are the—"

The maître d' interjected, "The Kellys, welcome back. We have your table waiting."

As they got close to their table, Getty was eating at his usual location. He stood and smiled. "Susan! Charlie, and Hank, it's so good to see you. Can we talk later?"

Susan pivoted to Paul and said, "Of course, join us later for a drink."

They took seats to give Charlie and Susan a view of the room, and Hank faced them.

Hank couldn't wait. "Because of what happened in Burbank, I knew you had met Getty, but you guys seemed friendly. And I know we're meetin' Sinclair tomorrow. How did you suddenly become friends with him?"

Susan looked at Hank's puzzled face and said, "Getty introduced us last week."

Hank shook his head and said, "You two are swimmin' in mighty deep water. My experience tells me to keep my cards close to my vest. Guys like Sinclair didn't make a lot of friends gettin' where they are today."

Charlie reached over, put his hand on his friend's forearm, and said, "Hank, you need to understand this. Susan and I are worth more than Getty and Sinclair put together and then some. And Hank, everything I've learned about you and the oil business tells me you don't take a backseat to anyone with your ability to find oil. So, don't worry about the deep water. Okay?"

"Uh... Sure, buddy. I guess I'm just not used to all this yet."

Susan said, "Don't worry, we're careful. I'll bet you're an Oklahoma oil millionaire pretty soon yourself."

The waiter arrived, and they ordered their food and drinks. Charlie said, "Please bring the cabernet now, and whatever Mr. Getty has to drink, take him another on us."

"Can we talk Seminole and Earlsboro?" Hank asked.

Charlie sat straighter in his chair and said, "Yes, I want to hear what you are thinkin'."

"There are several people I respect starting to explore the area. I haven't been down there since before Yale, except when I visited your place, but we need to explore it soon."

Charlie leaned back. "Okay, the three of us can get together next week. Susan and I are plannin' to go to the ranch on the 25th. Why don't you plan to head down there after our meeting in Cushing on Monday? Check everythin' out and come to the ranch on the 25th."

"Okay. I may run up to Burbank first, but I can get down to Seminole and talk to ya on Thursday."

Getty walked over to the Kelly's table. "Hello Kellys and Hank. Mind if I join you?"

Charlie had seen him coming and said, "Paul, please sit down."

"By the way, thanks for the drink. Can I please return the favor? I see your bottle's empty. I'll have the waiter bring another." He waved the waiter over and ordered the wine.

Susan said, "I hear you've had trouble like us, Paul?"

"Well, I could have had a better week. But you could say it too. Susan, how was your Kansas City trip?"

Susan smiled. "Very successful. I'm happy with what I learned. But Charlie has some news."

Charlie said, "I know you drove Hank back to Burbank the other day, so Hank tell him about our well up there."

Hank sat a little taller. "Good to see you again. The well came in several days ago, a true gusher. I haven't measured everything yet, but experience tells me we should see as much as a thousand barrels of oil a day from Burbank #1. We have the new pump installed and arranged to transport the oil to Ponca City."

Getty said, "Congratulations. I hope my wells up there do just as good."

"I'm sure you will," Hank said. "This wasn't my first well. As I said on the drive the other day I've been drillin' for over twenty years. My father made his livin' as an oil field geologist, and I was barely off my momma's tit when he started takin' me to the oil fields."

Getty leaned back in his chair, took a sip of wine, and said, "I could use a man like you out in California."

"California?" Charlie asked.

"Have you ever considered drilling in California?" Getty asked.

Charlie said, "No. Should we?"

Hank interjected, "Paul, I have an old friend who went out there three years ago. He's workin' for an outfit around Bakersfield. I hear things about the San Joaquin Valley and the coast near Long Beach."

Getty's eyes sparkled. "Hank, I hear the same thing. I lived out there as a teenager. It's beautiful around Los Angeles. I'm going to go out there soon and explore some sites. I could use a man with your experience to take a look at the land with me."

Hank said, "I'd love to, but only if Charlie agrees it's worth payin' me to do it."

Charlie asked, "California oil is new to me; what do ya know about oil out there?"

Hank said, "For the last twenty years, California and Oklahoma have swapped being number one in oil production. I feel they are primed out there for another boom. I also think Oklahoma's sitting in the same situation. I like what I hear about Seminole. I want to spend some time there. I love goin' and findin' new oil fields, but if I'm gonna spend a lot of my time doin' it, we need to find a few people who can take the lead on our drillin' crews."

Charlie said, "Well, I suppose it would be good to let you go explore the possibilities out there. I don't plan on Kelly Oil bein' only an Oklahoma outfit."

Susan looked over her wine glass at Getty, letting the stem sit just above her cleavage. "Only if Paul promises to not steal Hank away from us like you did with Marland."

There were chuckles from Hank and Charlie, and Getty's eyes didn't leave Susan's chest. "I think I can promise that."

"I have some other things comin' up over the next few months," Hank said, unaware of Susan's pull on Getty, "but maybe by the first of the year I could travel out to California."

"Good," Getty said, finally pulling his eyes away from Susan. "We'll stay in touch."

They talked longer and finished the bottle of wine Getty ordered, then Getty left.

Susan spoke up. "Gentlemen, I don't think there's any question we need to be where the boom is. Hank, you should thoroughly check out Seminole and California over the next few months."

Charlie nodded his approval. "I agree with Hank; we need to free him up from drillin' so he can go explore. But I also need him to participate in plannin' and a meetin' once in a while. We need to set up abilities to drill for oil, and I want us to refine it, distribute it, and sell the end products. I want this capability as soon as we can develop it."

"It's a lot to do quickly. It could cost in the millions," Hank said.

Charlie smiled. "We'll recover the cost in less than three years. I've checked, and Sinclair made $5 million in profit last year. After what I've heard tonight, we need to look at havin' an end-to-end operation here in Oklahoma and California."

Susan said, "I'll say amen, Charlie; I like the way you think. Hank, it would be best if you started making a list of the best oil field operators. If we decide to do it, we need enough men to have multiple wells going here and in California."

"We'll need to add personnel as we build refineries, pipelines, oil field servicin', and retail sites. We must include it in our conversation with Harry Sinclair," Charlie said.

Hank sat back in his chair, began rubbing his hands together, took a deep breath, and with a tremble in his voice said, "I hope ya understand I've been thinkin' about these kinds of things for a few years now. I can't rightly put it into words the way I'm feelin'. But Charlie and Susan, ya guys are makin' me so happy I can contribute to such an important conversation. I'm excited to be with people who want to do great things."

Charlie looked at Susan and said, "Honey, he's like me when we met. He doesn't have two dimes to rub together sometimes. I didn't, either. But we both have dreams, and we both have good ideas. We—"

Susan interrupted, "You both are intelligent, I mean, brilliant guys. Charlie, I adore the person you are. You are my reason to get up every day. Hank, you have become like family to Charlie and me. We love how we can dream big together. The Kramer Group's a huge conglomerate, but we want to make it bigger. We want to give back to our country someday something special. I'm so glad we found each other."

Charlie said, "That's beautiful, Honey. Now we better call it a night. We have a breakfast meetin' here in the mornin'.

Chapter Thirty-Three
Sinclair
September 1919

CHARLIE WOKE UP THINKING about the meeting with Harry Sinclair. At least until he looked over at Susan. She was mostly uncovered and looked angelic. After a few moments, his mind returned to the business at hand. He realized Gordon would have arrived last night and would have a room somewhere in the hotel. He looked at the clock on his bedside table. *It's a little after 6:00 and too early to call him. I'll call in a half-hour.*

He rolled out of bed and headed for the bathroom.

"Where do you think you're going, big guy?"

He turned and said, "Mother Nature calls."

She threw the covers off the bed and patted the mattress. "Okay, but come back to bed; we have time..."

***

Charlie rolled out of bed again at 6:45 and called the front desk. "Please connect me with the room for Gordon Brayton, please."

"Hello, this is Gordon Brayton."

"Gordon, Charlie Kelly. I'm glad you're here safe and sound. I'd like ya to join Susan, Hank, and me for coffee."

"That sounds good. I can meet you in the lobby at 7:00."

"Fine, see ya then, goodbye."

"Yes, goodbye, sir."

Charlie turned to Susan. "He's an asset to Kramer. I know he's goin' to impress Sinclair."

"I agree. We better get dressed."

Gordon and Hank stood at the restaurant entrance when Charlie and Susan stepped off the elevator.

Charlie said, "Good morning, gentlemen. Are introductions needed?"

Hank said, "No, I knew you expected someone from Kansas City, so I asked him where he called home."

Gordon added, "I said Kansas City, and we've had a brief but interesting conversation."

Charlie said, "Let's go find our table. I need some coffee."

The maître d' put them in the executive dining room and said he would bring Mr. Sinclair to them when he arrived. There were already pastries and coffee on the table.

As soon as everyone had poured their coffee, Charlie said, "First, Gordon, I want to thank you for agreeing to come to Tulsa and meet with Harry Sinclair. I know that when we spoke the other day you were not happy with the idea."

"I'm still concerned by the idea," Gordon said as he drank his coffee. "But Susan has explained a bit more about your ideas, so I am willing to listen quietly to the proposal and see if it has merit."

"Thank you, Gordon," Susan said. "But I've never known you to be quiet about anything having to do with your banks. Father wouldn't expect you to keep your thoughts to yourself and I don't either."

Gordon nodded and let the barest hint of a smile cross his lips. "Thank you."

"I assume everything in St. Louis has been addressed?" Susan added. "The branch bank is doing well?"

"Yes, it was actually less serious than I thought it was. But I like to be hands on with these things, I'm sure you can understand that."

"Good," Charlie said, not missing the subtle poke at Susan from Gordon. "That's why Susan and I wanted you to meet directly with Sinclair, since you are so attentive to the operation of the banks."

Susan took a bite of a pastry and said, "We have Harry Sinclair all day unless something has changed. This morning, I want us to focus on banking. He's already part-owner of the Exchange National Bank here in Tulsa. He explained to us last week that he wants to expand the bank to take on the growing oil business in the state. Your banks, Gordon, have more assets and access to ready cash than what he has, and I want him to see that."

Hank shifted in his seat and made as if to ask a question. Charlie said, "What is it, Hank?"

"It may not be my place, I'm just a lowly oilman here, but just how big are Mr. Brayton's banks?"

Gordon turned to Hank and said, "Walter always taught that you are never out of place if you are trying to learn something new. The Kansas City Bank of Commerce is currently valued at $2.5 billion."

Hank had just taken a sip of coffee and it erupted from his mouth and covered the tablecloth in front of him. "My God, I don't think all the oil companies in Oklahoma combined are worth that much." He picked up his napkin and started to dab at the coffee.

Susan smiled and said, "It's certainly a lot more than what Sinclair's oil company is worth, right Charlie?"

"Yes, I think the last number I saw for him was $350 million."

"And that's why I believe," Susan continued, tipping her head to Gordon, "that if we can get him to ask for your assistance to expand his bank, he'll see us as more significant than his oil company. Gordon, I've let Sinclair know that your banks are in Missouri, Kansas, and Texas and that we're interested in expanding into Oklahoma."

Charlie said, "I want to transition to talkin' about his oil business as soon after lunch as we can. I'm hopin' we can get him to give us a tour of his refinery. We haven't discussed it, but I want to have time for it if it comes up."

Gordon had remained thoughtful but now said, "Why are we using this approach? In our recent Texas expansion, we went in and bought them out. As you have described, one of those banks in Dallas is larger than this Exchange Bank. I'm confused."

Charlie took a sip of coffee. "I hear ya. And yes, it would be easy for us to do. But, if we did that we wouldn't learn anything about how he built his very sophisticated oil business."

Gordon picked up a spoon and twirled it in his hand. "I think I'm beginning to understand what you want to do. You are hoping that, by giving Sinclair help with his bank and not just taking it over outright, that he will somehow feel indebted to you enough that he will be willing to share his knowledge about his oil business so you can make Kelly Oil a bigger player in the industry."

Charlie nodded. "That 'bout sums it up."

Gordon used the spoon to add some sugar to his coffee. "I will admit that is very unorthodox. I don't think any of my bankers would have thought of using one part of our business as leverage to get a leg up in a different industry altogether." He turned to Susan and smiled. "I think your father would have liked this idea."

Susan said, "Gordon, this approach may not work, and if we learn his bank is something we want, we may turn you loose to go after it anyway."

Gordon smiled. "Okay, you have a plan. But why would a guy like

Sinclair share his secrets?" He turned to Hank and said, "Hey, maybe I'll learn something new here too."

Charlie said, "Hopefully, we'll all learn something." He looked at the clock and said, "Sinclair should be arriving soon."

They discussed their strategy for a few more minutes. Charlie asked their waiter to bring in fresh coffee and pastries.

At 8:00 the clock in the room chimed the hour. A minute later the door to the dining room opened and in walked Harry Sinclair. He wore an expensive, tailored suit and had an expression on his face that said he was all-business as he walked across the room. It was not the same Harry Sinclair they'd had dinner with the other night. Charlie wondered how this day was going to turn out.

"Good morning, everyone. Susan, Charlie, it's so good to see you again. I hope all is well in Kansas City?" He took his seat at the table across from Charlie and Susan and poured himself a cup of coffee.

Charlie made the introductions of Gordon and Hank and Susan gave him a polite, but insubstantial, accounting of her trip to Kansas City.

Charlie said, "Harry, are you still available all day?"

Sinclair opened a leather-bound notebook and pulled out a fountain pen. "Yes, I had a feeling this might be an important day for all of us, so I'm yours all day, and you are mine, right?"

"Yes, and we have set everythin' up to allow you to ask about bankin', and we'll give ya our basic approach to it. This afternoon we would like to change our focus to the oil business. We want to learn anythin' you are willin' to share about creatin' and controllin' all aspects of the oil business, from exploration to retail. Whattaya think?"

"Charlie, I think it's a good place to start, but I must say that my partners in the bank and my directors of the different parts of the oil business all think I'm crazy for even talking to you about any of this. The bankers think you are just here sniffing around before you buy us out and they all lose their jobs. My oil men think I'm going to sell out our business to an 'uppity cowboy upstart' who is just playing at being an oilman." He added, "No offense. My head of pipeline operations was rather passionate about your Kelly Oil company."

Charlie laughed. "You know what, I caught the same attitude from Gordon, Hank, and I think most of the Board of the Kramer Group."

"You're right about that, Honey," Susan said. "But they had the good graces to not call you an 'uppity cowboy upstart.'"

"Not in front of you," Gordon added with a wink that told everyone he was pulling her leg.

They all had a laugh that did more to break the tension than hours of conversation would have.

"Okay, then let's turn the morning over to Mr. Brayton," Susan said.

"Thank you, Mrs. Kelly, and it's a pleasure to make your acquaintance, Mr. Sinclair. Our banking system has operated in Missouri and Kansas for several years, and this past year we added a system of banks in Texas to our enterprise. We are now valued at $2.5 billion and growing. From the beginning, when Walter Kramer started the bank, our mission has been to serve both the private citizen and the commercial world. We've positioned ourselves to keep the size of a potential customer's requirement manageable. We have very little debt, most of which is driven by having acquired our new Texas banks and their debt. They are a set of strong banks located in Austin, Dallas, Galveston, Houston, and many of the other smaller cities in Texas that are seeing the same growth from the oil business as Oklahoma is. Do you have any questions at this point?"

Sinclair leaned in and rubbed his hands together. "Yes, do you focus on any particular industry as you build your commercial portfolio?"

"We have not intended to, but our largest sector in Missouri and Kansas has historically been the construction industry. Both residential and commercial. Our Texas banks have strong relationships with the oil business, which is why we acquired them. We are very interested in Oklahoma for the same reason."

Sinclair's eyes narrowed as he ticked off an item on his notepad. "The Texas banks you acquired are larger than Exchange National here in Tulsa. By a large amount if my accountants are correct. If this meeting is just the first step in a buy out, then I think I should leave now."

Charlie felt his stomach jump like a bronc being saddle broke. *Uh oh, we can't let him leave like this.* He started to say something but Gordon beat him to it.

"My understanding, Mr. Sinclair, was that you had requested some assistance from Mr. and Mrs. Kelly to learn how the Kansas City Bank of Commerce has handled the transition to the large influx of cash and assets that our Texas banks have had to deal with from the oil boom there. I do not have any intention of buying out Exchange National."

Sinclair seemed to accept that there was no direct threat to his bank and continued to ask questions, and Gordon was able to provide general answers for the next several hours. Then Sinclair asked the big question everyone hoped would come eventually.

Sinclair picked up his coffee cup and took a long drink. He set the cup down, cleared his throat, and said, "Mr. Brayton, you're an impressive businessman. Charlie, Susan, you have a winner in Mr. Brayton and your banking business. I think you're making some excellent decisions on structuring your growth, and I can see where my bank can make some improvements in how we do things here in Oklahoma. But we do not have the assets or the ready cash that I need to make all the improvements I want to make to be successful here."

Gordon leaned forward. "What direction are you wanting to take Exchange National here in Oklahoma?"

"We need to expand our presence in the state. I want Exchange National to be the oilman's bank in the state. But to do that I need to be in places other than just Tulsa. We could open other branches, but doing that takes time and is not a guarantee of success. There are other small banks, like Exchange National, all over the state. The surest way to grow and to gain the customers we need is to buy those banks."

"Which is what we did in Texas," Gordon said.

"Exactly," Sinclair confirmed. "I already have a list of potential banks to acquire, and I've been using some similar criteria you just described, Gordon. What do you think of creating a way to a joint venture in banking here in Oklahoma?"

Charlie thought, *Good, we could buy you out, but let's see if another way works better.*

Susan said, "I had hoped we might explore this. I know Charlie and I are open to the idea of a joint partnership. However, we would like to discuss an alternate way of backing Exchange National in such a partnership."

"What do you mean? I thought I was pretty clear that I need financing to be able to make this happen with Exchange National."

Charlie said, "I want to learn everythin' I can about how you run Sinclair Oil. I want Kelly Oil to do the same thing you are doin'. I can do that, but it will take more time than I want, and there will be mistakes made along the way that I would rather not make. If I can learn from you, I can make the transition for Kelly Oil into a big player faster. Are you open to explorin' the idea?"

Sinclair nodded and said, "Charlie, I'm one of the largest and most successful men in the oil business. I'm no fool and I won't put my control of Sinclair Oil in jeopardy, or willingly create a competitor that will take away my market share." He turned to look at Susan. "But Susan, I know you could buy Exchange National from me without batting an eye. I think I have a better understanding now of what you want out of any possible partnership with the bank."

Charlie thought, *Okay, we need to be a little wary here.*

Charlie spoke up quickly and said, "Buyin' Exchange National was not our plan. We want to create a way to partner in bankin' and in the oil business that will benefit both of our companies. We are willin' to enter a partnership between our two banks so that you can make Exchange National the biggest bank in Oklahoma. In exchange for that financial assistance—"

"And some share of the profits," Gordon hastily added.

"We also want to create a way to learn how you made Sinclair Oil the best oil company in the country. By workin' together, not only will I avoid the same mistakes that you learned to overcome, but we can ensure that we both benefit and do not compete directly."

Sinclair slowly nodded then pushed his chair back and said, "Okay, I think I have a better idea now of where you want to take Kelly Oil."

He paused, and Charlie hoped that he wouldn't end the meeting right now.

"I'm hungry," Sinclair finally said. "Let's pause for a good lunch, and then let's talk about the oil business."

Chapter Thirty-Four
Make a Deal
September 1919

THEY ENJOYED A FINE meal from the Topaz and conversation avoided any talk of banking or the oil business.

After lunch, Sinclair stepped out for a few minutes to make a phone call, and the others discussed what they hoped the afternoon might bring as they moved to talking about the oil business.

When Sinclair returned, Charlie made sure they had a few pitchers of water and iced tea and then said, "I think we are ready to start our afternoon session. Harry, the room's all yours."

From his seat Harry said, "Before I start, let me thank all of you for your time. Charlie, you and Susan have been generous with your resources today. Thanks for sharing Gordon and his knowledge."

Harry stood and began walking around the table. "How did I build an oil company engaged from exploration to retailing? I started just like you have by going out and finding a place I thought looked good, and I drilled. I soon found out I wasn't always right. I decided the money in oil was too good not to get involved, but I needed to reduce my risk. That's when I decided to make money from oil in as many ways as possible."

Hank asked, "I'm interested in where you started your expansion and how did you reduce your risk as you built your oil business?"

"Excellent question, Hank. I decided to go into refining. I had worked in the area before, so I already knew something about it. It reduced my risk, but I still wanted to be more confident that I would succeed. After some investigation, I determined some refining companies had done well but could be persuaded to sell out because of a lack of resources or some other factor. There was no reason for me to start from scratch. I took ad-

185

vantage of situations where someone had created a refinery but could not expand it or, for some valid reason, needed financial help. I also did this when I got into distribution and retailing as well. In most cases, I bought existing companies. When I created Sinclair Oil and Refining a few years ago, I merged eleven companies I owned. I strongly recommend you follow the same method as you expand Kelly Oil."

Hank said, "Susan and Charlie have offered me a tremendous opportunity with our partnership. As you know, I bring over twenty years of experience to use growin' Kelly Oil. My experience comes mostly in exploration, drillin', and settin' up the initial pumpin' operation. I also know a little about refinin', but pipelines and retailin' are foreign to me. What you said about ownin' the entire process makes complete sense to me. What I need to know is, can we negotiate a way for you to guide us through addin' all those assets to Kelly Oil?"

Harry sat back down and placed his right hand over his heart, and said, "What you have already agreed to this morning has the potential to make me a lot of money. I'm very grateful and want to give Kelly Oil a chance to make a lot of money in the oil business. Like banking, I believe there is room for several big companies, and I think a partnership between us to make Kelly Oil become the next big one would benefit us both. What can I do for you?"

Charlie jumped in and said, "I'll let Hank give you his thoughts in a minute. I know I would like to see us gain access to some of your key people."

Hank said, "Especially in refinin', distribution, and retailin.'"

Harry looked shocked, smiled, and said, "I wasn't expecting that. Do you have any ideas about how it could happen and why I would want to do it?"

Charlie said, "I think I do. I've seen staff with a lead man and a sidekick next in line everywhere I've been. And when the lead leaves for whatever reason, the sidekick's ready and steps in. I imagine Sinclair Oil's no different. I propose you allow Kelly Oil access to attempt to hire your leads or their sidekicks. We would limit it to only staff workin' refinery, pipeline, and retail operations. Three men workin' at the top of those three areas. If we are successful in bringin' someone from each area over to us, I'll authorize you a 5% share of Kelly Oil's net profit startin' one year from now for two years."

Harry pondered the offer, then said, "So, you're asking me to authorize you to steal some of my top men? What a novel idea, Charlie. You've got more guts than I thought."

Susan said, "You have no idea, Harry."

Harry grinned at her. He took a drink of tea and said, "You two are pushing me to the limit. But, with the assets you already have and the business acumen you have shown me, you are starting to grow on me. I would prefer to have shares of preferred stock or a place on the Board of Kelly Oil."

"Kelly Oil is part of the Kramer Group which has no stockholders, as I'm sure you know," Susan said. "And I know that my Board would fire me if I proposed adding another Board member, even one as esteemed as yourself."

Gordon nodded but remained silent.

"I can see how Walter Kramer became such a successful business-man," Harry said. "Well, since you won't let me join the Board, then I'll agree to your terms if you make it five years."

"How about three?" Charlie said.

Sinclair narrowed his eyes. "After the auction at Pawhuska I should have expected that. Okay, three years. But you must include me in your selection process and negotiations. I know of a couple of situations where the lead will probably only work for another few years, and his experi-ences would have more value to you than me. I could pay his replacement much less. You would benefit from the lead's experience in building what you want, and he would add value by guiding your future acquisitions. What do you think?"

Hank immediately said, "I don't know about you, Charlie, but that's the kind of help I want."

Charlie stood and walked over to Harry. He offered his hand, and they shook. "Harry, we're gonna make a lot of money together."

Charlie sat back down and Gordon coughed to get their attention. "It seems that the oil side of the proposal for the banks to enter into a joint partnership has been concluded. I think we need to discuss some of the details of that partnership now."

Sinclair nodded and said, "I had hoped we would end the day this way."

They spent the next several hours hammering out the details of the partnership for the bank. Gordon and Sinclair seemed to anticipate the needs of the other as they negotiated the finer points of the deal. In the end they reached a decision that all sides thought worked out the best for them.

When they finished, Harry said, "My, what a day. This meeting has been my most productive in a long time."

Susan said, "How about we celebrate with some champagne?"

They all agreed and she went to ask the waiter to bring them a bottle.

Charlie walked over to Harry and shook his hand. "One more thing, Harry."

Harry made a show of being wounded in the heart, then chuckled. "What now, Charlie?"

"There are many refineries in Cushing, and I would like your opinion on them. Should we look to acquire one or more of them or build our own?"

"Charlie, I had my eye on some of them. My man Bunk Severs runs my Tulsa plant, and he went down there to look at what I might acquire. Now I need to use those funds to do our banking deal and something else I'm working on. If you want to grow Kelly Oil as rapidly as you have said you want to, you should purchase one or more of those refineries instead of building your own. Building takes too much time, and you'd still have those refineries as competitors. If you have the funds to purchase them, you'll be better served in the long run even if your upfront costs might be higher. I can have you talk with Bunk."

Charlie said, "Can he set up a trip for us to tour those refineries next week?"

"I'll call him. Let's plan on it."

Susan returned with a waiter who carried two bottles of champagne and several glasses. "Okay, Charlie. Now can we celebrate?"

Charlie laughed. "Yes."

Chapter Thirty-Five
Big Day in Sapulpa
September 1919

CHARLIE AND SUSAN ENJOYED a quiet weekend basking in their success. They only left their suite to eat in the restaurant, and Sunday afternoon, they walked around downtown Tulsa. On Sunday evening, Jim Townsley drove in from Kansas City, and Hank returned from a quick trip to Burbank for a check on the Burbank #1 well. Jim and Hank met Charlie and Susan for their evening meal at 7:00.

They sat and ordered then Hank said, "Before I forget to tell ya, the fifteen-hundred barrel holdin' tank's in place and connected to the pump's output. I hired two pumpers who'll monitor and maintain the pump. Marland agreed to buy our oil for the next six months. He added the well to his Osage County route. They'll stop by daily to make a pickup. Marland's truck stopped while I was there, and I trained our pumpers on the process and what to look for, so we don't get cheated by a shady trucker."

Charlie said, "Good, Hank. How much is oil sellin' for right now?"

"It's about $3 a barrel. We're talkin' about a thousand barrels a day out, so we're makin' about $3,000 a day gross. Our pump's barely necessary; there's still so much pressure behind the oil."

"Thanks, Hank. Jim, how was your trip?"

"I drove my Buick down. I bought a new Touring Sedan about a month ago. I enjoyed the drive. I used the route you recommended."

Charlie asked, "Are you ready to discuss cementin' wells tomorrow?"

"Yes, Charlie. I called Erle Halliburton a few days ago. He's more than willin' to talk to me and share ideas. He said there's way more work out there than he can handle. I have a good understandin' of what we could do."

Susan said, "Let's not talk all night about business, then go through it all again tomorrow. Here comes our food now."

Charlie looked over at Susan and smiled. She had worn the Isadora blouse from the night they'd had dinner with Getty, Sinclair, and Skelly. The blouse now showed him more of her cleavage because of how she had turned in her seat. He said, "I agree, and then we can make an early night of it. Both of you guys had a long drive today."

***

The next morning all four rode over to Sapulpa in Jim's new Buick to meet with Zane Krebs at the quarry. As they walked into the office, they saw Zane had coffee and donuts waiting for them.

"Happy to see everyone made it here safe and sound," Zane said. "Hey, Jim, is that your new Buick you told me about?"

"It sure is," Jim said. "What a great automobile. I could brag all day, but I'm dying to talk about cementing oil wells."

"Get yourself coffee and donuts and grab a seat," Zane said, walking over to a small table. He stood while the others took their seats.

Jim said, "I spoke to Erle Halliburton last week about his cementing process, and we also discussed the equipment needed. He designed the equipment and has used his process successfully at several locations. He has a pending patent and hopes it's approved by early next year."

Hank asked, "Is there a way we can access the information to create our cementing operation?"

"The short answer is yes. I've struck a deal with Erle to give us a leg up on everyone but him. If we fund the materials costs for building enough new equipment for the expansion he wants for his company, he'll produce the same amount of equipment for us for the material costs plus ten percent. He'll also train crews for us as part of the deal for the personnel cost plus ten percent."

Charlie asked, "Jim, am I understandin' you, right? If he adds five new systems to his equipment fleet and we fund just the material costs plus ten percent for those new systems, he'll build us five systems too? We basically pay for materials only on his new systems?"

"Close. If we pay the materials costs for the *ten* systems, Erle builds them, and we get *five* of those systems. He'll also train our staff on how to use them."

Zane said, "That still sounds like an amazing deal. I've been contacting some drillers, and more and more want the cementing process but they can't all afford the prices Erle is asking for the systems outright. It makes the drilling operation much smoother, and the inner zonal isolation of the bore is improved."

Susan said, "I have no idea what you just said, but it sounds like it improves safety and saves time. We all know time is money."

Charlie turned to Hank. "Do we need to send you and Jim down to Halliburton?"

"I would recommend it. Jim, did you get a cost on the equipment?"

"Erle said $2,000 per unit, and he can give me an itemized breakdown. If we funded Erle for ten units, we would cover $22,000 in materials and overhead and end up with five units. He has sold two to people in California, where he once worked. They paid him $7,500 each for them."

"So, we'd be savin' just over $15,000 with this deal?"

"Yes," Jim said. "He wants to raise capital, and he wants people to use his units. He wants to create a market for his manufacturing arm of Halliburton. Like I said last night, he knows there's more work than he can handle. He'll make money providing the service and also make money providing the equipment for others to service the oil fields.

"And someday, others will pay to use their patents and manufacture more equipment. I can't imagine Halliburton could manufacture enough equipment by himself to service the entire oil business."

"Should we look at creating a plant to manufacture cementing equipment?" Susan asked.

"Excellent question, Susan," Hank said. "It might prove useful, but it would require creatin' another business to set up and operate."

Charlie got up and walked to the coffee pot and donuts for a refill. He turned and said, "Folks, there's a lot of ways we can make money in the oil business. Let's get our equipment and some crews trained so we have some expertise in cementing. Then let's watch the demand for the equipment a year or two from now. If it's strong, we need to hire one of Halliburton's best and build a manufacturing plant to make more of his machines."

Jim said, "Zane, I plan to either get the formula or bring back a sample of the cement they use in their machine. I'll give it to you to analyze and prepare to create it here in Sapulpa."

"Great. I'll put our lab to work on it immediately," Zane said. He looked over at Charlie. "When do you want to have a cementing capability in place? I mean, with equipment, training, and cement?"

Charlie leaned back against the wall and thought for a moment. "It's Monday, September 22nd. I want Kelly Oil to provide cementin' service to our wells and others by January. It may mean we buy additional machines. If we decide next year, we want to manufacture the machines. I want in the business by 1921."

Susan said, "That timeline makes perfect sense if Jim and Hank's trip to meet with Halliburton is successful."

"When do you want us to leave for Duncan, Charlie?" Jim asked.

Charlie scratched his chin and looked at Susan. "Susan, I think we send them this week. But I want Hank on the tour of the refineries in Cushing. It wouldn't hurt for Jim to see it as well. Then they can leave Cushing to go to Duncan. We should allow Hank to commit to Halliburton for the machines. Do ya agree?"

"I do. Jim, how's your schedule? Can you spend another week or so in Oklahoma?"

"I can. My man in Kansas City can handle the place. This business is all new and exciting for me. I'm so glad to participate in this effort. Zane and I are tied up tomorrow, acquiring another quarry. We'll certainly need one with all this new oil business support coming at us."

Charlie looked around the room and made eye contact with everyone. He spoke with a strong, confident tone. "This has been a special mornin' for the Kramer Group and Kelly Oil. We've created a plan for growth in the cement and oil businesses, which will likely spawn a manufacturing business. How excitin'!" Charlie's voice cracked with emotion. "I agree with Jim, and I'm glad we're gittin' in this business. We're headin' into some excitin' times. We'll likely have some challenges, but the talent in this room can handle whatever we face.

"It's lunchtime. Let's pack up and head to the Harvey Hotel at the railroad station."

Susan added, "Gentlemen, this has been a great day. I know my father would have enjoyed being here with you. Charlie and I certainly did. I heard it in his voice and felt it in my heart."

"Thank you, Sweetheart; let's go," Charlie said.

Chapter Thirty-Six
Hiring
September 1919

BEFORE CHARLIE LEFT THE cement plant in Sapulpa, he called Sinclair. "Harry, can you confirm your refinery manager's meeting me for breakfast at the hotel on Wednesday to guide our trip to the Cushing refineries?"

"Sure, Charlie. Bunk Severs is my most experienced refiner."

"Thanks, Harry. Do you want to come to Cushing with us?"

"I would enjoy that," he laughed, "but I'm working on the tasks Gordon left for me for the bank deal, remember?"

"I remember, and it's where ya should focus. I hope to see ya soon. Goodbye."

The group had a great lunch in Sapulpa, then Hank, Charlie, and Susan returned to the Hotel Tulsa. Charlie and Susan went directly to their suite.

Charlie sat and watched Susan undress and prepare to shower. "Sweetheart, would you like to go for a walk this evenin'?"

"Sounds like fun. I want to shower and cool off first. Want to join me?"

"I'm there."

***

As they crossed the lobby and walked outside, Charlie said, "Getty told me the other night about Bishop's Restaurant. I guess it's where he, Sinclair, and Skelly often go when they don't wanna eat in the Topaz Room. Let's find it tonight."

"Sure, let's give it a try. Is it close by?"

"A few blocks away. Let's walk around and check out the stores first."

"I would like to find Hunt's Department store. I've been wearing the same blouses for the second and third time since we left the ranch. I know I'm spoiled, but I would like something new."

"We'll find the store, and you can have fun findin' a few new things."

They walked around for about thirty minutes and stopped for Susan to shop at Hunt's. Susan found a white silk blouse that seemed uniquely tailored for her; it fit her perfectly.

"I love this, Charlie. It flatters me when buttoned for the office and unbuttoned for a sexy casual night out. What do you think?"

"I love it. It shows off your curves, which always makes me smile. We're buyin' it."

She found and bought several more things before they went to Bishop's for supper. They sat at the counter, and Susan captivated the waiter. He gave Charlie and Susan a few minutes to look at the menu while he got their drinks and gathered his wits.

Charlie said, "Getty told me to order either the cheeseburger and fries or the Brown Derby. I guess Bishop's is famous for both."

Susan said, "Why don't you order one, and I'll order the other, and we can try both."

"Good idea."

As they finished their food, Susan said, "I think we owe Paul another thanks. That was the best cheeseburger I've ever eaten. The Brown Derby with the grilled onions and the hot rolls would bring me here at least once every week if I lived in the hotel as Getty does."

"We ate some mighty fine food, alright. I'm gonna sleep well tonight. Let's see if we can walk back to the hotel or need someone to carry us back in a wheelbarrow."

Susan laughed as they left the restaurant.

***

Wednesday morning, Charlie and Susan arrived at the Topaz a little before 8:00, and a few minutes later, Rice Coburn, Hank, and Jim walked in.

"Rice, I'm glad you could change your plans and meet us here in Tulsa," Charlie said.

"Sure. Susan insisted I see Tulsa for the opportunities in construction here. But I'm interested in what you are thinking about with these refineries. I assume that whatever you decide, some construction work may be involved with them."

As they waited for the maître d', an older man walked up wearing a simple gray suit. He had thinning hair and wore glasses. He held out his hand. "Morning. I'm Bunk Severs, the Refinery Manager for Sinclair Oil. Are you Charlie and Susan Kelly?"

Charlie shook his hand and said, "Yep." He made the other introductions as the maître d' led them to the private room in the restaurant. The waiter already had coffee waiting and took their orders.

Charlie opened the meeting with, "Susan and I are glad to see all of you. We'll eat first, of course, but I would like us on the road to Cushing by 9:00. I'm lookin' forward to listenin' and learnin' today. What have you got planned, Mr. Severs?"

"I made arrangements with some refinery owners I know in Cushing. We'll start at the refinery owned by Cornell Oil Company. I once worked with the founder of Cornell. When we get to the refinery, I'll guide you through the process from start to finish, where the oil comes in, how it's refined, and how it goes out the door as the different products."

He turned and looked at Susan. "You expected to go with us, ma'am?"

"Of course," Susan said, irritation in her voice.

"Well, it's just a refinery is no place for a woman, is all. It's a rough and dirty place, and I don't mean just the equipment."

"Susan's the head of the Kramer Group," Charlie said.

Bunk replied, "And I've spent plenty of time around workmen. I know how 'well-behaved' they are around a woman. Am I right, Rice?"

Coburn laughed. "Yep. Sometimes I think you grew up at the construction sites when your father brought you along."

Bunk shrugged. "Well, I suggest you at least get some coveralls to put on, ma'am. Otherwise, you might get oil and grease on your clothes. I'd hate for you to have to buy a new outfit."

"I don't know, Mr. Severs. I could always use an excuse to do more shopping. But I take your point."

Just then, the waiter arrived with their food. They made arrangements over the meal for who would ride with whom to Cushing, and Hank started the process of getting as much information from Bunk Severs as he could.

***

The group arrived in Cushing at noon and went straight to the refinery. Everyone got out of the cars and waited for Bunk.

Bunk said, "Mr. Sinclair told me you might be interested in acquiring a refinery. As I said at breakfast, I know the owner here, and he's open to an offer."

Charlie replied, "Good, and do ya think this place is a good example of a quality approach to refinin' oil and gas?"

"Yes, they use our process from the Sinclair refinery in Tulsa. Every company we'll look at today does."

"Good, and I want you to describe what improvements, including expansions, you would recommend to these sites as we tour them."

Bunk raised his voice to ensure he had everyone's attention. "Let's go inside and let them know we are here. They're expecting us. For your safety, we must stay together, and don't touch anything without asking me first."

The first location in the refinery they visited was where they heated the crude oil. Bunk described refining the petroleum into products using an inexpensive fractional distillation process. He said, "It's a mechanical operation involving heating crude oil. As it heats, its various hydrocarbon components, called 'fractions,' boil at different temperatures. As the fractions boil off, vapors are recovered and distilled into liquids. The fractions recovered from the lowest boiling point to the highest include butane, gasoline, kerosene, diesel, heating oil, and lubricants. Distillation typically produces about forty percent gasoline from each barrel of crude oil."

As he described the refining process, Bunk's knowledge and confidence impressed Charlie. "How long have you worked in refinin'?" he asked.

"I started in the oil business around 1890. I got into refining in 1904, so it's been fifteen years. Over the last two or three years, big improvements have happened in the equipment supporting refining."

They finished the Cornell refinery tour and headed to the next facility. They were within a mile of each other and shared the same approach to processing crude oil. After about four hours, they had finished touring the last refinery.

As they returned to their cars after the last tour, Charlie asked, "Could these four refineries be tied together and store oil in the same tanks?"

Bunk answered, "They could, and the fact you asked the question tells me you see the process and are thinking of refining on a large scale." Bunk smiled. "Charlie, you're rapidly becoming a man to be reckoned with in the oil business. I'm sorry I ever said you were an 'uppity cowboy upstart' to Mr. Sinclair."

Charlie laughed and patted Bunk on the back. "Thanks, Mr. Severs, I've been called worse. But I won't become a man to be reckoned with alone. I'll need some men around me willin' to take some risks. We need to talk."

"Yes, we do. Sinclair's impressed with you and Hank after your long meeting with him the other day. He expected you might want to talk to me."

"We do." Charlie then turned to Coburn and said, "Rice, you looked mighty busy takin' notes today. Do you have any questions for Bunk?"

Rice opened his notebook. "I have a long list; do you want me to start asking them now?"

Charlie raised his right hand, palm out, and said, "I thought you might have a lot based on what we saw on the tours. Why don't you and Mr. Severs discuss your questions as we drive back to Tulsa?

"Mr. Severs, when we get to the hotel, let's get a table at the restaurant and talk. Susan, you and Rice and Hank can join us after our meeting. We won't take too long. It'll be about time to eat by then, and we can eat and talk more about refining oil."

Lively conversations continued in the front and back seats during the drive back to Tulsa.

***

As they walked into the hotel lobby, Charlie looked at Susan, Rice, and Hank and said, "You guys give us thirty minutes, then we'll have dinner." Susan kissed Charlie and headed for the room.

Charlie turned and said, "Now, Mr. Severs, let's have that discussion."

Bunk asked, "What's on your mind, Charlie?"

"I think you know. Surely, Harry has told you we want to use his model to build Kelly Oil."

"Yes, he mentioned it and indicated he had approved for you to talk to me if you wanted to. I took it the tour today had two agendas. One, for me to educate you on refineries and, two, for you to take a look at me and decide whether you wanted me to join Kelly Oil."

"That about sizes it up. Harry wanted to get bigger in banking, so we're goin' into the banking business together. As part of the deal, I wanted a few key people who helped him build and run Sinclair Oil to help me build Kelly Oil. He told me you are his top man in refining. I liked everythin' I heard today. I want to put you in charge of creatin' the entire refining division of Kelly Oil. The position justifies a bigger salary than you make now, and I'll give you a percentage of the profits from refining every year. Do you want to become part of Kelly Oil?"

"Before I answer, let me say the amount of money it takes to create a refining capability is substantial. I know Kramer's much bigger than Sinclair, but are you planning to do as little as possible to get into refining, or are you planning to do what it takes to lead the industry?"

"Another fair question. The answer is this: Kelly Oil's refining division must become the industry's model and the nation's biggest refinery system. I want refining capabilities in Oklahoma, Texas, and California as soon as possible. You would lead the establishment of all of it."

Bunk nodded. "The other thing is I was looking to retire from Sinclair in a few years. I'm in my mid-fifties now and I was hoping to be able to retire in the next five years."

"That's exactly what I want," Charlie said. "I want people with experience who can pass their knowledge on to others. You'll be well compensated not only for what you bring to Kelly Oil, but who you train to replace you. Your own legacy, so to speak."

Bunk glowed with excitement. "Charlie, I'm in. Where do I sign?"

"We can discuss the details later, but what's your salary now?"

"I make $10,000 a year."

"It's a good salary. I'll pay you $20,000 for now as you create the first refinery system for us. Once it's operational, you'll get three percent of the annual net profits every Christmas. We'll find some incentives for you to create refineries in Texas and California."

"I'm excited by all of this and can't wait to start."

Charlie looked up to see Susan, Rice, and Hank walking into the restaurant. "Susan, your timin' is perfect, or maybe Mr. Severs' is."

Susan beamed as she asked, "He said yes?"

"Of course he said yes. Now we have our lead for the refining division of Kelly Oil."

They ordered their meals, and Charlie said, "Let's hear your questions, Rice."

"Mr. Severs answered all of them for me on the drive back to Tulsa."

"Call me Bunk since I'm now part of the family."

Everyone laughed.

"Let me ask it another way," Charlie said. "What are your questions, Rice?"

"The big one's about how each of the four refineries is similar, and I wanted to know if we could easily tie them together."

Bunk said, "The answer is yes, but some challenges are involved. If we want to not only service Kelly Oil but also process oil products for other companies, then it's less expensive to modify those sites instead of building from scratch. The oldest is T-C Oil Company's site, and it's only five years old. Cornell is three, and Eagle Oil and Panhandle are less than two years old. They all built solid refineries from an equipment standpoint, but they are dependent on the Cushing-Drumright oil fields, and they are underfunded. Sinclair told me he strongly considered buying them. Now he needs his cash on hand for something else. I guess his need has something to do with you guys."

Susan said, "Okay. What are the pitfalls?"

"There are none. You can get all four for around $200,000. You'll need more to integrate the refineries. But it's what you should do. You should consider buying a pipeline company already putting the pipe into the Drumright field and Osage County. We hear the next big one is likely south of here. I would prepare to lay pipe for the next big one. Cushing's location is better than any other refining operation to serve the entire state of Oklahoma."

Rice said, "I heard you say, to create what we need we should look at $250,000 to invest in the refining and pipeline infrastructure to support growth. Right?"

"Yes. It'll likely take a year to get everything up and running. I'd approach this in two phases. I would take two refineries offline, integrate them, then do the other two, and create the interface for all four as you end this second phase. At the same time, I would create the pipeline-interface necessary to minimize trucking the oil."

Charlie asked, "Is there a pipeline company you think is prime to do this?"

"The Mid-America Pipeline Company is the one I would go after. They already have pipe laid to Drumright, and we would likely want to tie into them anyway. They have done work for Sinclair, and they're on time and under budget with us."

Rice asked, "How much modification to the buildings and tie-in to Cushing's electrical and plumbing systems is required?"

"Quite a bit, but I'm certain after our conversation this afternoon you have the experience and resources to do the work."

Charlie said, "Bunk, you said you knew the owners of each of the refineries. Can you call them and set up a meeting for tomorrow in Cushing?"

Bunk smiled. "I'll give them each a call after dinner. I'm sure they will want to hear your offer."

Susan said, "Our food's coming, and I've heard enough to know we have what we need. Charlie, the income from Burbank #1 will build us a refinery system."

"I agree, and I'm confident we have the right people, place, and time to do this."

Chapter Thirty-Seven
Refineries and Pipelines
September 1919

THEY LEFT TULSA EARLY the following day and arrived at the Cushing Hotel around 8:00.

As they walked into the hotel, Bunk said, "I've drawn up a schedule and told each company head to show up ahead of their appointed time." He showed Charlie the schedule.

"We'll start with Cornell first. I planned on taking a couple of hours for each of them, but also told them to come early in case we were moving quicker. T-C will be second, then Eagle Oil, and we'll end with Panhandle."

"I see you have Mid-America on the schedule," Charlie said.

"After our discussion last night, I figured you'd want to talk to them today as well."

"Good thinkin'," Charlie said. "You're already readin' my mind."

Bunk said, "I mentioned to the owners this was a preliminary meeting, just a chance to get to know them and thank them for the tours in person."

Charlie replied, "Good. They won't expect us to make an offer right away. I'm glad you're givin' us two hours for each one. I don't plan to use much time. I'll know within fifteen minutes if someone is willin' to sell to us. Harry told me last night each of these companies is worth buyin', and he wanted them for the additional refinin' capability. We talked about what he would have paid for each company, and I'll use the information to guide me as we talk. I guess what I'm sayin' is, I'm prepared to wrap up all of the hagglin' in an hour or less, but we'll see how it goes."

Based on what Sinclair had shared with him, Charlie wanted to get the four refineries for well under $200,000 and wanted to keep it under

$150,000 if he could. He sat in the middle chair with his back to the wall in the banquet room. Susan and Hank sat on his right, and Bunk and Rice were to his left.

***

Bunk pointed across the room at a man about fifty years old with gray hair, a handlebar mustache, medium build, and in a suit and tie. He said, "That's Ben Cornell, owner of Cornell Oil."

Charlie laughed. "Well, he's out-dressin' me. I wonder if he can out-talk me. I guess we'll see."

Ben Cornell from Cornell Oil was an excellent negotiator. Ben said, "I need $60,000, Mr. Kelly."

Bunk leaned over to Charlie and quietly said, "Of the four, you're going to see this is the one you should want most. If it takes $60,000 to get him to part with his company, it's worth it."

Charlie smiled and said, "If I agree, you'll sell it right now?"

"Yes, which makes the company free and clear and puts a little in my pocket."

Charlie leaned back and thought for a minute, then said, "Well then, consider it done. We have memorandums of agreement here to fill in, sign, and witness. My corporate attorney will use it to create our contract and cut you a cashier's check."

***

Trace Catchings of T-C Oil was young, six feet tall, with dark hair and striking green eyes. He sold his company for $45,000. Although high quality, his operation produced less than Cornell's.

Bunk commented, "Trace, I would like you to consider staying on and helping me run the refinery. What do you think?"

"I'm willin' to talk about it."

Bunk said, "Good, I'll buy you dinner tonight."

***

Delbert McDaniel of Eagle Oil and Gas was next. He was about forty years old, average sized, and carried himself with confidence.

Kelly Oil had already bought two companies, and Charlie felt things were going his way.

Charlie said, "Delbert, I'm Charles Kelly. Happy to meet ya. I've got some McDaniels in my family. They're mostly down in Pontotoc County. Where ya from?"

Delbert grinned and said, "I grew up in Ada, the county seat of Pontotoc County. Good to meet ya, cuz."

Charlie laughed. "We might be cousins. Well, let's talk business first."

After forty-five minutes, Delbert still wanted more than Charlie planned on paying. Susan suggested a short break to use the lady's room, a tactic she had used before in negotiations to give them time to talk strategy. Delbert got up from the table to get some coffee.

Charlie and the others huddled together. He turned to Bunk and quietly said, "What do ya think? Is there a way he might take the $50,000 I'm willin' to pay?"

Hank whispered, "I know Delbert well, and he's a solid guy. He knows the business, and he's refining gasoline more than the others. Panhandle has recently refined oil into gasoline, but you want Delbert and Eagle. He may take the $50,000 if you sweetin' it with a contract to help Bunk run the operation."

Charlie said, "Okay. I'll make him the offer."

Susan returned, Charlie gave her a nod, and they all resumed their seats.

Charlie looked at Delbert. "I think we can find some common ground here and make us both happy. I'll pay you $50,000 for your plant and offer you a contract to help Bunk run the place with a salary that'll make ya happy."

Delbert stroked his chin. "What salary you thinkin' about?"

Charlie looked at Bunk as if looking for confirmation, though Charlie already knew he had hooked his next fish. Bunk leaned in and whispered, "He's ours. I'll negotiate a fair salary for him."

Charlie turned back to Delbert with a smile. "I think you and Bunk can negotiate a salary to make you a happy man."

Delbert looked over at Bunk, who nodded, then Delbert asked Hank, "Is this as fair as it seems?"

Hank nodded. "Yes, the Kellys are fine people and always fair to their team."

Delbert looked back at Charlie. "Done."

***

Bunk pulled Charlie aside after they signed the memorandum for Eagle Oil and Gas. "I want to offer Ben Cornell a job as my Vice-President. After Sinclair and Marland, he's the best refinery manager I know. I have no idea whether he's interested. He sold his company to us only because he had gone as far as he could without further financial backing. Marland barely beat him out on a refining contract three months ago. If Ben had won the contract, it would have changed everything."

"I assume you are goin' to offer Trace and Delbert around $10,000 each to come work for us. What's Ben worth to you?"

"$15,000 plus a two percent bonus."

"Make him the offer. If he doesn't create enough business to cover his costs, it's cutting into your bonus."

"Charlie, his contacts and ability to create business will more than offset his salary. As I said, he came very close to beating out Sinclair. He needed money to expand his production line, and then he would have got the contract. Remember, I was on Sinclair's staff and at those negotiations. Sinclair's new client told me it made the difference. Ben's bid per barrel beat us. He just couldn't handle the volume. Money isn't a problem with us; he knows how to create efficiencies without giving up effectiveness."

"As I said, make him an offer. He probably wasn't paying himself $15,000 a year."

***

Max Stiles from Panhandle Oil and Gas arrived right on time. Friendly and outgoing, Max was short and shaped like a basketball.

"Max, I'm Charles Kelly, and I understand you're acquainted with Bunk and Hank. They speak highly of you, and your vision for how refineries integrate with pipelines is also how I see oils should be processed and moved across the nation."

Max said, "It's great to meet you. Yes, I see refineries and pipelines working hand in hand more and more. Trucks and railroads will still play a big role in moving oil around the country. But I see both having their role diminishing in transporting petroleum products. Long term, refineries coupled with pipelines will lead the industry. Cushing will still play a significant role in distribution even a hundred years from now.

"We agree with you and want to help you to lead the effort to create your vision."

"That all sounds too good to be true. Where are we gonna get the money needed anytime soon?"

Hank said, "Max, you always do your homework. You know who Charlie and Susan are, don't you?"

Max sat straight in his chair with a big grin and replied, "Yes, they own Kelly Oil with you. Right?"

"Well, yes, but it's not all they own. Ever hear of the Kramer Group out of Kansas City?"

"I've heard of it but don't know anything about it. I've lived oil and piping all my life and had one banker and my crew. We've done very well for ourselves, but I'll admit, I've gone about as far as me and my banker can take us."

Bunk said, "We consider you the best pipin' man out here, and we like what you are tryin' to do. The Kellys are the richest people west of the

Mississippi and maybe east. They have the money, Max. Listen to them, please."

Max perked up and said, "Oh, I'm all ears, Mr. Kelly."

Charlie looked Max in the eye and asked, "What do you think your company's worth? And how much do you pay yourself each year?"

"My equipment and material are worth about $30,000. I have contracts worth about $25,000. I have about two dozen men who work for me. I pay myself about $10,000 a year."

"Okay, do ya have debt?"

"I owe my banker about $20,000 on a two-year note."

Charlie leaned back as he often did when mulling things over. "Max, here are my thoughts. I'm puttin' together a set of refineries here in Cushing. We'll integrate them and the pipelines servicin' the oil business around Oklahoma. I want your refinery and your men to become part of it. Here's my offer to you. I'll buy your refinery for $40,000 and pay off your debt if you'll come to work with Bunk and help him by continuin' to run your place and to integrate all the refineries into one large refinin' system."

Max tried to keep his face neutral, but Charlie could see his Adam's apple bobbing up and down. "What… would you pay me?"

"I'll let Bunk and you settle it. But I'll say you won't have to worry about findin' customers and payin' bills anymore. We'll pay you well for your experience."

Bunk smiled and said, "I promise the salary will make you happy."

Max smiled and asked, "You'll pay off the $20,000 note and give me $40,000, right?"

Hank said, "Yes, Max, that's what Charlie said."

"Okay, I'll do it. Where do I sign?"

***

After they'd wrapped up everything with Max, Charlie asked, "Has anybody seen Karl Webb of Mid-America Pipeline yet?"

Hank said, "I thought he was standing in the doorway a few minutes ago. I'll go check and see."

Five minutes later, Hank walked in with Karl Webb. Karl was in his late fifties, slender and not much under six feet tall, with a full head of silver hair.

Hank said, "Karl, have a seat right there. He's Charles Kelly, and she's his wife, Susan."

Charlie and Susan both smiled and nodded. Charlie said, "It's a pleasure to meet you." He pointed at Bunk and Hank. "I've heard nothin' but good things from these two guys about ya and your company. Last week over dinner with Harry Sinclair, he described you as the person who would come as close to anyone to sharin' my ideas for pipelines."

"Honestly, I had not heard of Kelly Oil before Bunk talked to me about this meeting. I've been at this for over five years and have connections from Cushing out to most current hot spots. Are you hoping to discuss a contract for me to pipe your oil to Cushing?"

Hank interjected, "Karl, it's good to see ya. It's been six months or more, hasn't it?"

Karl nodded.

Hank continued. "You're right; Charlie and Susan started Kelly Oil earlier this year. I joined them from the start. We've drilled only one well so far as Kelly Oil. A gusher up at Burbank."

Karl said, "Congratulations, guys."

Hank said, "Thanks, but what you don't know is we didn't start with nothing. We set up an initial bank account with over $100,000 in it. Today, Charlie has spent about $200,000 to buy four refineries. I'll let Charlie or Susan share the rest."

Charlie said, "I've done all the talkin' today. I'll let Susan describe more about us."

Susan said, "It seems we must tell our story a lot. We own the Kramer Group out of Kansas City. We own banks across several states, department stores, railroads, construction companies, and—..."

Karl said, "Meaning no disrespect; just the opposite. You don't need to go any further. I now know who you are; if you own only some of those businesses, it's all I need."

Charlie responded, "Well, great, but it seemed like you missed something. We're the sole owners of Kramer."

Shocked, Karl slumped back in his chair. He gathered himself and said, "Oh my God, I'm sorry, I missed that. So, you own it all?"

Susan said, "Yes, we do, and we want to bring you and your company with us as we become one of the largest oil companies in the country. We'll own successful companies in all aspects of the oil business."

Charlie said, "Now we know each other. Can we do business?"

Karl said, "Maybe so. I've done well, but there have been times when I had a great opportunity and didn't have the resources to jump on it. I'm not exaggerating when I say every time the opportunity turned out just as good for the person who took advantage of it as I thought it would."

Charlie asked, "We want to buy your company and make it a part of Kelly Oil. You'll run it as the President. What would it take for you to sell, and what are you paying yourself?"

"I'm guessing you already know or have an expectation as to how

I would answer the question. You know me and my company, or you wouldn't have invited me here. What are you offering me?"

Susan said, "You're right. We have a good idea about your assets and debts, but do you have any future contracts?"

"I'm fulfilling one for Sinclair Oil as we speak, and I have a large one with Marland following this one. If I had more staff, I would have already started on the Marland work. He's willing to wait for me."

Charlie said, "Karl, here's what I'll do. I'll pay you $60,000 clear for your company and pay off your debt. I want you to stay and run the company as a division of Kelly Oil. We'll pay you $20,000 in salary plus a three percent bonus of the net profits each year at Christmas. You'll have a reserve fund available to take advantage of those opportunities when they come along. How does my offer sound?"

"Unbelievable; you described my dream. Are you sure?"

"I'm sure." Charlie grinned. "It's a yes or no question, Karl; what's your answer?"

"Yes, of course, yes. We need to sign something."

Susan said, "We'll have the memorandum ready shortly. Welcome to the Kramer Group."

Chapter Thirty-Eight
Explorations and Possibilities
September 1919

RICE COBURN JOINED CHARLIE and Susan for breakfast on Friday morning before they went on a tour of Tulsa to look for a potential site to create a residential development like the Country Club area in Kansas City.

Rice took his place at the table and looked at Charlie. "Is something wrong?"

Charlie's nostrils flared as he said, "I received a phone call earlier from Hank. He and Jim decided to go to Burbank before going down to Duncan to meet with Halliburton. We had damage done at our well site in Burbank a while back."

"I heard Hank mention something about it in Cushing. Sorry, Charlie."

Susan said, "The good news is there's no new damage to the well, but the sheriff has had no luck at all finding and arresting who did the crime."

Charlie's tone evened out as he continued. "I know who the scumbag is who did it. His name is Willard. He and his man have been a problem for us for a year. I'm sure they're in Kansas. Hopefully, Bailey Muldoon and his guys can go up there and find 'em."

Rice shook his head. "It sounds like a real problem. But you said you knew who was likely behind this, right?"

"Right, and we need to catch him or his thug red-handed. Willard pays people to do his dirty work."

Susan said, "Okay, let's get the waiter over here and order. We need to find this Maple Ridge area. I want to see some beautiful homes."

***

Before leaving the hotel, they got a city map from the concierge, then they climbed into the Cadillac to explore Tulsa.

Charlie said, "Getty told me Maple Ridge is south of downtown."

Susan looked at the map and said, "We need to go over to Main, about three blocks west, and then south for a mile or two and go west at 21st Street. A few streets over, we turn south on Madison Avenue into the neighborhood."

It took about five minutes to get to 21st and Madison.

Charlie turned south onto Madison Avenue, and they started seeing a few occupied homes and some under construction. The houses sat on large plots of land, and Getty had said oil money probably paid for most of them.

Susan said, "This is a nice neighborhood like Ward Estates in Kansas City. There are more homes north of 21st. Let's turn around and drive into there and have a look."

Rice said, "I noticed those homes, too, from where we turned. I'm amazed at the craftsmanship I'm seeing."

Charlie drove across 21st Street and into a neighborhood with more than a dozen large estates within a few blocks. The builder of these homes had used a mixture of styles, but they shared one characteristic: each was grand and made a powerful statement.

Charlie pulled over and stopped at 1030 East 18th to look at the house and yard. He said, "This place tells a story. To me, it says I'm livin' my dream. I know we could buy this house right now, and Tulsa is where we should live to wheel and deal in the oil business. If we move here, we need to live in this neighborhood."

Rice said, "This neighborhood says there's a lot of money in Tulsa. These homes go on for blocks. These are larger than those in some parts of the Country Club district. The Wards Estates area where you live is like this. Your place is larger than this one we are sitting at."

Charlie asked, "Are you interested in puttin' an office here and buildin' custom homes and estates?"

"I would like to investigate it. It does appear there is a market for it, and we already have the Townsley outfit down here to support us."

They explored for another few hours then returned to the hotel for lunch.

At the table, Charlie said, "Rice, take all the time required to find out what you need to put together a proposal for establishin' an office of Strawberry Hill Construction here in Tulsa. It's not somethin' we need to do immediately. I want you to have a crew here to support Bunk as we begin creatin' our refinin' capability. I hope it starts soon. You may need to stay here a while longer."

Rice pushed himself away from the table and said, "The pork chops tasted good. I need to call my office because you've given me some more work. Let me know what's happening with the refineries. If nothing's happening soon, I'll return to Kansas City this weekend."

Charlie replied, "Makes sense."

Susan asked Charlie, "Are you done? If so, let's go to our suite. You can work and make your calls from there, and I can get more comfortable."

"Sure, Sweetheart. Let's go."

***

As they walked in the door, the telephone rang. Charlie picked up the receiver. "Hello. Charles Kelly."

"Charlie, it's Hank again. Bailey Muldoon, Jim, and I had a drink at the Arcade Hotel. Willard's still up to his old tricks but doing it in Kansas. He's managed to stay one step ahead of Pinkerton and the law. Bailey said they'll stay after him, and he's still usin' the Arcade as his headquarters in case ya need him."

"Thanks, Hank. Tell Jim hello for me, and you two drive safely to Duncan."

"I'll still call you tonight when we get there. It should take us about five or six hours."

"Okay, Hank. I'll feel better if ya do. Goodbye."

Susan asked, "Who were you talking to?"

"Hank called from Burbank. The pump at the well's still workin', and it appears no additional vandalism is happenin' in that area. He had talked with Bailey Muldoon, and there are some similar crimes up in Kansas, so Willard may be up there. Hank and Jim should be headin' to Duncan now."

Her face turned serious as Susan said, "I know I said this before, but we must get that asshole Willard behind bars."

Chapter Thirty-Nine
Corporate Strategy
September 1919

CHARLIE SAT IN THE front room of their suite as Susan walked into the room. She dripped water on the hardwood floors as she dried her hair and said, "What are you doing, Sweetheart? It looks like you're deep in thought."

"I'm making a list of things needin' attention as soon as I or we can get to them. Did you realize we have over a dozen things goin' on right now?"

"I hadn't stopped to think about it, but it doesn't surprise me. We're about as busy as possible."

"It's true. I'm glad Hank called last night. He and Jim are meetin' with Erle Halliburton this mornin'. We should hear from Hank or Jim sometime after lunch with their report on the deal's progress. I sure want in the oil field cementin' business by the end of the year."

Susan turned to return to the bathroom. She hesitated and looked back. "I would like to spend some time this afternoon talking about what you've got listed."

"I would like to. There's a lot to discuss. I'll finish puttin' the list together. You may have some ideas I haven't thought of when we talk, and we'll add them to the list."

They called and had room service bring lunch up to the room.

Susan asked, "Charlie, do you have the list ready? I'm ready to talk, Sweetheart."

"I'm ready. There's no order; I just wrote them down as I thought of them."

"Okay, let's start."

"First is finalizin' the purchase of the refineries in Cushing and puttin' the financial backin' in place for Bunk and his team to draw on as needed."

Susan leaned in. "I don't know what you've read in the Kramer by-laws and policies, but my father set it up so each company within the Group would never let their cash reserves fall below ten percent of the company's value. So, the banking system must have around $200 million in liquid cash reserves. They won't have all of it sitting somewhere, not making money, but they would not tie it up in real estate or something requiring a significant transaction to get to the asset. My father always had an additional reserve held at the Group level similarly. The Presidents do not know this, but if their collective value is the $5.9 billion we estimated, there's about $500 million in reserve managed by me and you with the help of Uncle Curt."

Charlie's jaw dropped as he leaned back. "I had no idea, Susan. Why haven't we discussed this reserve before?"

"I didn't intentionally keep it from you. Since we married, there has not been a decision to make regarding the reserve fund. After acquiring the Texas banks a few months back, Gordon wouldn't have enough in his reserves to buy Exchange National, even if we had wanted to buy it from Sinclair at this time. We likely would need to give him some support from the Group level. You and I would make the decision together."

Charlie pulled himself together and said, "Okay, I see what you mean. Then the $250,000 to $300,000 spent on refineries and pipelines is nothin' compared to what we have in reserve. But it's still a lot of money, and we must carefully use it."

"I agree; you're not mad at me, are you?"

"A little. Ya can't keep things from me, Honey."

"I'm sorry. You're right; I should have shared that information months ago. I'm surprised Father hadn't shared it with you. And to your point, he often said he treats a dollar bill like real money because it is. What's next on the list?"

"The Halliburton deal's next. I hope to hear from Hank sometime this afternoon. Jim negotiated a potential deal over the phone. It should amount to a purchase of ten machines with five coming to us with some trainin'. Hank can write them a check if everythin' goes well. The estimated cost is under $25,000."

"Well, Charlie, we've spent about $320,000 so far. I'm pleased, looking at what we're getting. What's next?"

"The new quarry at Sapulpa. Zane was supposed to meet with them to close the deal. He estimated about $20,000 to buy it. I told him to buy it even if he had to go above his estimate but to keep it down as much as possible."

"Won't we make a lot of money from the quarry?"

"Yes, but it takes a lot of money to get the cement product out of there, so the number of people who could buy it is limited. I hope we don't have a competitor bidding against us.

The waiter from the Topaz arrived with their food for lunch.

Charlie sat down after placing the food and drinks so they could reach them. "Next is the bankin' deal with Sinclair."

Susan said, "Charlie, it's in Harry's hands right now, isn't it?"

"Yes. Exchange National focuses on supportin' the oil business, but it has other commercial clients. You and Gordon looked at their books; what did you think?"

Susan sipped tea. "Harry and his fellow investors have done a good job over the past ten years. They bought a failing Farmers National and have created a profitable asset."

"I agree. It's up to Harry to make the deal work. Next on the list is lookin' into the oil business in California and Texas. Getty's goin' to California soon, and I hear there is activity out in west Texas we might need to explore."

Susan leaned back and crossed her arms. "Have you ever been to California? I went out there with my father when I was about sixteen. Los Angeles is a pretty place. We enjoyed the trip. I assume you may send Hank out there. He needs to get some more wells started somewhere, right?"

Charlie swallowed his first bite of sandwich and said, "It's the question we need to answer. Hank has said we need to look into Seminole and even Garvin County in Oklahoma but agreed with Getty; California looks great for oil. He's our expert, and he's just one guy."

"Charlie, let's invite him back down to the ranch and spend some time building a strategy. We need experts in every part of the oil business, and each of them needs staff they can manage. We have the ideas, and we have the financial resources. What we need is the people to help us reach our goals."

Charlie looked her in the eyes and said, "You're amazin'. You're sweet and so beautiful. You're so smart and decisive and have a wonderful way with words. I have to step back from time to time and catch my breath. I'm so thankful you're my wife."

"Oh, Charlie, quit it. I sometimes get carried away with myself. You're the special one."

Charlie grinned. "If you say so. I know I'm very comfortable with you and see you sometimes intimidate powerful men. We've discussed this before, so I won't go through it now."

Susan picked up the list. "You do have this Willard situation on the list.

Good. I think we should investigate the creation of a security company. We could use it to support our banks, other businesses, and the oil business."

Charlie nodded. "You're thinkin' along the same lines as me. I want to meet with the Pinkerton lead on this Willard case. He's the guy we had at Yale. I might offer him a chance to lead a security business for us. I'll want to know more about his background first."

Susan reached over and squeezed Charlie's bicep. "Honey, I'll leave it to you to handle the security issues, but we need to determine who we trust in that world slowly. By the way, I bet Boss has some ideas for you about expanding the ranches; let's talk to him next week." She pointed to the list. "And I see purchasing a home in Tulsa on this list. Are we going to buy another house? Are you not happy with the ranch we just bought?"

Charlie smiled. "I'd rather sit on our Maple Ridge patio than in a hotel room. If we're goin' to run Kelly Oil out of anywhere, Tulsa makes more sense than a cattle ranch in the middle of Pottawatomie County, don't ya think?"

"I think so. When are we going to make the decision?"

Charlie said, "Not today, but I think we'll be here a lot more than six months to a year as we get everythin' finalized and workin' as smoothly as our bankin' is with Gordon. At some point, this may feel as much like home as anywhere."

Susan leaned back, sighed, and said, "I could see us being here more than the ranch and Kansas City, so I'm open to buying a house sometime soon."

"I have addin' a construction company here in Tulsa on the list. Let's talk to Rice about it tonight. The final thing is restructurin' the Kramer Group. I mean, formally puttin' Kelly Oil, the ranches, and anything else we start under the organization. What do you think?"

Susan looked directly at Charlie. "I want to have this conversation with Uncle Curt sitting with us. I think doing it is the smartest thing we could do, and he can guide us through making a good decision and a legal one. Would we change the name?"

"I hadn't thought about it. The world knows the Kramer Group. I would be careful about losing the name recognition."

Susan smiled and said, "You're right; we need to be careful and keep it to honor my father's legacy. We meet in the dining room in a little over an hour. We better start getting ready."

Chapter Forty
Closed a Deal
September 1919

LATER, THE TELEPHONE RANG, and Charlie answered, "Hello, this is Charles."

"Charlie, it's Hank, and we got the deal, buddy. We'll have five units by November 30th. When they complete the equipment, they'll schedule trainin' for our people and deliver the units to our designated location."

"What's the cost, Hank?"

"$20,000, and that includes the ten percent overhead he wanted and training. Halliburton wanted $7,500 upfront and the balance at the end. I wrote them a check before they could change their mind. Jim wants to say something."

Charlie waited while Hank handed the phone to Jim.

"Charlie, this is Jim. Hank's great. They wanted to get more money out of him and push out the delivery date. Hank stood up and said, 'Well, we wasted our time coming down here. We won't waste any more.' He turned to leave, and they scrambled and gave us everything we wanted at a better deal than we had originally discussed. It's all in a notarized contract we'll bring back."

"Thanks, Jim. Yes, he's good. I assume you'll come back tomorrow?"

"We'll make it to Oklahoma City and stop for the night. We'll get back in Tulsa by lunch tomorrow."

"Come to the hotel, and we'll buy ya lunch. Drive safe."

Speaking from the bedroom, Susan said, "It sounded like good news. Was it Hank?"

"Yes, and Jim. The deal's closed. We got what we wanted from Halliburton at a bit lower than we had expected because Hank's good at negotiating. He always seems to know the right thing to do or say and when to do or say it."

Susan asked, "I guess we got all five machines for $22,000?"

"No, we got them for $20,000, and the deal includes training our crews. They estimate we'll have the machines by the end of the year."

"Great! Charlie, we have thirty minutes to get downstairs to meet our guys for dinner. It would be best if you took a shower. I'm almost ready."

"Okay, I'll be ready in fifteen minutes. I already know what I'll wear."

"What are you wearing? I'll lay it out for you."

"My beige seersucker suit, with a white shirt."

"I'm wearing the white off-the-shoulder cotton sundress."

As he turned on the shower, Charlie said, "You're beautiful in anything."

They arrived five minutes early, and the maître d' ushered them to their table in the private dining room. When Rice, Bunk, and Paul arrived a few minutes later, Charlie and Susan were surprised that Zane wasn't with them.

Susan held her arms out, welcoming everyone, and said, "Where's Zane? We expected him too."

Rice said, "I don't know..."

Charlie pointed toward the front door. "Here he comes now."

Zane rushed up to the group, sighed, and slowly shook his head as he said, "Sorry I'm late. As I was walking toward my office door to leave, a worker ran in the front door saying we had an employee hurt. I called for an ambulance and went to the quarry to see what happened. That was about an hour ago. I apologize."

Charlie said, "No apology necessary. Is your man okay?"

"He will be. He's at the Sapulpa Hospital. He took a serious fall, broke a leg, and scraped himself up. He fell into a deep pit. It took a while to get help to him and then get him out. I hate that we got this evening off on a negative note."

Susan pointed to the empty chairs and said, "Okay, everyone, sit, and let's order our drinks and food. Then we can have a business discussion. Afterward, we can stay and enjoy ourselves as we can get to know each other a little better, or if you need to, feel free to go."

Paul smiled and said, "Susan, you look amazing as always. Let me cover this tonight. I have much to discuss, so I want to do it."

Susan looked at Charlie, shrugged, turned back to Paul, and said, "Okay. Gentlemen, eat and drink up; Mr. J. Paul Getty's buying tonight."

The waiter came and took their orders. Rice, Bunk, and Zane ordered beers, while Charlie, Susan, and Paul ordered their usual bottle of cabernet.

Paul asked, "You two seem to spend a lot of time here. Have you arranged to lease the suite? I'm sorry, I don't mean to get too personal, but it's much cheaper than day-to-day or week-to-week. I would love to have you as neighbors."

Charlie responded, "No offense taken, Paul. We started discussin' it this week. We see a strong possibility of setting up an office here in Tulsa. We would need to have a place for us to live. Our best options are a suite at the hotel or purchasin' a home here in Tulsa."

Paul nodded and said, "A home, maybe something in Maple Ridge?"

Susan's eyes sparkled as she said, "Oh yes! I love the new street called Madison Avenue. The lots are like what we have in Kansas City."

Charlie said, "Our discussion tonight could have a lot of influence on what we decide to do about housing. I see Tulsa as the center of all things oil."

Paul looked serious for a moment. He focused on Charlie and said, "Tulsa is where things are happening and will for some time. It seems wise to have a permanent presence here. But Texas and California are important too. We'll talk more about this later this evening."

Their drinks arrived, and the waiter said, "I'm sorry for the delay in getting this to you. Your food's ready. It should only... Oh, wait; I see it coming now."

After everyone had their food, Susan said, "Okay, let's eat, and we'll start our business meeting after I finish eating." She laughed and said, "I know I'll finish last, and I don't talk with my mouth full."

Everyone enjoyed a laugh. Then they all dug in.

Everyone but Susan had finished in about ten minutes, so she said, "Charlie, it's time to get the meeting started. I'll finish up here shortly."

"Zane, why don't you start things off with an update on the quarry purchase."

"Glad to Charlie. The news is we purchased the quarry. I paid a little more than I'd hoped, but it's a good deal because we need the quarry to support the oil field cementing effort. We had an opposing bidder, and it drove up the price. He became agitated when I kept bidding against him. He intimidated several others to stop bidding with a look that would kill. I later found out he represented a company backed by the Chicago Outfit."

Charlie looked around the table and back to Zane, then said, "Good job. I'm glad you hung in there and got the quarry. But I've heard that those Chicago people may not let things rest, Zane. We shouldn't expect them to just go away. Don't worry; we have your back. Anythin' else?"

"No. I'll let you know if we have any repercussions."

"Okay, Rice, what do you have for us?"

"I don't have any cost figures for you, but I have spent enough time on this to know we need to create an office for Strawberry Hill in Tulsa. I've learned Tulsa is one of the fastest-growing cities in this part of the country. And many of the new people are people in business with money. I can have something set up here in less than ninety days."

"Send Susan and me a packet with your recommendation and those cost figures. My gut's sayin' go for it, but we'll wait for your packet. Bunk, you're next."

"This report's my first task as an employee of the Kramer Group. I'm happy to say it's a positive message. As you already know, we've agreed in principle to acquire the four refineries in Cushing and Mid-America Pipeline Company. There are some details to work out and put on contract. I told them you plan to come back to Cushing on Monday for other business. They agreed to meet at your convenience. They'll have all their ducks in a row so we can discuss the final details."

"And I'm happy to meet with them. Anything else, Bunk?"

"No. That's it."

"Rice, can ya stay over this weekend and join us in Cushing on Monday?"

"Sure, Charlie. Do you want me there for the refinery talk *and* the Abrams meeting?"

"Ya bet. And, Paul, what do you have to discuss?"

"I hear you have Pinkerton working for you and with the authorities in Burbank. I'm glad, but I'm considering selling out up there. I want to talk to you about it. I need to focus on California in the first part of next year. Can we meet tomorrow morning? We can talk then. Let's relax tonight and enjoy our wine."

Susan said, "What a great idea."

Chapter Forty-One
Maple Ridge
September 1919

GETTY ARRIVED THE NEXT morning to find Charlie and Susan pouring their second cup of coffee. "I hope you haven't been waiting long," Paul said.

Susan shook her head. "No, Paul, we've only been here long enough to enjoy a cup of coffee and wake up."

Charlie grinned and said, "Maybe she's awake. I'm not sure about me yet. The last bottle of wine we drank was probably one too many."

Paul looked away for a second, cleared his throat, then said, "Sorry, my fault. We'll not do it next time."

Susan giggled. "No one forced us to finish the bottle, so, Paul, it's not anyone's fault. Let's get the waiter over here and order."

As he poured another cup of coffee, Charlie asked, "Are ya ready to talk about Osage County?"

Paul reached for the carafe, and he said, "Absolutely. I talked about it briefly with Hank. It's not just because of this Willard fellow and the vandalism; I'm ready to move my focus to California. I think the California oil business is ready to explode. I want to be there when it does."

"What do you own in Osage County you're ready to sell?"

"I have ten thousand acres with mineral rights in the Shidler, Oklahoma area. Based on what Hank told me the other day, it's less than five miles from your Burbank well. I have drilled two wells, and they will produce for whoever buys me out. There's still a big field worth finding up there. But I want to go to California as soon as I can."

Susan didn't wait for Charlie, "How much do you need for it?"

"I want $20,000. The deal will include all the equipment and build-

218

ings. Everything up there goes with the land and minerals."

Charlie scratched his neck, smiled, and said, "Your price seems a little strong, but I'll tell you what I'll do. You come down to our ranch next week when Hank's there and help us plan our expansion into California, and I'll pay you the $20,000. Do we have a deal?"

"Your offer's fair, so it's a deal. I'm excited to discuss California with you guys. I'll come down there next week."

Susan said, "We'll have Uncle Curt contact you and draw up the papers. We're in Cushing tomorrow night for some meetings on Monday. The business may require that we stay there for several days. We'll call you from Cushing when we leave for the ranch."

"Okay, I'm here, or I'll leave word with the desk where you can find me. I've got a call coming from my mother about a project she wants me involved in, so I better go. Have a great weekend and productive meetings in Cushing. I'll see you next week."

After Paul left, Charlie looked at Susan. "Let's drive over to Maple Ridge again. Several construction crews were workin', and there's a sales office south of the corner of Madison and 21st. I want to check it out."

"Sure, Sweetheart. I need to go back to the suite and freshen up. Then I'm ready when you are."

Charlie and Susan drove down Madison Avenue, and the elegance of the completed homes on the street impressed them. On an open lot was the sales office building with a sign which read Stebbins Company. Someone had parked an expensive-looking car next to the office, so Charlie stopped. They got out, knocked on the front door, and heard, "Please come in."

They stepped inside, and a man, about forty-five years old, with a mustache and a friendly smile, sat behind a desk. He rose and offered his hand to Charlie. "I'm Grant Stebbins; welcome to Maple Ridge."

Charlie stepped aside. "Thank you. We're the Kellys. I'm Charles, and this is Susan."

"Please have a seat. Can I get you something cool to drink?"

Susan raised her hand and nodded. "A glass of water if you have it."

He walked over to an icebox and brought back a cold glass of ice water. "Here you go, Mrs. Kelly."

"Susan, please. May I call you Grant?"

"Please do, and Charles—"

"Charlie, my friends call me Charlie."

"Charlie, it is. Are you folks looking to find a new home?"

Before Charlie could respond, Susan said, "We have a home in Kansas City and a pair of ranches in Pottawatomie County here in Oklahoma. We're considering adding a place here in Tulsa. This area looks promising."

Charlie had difficulty keeping a grin from breaking out across his face. He added, "We're beginnin' to see we may need to live in Tulsa. Like some of our friends, we may buy a house rather than operate from the Hotel Tulsa. We'll likely have some social events, and we'd also like to create a sanctuary so we can leave our business at the office."

"If you don't mind me asking, who are your friends you mentioned?"

Susan replied, "Harry Sinclair, J. Paul Getty, and Bill Skelly, and we're meeting others."

Grant quickly responded, "Mr. Skelly and his wife Gertrude are discussing buying the lot at 21st and Madison to build their permanent home. You folks could be neighbors if you move in here." Stebbins hesitated, looked at each of them as his face took on a soft demeanor, and said, "I don't mean to offend you, but you're young compared to my typical clients. Our clients building in Maple Ridge must build on a large lot and build a large house. The total costs run from $75,000 to more than $250,000. Maybe you should look at another area for your needs."

Susan raised her left hand to quiet Charlie and responded, "I'm sorry; this is our fault. We didn't adequately introduce ourselves. My husband's Charles Ashley Kelly and I'm Susan Elizabeth Kramer-Kelly. We are the sole owners of the Kramer Group in Kansas City. You have heard of us, haven't you?"

"Y-Yes, ma'am. I... have h-heard of your company." Grant gathered himself and continued. "I'm sorry, but we don't get many people your age—"

Charlie stopped him. "Grant, we understand. As Susan said, we should have said somethin' at the beginnin'. We have a new oil company growin' fast, and we'll likely place its home office in Tulsa. That's why we're lookin' here. The homes we see in Maple Ridge remind us of our home on Westover Road in Kansas City."

Susan asked, "If we wanted to build here, what's the process?"

Grant got up from his chair and walked around to a mechanical drawing mounted on the wall depicting the layout of Maple Ridge. He pointed to the drawing and said, "This is the area. You would select the lot, and you can use your architect and construction company or work through me. I have several on retainer and could arrange for you to meet with them and select whomever you want. Though, you must meet certain requirements."

Susan said, "We own a construction company, but we might want to sit down with one of your architects if and when we decide to get serious. If we wanted to reserve a lot, what's the cost?"

"Susan, it's $10,000, to hold the lot for no more than six months. We'll apply it to the purchase of the lot. We require you to start construction by then. We see it taking six months to a year to complete construction. There have been a few who take longer."

Charlie said, "I would like to go tour some of the lots, and do you have any homes for sale? I thought it possible someone might need to sell because of an unexpected tragedy causing a move out of Tulsa."

Grant looked a little surprised and pleased as he responded, "Ironically, I received a call from the folks who had planned to move into their new home next month. An emergency is forcing them to move back to New York City. Would you like to look at it?"

Susan said, "Yes, can we look at the house now?"

"I have a key. There's a small amount of clean-up I'm overseeing for the owners. It's only about a block from here. We can walk there if you like?"

Charlie smiled. "I need to walk some stiffness out, so yes, let's walk."

As the property came into view, Susan said, "Charlie, it's the house I said reminded me of our home in Kansas City. Grant, how large is this place?"

"It's fifty-nine hundred square feet. It sits on almost three-quarters of an acre of land. They have done a lot of brickwork, and there's a pool in a very private backyard. I'm amazed at the expense they went to on the landscaping. It already looks mature."

Charlie couldn't wait to ask, "What are the owners goin' to want for the place?"

Susan said, "Honey, can we look at the house first?"

"Sweetheart, I guess we're here, so let's look."

Grant walked ahead of them and unlocked the front door. He stepped aside and let Susan walk in first.

"Oh my, it's lovely. Look at the staircase, Honey, which winds like ours at Westover. Look at this beautiful sitting area. We could do so much with this."

She continued walking through the room and into a beautiful office.

Charlie said, "This would work perfectly for my office."

Susan looked at him and said, "Did I hear a little excitement in your voice?"

"Honey, the place is nice. I want the first house we buy to be somethin' we want and not settle for less."

Grant asked, "Did you have a size in mind or a minimum number of bedrooms?"

Susan said, "I want something similar to our home in Kansas City. This house is smaller, but it does remind me of home. Oh, Charlie, look at the pool."

They stepped into the backyard, and Susan said, "It's private. I love this. The house surrounds the yard and pool area. It's like a courtyard; it's amazing."

Charlie looked at Grant and said, "I thought we would buy in here, but I figured we would wait another six months. We'll probably take this if the kitchen, bedrooms, and baths measure up to what we've seen."

They finished the tour and were walking toward the office when Susan looked at Charlie and said, "Honey, I—"

"We're buyin' the house. I knew it at the swimmin' pool. I like it too. It's smaller than Westover, but it meets our needs, and the patio and pool area are perfect for us. My only concern is there's only a two-stall garage."

"We can get by with two cars, can't we? The staff quarters are huge in their separate wing, with three bedrooms and baths upstairs. The kitchen's amazing. The staff quarters area shares a wall with the garage. We could take the wall out someday and add another stall to the garage."

"No, two automobiles are enough anyway. So, you want the house, right?"

"I do. We would live less than a block from the Skelly's, and living on Madison Avenue sounds nice."

Charlie looked at Grant and said, "What cash offer buys the place this afternoon?"

Grant swallowed, smiled, and said, "I have an idea, but they didn't give me a figure this morning. Can you give me a few minutes to call them? If you don't mind, I'll tell them you can write a check for the full amount today and you want a closing date as soon as possible. They're leaving the area in a few days, so you're in the perfect situation. Do you have an offer you want to make?"

Charlie said, "You mentioned people are spending as low as $50,000 and as much as $250,000 on homes here. From what I can see, this house is not the largest but among the larger houses. I'd say $175,000 is a fair offer, and we can leave them a check for the full amount with you today. We'll swap a cashier's check for it at closing."

Grant said, "I think you may have bought a house. Your offer's fair. Can you give me some time?"

Susan said, "We'll get a Coca-Cola somewhere and return in a half-hour. Okay?"

"A half-hour is fine."

Charlie pulled the Cadillac back into its parking spot at Grant's office in thirty minutes, almost to the second.

Susan bounded into the office and asked, "Well? Is it ours?"

Grant smiled and said, "Yes. At first, they wantedfor $200,000. If they could have waited six months, they might have gotten it. I told them your offer was fair and covered their expenses, including some debt. They would have the place sold and some money in their pocket. I'll get this closed in ten days. They need it, and I gather you want it. Right?"

Susan said, "We do. Today's the 30th. You set a closing date of Tuesday, October 7th, and we'll be here. Do you need a check for $175,000 to hold for the seller?"

"No, but I need you to sign a formal offer sheet and leave me a check for an appropriate amount as earnest money."

They signed a check for $17,500 and the paperwork for the purchase. They would own the estate at 2110 Madison Avenue, Tulsa, Oklahoma, in a few days.

Chapter Forty-Two
Celebration
September 1919

CHARLIE AND SUSAN WANTED to celebrate after the Maple Ridge trip and purchasing the Madison Avenue house. Charlie put the newspaper down in their suite at the Hotel Tulsa and said, "Let's invite our friends and workers to join us for dinner and celebrate."

Susan walked over, sat beside him, hugged his neck, and kissed him before responding, "Oh yes, Sweetheart, let's have a party. Invite Harry, Bill and their wives, Paul, and all our company people here for the meetings."

Charlie called the Topaz Room and reserved the private dining room for the evening. Then he called the group. He didn't tell them anything other than this was his and Susan's last night in town for a while, and they wanted to get together.

Susan asked, "Do you have a favorite outfit you want me to wear? Since we're celebrating, I thought I would wear something special."

"You look great in anythin'. There's one you haven't worn for a while I like a lot. Your beige slacks with the thin white silk button-up blouse. You didn't have a camisole under the blouse the last time you wore it, and you looked gorgeous."

"I have the outfit with me, so I'll wear it tonight. You can match me with your beige slacks and white shirt."

"Okay, we'll look great together."

Susan said, "Yes, we will. Let's get to the dining room early to set it up how we want. There's at least nine of us, and I want our workers to meet and talk with Paul, Harry, and Bill."

"Good idea, Beautiful. We have a little over an hour, and I need a shower. Care to join me?"

Susan gave Charlie a demur smile. "I thought you'd never ask."

***

Charlie looked up, and Harry, Bill, and Paul were walking into the dining room. Susan stepped forward and said, "I'm so glad you're here tonight. Harry, Bill, I don't see your wives."

Harry said, "She's in Kansas and couldn't get here tonight." He grinned, "Hey, Charlie made this sound like a party."

Bill added, "Gertrude's visiting her mother and sends her regrets. I know Harry and I aren't kids anymore, but we like a good time."

Paul leaned in and quietly said, "You look wonderful, Susan." He turned, looked at Charlie, and teased, "Sorry buddy, you're still homely." He laughed and squeezed Charlie's shoulder.

Charlie said, "I'll git ya, Getty." He looked at them, "Fellas, we wanted ya here tonight. You'll see why later."

Bill said, "So, you're going to share something special with us?"

"We'll see; go find your seat; we've put name cards out," said Susan.

The others straggled in and got seated around the large table.

A few minutes later, Charlie stood and welcomed everyone. "Susan and I wanted to invite you here tonight for two or three reasons. It's our last night in Tulsa for a while. Several of us are travelin' to Cushing tomorrow on business, which will also prepare us for the trip. We'll try to minimize business as much as we can. But the main reason, I'll let Susan share with ya."

Susan stood and shouted excitedly, "We bought a new house here in Tulsa today! It's on Madison Avenue in the Maple Ridge area. We're thrilled to own a home here."

Bill asked, "Is the house finished? What's the address?"

Charlie replied, "There are a few small things to finish. Maybe two days' work by one man. Our address is 2110 S. Madison. Grant Stebbins said you and Gertrude are building close by."

Bill said, "I believe we're neighbors. You're right across the street from where we are building our house."

"Grant mentioned you're building a large home. I can't wait to see it. According to him, ours is smaller than yours and smaller than our home in Kansas City, but we will love it. It has a nice pool. We love to swim."

The room had erupted when Susan shared the news and now settled down to conversation level. Two waiters took orders for food and drink.

Harry leaned over to Charlie and said, "I'm happy for you. I continue to rent a suite at the hotel. My wife and children are in Independence, Kansas. I'm looking forward to moving us to New York next year. So, I'll not join you on Madison, but it's where I would buy here in Tulsa."

Charlie said, "Susan and I are excited to have found a place we're sure to love. We close on the deal in about a week. As we said, we're headin' to Cushing tomorrow for meetings on Thursday with our team and the contractors building the storefront we'll put our new department store in."

Harry wiped his mouth with his napkin, "I guess everything went well down there regarding the refineries and pipeline acquisitions?"

Charlie took a sip of wine, "Yep, it went about as good as we could have hoped. Where are ya on the bank acquisition?"

Sinclair smiled, "I'll have it done by the end of next week."

"Good; as I mentioned, we'll come back here next week to close on the house. You send Curt the figures, and we'll have him draw up the contracts, and we can sign them next week."

"Sounds doable. I have all the telephone numbers and addresses I need."

Susan joined them and said, "Harry, we need to have you and Elizabeth down to the ranch sometime soon. I think you will like it. Paul's coming down next week."

Charlie said, "Speakin' of Paul, he and Hank have been standin' off to themselves talkin' ever since Hank got here. I wonder what they're plannin' this time?"

Harry said, "Paul told me he has a lot of respect for Hank. I think he wishes they were partners. Kelly Oil has a good lead man. I'm convinced you have a knack for talent evaluation. What's amazing to me is how you find such loyal staff."

Susan quickly said, "Charlie's genuine. He's not a game player and is willing to share the benefits of hard work with those who share in the work. It creates a strong and long-lasting bond."

"You two are figuring a lot out at a young age, but you both have a lot of natural ability. I see you becoming the next Rockefeller, Rothschild, or Vanderbilt dynasty."

Susan responded, "We certainly want their success, but Charlie wants it done differently. Each of those families made their wealth in one area of the economy. I agree with my smart husband, and we'll continue investing in several segments of our economy."

Harry said, "I think he's right, and your father agreed. I'm hoping two areas are enough for me. I'll keep working hard and look for ways to grow what I have."

Susan said, "I'm looking forward to growing through banking with you."

Skelly had listened to the last part of the conversation and said, "I'm still hoping to show you my aviation plans sometime soon. Charlie, you seemed interested."

"Bill, I'm interested. As I told Harry, we're back next week. I hope we can get together then and talk. We have our hands in a lot right now, but we still need to talk about your vision. As I said, I'm interested."

"Good, then I hope to hear from you soon."

The party continued, and Charlie told the group going to Cushing to meet for breakfast, packed and ready to leave.

Susan, popular as always, engrossed the room with her beauty, personality, and wit. The white, thin, snug-fitting blouse perfectly displayed every inch of her curves. Charlie watched as her beauty and charms captivated everyone in the room, including the hotel staff.

Back in their suite, they packed to move out in the morning.

Charlie raised his voice a little to talk to Susan in the next room and said, "What a great day. We started wondering how we might live and operate out of Tulsa and found the perfect solution. Tonight, we solidified ourselves with our new friends and our employees."

Susan was naked when she walked out of the bathroom. "You were magnificent today as we negotiated for our house and tonight with Harry and Bill. They want to do business with us, and the main reason is you, Darling. I love and appreciate you so much."

She gently pushed him onto the sofa. Charlie was happy to take a break from packing.

Chapter Forty-Three
Trouble in Cushing
October 1919

CHARLIE AND SUSAN DROVE alone in their Cadillac and arrived in Cushing to a warm welcome by Anson Peabody, Chester Abrams, and Jess Kelly at the Cushing Hotel. Sam Holder came later, and the group walked to the construction site and found the project nearing completion. The only thing left was installing the fixtures and stocking the shelves.

Charlie looked at Rice walking toward them. "Rice, I'm glad you've made it. Whattaya think?"

Rice said, "This looks interesting." He smiled. "How about letting me and Sam have a few minutes together."

"Go ahead, gentlemen, we'll meet you back at the hotel restaurant in a few."

Once Rice and Sam had joined Charlie and Susan at the hotel restaurant, Rice said, "I'm very impressed with the quality of work performed by Sam's crew. We also discussed the idea of some future projects across Oklahoma our two companies could work on together."

Sam nodded. "I look forward to exploring this. It will involve commercial sites across the state. I've had to pass up work I didn't have the resources to do. With Rice's help, we'll bid on most everything."

Susan looked at Rice and Charlie and said, "Cushing continues to give us new opportunities. I'm thrilled to hear this."

Charlie stood and offered his hand to Sam. "Chester and Anson showed us their progress, and we're plannin' a party to celebrate it and our successes with Kelly Oil's growth tomorrow afternoon. Now we have a third reason to have the party."

***

Charlie looked at his watch. "Susan, it's 3:45. I want to start the party with everyone as soon as possible. I don't see Anson and the folks involved with the store. I would love an early dinner and get to bed so we're outta here at sunrise tomorrow mornin'."

She replied, "I'll find Anson, Chester, and Jess. Rice is over there." She pointed across the room.

"Great, I'll go grab Rice, and we'll wait with the rest of the folks." He walked over and told Rice they would start the party as soon as Susan returned with the department store folks.

A few minutes after 4:00, Charlie became concerned. He walked out to the lobby and didn't see Susan. Anson stepped off the elevator with Jess beside him.

Charlie asked, "Have you seen Susan?"

Anson replied, "No; she's not with you? She called me, and I apologized and said we would come to the banquet room immediately."

Charlie walked to the registration desk and asked, "You know my wife, don't you?"

The young blond-haired clerk said, "Yes, sir, she was here about twenty minutes ago. She used the house phone over there. A man joined her. Then they were gone. I found this envelope on our counter a few minutes later. I have no idea who left it. It's addressed to you."

"Okay, thank you. You didn't see where they went?"

"No, sir. I had started to register a new arrival."

Charlie nodded, turned around, looked at Anson, and said, "This isn't like Susan. I wonder what's goin' on?"

Jesse said, "What's in the envelope, Charlie?"

"Probably nothing."

Anson said, "Open it and see. We're just waiting for Susan."

Charlie opened it, read the first line, shuddered, and shouted, "Holy shit!"

Anson said, "What's wrong? What's it say?"

Charlie's anger almost overwhelmed him as he crumpled the letter and threw it to the floor.

Initially startled at Charlie's response, Anson stepped over, retrieved the letter, and read it aloud.

"We have your wife. We'll not hurt her if you follow these instructions perfectly. We want $2 million delivered at exactly midnight tomorrow. We'll leave a note on the bench telling you where and when you can pick up your wife. NO POLICE and no games. Follow these instructions, and no one, especially your wife, will be hurt."

Charlie stood very still, breathing heavily, appearing like he could explode at any moment.

Jess reached over and placed his hand on Charlie's shoulder. "Brother, it'll be alright. We'll get Susan back safely. Let's go back with the group."

Charlie nodded. They returned to the banquet room. Jess guided Charlie to a chair.

Anson raised his hands to gather everyone's attention. "There has been an emergency, and Charlie has canceled the party. He's limiting the group to remain here to himself, me, Jess, Chester, and Rice. The rest of you need to go, and we'll reschedule the party."

After the room emptied, Anson looked at Charlie and said, "What can we do to help?"

By this time, Charlie had gathered his emotions. He focused on controlling his anger and thinking as clearly as possible.

"I need to make two phone calls. One to Uncle Curt and then to Pinkerton. Stay here, and I'll come back soon."

Jess said, "Where are ya goin'?"

"To our suite to make the calls."

"Ya don't need to be alone. I'm goin' with ya."

"Oh, alright. Let's go."

In the suite, Charlie called Curt's office, knowing he typically worked late.

It felt like an eternity for Charlie to wait as the operator connected to the Kramer office in Kansas City and then for the switchboard operator to connect him to Curt's office. By the time Curt picked up, Charlie was about to jump out of his seat.

"Hello, Curt Schlegell speaking."

"Curt, it's Charlie. Are you sittin' down? I have somethin' I need to tell ya. It's hard for me to say this. Someone has kidnapped Susan, and they want $2 million for her return."

"Oh my God. Charlie, what happened?"

Charlie briefly explained what had happened, what the hotel clerk had told him, and about receiving the ransom letter. It was hard to control his anger as he recounted the events.

After he finished, Curt said, "Charlie, of course, the money's no problem, but do you trust Susan won't get hurt or killed anyway?"

"No, I don't. The hoodlums said no police, but I'm callin' Pinkerton after we finish this call."

"Charlie, I will call our Attorney General here in Missouri. He's a good man and has been helpful in the past, though not on something this serious. But he can reach out to the Oklahoma AG.

"Okay, but I'm in charge and lookin' for support and advice. My biggest concern's nothin' happens to Susan, so I'll make the final decisions, period."

"Agreed. You have the most at stake here and have already handled more than your share of tough situations. I'll get the money wired to you. Where are you?"

"I'm at the Cushing Hotel in Cushing, Oklahoma. I'll use this place as my headquarters for now. I need to call Pinkerton, so I'll call you at home later."

Charlie placed the call to the Pinkerton office in Oklahoma City. "Hello, this is Charles Kelly. I need to contact Bailey Muldoon as soon as possible. How can I reach him?"

The Pinkerton person said, "I have not heard from Mr. Muldoon today." Charlie did his best not to yell at the man on the other end of the phone. "His assignment log," the man continued, "shows he's in Ponca City today. If he's there, he's at the Jenns-Marie Hotel."

Charlie thanked the man and immediately tapped the hook on his phone several times to clear the line and get the operator. He placed the call to the hotel in Ponca City. Charlie breathed a sigh of relief when the front desk clerk said Muldoon had checked into the hotel and put the call through to his room. The phone rang several times, and Charlie began to worry Muldoon had gone to dinner or something when, finally, he picked up the phone.

"Hello, Muldoon speaking."

"Muldoon, it's Charlie Kelly. I need you in Cushing as soon as you can get here."

"Whoa, what's going on?"

"Susan's been kidnapped. I need your help."

"Of course, but I'm workin' the Willard case up here. Shit, listen to me. I'll be there in two to three hours. Where in town are you?"

"The Cushing Hotel, in the banquet room or the Presidential Suite."

"I'll pack and drive directly there."

"Thanks, Muldoon."

Charlie and Jess rejoin the others in the banquet room. Everyone was seated around a table, and Jess said, "I see they brought in coffee. Want some Charlie?"

Charlie was shaking with nerves. "Uh, yep, sounds good." He gathered himself again, forced a smile, and said, "We've gotta long night ahead of us, folks. We all better tank up on coffee."

The man from the registration desk ran into the room. "Mr. Kelly, there's another call for you."

Charlie went to the lobby. The clerk pointed to a phone on the wall. "Hello, this is Charles Kelly."

"It's Hank. After you guys left, I drove to Burbank. When I arrived, I found our crew workin' hard to repair damage to our holding tank. Someone shot it full of holes last night. We're lucky the tank wasn't full. The truck had come and done a pickup earlier in the day. One more thing, I don't think Willard did this. Somebody painted a message on the tank. It said: 'Get out of Oklahoma and go back to Kansas City.' Does that make any sense to you?"

Charlie said, "Damn it, what next?"

"Charlie, are you okay? What's wrong?"

"Susan's been kidnapped. I'm workin' to git the money here, and by the way, ya won't find Muldoon in Ponca. He's on his way here."

"Kidnapping Susan does sound like Willard."

"It does."

"I'm on my way too, Charlie. I've got things goin' here. We can handle bullet holes and this threat later. Goodbye."

Charlie went back into the banquet room and was greeted with questions.

Charlie raised his hands and said, "Hold on. It wasn't the kidnappers; it was Hank. We've had another act of vandalism up at Burbank. He's got it under control and is headin' this way." He wrung his hands as he said, "I must have messed up somethin' awful to put Susan and others in this kind of jeopardy."

Anson said, "Charlie, none of this is your fault. And we'll figure something out."

The group drank coffee and continued discussing different what-ifs. Charlie had the hotel bring in two phones so they could answer calls in the banquet room.

It was nearly 8:00 before Muldoon arrived and joined Charlie and the others in the banquet room. Over his first cup of coffee, Charlie shared the ransom note with him. He read it in silence, then he asked, "Any news? Has anything changed?"

Charlie leaned back and shook his head. "Nothing. I would have thought we'd git a call or somethin' to ask us if we got the note about Susan and the ransom."

Muldoon nodded. "You should, and soon. We need to get them to talk as long as possible when they call. The longer they gab, the more likely they'll slip up and give us some clues about their whereabouts."

Elbows on the table, Charlie said, "Why do you say soon?"

"They know you'll need time to gather up the money. There weren't clear instructions in the note, so they'll have to give them to you. They know you are here at the hotel, so they will probably call here. In these situations, I advise my client to pay the ransom."

"The money's not the problem. I'll have it by the morning. But I don't trust those assholes."

Muldoon took a sip of coffee. "Good, you shouldn't. They know you've got access to money. If it's just the money they want, they'll make sure Susan's safe and can't identify any of them. They'll treat it as a business transaction. But if they have darker intentions, and want to hurt you directly, then Susan is in danger no matter if they get the money or not. That's what concerns me."

One of the phones rang. Charlie quickly picked up the receiver. "Kelly."

"Did you get our letter, Mr. Kelly?"

Charlie did not recognize the voice.

"Yes, I got your note. I've arranged for the money."

"Good. You will deliver the money to the train station on Broadway at midnight tomorrow. Alone. Place it on the bench outside the front entrance to the station and walk away. Somebody will pick it up. Five minutes after midnight, you will walk back to the bench. We'll leave a note there telling you where you can find your wife."

"Let me speak to Susan."

"No dice, cowboy. You got just one job here: to get us the money. Or we'll hurt her."

Charlie gripped the phone's body so tight it looked like it would snap in two. "If I don't know she's safe, then I ain't bringin' the money. You said you wouldn't harm her, so prove it, and you'll get your money."

There was a pause, and Charlie could make out muffled noises, maybe someone giving orders to someone else. Then he heard, "Charlie?"

"Susan!" Relief flooded into Charlie like oil gushing from a well. "Are you okay, Darlin'? Have they hurt you?"

"They haven't hurt me. Did you contact Uncle Will about the money?"

"Uncle... Who? Susan, what did ya say?"

"Make sure Uncle Will brings the money on the train—"

Suddenly there was a scream from Susan and the sound of something hitting the floor. Then the line went dead.

Charlie pounded on the hook and yelled into the mouthpiece, "Susan! Susan!"

Finally, he set the phone down, replaced the receiver on the hook, and sat back in his chair.

Muldoon asked, "What happened?"

"I spoke to Susan, but then something happened, and she screamed, and the line went dead."

"What did she say?" asked Jess.

"She asked if I had contacted Uncle Will about the money, and he needed to bring it on the train. It doesn't make any sense to me."

"Isn't Susan's uncle named Curt?" asked Jess.

"Yes, and she would know he wouldn't bring the money here. Not on the train."

"Did they say anything about delivering the money?" Muldoon asked.

"They said I was to deliver it to a bench outside the Broadway station at midnight tomorrow," Charlie said.

Muldoon rubbed his chin. "The station here in Cushing is on Broadway. It makes sense to have you deliver it in an open space like the station."

Charlie had been chewing on Susan's words. "Wait, do you think Susan was trying to tell me who was involved? Maybe she was trying to tell me who had kidnapped her."

"So, who's Will?" Rice asked.

Charlie and Muldoon looked at each other and said, "Willard," at the same time.

"The phone disconnected as soon as Susan mentioned the train. Do you think she was tryin' to tell us where she was at?"

"I think so," Muldoon said. "You have a brilliant and courageous wife."

"Who's this Willard person?" asked Anson.

"He's a no-good varmint who tried to sabotage one of Marland's oil wells last year. I brought in Pinkerton, and Muldoon here helped drive him off."

Muldoon nodded and added, "Willard made other sabotage attacks against wells here in Osage County, not only against Mr. Kelly's but other oil wells as well. We've been trying to track him down so the police could arrest him, but he's slippery."

"And you think he's stooped this low to kidnap Susan to get a ransom from you?" asked Chester.

"I do," said Charlie. "He's a greedy son-of-a-bitch. And he's mad at me for standin' up to him and puttin' the Pinkertons on him last year. And this year, I outbid him on some prime leases in Burbank. I'd say he's got no love for me."

"Well, he's a coward for goin' after your wife," said Jess. "He's too scared of you, Charlie."

"You're right, Jess. And he better not hurt Susan one bit." Charlie clinched his fists together.

"Charlie, you've kept it together so far, don't lose focus now," Muldoon said. "It does make sense that it's Willard. Things have been quiet in Osage

County for days. Do you have any idea how he could have known about you being here?"

"I have no idea. We haven't tried to keep the new department store a secret, but we hadn't announced bein' in town today."

Just then, four men walked into the room. They all had short haircuts and wore similar grey business suits.

A tall, gray-haired man of about fifty asked, "Which one of you is Charles Kelly?"

"That's me. And you are?"

"I'm Captain Richard Murphy of the Oklahoma State Bureau of Investigation. I have been sent here by the Oklahoma Attorney General to help you get your wife back safely. What can you tell me?"

Charlie walked over and shook Captain Murphy's hand. "Glad you could come." He made introductions to all the others and then motioned to the table. "Have a seat, and I'll tell you what we know. Jess, can you have the hotel bring in a fresh pot of coffee and some mugs?"

Jess hurried out as Captain Murphy and his men sat down.

Charlie gave the OBI folks a complete history of what had happened, including the details of the phone call and the possible clues Susan had given him on the phone before being cut off. Because of the possibility it was Willard, he shared what happened at the Yale well site last year. Muldoon added in the ongoing investigation in Osage County for the sabotage this year and why they suspected Willard. During all this, Jess had returned not only with coffee but had found some pastries as well.

Captain Murphy asked, "Are you sure your wife said Willard?"

"She didn't say his full name," Charlie said, "but asked if I had contacted Uncle Will about the ransom. Her uncle's name is Curt, Curt Schlegell."

"Mrs. Kelly is a smart woman, Captain," Muldoon added. "She'd know better than to use Willard's name directly and was giving Charlie here a clue. Based on Willard's history with Mr. Kelly, I'm confident he's our kidnapper."

"She also insisted 'Uncle Will' take the train to bring the ransom. Then the line got cut off," Charlie said.

"Susan would know Curt would wire the money to a bank here," Rice said.

"I think you're correct in your assessment of Mrs. Kelly," Captain Murphy said to Muldoon. "Sounds like she was offering up another clue."

"Yes, we're thinking so, too," Muldoon confirmed.

"I think their drop point is close to where they have her. It might even be in view of the bench at the station." Captain Murphy motioned to one of his men, who stood up. "Go down to the station and watch for a while.

Act casual, and don't draw any attention to yourself. We don't want to tip our hand."

The OBI agent nodded, but before he could leave, Muldoon put his hand up to stop him and asked, "Has anybody talked to the local police yet?"

"I haven't," Charlie said,

Captain Murphy said, "As a courtesy, I stopped to let them know we're in town to investigate a potential crime. I'm required to do it. But I said we didn't need their assistance at this time. I know these cases are sensitive, so I did not give them specific information."

"I'd like to ride with your man, Captain," Muldoon said. "I've interacted with Willard and his man, so if it's them, I will recognize them."

The Captain nodded as he got up to refill his coffee. "Good idea."

Muldoon got up, and he and the OBI agent left the banquet room.

"Charlie, how do you prefer to handle this?" Captain Murphy asked.

"If there's any chance we can find where they are holding Susan, I want to get her out before the drop time. I'm afraid if it's Willard, they may hurt or even kill her once they have the money."

"The fact they won't do it as an exchange, cash for wife at the same time, strongly suggests they are not invested in her safety," Captain Murphy said.

"In my experience with this son-of-a-bitch, Willard's not the brightest heifer in the herd. And his goon makes him look as smart as Thomas Edison. If this goes sideways, I'm afraid the goon will just shoot. As to the police, I think involvin' them will get them in the way. And since the note said not to involve them, I wouldn't rule out Willard has someone on the inside who could tip him off to what we're doin'. Do we need to involve them?"

The OBI captain shook his head. "No. As I said, I was vague as to why I was here. And the Oklahoma statute gives me a lot of freedom to operate independently of local police departments. As long as I inform them after the fact of an arrest, then we are covered."

"Good," Charlie said. He looked at the clock in the room; it was well past 9:00. The day had felt like an eternity to him. He went and poured himself a coffee when one of the phones rang.

"Is this Willard character calling back?" asked Captain Murphy.

"No, it's the line I asked the hotel to set up for my lawyer to call on," Charlie said.

He set the coffee down and picked up the phone. "Charlie."

"It's Curt. I've got the money ready for you. You can pick it up in the morning at the Farmers Bank in Cushing. Talk to the bank manager, Mr.

Gregory."

"Thank you, Curt."

"Any news?"

Charlie filled him in on what had happened since they last spoke. He told Curt to thank Missouri AG for calling in the favor, as the Oklahoma agents were very helpful.

"Do anything you can to get Susan back," Curt said, and Charlie could hear the emotion in his voice over the line.

"I will."

Chapter Forty-Four
Rescue
October 1919

CHARLIE GOT UP AFTER the call with Uncle Curt and started to pace the room. He wished he had Tony with him and could ride out with a Winchester in his holster to hunt down Willard and his man. Having to wait for information and not actively doing anything was wearing on him more than when he'd faced down the rustlers last year.

"Charlie, why don't you get some rest," Rice suggested.

"I'd just pace in the suite if I weren't here," Charlie replied.

"If I know my younger brother," Jess said, rubbing his leg, "he won't sleep until this is over."

Charlie nodded and kept on pacing the room.

"Though if you keep it up," Jess added, "you'll wear a hole in the carpet. The hotel might bill ya for it."

It was a moment of fun and caused Charlie to change direction, but he didn't stop pacing.

Despite suggestions from Charlie, the others also stayed in the room. Captain Murphy sat and conferred with the two other agents who had remained behind, making their plans. Rice, Anson, and Chester sat at the table, clearly weary, but stayed to offer moral support to their boss and friend. Jess got up, found the night clerk, and convinced him to refill the coffee urn.

The clock's chimes rang out the hour; eleven deep bongs filled the room. As the last chime spread across the room, Muldoon and the OBI agent walked back in. Charlie pounced on them like a coyote on a rabbit.

"What did you learn?"

The OBI agent said, "We checked out the station. There's a bench located outside facing Broadway. We milled about with the crowd waiting for the evening train. We acted like we were checking the schedule and blended in."

Muldoon added, "It gave us a chance to check out the buildings across from the station. There are some buildings a block up Broadway with a view of the bench. Most of them are storefronts and closed for the evening."

"Did you check anywhere closer?" Charlie asked, not noticing the irritation in his own voice.

"Of course we did," Muldoon soothed. "When the train arrived, we blended in again with the crowd and walked out of the station.

"As I said, all the businesses seemed closed up, no lights or anything. But there was a building about a block east of the station. It's on the corner of Broadway and Seay Street. Lights were on in the back, and I could see people moving.

"The building looks like it might have been a smithy shop at some point. It has a big door facing Broadway and a side door facing Seay Street. A big, rough-looking character came out of the side door to get something from a Model T."

"Sounds like the same car Willard had when they clocked me and gave me the goose egg up by Ponca City," Charlie said.

"Well, whoever was inside seemed okay with keeping the door propped open. It's probably because it was hotter than usual today and hadn't cooled down much after the sun went down," the agent said.

Charlie asked, "How close did ya git to the place?"

"We had to blend in with the people leaving the station and didn't want to draw any attention. We could go back and come in from the north and get to the side door, and no one would see or hear us."

The agent looked at Captain Murphy. "Mr. Muldoon's right. It's the best way to approach the building. But we don't know for sure if it's their hideout. It could be some guy just working late."

Muldoon shook his head. "Even half a block away, I could judge the size and the way the guy walked. He sure made me think of Willard's sidekick. Plus, Mr. Kelly is right. They drive a Model T. I would bet it's them."

"We could try and get a man closer to the door and try and listen in," Captain Murphy said.

Charlie put his hand on Muldoon's shoulder, looked him in the eye, and said, "You and I are the only ones here who have seen those two assholes. It's us who pays them a visit. At least we'll get closer than you did earlier."

Captain Murphy crossed his arms. "I don't like you, as a civilian, putting yourself in danger."

Charlie looked at the Captain. "I've already confronted those two once before. And I corralled rustlers out on the 101 Ranch last year, and they were much smarter and tougher than these two yahoos. Captain Murphy, my wife's in there. Susan's my life. I won't be foolish."

"Of course you won't. But we'll position ourselves nearby so we can give you immediate support. What do you have in mind?"

"If Bailey agrees, I would like him and me to get close enough so I can hear and hopefully see if it's them. I want to surprise them, use it to overwhelm them, and get this over tonight. We can do it in two stages. If they have the side door open, we'll get close enough to hear them and identify who's there in the first stage. We can then regroup back a block or so and discuss a straightforward way to overwhelm them. I have an idea, but I want to see the location first. What do ya think?"

Muldoon said, "I'm in."

Captain Murphy said, "My men and I'll back you up."

Charlie offered his right hand to the Captain. "Great, where should we meet up?"

Chester stepped up and said, "The corner of Moses and Seay is the best spot. It's one block north of the building."

Charlie nodded. "I'm glad you've been getting a feel for the town as you get our department store ready."

"Jess and I have been walking all over the area to get a feel for the competition and the best products to carry in the store. I'm glad I can do something, even a small thing, to help get Susan back safely."

Charlie patted Chester on the back. "This is certainly more than a small thing. I'm glad to have you here." He looked up at the others from the Kramer Group and his brother. "All of you."

They quickly discussed the plan. Captain Murphy and his men would drive to the corner of Moses and Seay. Charlie and Muldoon would walk there since the hotel was only three and a half blocks from the building of interest. Then if there was any trouble, the OBI agents could signal Charlie and Muldoon. The others would wait in the hotel in case of any calls.

Captain Murphy and his men left. Charlie and Muldoon waited five minutes and then started walking to the meeting spot. The clock in the banquet room began to chime out midnight as they left the room.

It took about ten minutes for them to walk to the spot. It was dark, and there were no streetlamps. As they approached the area, the OBI agents gave the all-clear signal. Charlie and Muldoon continued walking, and they arrived at the northwest corner of the building, where they hoped to find Willard and his man and Susan.

The side door stood propped open even though the night had cooled down. From the corner, they could hear muffled voices. Charlie moved in first, with Muldoon close behind him as they neared the partially open door.

Charlie stopped and listened for a moment. The voices were still muffled, but he could make out part of the conversation. He put his lips as close to Muldoon's ear as he could and whispered. "It's Willard."

Willard was saying, "Keep your cool, you fool."

"But, Boss, she's so beautiful. I want to touch her tits once."

"Leave her alone and her clothes on her. For now. I told you you'd get your chance before this is over."

Charlie struggled to keep from crashing into the room immediately. He and Muldoon quietly slipped away from the building and returned to the group waiting at Moses.

Captain Murphy asked, "Well, is it them? Do they have her?"

Charley put his hands on his hips and said, "It's them, and they have Susan. They must have her tied up and gagged."

"How do you want to do this?" Muldoon asked.

"We should wait until they fall asleep," said Captain Murphy. "Our odds are improved."

Charlie shook his head. "We heard them talkin'. Willard's goon's plannin' on rapin' my wife if he gets his chance. I ain't gonna wait for it to happen."

The Captain looked at Charlie in the dark night, and clearly could see the only way he'd stop Charlie was to tie him up or shoot him. "Then what do you propose?"

"My plan's for Muldoon and me to loudly approach the buildin's side door and appear to be two drunks wantin' a bathroom. I'll pound on the door until someone comes to it. When the door opens, I'll pounce on him, and Muldoon will follow me. You guys stay close enough to get inside within a few seconds."

Captain Murphy looked at Muldoon, one professional to another, and said, "Yes, it might just work. I can't think of a better plan."

Muldoon pulled out his sidearm and checked it. He put it back in its holster and said, "Then let's do it."

It took Charlie and Muldoon a few minutes to quietly return to the corner across from their target. Then they started their act, singing, "Rye whiskey, rye whiskey, rye whiskey, I cry. If I don't get rye whiskey, I surely will die."

They stumbled and wobbled as they crossed the street. Charlie slurred out, "Hey, buddy, I need to piss. Let's see if we can use the bathroom in here." He approached the door and began to pound on it. Bang!

Bang! Bang! "Hey, can I use—"

"Whattaya want?"

Charlie grabbed the door and yanked it open. The goon stood there, a gun in his hand. Charlie swung a right to the goon's jaw and dropped him like a dishrag. Muldoon rushed in behind Charlie. Willard stood across the small room and had his gun out. Muldoon reached for his gun, and Willard fired. The bullet missed Muldoon, who had already dived for cover behind a coal forge. Willard aimed again, but immediately there was a series of blasts from the doorway. Captain Murphy stood there, his old-style Colt Peacemaker pistol in his hands, smoke rising from the barrel. Willard was dead.

Muldoon stood up and gave a salute to the OBI captain. They both walked over to check on Willard as the other OBI agents arrived to put Willard's man into handcuffs.

Charlie was already moving across the room, calling out, "Susan! Susan!"

He saw a door to a closet off to the side. Inside, he found his beautiful wife bound to a chair, her arms tied behind her back, and a grimy rag tied around her mouth as a gag. He immediately pulled off the rag.

He gave her a kiss that tasted sweeter than any before.

He pulled out a pocketknife to cut the ropes.

Susan cried, "Oh, Sweetheart, you're bleeding!"

Charlie paused and looked at his right shoulder. Blood had soaked into the shirt. "Must've been Willard's bullet clipped me."

"Does it hurt?"

"Nah, it's just a scratch. And I don't feel a thing now since I have you back." He finished getting the ropes cut and pulled Susan out of the chair and into the room, giving her a tight hug.

Susan hugged back but let out a soft, "Oww."

Charlie let go and looked at her. "Did they hurt you? Let me look at you."

"Willard's goon knocked the phone out of my hands hard enough to leave a bruise, that's all. I'm fine."

"You sure?"

Susan gave him a long kiss to reassure him. When their lips parted, she said, "I'm so glad to see you. You're amazing." She turned to look at the others. "You too fellas. Thanks for helping my wonderful man. But who are you?"

Charlie put his arm across his shoulder. "Susan, meet Mr. Bailey Muldoon of the Pinkerton Detective Agency. He's been investigatin' the sabotage at the wells."

"Pleasure to finally meet you, Mr. Muldoon," Susan said.

"And this," Charlie continued, "is Captain Richard Murphy of the Oklahoma Bureau of Investigation. He brought some fine men with him, and we decided to come to get ya."

Susan walked over and hugged the Captain, who was startled by the gesture. She said, "Words can't describe my gratitude for your bravery and support tonight."

"Just doing my part, Mrs. Kelly. Charlie's the real hero here tonight."

"Anybody who saves my life can call me Susan," she said. "And you too, Mr. Muldoon."

"Only if you drop the mister for me," Muldoon said.

"Deal."

Susan turned back to Charlie. "How did the Oklahoma Bureau of Investigation get involved? I overheard Willard and his man talking about the ransom. Didn't they say no police?"

"They did. And I didn't call them. Uncle Curt did."

"Uncle Curt?"

"Ma'am... Susan," Captain Murphy said, "it seems your uncle is friends with the Missouri Attorney General, who is friends with my Attorney General. He told me you'd been kidnapped, and we hurried here to do what we could."

"We couldn't have done it without Charlie's help," Muldoon added. "You have quite a husband."

"I know I do, and I love him so much," Susan said, confirming it with another kiss.

Captain Murphy smiled and said, "Pardon me, but I have a crime scene to work."

Charlie and Susan reluctantly broke the kiss and walked out of the building with Muldoon. Behind them, the Captain was giving orders to get the Cushing Police and his coroner to bring their equipment out of their car and to take their prisoner away.

Muldoon turned to Charlie and Susan and said, "I'm sure the Captain will need to get statements from each of you. I think it can wait until later today. Go get some rest and make sure your wife's fine."

Susan looked up into Charlie's eyes. "I don't want to rest. I'm starving. Those two thugs didn't give me anything to eat. I could devour a ribeye and a bottle of cabernet."

Charlie smiled at Muldoon and said, "My lady's doin' just fine."

Together they walked back to the hotel, arms around each other's waist.

Chapter Forty-Five
Recovery
October 1919

CHARLIE WOKE TO A bird chirping. It perched outside the screen on the sill of the window overlooking Broadway. He gazed with sleepy eyes at the wall clock; it was 11:55. His shoulder, where the bullet had grazed him, ached, and the bandage Susan had insisted he get when they returned to the hotel last night—or more accurately, this morning—itched.

He rolled over and gazed at Susan, marveling for the millionth time at her beauty and how lucky he was. He had come close to losing her forever yesterday and made a silent vow to himself that he'd never let it happen again.

After returning to the hotel, they'd found some hotel staff who allowed them to use the kitchen. The chef had gone home, but Charlie had found the ingredients and grilled the steaks himself. They had eaten in the banquet room, where Charlie told everyone what had happened at the building while Susan ate. They finally all went to bed around 4:00.

Now, as he watched Susan's naked breasts rise and fall as she breathed he realized how lucky a man he was. Slowly he reached over and lovingly caressed her breasts. Her eyes flickered as she awoke.

He moaned, "I'm sorry. I didn't mean to wake you up."

Susan giggled. "Yeah, but you couldn't control yourself, right?"

"There's no denying it. Are we ready to git this day goin'?"

Susan brought her hand down and stroked his chest, then his stomach, then around his groin. Charlie instantly rose to the occasion. They kissed and made love, slowly and passionately, each excited to be back in the other's arms.

When they finished, Susan lay with her head resting against Charlie's neck, her arm draped across his muscular chest. Charlie traced circles around her nipples.

"I guess now we need to git this day goin'," Charlie said.

"I would rather lay in bed all day, but you're right." She paused for a moment, then said, "Oh my, did we let Uncle Curt know? I was so wound up last night that it totally slipped my mind."

Charlie patted her shoulder. "Yes. Anson placed a call to Curt while I was fixing dinner. He knows you're safe."

Susan smiled and kissed Charlie. "I love you. I'll get cleaned up, and we'll go have a late lunch." She slid out of bed, and Charlie watched her naked form walk across the room to the shower.

Susan asked over her shoulder, "Can you have everyone from last night meet us after lunch?"

"I think so. Why?"

"I want to thank everyone for supporting you and saving me."

"I'll make it happen."

***

They headed downstairs and enjoyed a late lunch. At one point, the chef, Gregory, stopped by to apologize for not being there when they returned. He said the entire staff was distraught when they learned what had happened and was now glad Susan was safe. Then he turned to Charlie.

"And you, sir," sounding serious and making Charlie wonder if he had offended the chef, "must give me your biscuit recipe. Some remained out this morning when I arrived, and I tried one." He brought his fingers to his lips and gave a chef's kiss. "The best biscuits I have ever had. When I asked who had made them, the night clerk said you."

"Why thank you," Charlie said. "I hope you don't mind we used your kitchen last night."

"Mind? Not at all. I want to know if I can hire you away from your big, important oil job to come cook for me."

They all laughed, and Gregory returned to the kitchen as Charlie and Susan continued eating.

"Seems like you've made another friend with your biscuit recipe," Susan said.

"Yep. I guess Grandma McDaniel is smilin' down from heaven at how many people love her biscuits."

Captain Murphy spotted Charlie and Susan sitting by the front window as he walked into the restaurant and waved.

Charlie pointed to an empty chair. "Have a seat, Captain."

Murphy sat, and the waiter asked if he wanted a menu.

"No, but a glass of sweet tea sounds nice."

The waiter left, and Charlie said, "We're meetin' with the folks here last night after lunch in the banquet room. Susan wants to thank them for their support last night."

"Very nice of you," Murphy said. "But I'm sure they'll say no formal thanks is expected or required."

"It's for me," Susan said. "I want to say a few things, and I need to do it today."

"If it's okay with you, we'd like to wait until after her talk to make our formal statements," Charlie said.

The waiter returned with Murphy's tea. He took a long drink, draining half the glass in one pull. "Mmm, boy, hits the spot. Yes indeed. We documented the crime scene and have pictures with a thorough report of what happened from Mr. Muldoon. We'd like both of you to give your versions of what happened. Susan, are you prepared to do it?"

Susan set her napkin down and placed her hand on Charlie's, and he squeezed her hand. "I won't enjoy reliving it. But I can give you all you'll need to put the idiot Brady Tompkins away for a long time. I'm happy to do it."

Charlie said, "Brady Tompkins's his name? I don't think I ever knew it."

"Before they gagged me, I asked him his name. The fool told me."

Captain Murphy finished his tea and told them he'd see them later in the afternoon. Charlie and Susan finished their lunch in peace.

***

After lunch, Charlie and Susan headed over to the banquet room. Everyone who had been there last night for the search for Susan was there. The ongoing conversations slowly ended as Charlie and Susan walked in. Susan smiled at all of them and walked to the head of the banquet table. Everybody gathered around.

Susan wiped away tears as she met everybody's eyes, then gathered her emotions and said, "I'm not able to satisfy myself that I can adequately thank you, folks, for the support you gave Charlie and me last night. But every one of you has a place in my heart forever. I was concerned and more than a little scared. But I knew my Charlie would come to get me. I would have been comforted if I had known he had all your support. If any of you are ever in a similar situation anywhere in the world, I want you to know this: Charlie and I'll come to help you as fast as we can get there. I love you, and thank you from the bottom of my heart."

The group erupted into applause and shouted, "We love you, Susan."

Chapter Forty-Six
Closer for Last Night
October 1919

AFTER THINGS SETTLED DOWN, Charlie raised his hands and said, "Susan and I need some time with Captain Murphy to give him our formal statements about last night. We can reconvene here afterward. We'll end the day over dinner together here. I have the restaurant prepared to support us. We need the room alone for our statements, so we'll see you later."

Captain Murphy walked in as the others walked out to wait in the bar. He greeted Susan and Charlie and took a seat at the table. One of his men followed him in, sat down next to the captain, and pulled out a notebook and pen to take notes.

"I'm sure you would want Charlie with you for support, Susan," Captain Murphy said. Susan nodded. "However, to make this legal, I need to have you give your statements separately and without any influence from each other."

"Makes sense," Charlie said. He turned to Susan. "Are you okay with everythin'. I think we can delay this if you need more time."

She squeezed his hand. "No, I'm alright. I want to get this over with."

They split up, with Charlie going with the other agent across the large banquet room. Murphy stayed with Susan. It took over an hour to guide Charlie and Susan through the process.

After reading each statement, Captain Murphy said, "I want to compliment you all on being thorough, and I'm amazed at how your descriptions show a uniform story. Each of you had parts of the evening only you could see, but when you blend them as I just did, you have the whole story, and it gives me confidence this Tompkins fella goes to jail for a long time.

Thank you."

Murphy handed the statements to the agent, who filed them into a briefcase. The captain stood up and put his hand out to Charlie.

"It's a pleasure to meet you, and I'm glad this worked out for the best. Too many times, these kinds of events end in tragedy."

Charlie shook Murphy's hand and said, "Thanks for your help. Now promise to stay for dinner. I have a question for you later tonight."

Captain Murphy gave this some thought and said, "I'll stay. I'll see you later."

***

As requested, Anson, Chester, Jess, and Rice returned after Captain Murphy left. It took a few minutes as Anson, Chester, and Rice each wanted to say a few words to Susan. Finally, they all sat down, and Charlie started the meeting.

"Susan and I are excited to hear what you have planned for Abrams Department Stores. Are you ready to give us your plans?"

Anson stood and responded, "Yes, we are. Chester and Jess will do most of the presentation. I'm speaking now because I want to say if you approve this effort, the funds to support it will come from the reserve funds within my accounts. Chester, it's all yours."

"Over the last several months, we have been continuously asked when this store will open. This interest and some research by Jess have convinced us the concept of a store sized appropriately and aimed at a community similar to Cushing, serving the typical family with a median income of $3,000 to $4,000, can be successful. There are several dozen communities like this in Oklahoma, and we have targeted our next five locations as Shawnee, Ada, Norman, Chickasha, and Anadarko. Each is a County Seat with a stable economy that will strengthen and grow over the next decade. Jess, can you discuss the research you completed?"

"Thank you, Chester. After selecting these five locations based on their size, standing within their counties, and the current economy, I talked with Hank Thomas and Rice Coburn to get their opinion on two critical items. They're the oil industry's impact over the next decade on Oklahoma and these cities and the construction costs to build a store to serve these communities best."

Charlie interrupted Jess, "Well done. Those are two key influences on business in Oklahoma for the foreseeable future. I'll let you tell us what you found out."

Jess grinned. "Thank you, Charlie. I should have said, Mr. Kelly."

"I'll always be Charlie to you. Just don't call me little brother."

The room filled with laughter.

"A while back, we had Hank look at the locations, and he said every one of them would be impacted positively by the oil business. He already has plans to drill Kelly Oil Company wells around Shawnee, and he sees good possibilities in the rest. Rice gave us estimates for construction costs if Strawberry Hill builds our stores. We'll reduce our monthly costs by amortizing the cost over ten years. We can expand into these five locations and become operational within eighteen to twenty-four months. Any questions?"

Susan asked, "What are your concerns, if any?"

Jess answered, "Personnel acquisition and training tops the list for me. I'm not concerned to the point I wouldn't support proceeding. I'm excited about the possibilities we see. But the biggest unknown is the people. I'm confident we'll find them, but we may have to reach beyond those cities to find them."

Anson spoke up and said, "Some staff out of Missouri, ready to advance into a leadership role, might volunteer to transfer to Oklahoma. We have some native Oklahomans working for us in Missouri. I agree with Jess. Whenever we opened a new store or set of stores, we had to find the people to run it. You can't find and train staff and then build the store. It doesn't work."

Abrams said, "We feel the plan's executable—Jess has been the prime mover on this initiative—and I think he has a plan worthy of your support."

Charlie said, "I couldn't agree more. Good job, Jess. Susan, your thoughts?"

"I'm very impressed. I love what I'm hearing from you today; I say go for it. You'll be successful. Anson, you have some true stars here."

"I couldn't agree more. The smartest thing I can do is get out of their way and let them go."

Charlie added, "You also have my complete support on this expansion project. Let's take a break and come back for dinner."

Chapter Forty-Seven
New Kramer Addition
October 1919

WITH THE EVENING DINNER party well underway, Charlie noticed most of the people he needed to speak to had finished eating. He rounded up Susan, Hank, Anson, Rice, Abrams, and Jess and brought them to a separate table at the other end of the room.

"I need some time with you folks to discuss an idea Susan, Hank, and I have been tossing around. Even before last night, we discussed creating a company within the Kramer Group dedicated to security. Over the past year or two, we have had issues in Kansas City and Oklahoma and have had to call in Pinkerton and law enforcement organizations. Since we own many unique assets, not the least of which are banks, we need security and investigative work daily. I want feedback from this group on whether we should have this capability within the company or continue to hire from other sources."

Anson said, "I'm not an expert, but I know we have enough of what we call shrinkage in the retail industry to cover a few security people in each store. If the Group can provide a security staff and it's another moneymaker for us, it could become a smart move. But I'm skeptical."

Hank said, "We've had enough issues out at our well sites for me to support havin' our own security. And Charlie, we need to discuss the last incident at Burbank."

Charlie nodded. "We will, today."

Rice added, "You know we've had vandalism at our construction sites in the past in Kansas City. I'm starting to think this hasn't been random. We need to investigate this. Could we maybe create a company to hire out to others, too?"

Susan spoke up. "Charlie, this was too easy." She tried to keep from grinning as she said, "Which means it shouldn't have taken someone kidnapping me for us to see a need. We better do this now before someone kidnaps you."

Everyone laughed, which helped them to become a little more removed from the events of the previous night.

Charlie said, "Thanks, everyone. We're gonna bring Richard and Bailey over here and git their ideas on this. You guys can return to the party."

Charlie found Murphy and Muldoon and brought them over to join him and Susan at their table.

Charlie said, "Thanks for joinin' us. We had a short meetin' with some of our folks regardin' security and how we should approach it within the Kramer Group. In light of dealin' with everythin' from theft, vandalism, and even kidnappin' over the past few years, it seems smart for us to do somethin'."

Richard immediately offered, "First, as you already know, I'm an Oklahoma Bureau of Investigation employee, and anyone should comfortably depend on the Bureau to protect them and their interests. But I think it's prudent for you to create your own security company and not limit it to your requirements. Have a division within it to address your company's specific needs. But also hire out to other companies and individuals with security needs."

Bailey said, "Richard's right. You have the resources and plenty of requirements within your company to drive a security company's creation and sustainment. Creating an additional segment to hire out to others would likely create pure profit."

Charlie looked at Susan and said, "Well then, this turned out as expected. Our staff and these guys think we should create a security company within the Kramer Group." He looked at Murphy and Muldoon. "Now, we're not done here."

Bailey said, "Whattaya need, Charlie?"

Richard asked, "Do you want some specific advice from us?"

Susan replied, "No. Now we're looking for the person to become President of the Kramer National Security Company."

Richard said, "It's not me. I'm within five years of retirement. It would not make sense for me at my age to not stay where I will retire at fifty-five with full benefits. Buying out my retirement would cost you a fortune, so that wouldn't make sense. Now, I recommend you consider my new friend, Mr. Bailey Muldoon."

Charley said, "Susan and I respect your answer regardin' the timin' within your career with OBI. But we wanted you included in this conversation. After talkin' with Bailey, we wanted to ask your opinion. We have it now. Bailey, you're our target for the position. We already knew you spent time in the U.S. Army. You're twenty-six years old. You're a regional manager for Pinkerton, with several hundred people reportin' to you. We want to offer you the job of creatin' and runnin' a security company. We have been doin' some work preparin' for this decision after the last vandalism incident. We know what you make at Pinkerton because we also wanted their recommendation. We got it. They love you and are plannin' to give you a raise to try and keep you. They're payin' you $15,000 a year, and you received a nice $1,000 bonus at Christmas last year. Our offer's this: $25,000 the first year as you create the company plus a $2,000 bonus if you get the company formed and ready to operate by December 1920. Once the company is running we'll pay you $35,000 a year afterward plus an annual bonus of three percent of net profit given at Christmas. The deal includes a benefits package, including insurance and vacation time off. I don't think Pinkerton can match us; whattaya think?"

Richard laughed as he said, "Bailey, if you don't take their offer, I'll have you taken out behind the barn." He looked Bailey in the eye. "It's a wonderful package, and it's fair. You'll earn it, but you can set your pay with the bonus."

"I think you just hired yourself a new President," Bailey said with a smile. "You and Susan must also discuss whether you want a security detail dedicated to you two. Don't answer now; think about it."

Richard turned his gaze to Charlie and said, "Charlie, you and Susan should consider his suggestion to discuss a security detail. Call me if you want to talk about it. I have some experiences we can draw some perspective from."

Susan stood and offered her hand. "Thanks, Richard, stay in touch."

***

The meeting ended a productive day. Charlie and Susan returned to the party, picked up an open bottle of cabernet, two glasses, and found an empty table for two. Charlie poured their wine as he said, "I'm so happy we can do this."

"Me too, Sweetheart, but something's still bothering my wonderful cowboy."

He looked lovingly into her eyes, then grimaced. "I think the people who shot up the tank at the well may be related to the issue Zane had with buying the quarry. I don't think we're done yet with the Chicago Outfit."

About the Author

E. Joe Brown has published six short story/memoirs, and his writing has been included in the National Baseball Hall of Fame. He's a member of Western Writers of America, SouthWest Writers, the International Western Music Association, Military Writers Society of America, and President of New Mexico Westerners. He's served as a New Mexico State Music Commissioner and on the International Western Music Association Board of Directors where he's influenced the culture of New Mexico and the Southwest through music, poetry, literature, and education. He is a proud retiree of the USAF. Joe lives in Rio Rancho, New Mexico with his wife.